MUTE WITNESS

Rick R. Reed

A NineStar Press Publication

www.ninestarpress.com

Mute Witness

Printed in the USA

Print ISBN: 978-1-64890-138-6

First Edition, November, 2020
Originally Published in October 2009

Also available in eBook, ISBN: 978-1-64890-135-5

WARNING:

This book contains sexually explicit content, which may only be suitable for mature readers, graphic violence, off-page child molestation, rape, homophobia, kidnapping, and memories of past child abuse.

Sean and Austin have the perfect life. Their new relationship is only made more joyous by weekend visits from Sean's eight-year-old son, Jason.

And then their perfect world shatters.

Jason is missing.

When the boy turns up days later, he has been abused and has lost the power to speak. Small town minds turn to the boy's gay father and his lover as the likely culprits. Sean and Austin struggle to maintain their relationship amid the innuendo and the threat that Sean will lose the son he loves. Meanwhile, the real villain is close to home, intent on ensuring the boy's muteness is permanent.

For my son, my heart, Nicholas

Chapter One

It was one of their rare lazy evenings. Summer, and the evening air was fresh and clean after an afternoon thunderstorm, with just a hint of a breeze. Normally, Sean and Austin were so busy that if they weren't trying to change something about the little Cape Cod on the Ohio River they had bought a year before—adding a deck, putting in a new kitchen, stripping away years of white paint from the woodwork downstairs—they were too tired to do anything but crawl into bed and pass out, usually before eleven o'clock. Lovemaking, since they had bought the money- and-time-sucking house, had become relegated to weekend afternoons and the occasional early morning.

But today, Thursday, had been an easy one. Austin had called into work—the Benson Pottery, where he was a caster—and taken a mental health day. Things had just been too damn busy lately, and he needed the break. Waiting until Saturday was out of the question. Sunday seemed further away than the next millennium.

Sean, a reporter for the *Evening View*, the local thrice-weekly compilation of ads sandwiched in with a little editorial, had the day off. The couple spent the day in Pittsburgh, at the Andy Warhol museum, then had an early dinner at the Grand Concourse (the best paella on the Monongahela and Allegheny rivers), beat the brutal thunderstorm home, made love (acrobatically, in the kitchen, atop a butcher block), and now the two were curled up in front of the TV. Sean had rented *Who's Afraid of Virginia Woolf?* and, after a bowl of Jamaican and a couple of vodka and tonics, the two were teary-eyed with laughter.

Sean looked over at his younger boyfriend and thought how lucky he was to have found Austin, especially in a town the size of Summitville, where the population hovered just above ten thousand. Even better, Austin was his fantasy man, with a broad, beefy body that his mother and her friends would have called strapping, sandy blond hair, and the bluest eyes he had ever seen. When Sean first met him, he thought Austin's eyes had to be fake, enhanced by those tinted contacts that never looked real. But he found quickly that the young man was simply blessed with arresting eyes to go along with his broad shoulders, dimpled chin, and infectious smile. He wore that smile right now, coming down from a fit of inappropriate laughter after hearing Elizabeth Taylor tell Richard Burton something along the lines of "I'd divorce you if I thought you were alive."

A sick sense of humor was yet another thing the pair had in common.

It was what they both would have agreed was a perfect day. Well, Sean might have had one more item to add to the "perfection" list. Having his son, Jason, around for at least part of the time would have been all it would have taken to make the day ideal, but these days, Jason was for the weekends only.

In any case, this was close enough to nirvana. He closed his eyes and let his head loll back on Austin's shoulder.

Sean was just thinking about slowly undressing Austin and then leading him into the bedroom for round two when the phone rang. Its chirp startled both of them out of the cocoon of warmth that had surrounded them, a cocoon built from good sex, supreme relaxation, and the aforementioned Jamaican weed.

Austin said, sleepily from under Sean's arm on the couch, "Don't get it. Please don't get it. Just let the machine pick up. I don't want to talk to anyone. And I don't want you to either." Sean eyed the little answering machine next to the cordless, wondering when they would enter the twenty-first century and use voice mail like everyone else. But, unlike voice mail, the machine did allow them to screen calls, and for two men who appreciated their privacy, this feature had voice mail beat all to hell.

Sean let the phone ring its customary four rings, although his tendency would have been to answer it. But if this would make Austin happy, then he was willing to do it. Especially since he had things in mind for Austin that did not involve the telephone. Things that would erase their fatigue and perhaps keep them up the better part of the night. Sean grinned.

On the fourth ring, Sean pressed the pause button on the remote control and sat up straighter to listen.

"Whatever it is, it can wait," Austin whispered in Sean's ear, flicking his earlobe with his tongue and giving his crotch a playful squeeze.

And then the moment shattered.

Shelley's voice, almost unfamiliar under the veneer of tension that made it higher, quicker, came through. Shelley and Sean had been married once upon a time and their union had produced Jason, the best little boy in the world. As soon as Sean heard Shelley's voice, he thought of his son, who shared his dark hair, green eyes, wiry frame, and his fascination with stories.

"Sean? Sean, I hope you're there. This is important. Please pick up." There was a slight pause. "It's about Jason. He—"

Before she could say anything else, Sean sprinted for the phone in the entryway. "Shelley? Sorry, I was—"

"Jason is missing."

"What?"

And then Sean heard her begin to sob and the relaxation in all of his muscles vanished, replaced by a tightness that felt like steel bands snapping taut. Blood rushed in his ears; his heart began to pound. A queasy nausea rose in his gut.

"Jason never came home tonight," Shelley sobbed. "I don't know where he is. Please say he's with you."

Sean sat on the little oak chair in front of the desk. Well, collapsed into the chair was more like it. "Shelley, I'm sorry, but he's not here. Don't you think I would have called if he had come here? How long's he been gone?" Sean rubbed the back of his neck, his mouth curiously dry. He glanced out the window at the complete darkness.

"I went to work at six and he wasn't home yet." She blew out a sigh. "But, you know, we just thought he was horsing around in the woods or something and lost track of time. Then I called Paul and..."

"Wait a minute, Shelley. It's a quarter to eleven."

"I know. I know."

"Why didn't you call sooner? You mean to tell me you're just starting to look? Christ, he's eight years old."

"I thought he would've come home while I was on my shift. Paul was here and he fell asleep and..."

"Paul. Great." Sean rubbed his sweaty palms against his thighs.

"Please, Sean, it's not the time. I fucked up. Okay? Now that we've got that out of the way, I need some help finding our son."

She was right. In spite of the thoughts running through his head—most of them centering around how he and Austin would have been better parents but the courts couldn't see that, all they could see was a little boy growing up under the wings of two queers—Sean knew she was right.

This was an emergency.

He looked over at his partner, who was sitting up, alert on the couch, concern making his fair features somehow darker, eyebrows pulling together, mouth open as if to say something. Austin mouthed, "What's wrong?"

"Just a minute, Shelley." Sean covered the receiver with his hand. "Jason has disappeared. They haven't seen him since this afternoon." Sean closed his eyes to try to center himself; this was feeling unreal, like a nightmare come to life. The room shifted, like he was drunk. He wished away any high the Jamaican he had smoked earlier brought on, but it wasn't that easy. A feeling of giddy dread pulsed through his veins, electric.

This is how it feels to be totally helpless.

Austin got up from the couch and began rubbing the cords in Sean's neck, which had tightened into iron.

Sean swallowed, trying to summon up some spit. "You haven't seen him all day?"

"That's right, and I don't need the accusations. You know how it is around here in the summertime. Kids play outside until it starts getting dark. It was like that for you. It was like that for me."

"I'm sorry. Listen, we'll be right over."

"'Kay." There was a pause. "Sean? Would you mind just coming alone? Paul..."

"For Christ's sake, Shelley." Sean hung the phone up. "I'm going over there. See what I can do to help."

"Let me throw something on." Austin stood, his blue eyes alive with concern and sympathy.

"No." Sean practically winced at the look of surprise on his lover's face. He bit his lower lip and added, "I mean, maybe you should stay here in case anyone calls." Austin frowned.

"Like Jason, Austin. Like Jason." Sean groped in a desk drawer near the front door and pulled out his cell. "I'll have this on me so you can reach me. Okay?"

Sean was out the door before Austin had the chance to offer any sort of rebuttal.

*

By the time he pulled up in the driveway, Sean was hoping, without much optimism, that Jason would have come home during the time it took him to drive over to Shelley's. He even had a vision of his knobby-kneed little son running out the back, screen door slamming behind him, and calling, "Daddy!" He ran a trembling hand through his close-cropped dark hair and yanked on his mustache. Even under the best of circumstances, he didn't particularly like going in that house: Paul and Shelley had done their best to make sure he never felt comfortable there. When was the last time he'd been inside? He couldn't remember. Usually he just gave a couple of toots on the horn when he picked up Jason and out the boy would run, nylon weekend bag in hand.

It had been easy. Unlike his divorce from Shelley six years ago...

But thoughts like that were for another time. Weren't crises supposed to draw people together?

He took the back porch steps two at a time and could see them both waiting through the screen door. The light in the kitchen seemed unusually bright, and the silence of his ex-wife and her husband, sitting at the table, heads bowed, erased any hope that Jason had already returned home.

Sean gave a couple of taps on the screen door to alert them to his presence and went inside.

Shelley stood. "Sean! God, I'm so glad you're here." Then she glanced over at Paul to see how he would take what she had just said, but he was looking at once bleary-eyed and dour. "I mean, Paul and I have been worried sick."

"Have you called the police and reported him missing yet?"

Paul stood. "Of course we did that. As soon as Shel got home from the diner. What do you think?" Paul's large frame looked imposing. He was the kind of man at whose hands Sean had always received taunting and torture, a man's man, with no tolerance for sissies like him. He had heard from Jason the names Paul called Sean, the snide remarks about his masculinity, and the none-too-subtle hints that he, Paul, would make a fitter father for Jason.

Sean ignored the big man, with his glowering good looks and the smell of beer and perspiration that wafted off him. Sean caught his ex-wife's gaze. "What do you say we take a little ride? Check out his favorite haunts? Just do a little searching on our own?"

Shelley was already heading toward the door. Paul was behind her. Shelley stopped and turned at the sound of his footfalls. "No."

Paul's mouth dropped open.

Shelley grinned, the little half smile looking sickly on her pale, worried features. Sean wondered then if he ever beat her. "I mean, someone has to be here in case he comes home or the police call." She then turned back to Sean. "They're on the way over here right now. Paul, you've got his school picture, right?"

Paul consulted the ceiling. "It's right where you left it, dear. On the kitchen cabinet."

Sean could see the five-by-seven color photo lying near a stack of newspapers.

"Just give them the picture. The guy I talked to on the phone said they could make signs—" She paused. "—if necessary."

*

As Sean drove through the night, he battled a feeling of sick helplessness. If something horrible had happened to Jason, he couldn't bear the thought of it. The loss would rob him of more than just an only son. It would rob him of a life.

He didn't know how he could go on.

He had to fight back accusatory words, so he turned the radio on. He pushed the button that was set on the classical station in Pittsburgh and the car was filled with trumpets: Pachelbel's *Canon*. Shelley had always despised his love of classical music, but tonight he thought she might find it soothing.

And it gave them a way to deal with the silence and the anxiety, which thrummed in the car like a third presence.

"Have you checked the woods across from the house?"

"Paul went out there a little while ago with a flashlight. He knows right where Jason has his little fort built." She brushed away a tear. "There was nothing there, except for his iPad and a couple apples in a plastic bag."

Sean bit his lower lip. "He would never leave the iPad. He loved it. *Loves* it." Sean and Austin had given him the iPad Mini just last Christmas, and the little boy went everywhere with it.

"I know," Shelley whispered. "I know."

"How about his friends? I suppose you've called around."

Shelley answered in a voice barely above a whisper. "Friends, classmates. Christ, practically everyone he's ever bumped into in his whole life."

"No luck?"

"Yes, Sean, I had a lot of luck. Actually, this is just a ploy to get you alone. I thought I'd take another crack at seeing if I could convert you."

Sean sighed.

"I'm sorry. I didn't mean that. It's just that I'm so damn worried. This is the worst thing that's ever happened to me."

Sean pointed the car toward the river, deciding not to call Shelley on saying that it was the worst thing that ever happened to *her*. She was upset; her terror and anxiety wafted off her like a scent. The Ohio curved along the town of Summitville, and even though Jason had been warned, over and over, to keep away from its muddy banks, both parents were certain that wouldn't keep him away. Parental warnings had failed to keep generations of boys, including Sean, away from the allure of the river.

Both grew silent, thinking things they didn't want to: the number of boys over the years who had been claimed by the Ohio's treacherous and unpredictable currents.

Would they find Jason washed up on a bank? Or worse, would the current carry his body downstream, to turn up days later when everyone concerned would be fragile from lack of sleep and worry?

Sean steered the car down a bumpy road, filled with potholes, and headed toward the river. In front of the two of them, cooling towers from Summitville Power, one of the nation's first nuclear power plants, rose up against the night sky, tiny lights on the towers blinking in the darkness. The towers, sentinels against the dark and starless night, gave an almost surreal feel to their venture. Wafts of steam came off the tops of the two towers, to be snatched up by the wind.

After they had passed the small neighborhood filled with decrepit, tiny homes, sheathed in peeling paint or tar paper masquerading as brick, called Little England for as long as anyone could remember, Sean pulled the car over to the side of the road. Just ahead of them, the road dead-ended. Beyond where the cinders ended was a large grassy field that backed up to Summitville Power. For as long as Sean could remember, kids had been coming here: as prepubescents to explore the tall grassy fields nourished by the river, and later to smoke and make out.

Sean swallowed hard. If Jason was in this field, there was no way they would find him safe. Sean was gripped by a numbness that made his movements those of an automaton, doing each action separately, right down to putting one foot in front of the other.

He wished he had some optimistic words for Shelley, wished he had some optimism for himself. But what answer could there possibly be for an eight-year-old boy, smart and always well-behaved, to be out now, after a thunderstorm and hedging in on midnight? Still, he kept a part of his mind open for something he hadn't thought of.

The air, after the storm, had a slight chill to it. Shelley wrapped her arms around herself and Sean noticed for the first time how much she still looked like a child. Her thin build, barely clinging to a frame little more than five feet tall, gave her a waifish appearance. The baggy T-shirt and jeans she wore did little to dispel the illusion that Sean had a child along with him. Her reddish-brown hair was pulled back away from her face, a face unlined, but now creased by worry and dread.

"It's going to be okay," Sean said to his ex-wife. "There's got to be something we're not thinking of."

Shelley said nothing as the two of them stepped over a chain that supposedly barred anyone from entering the field.

The ground beneath them squished with each step they took, and as they progressed their feet sank deeper into the mud, causing them to have to pull them out sometimes, with a loud sucking noise once the foot was freed. An odor of fish wafted up from the river.

"He's not here," Shelley said. "This is pointless. We should be home so we can talk to the police when they get there."

"Paul can handle that. Besides, I've got my cell phone, and I assume you do too."

Shelley looked at him then, her eyes bright with tears in the darkness. She didn't need to say anything.

"Let's hurry."

Movement was tough, what with the damp and the sliver of a moon hidden behind slate gray clouds.

As their gaze roamed the darkened empty fields, Shelley grabbed Sean's arm suddenly. "There! Oh God, do you see it?"

And Sean followed Shelley's gaze and her trembling finger to what he first saw as just more high, yellowing grass and weeds. And then he noticed how some of the vegetation was tramped down.

And then he saw the little red Converse shoe.

Shelley collapsed against Sean, and he wrapped his arms around her. "It's his shoe! Sean, it's his shoe!" She sobbed against his chest, and Sean feared he would vomit. But he knew one of them needed to stay strong. "Shh." He stroked Shelley's hair. "It's just a shoe. It doesn't have to be Jason's. It could be anyone's. You know how people dump trash around here." Even as he voiced the reassurances, Sean doubted them himself. The shoe, almost glinting in the dull light, was exactly the right size. And his son wore little else besides red Chuck Taylors. When he outgrew one pair, he demanded another.

They trudged on through the darkness and the damp, silent. Shelley scooped up the shoe and held it, muddy, to her chest. What other horrors awaited them? Perhaps just beyond where the tree line started? Sean couldn't bear to think that his son was dead. That just couldn't be. God wouldn't do that to them. To him. Sean was thinking even if they found Jason lying unconscious somewhere, it would be better than this not knowing. He flashed forward to coming through the doors of City Hospital with Jason in his arms. The emergency staff would take Jason from them. They would fix him up and everything would be all right. Tomorrow, he and Austin would visit Jason in a hospital room, with the Audubon bird guide they had put back for his birthday next month. Jason would complain about being confined, wondering when they would let him go. There would be appeasements made, promises of ice cream and new toys.

Things would slowly come back to normal. Sure, Jason had fallen, bumped his head, passed out. Things like that happened all the time.

Didn't they?

Shelley stumbled and fell to the ground. She grunted as the air was knocked out of her. "What the hell?" she groaned, when she found enough breath to put behind her words.

The two looked down to see a mound of fresh dirt. Drying weeds and branches had been pulled over it, but the dirt looked freshly dug; nothing could hide that. All around them, weeds and various grasses grew unchecked. But there was this spot, a rough rectangle in shape, about as long as Shelley was tall.

Both stood and stared at what looked like a fairly fresh-dug grave with horror. Shelley chewed on her thumb. She whispered, "Do you know what that looks like?"

"Yeah." Sean's gut twisted itself into a knot.

Shelley dropped to her knees in the mud and began digging.

Sean grabbed her shoulder and pulled out his cell. "Maybe we should call the cops."

"I can't!" Shelley shrieked. "I can't wait for them to get here. I have to know." She threw up clumps of wet dirt behind her as her hands went deeper and deeper into the moist soil.

Sean couldn't wait either. He put his cell back in his pocket, knelt beside his ex-wife, and began to help her. From the recent rain, the earth was moist and easy to move.

They dug for about a half hour before Sean's hand hit on something. He recoiled, wanting to vomit, yanking his muddy hand back from what he had just touched.

"Shelley, stop." He pulled her hands out of the dirt. She turned to him, her lower lip quivering.

"What is it?"

"I hit something."

"What?"

"I don't know," Sean said, but he was lying. He knew all too well what he had felt: flesh and bone. "Please, let's go call the cops. I think we need to."

"I won't stop, Sean." Shelley buried her hands in the earth once more.

Only seconds passed before she stopped as if stunned and screamed. She then began to laugh, first in little hiccups, then in an all-out hysteria, beating the ground, the tears pouring down her face.

Sean looked over her shoulder and a kind of sickening horror and giddy relief rushed through him.

Someone had chosen this spot as the final resting place for a dog. The moon appeared from behind a cloud, revealing that the animal was far gone in decomposition. Bits of flesh and fur still clung to the bones, but maggots were busy erasing even those traces.

Shelley turned away from the stench and the ruin and grabbed Sean, burrowing her head into his chest, whispering breathlessly, "It's not him. It's not him."

And Sean stroked her hair, wondering: *Where is Jason, then? Where could he be?* He clutched the little red shoe tighter in his hand, behind Shelley's back.

Shelley pulled away and looked up at Sean. "Oh God, where is my boy?"

Chapter Two

It was no use. Sean swung his legs over the side of the bed, gray light of dawn filtering into the room, giving form and definition to the furniture in the bedroom, making of them sinister shapes, huddled creatures waiting in the half light.

He hadn't slept. Austin, comforter pulled up to his chin, lay on his side, mouth open. His sandy hair hung down over one of his closed eyes. A line of drool stained the pillowcase beneath him. Sean wondered how he did it. Sean had not slept at all the few hours that remained after dropping Shelley off at her house.

But then, Jason wasn't Austin's son. Not really. In spite of all Sean's wishing to the contrary, he often suspected his handsome boyfriend's interest in Sean's son was only to score points with Sean.

The night before, they had spoken to the police who were organizing a hunt for the boy at first light. Media had already gotten wind of the story, and Shelley was set up to do a plea for a Pittsburgh station, should it come to that. They were told there was nothing the police could do until morning, to try to get some rest. In the meantime they would be faxing out the boy's photo to area hospitals, to see if anything turned up. But how could any parent rest when he or she knew their child was out there somewhere, beyond protection and vulnerable?

He was just a little boy.

Enough. Sean slipped from the bedroom, soundless, and went downstairs to make himself some coffee. Outside, the sky was lightening to a dull gray. As he listened to the water trickle through the Mr. Coffee, he didn't know how he'd keep the stuff down, but he needed something to jar him out of the numbness he'd been feeling since he and Shelley found the buried dog...and Jason's shoe.

You don't know that it's Jason's shoe. Not really. Jason may not be the only little boy in Summitville who wears red Cons, for cryin' out loud.

He had to find the energy to go back. Help the search team. He knew the police force, small as it was, would corral anyone who was able to walk in their small town to help hunt for his little boy. They planned to start the search in the field where he and Shelley had made their grim discoveries the night before. He wanted to be there if—*Oh God, how could he even think this*—if Jason was discovered. He couldn't stand waiting around the house, dreading a call that might never come.

He wondered if Shelley had been able to sleep at all. And if she had, if it had been worth it. Or had she awakened, screaming, images of the buried dog replaced by images of Jason's decaying corpse? Wasn't life awful when reality and slumber meshed into one big horrible nightmare? But at least with a dream, one could always wake up.

Outside, the sky was lightening more, and Sean could see, as he looked out the window, pouring himself a cup of coffee he knew he wouldn't drink, that it would be another scorching day. The sky was already that milky white that foretold unrelenting heat and humidity.

What would this day bring? He looked around the kitchen, at the new oak cabinets he and Austin had hung barely a month ago, at the wallpaper they had put up, only after arguing for weeks over which pattern would look best. Outside, the deck was almost completed.

All of it seemed pointless now. If something had happened to Jason, and with dread he thought something most assuredly had, none of these things would matter. Not even Austin, who slumbered upstairs, unaware of how the loss of Sean's child could have affected his feelings not only for his lover, but for everyone.

He wondered if Shelley was awake yet. He wished he could be there to comfort her. He had thought that, after the divorce, he was completely indifferent to her, but now the thought occurred to him that the two of them could be merged in another unbreakable tie: sharing the loss of their child.

Stop it! he told himself. It wasn't Jason's body they'd discovered. No one had called yet and said that the body of a small boy had been found and could he come down and make an ID.

There was still hope. And as irrational as it was, that hope was all he had to cling to.

*

Shelley awakened from a dead sleep, feeling as if she was rising up with a great weight upon her chest. She turned, twisted up in sheets damp with sweat, to find Paul looking down at her.

He nudged her below her hips, and she could feel his erection pressing against her thigh.

"C'mon, honey. I've got something to take your mind off this whole fuckin' business."

Shelley looked up at him, awed, and stared into eyes that seemed paler than usual, almost colorless. She wondered how she had ever loved this man. "Paul, Paul, I can't." She pushed against him, trying to get out of bed, but his arm whipped around her and held her against him.

"No. Jason hasn't come home."

"Sure, he has, honey. He's in his bedroom. I didn't want to wake you up. Now, come on." His head dropped to her breast and she felt the warm wet of his tongue.

Revulsion burned. "I can't right now. Just let me go see that Jason is okay, and then maybe we can…"

"What? My word isn't good enough for you?" Paul slid the length of his body over hers, and his weight almost took her breath away. The coarse hair on his chest and stomach felt almost crawly against her skin, like insect legs. She reached up and placed her palms on his chest, pushing, struggling to slide out from beneath him. His face was almost impassive, but the set of his mouth told a tale of determination.

Shelley felt nothing. Sex right now seemed impossible. She felt dead.

And then she could feel the insistence of his sex against her belly, lower, trying to push between her legs. How could he do this to her? He had always been the macho man, careful that nothing but the toughest emotions showed, but even she never expected him to sink this low.

The head of his sex pushed against her and entered, the dry pain of it making her wince. "No!" she shrieked and began hitting his back with her fists. "Get off me."

"A little challenge? Ah, I like that." He pushed deeper into her, and the pain caused Shelley to suck in her breath.

"God, girl, you feel good," Paul whispered, his breath rank. Then he savagely shoved himself into her, and Shelley could almost feel herself tearing. For once she wished it was Sean who was with her. Sean, who shared in her horror and dread. "Stop." Her voice was weak from pain.

He continued to thrust, savagely driving his hips into her pelvis, sending hot tendrils of pain through her whole being.

Shelley couldn't determine how long it went on. The pain lessened as her body took over and she began lubricating. But the psychological pain deepened, making her feel nauseated. Why had she married this man? How could she be with someone so insensitive?

At last he finished, body stiffening above her as he bucked into her, his penis feeling like a club, something with which to rip her apart. He rolled off her, panting. "Damn," he wondered.

Shelley reached down. A sticky mess pooled over her thighs and on the sheet beneath her. When she raised her hand, she saw it was covered with blood.

"Paul," she whined, "look what you've done." He glanced over at her bloody fingers.

"Now you know what it's like to be fucked by a real man."

Shelley couldn't move for several minutes. She was trembling, stunned by this outrage.

Finally, she was able to quell the trembling enough to swing her legs over the side of the bed. Outside, it was light and the sky was a milky white color. The temperature must already be in the nineties, but Shelley felt cold.

It hurt to stand; her whole lower body felt as if it had been beaten, bruised. He said Jason had come back. Was that the truth?

Naked, Shelley hobbled to the door, still leaking, and grabbed her robe from the back of it. She could deal with the pain later.

Holding on to the wall for support, Shelley made her way down the hall toward Jason's room. He had a TV in there, and Shelley closed her eyes when she heard it on. Canned laughter came from the room and Ricky's and Lucy's voices, telling a tale of comic marital discord, wafted out from behind Jason's closed door.

Shelley paused at the tinny sound of the portable TV. "Thank you," she whispered. "Oh God, thank you."

She managed to get herself down the remainder of the hallway and paused outside his door to listen, hand on doorknob.

"But Ricky, you promised!" Lucy whined.

Shelley turned the handle and went inside.

There was no scream. The voice had been stunned out of her.

Jason lay on his bed, illuminated by the harsh glare of the sun outside. His bedclothes were covered with soil, as was his naked body. Clumps of dirt littered the bed. He had been opened up from navel to neck with some kind of knife, something that would cut jaggedly, leaving pieces of skin and muscle in pieces on his too-white skin. His green eyes were still rimmed in the black lashes Paul found too long ("like a little girl's"), but they stared dully at the ceiling, covered with a milky white substance. His mouth hung open; a trickle of blood seeped from one corner of it. All his teeth had been broken and stuck out of his gums, jagged stumps.

And his tongue, ripped or cut from his mouth, lay on the pillow beside his head.

*

Shelley awakened from a dead sleep, feeling as if she was rising up with a great weight upon her chest. She turned, twisted up in sheets damp with sweat, to find Paul looking down at her.

She jumped from the bed, searching on the floor for her clothes from the night before. She struggled into shorts, a T-shirt, and a pair of running shoes, pulling her amber hair back with a scrunchy, staring at Paul the whole time, as if holding him at bay.

"They said to meet down at City Hall to help with the search party. You're coming, aren't you?"

Shelley didn't wait for an answer. She turned and left Paul in bed.

Chapter Three

Junior Parsons had waited long enough. He couldn't be bothered with their confounded laws and stupid fuckin' rules. It was early morning, and he was hungry. And when Junior was hungry, he knew of only two ways to get food, the way his daddy and his grandpa had gotten it before him, the way all animals satisfied their hunger: by hunting and gathering.

Junior lived in a shack in the hills above Summitville. The shack had a tin roof and its walls were nothing more than old boards, turned gray by the wind, rain, heat, and snow that besieged it every day. In the small clearing, the shack he had built from metal parts, from cars, from old washing machines and other appliances, rusted. Junior had driven a stake into the ground and from it snaked a long coil of rope. Attached to the rope was Eunice, his beagle mix and the best hunting dog he had ever had. She was an old thing, with a baleful bark and a muzzle that was turning gray, but she knew how to ferret out a rabbit or a squirrel better than any purebred.

Now, as he stood outside his shack, he looked up at a greenish-colored sky. Down in the valley, near the river and hanging over the little town down there, a bank of slate blue storm clouds gathered, moving into position to assault the town with one hell of a storm. Hadn't they just had one yesterday? The weather sure was getting stranger with every year. Junior spit on his finger and held it up to catch the breeze. The storm was moving in from the south, and from the occasional grumbles of thunder and the flashes of heat lightning, Junior knew he and Eunice wouldn't have long to find a good piece of meat.

Junior ran a hand through his coarse red hair, making it stand on end. His face was a grizzled mass of scars, crowned by a crooked smile and a chipped front tooth. He would never be called handsome. In fact, he would never be called anything. For him, Eunice was company enough. She scared strangers off, usually little boys wandering the woods, and when she didn't manage to scare them off, at least warned Junior of their presence. To his way of thinking, what more did a man need?

He leaned back inside his front door and snatched the double-gauge shotgun from its rack on the wall. Even though it was still August and the official hunting season did not begin for another couple of months, Junior felt he was above the law when it came to hunting. After all, he wasn't one of those weekend sissies, in their fluorescent orange or camouflage, out for some kind of he-man adventure; he needed to hunt to eat. If he didn't, he would starve.

His daddy had told him once that when laws were wrong, the place for a just man was in jail. And Junior agreed completely: if he got arrested for poaching today, it wouldn't be the first time he went off for a few days' vacation in the county jail. Hell, at least there he got three squares a day without having to lift a finger.

Not too shabby.

Besides, with the rain approaching, it was unlikely any of the law would be out, trying to make life difficult for a little guy like him, who wanted only to put a decent meal on his table.

Enough with thinkin'. If he didn't get out there in those woods, with the brush and the trees and the briars, his food for the day might consist only of a few roots and if he was lucky, some mulberries. The growl in Junior's stomach told him that was just unacceptable fare for a full-grown man.

Junior positioned his gun under the crook of his arm and stooped to untie Eunice from her stake. Immediately the yellow, white, and black hound was off into the brush, her paws beating down the weeds and lifting her mournful cry to the storm-cloud crowded sky.

Junior followed, alert for the change in Eunice's bark that would let him know she had trapped a rabbit or treed a squirrel or raccoon. The dog was already well ahead of him, her barks sounding weaker, lifted up on the wind that had a sudden chill to it.

Damn all this rain they'd been having lately. It made it hard to get out to hunt, not to mention the mud he had to tramp through to do as little as forage.

In the woods, Junior was confronted with a pale darkness. Bright enough to see, but decidedly unpleasant. There was a cold, electric tang in the air and the leaves at the tops of the trees rustled, whispering to one another, warning of the coming storm.

Junior pressed on, the cold barrel of the gun his only comfort.

And then, when he was well into the woods, Eunice's cries changed. She began yapping furiously, her yelps coming out more high-pitched than usual.

"Hot damn!" Junior shouted, quickening his pace. That bitch was the best dog he ever had. Whatever it was she had cornered, she was going to get some of it today. "Good girl," Junior whispered, "good girl." It was almost as if the dog knew he had to find his prey in a hurry and she had taken care of the matter. One good shot to the head and he would be having a great supper tonight.

Junior tramped through the woods, following the sound of his dog's furious barking, changing his course every so often so that her yaps grew louder instead of softer.

And there, up ahead, was Eunice, head lowered to the ground, growling, then jumping up and barking.

What the hell had she found this time? Junior stepped closer, ducking beneath the branch of a low-hanging maple before getting to the clearing where Eunice was sending up such a clamor.

Junior stopped when he actually neared the dog. Stopped, and his mouth dropped open. He had never seen anything like this before. Hell, this wasn't what he had expected at all.

On the ground, near Eunice, was a little boy. Couldn't have been more than seven or eight years old. The boy sat in the brush with his knees drawn up to his chin, his skin white with terror, his eyes wide and sparkling, even in the dim light, which was growing darker by the moment. The poor little guy was white as a sheet; the only thing about him that seemed bright at all was the red tennis shoes he wore. The kid wasn't making any noise, except for a tiny whimpering that Junior didn't even hear until he got up real close. The kid was staring at Eunice as if she were some kind of fuckin' monster, for Christ's sake. Junior conceded Eunice could be pretty scary when she set her mind to it. And now, with her fangs bared and her yelps and growls coming out like she was express delivered here from hell, he didn't blame the little guy for his terror.

"Eunice!" Junior shouted, his voice tinged with rage, coming out in a gruff baritone. His command caused the dog to stop in midbark and slink over to him, tail between her legs. She sat down, keeping herself low, by his feet and waited.

"Good dog." Junior patted Eunice on the head and moved close to look at the little boy once more.

What he saw filled him with sadness.

This was no little boy who had wandered into the woods, as so many of them did, in search of adventure or an appropriate place to build a shelter. Something awful bad had happened to this kid.

To begin with, his clothes were ripped and covered with mud. His dark brown hair was wild, dirty, and sticking up. A big shiner caused one eye to swell almost shut, making the other one appear even wider than it was. Dried blood crusted under his nose.

Somebody sure as hell had done a number on this little guy.

As Junior drew closer, the kid drew up into himself even more, leaning back into the brush behind him, trying to disappear. His whimpering was one of the most pathetic sounds Junior had ever heard.

When he got to within three or four steps, the kid leaned way back and let out a cry that sounded like the howls Eunice made when she heard an ambulance's siren down the valley below.

Junior smiled and hunkered down on his haunches. "Hey, kid," he said, making sure his voice came out real soft, but distinct enough for the boy to hear. "What the hell happened to you?"

The little boy stared wide-eyed at him, lower lip trembling and his whole body shaking.

"Hey, I ain't gonna hurt you."

His reassurance seemed to do nothing to comfort the boy. It was almost as if the kid couldn't hear him.

"C'mon, son, why don't you tell me your name so I can get you back to your folks."

But the boy said nothing. He quickly wrapped his arms around his knees and lowered his head. Junior was once again struck by the fact that the poor little guy was trying to make himself small enough to disappear.

Junior wasn't sure what to do. He felt if he reached out a hand, the gesture would send the boy over the edge. His terror seemed so great.

What had happened? This was more than a case of just being lost in the woods. Someone had hurt this kid, hurt him bad, and from the looks of him, all the little boy could think of was that someone might do it again.

Junior repeated his reassurance while, at the same time, he slowly extended his right hand. "C'mon now, I ain't gonna hurt you. My name's Junior."

A drop of rain, heavy, splashed on Junior's forehead. The sky had become like night. The boy had been through enough, he decided, and didn't need to be left out here at the mercy of the storm. He had to get him back to his shack, and soon.

And then, Junior thought with dread, he would have to somehow get this boy back into town, where his parents were probably looking for him. The thought was almost enough for Junior to think, for one split second only, of just leaving the boy here for someone else to find. After all, the town's business had always been the town's business; he had been taught that since he was just so high. "They don't want us, and we don't need any of them," his grandpa had always told him.

But Junior wasn't that kind of man. He didn't think his grandpa was either. Extraordinary circumstances called for extraordinary measures.

Junior moved slowly to the boy, whose one good eye widened as he approached. "Don't be scared now. You don't wanna be caught out in this storm, now do you?" The boy leaned back as Junior drew closer, leaned so far Junior imagined him toppling over. "It's okay there, son. I'm gonna help you. Won't you tell me your name?"

But the boy stared at him, as if such a question were out of the grasp of his knowledge.

Finally, Junior reached him and gently laid a hand on his shoulder. "Now, I'm gonna pick you up and carry you back to my place. I ain't gonna hurt you, and that's a promise. We'll wait out the storm, and then I'm gonna get you down to the hospital. They'll treat you right." Junior was guessing at this last part; he had never actually seen the inside of a hospital in his forty-two years and had little knowledge of what went on within the walls of one.

Even though the boy's trembling had reached such a frenzy that Junior was afraid he might start pitching some kind of fit, he reached down and swooped the boy up in his arms, no easy task with the shotgun to carry as well.

And when he picked him up, he noticed the back of the boy's shorts was covered with a dark stain.

Blood.

Junior shivered.

The rain started coming down hard now, pelting Junior as he dashed through the woods, alarmed and afraid.

What had happened to this kid? Who the hell would do such a thing to such a sweet little guy?

Chapter Four

A cloud of dumb terror surrounded her. Today was the third day Jason had been missing, and Shelley had grown almost accustomed to the cloud. It had become her friend. Yes, it was painful, but it was also numbing. She moved through days and nights as if wrapped in a cocoon. The cocoon made everything she touched, everything she tasted, everything she saw dull, as if she were experiencing life secondhand.

There had been the search down by the river. It still brought tears to Shelley's eyes to remember the crowds of people, young and old, who had turned up to look for her boy. They had divided the fields and woods surrounding the nuclear power plant into quadrants, and they had all gone hunting, using long sticks to poke through the tall grass and weeds.

But other than discarded tires and similar unwanted detritus, they had found nothing—not Jason or any other child—on the property.

Bulletins had gone out over wires, and Jason's picture appeared on televisions and newspapers across the tristate area, in Pittsburgh, Youngstown, Steubenville, and Wheeling.

Shelley herself had appeared on Youngstown and Pittsburgh affiliate news stations, pleading for the return of her child. She barely recognized the waifish, tearful young woman on the screen as herself.

She had been certain Jason's body would be found. As much as she wanted to hope he was still alive, as the hours, and then the days passed with no result, she knew rationally there was little other explanation than that Jason was dead. Emotionally, though, hope still clung on, like a flame that could not be extinguished. She had tried to prepare herself for the call, allowed herself to wonder what it would be like to be suddenly without him.

There was a tiny part of her that would have been relieved to hear the news. Not that such news wouldn't send the world crashing down around her, not that such news wouldn't make her wonder if there was enough left to make her want to go on living. But at least she would have known something, and that would have been better than not knowing at all. Not knowing haunted her like the most vengeful of spirits, conjuring up all sorts of scenarios, the kind of things most mothers never even let their conscious minds come close to.

The police had made a thorough search of the field that backed up to Summitville Power and had found nothing else. At least he wasn't there. But Shelley was tormented by the thought that he was merely buried elsewhere.

And then optimism would raise its ugly head and Shelley would begin thinking, with a peculiar kind of pain in her gut, that her boy was still out there, alive, and would one day come back.

She pictured the reunion, tearful, over and over, until the fantasy brought on real tears and Shelley would have to do something, some robotic action to try to take her mind off all of this.

Like right now. Shelley stood in the kitchen, peeling apples. Royal Gala apples, Jason's favorite kind. She would bake a pie. But even this small action made her think of him, made her think of how the pie would be a wonderful homecoming gift.

In the harvest gold, brown, and maple kitchen, Shelley had the radio tuned to one of Pittsburgh's easy-listening stations. Celine Dion, Michael Bolton, Kenny G, and other musical pabulum filled the kitchen and if the song was an oldie, say, Carole King singing "It's Too Late," Shelley could sing along and concentrate only on what verse was coming up next. It was three or four minutes of oblivion.

But then a commercial would come on and Shelley would be back at the kitchen window, imagining Jason walking up the driveway, head hung low, sheepish at this awful transgression he had made.

But nothing stirred outside the window, save for the heat shimmering up from the concrete.

Shelley sliced the apples and put them in the crust, sprinkling them with raisins, walnuts, butter, and brown sugar. She started to mix up a crumb topping, sniffling and trying to hold back another onslaught of tears. The past couple of days, she had walked around, eyes puffy and watery, looking as if she had the worst of colds.

Paul, of course, was little help. He paid lip service to her concern but didn't really seem to share in it. Since Jason had disappeared, he spent more and more time away from her. He could be found at the VFW or the American Legion, downing beer after beer and, Shelley supposed with a hateful chill, basking in the newfound attention the loss of his stepson afforded him.

She wondered who Paul was, wondered why she even stayed with him. But, she thought, finishing sprinkling the crumb topping on the pie, she couldn't think that way. She already had one failed marriage through no fault of her own. No matter what, this one would survive. After all, she had taken the vows...for better or worse...

Shelley put a foil-wrapped baking sheet on the bottom of the oven and set the pie on the rack above it. Just as she was closing the door, the telephone rang.

Every time it rang these days, Shelley screamed. Even when her cell phone chirped, it sent a jolt of electricity through her. Her nerves were on alert and the shrieking jangle of the telephone caused the cocoon to fall away, exposing raw nerve endings. She knew, just knew, someone from the police would call and tell her Jason's body had been found.

When it was only her mother, or Paul telling her he would be a little late through alcohol-slurred words, or even Sean, seeing if she had heard anything yet, Shelley couldn't keep the disappointment out of her voice.

The phone screamed, demanding attention, and for just a moment Shelley thought of ripping the damn thing out of the wall. Thought of just crawling under the kitchen table until she saw a pair of little red Chuck Taylors coming in the kitchen door.

"Hello."

"Mrs. Thompson?"

"Yes?" The man's voice had the ring of authority to it. Was this Hugh Allen, the detective who had visited them, who had collected Jason's school picture from them?

"This is Hugh Allen."

"Have you found something out?"

There was a pause. "Maybe. About an hour ago, someone left a little boy by the emergency room doors down at City Hospital."

"Someone?"

"One of the nurses saw a bum hurrying away, but he wouldn't stop when she called out."

"But was it Jason?" Shelley tried to keep the wheedling high tone out of her voice.

"We don't know."

"Well, hasn't anyone asked?"

"Mrs. Thompson, the boy can't or won't speak. There's no ID on him, so we don't know who he is."

"Describe him."

"Um, he appears to be eight or nine, with dark-brown hair, green eyes, slight frame." He continued to talk about what he was last seen wearing.

That could be Jason, Shelley thought, but it could also be any number of boys. And what was this business about not being able to talk? If there was one thing Jason was good at it, it was talking. One of her greatest challenges was trying to get him to shut up for five minutes. But, oh, how wonderful it would be to hear him ramble on about the solar system again, or Greek mythology, or whatever had happened to catch his interest that week.

"Well, Jason fits that description. Is he okay?" If he was dead, if he was dead, Hugh Allen would have told her that right off.

"Mrs. Thompson, I think you should come down to the hospital. Can you do that?"

Shelley caught on to how he had ignored her question about the boy's well-being, and it caused a chill to run through her. She sat down heavily in a kitchen chair, whispering, "Is he all right?"

There was a pause. "The boy is recovering. But he was beaten and..." The detective's voice trailed off.

"What is it?"

"I don't know quite how to put this."

"Baldly, Mr. Allen. Put it baldly. Do you know the hell I've been through?"

There was a pause. "He was raped."

"What?"

There was another long pause. "He was anally raped, Mrs. Thompson."

"Oh God."

"Can you come down? Do you need someone to come out and get you? I could send—"

"I can get there okay, thanks."

"Is there someone you could call to come with you? Your husband?"

Shelley immediately thought of Sean. "Yeah, that's probably a good idea." She sucked in some breath. "Do you think it's Jason?"

"This boy has quite a few facial bruises, so it's hard..."

"Is it Jason?"

"Yes, Mrs. Thompson, we think it probably is."

Shelley hung the up phone, rushed to the sink, and vomited.

After she cleaned up the mess she had made and went upstairs and put on a fresh pair of jeans and a plain white blouse, she went into the bedroom and stared at the phone.

Who should she call? Paul was at the American Legion, of that much she was sure. She could see him now, sitting in the dim light at the bar, a longneck in front of him, along with a couple of shot glasses. He would come if she called him. She knew that. Knew his large frame would come staggering through the door within ten minutes if she would pick up the phone and dial the familiar number, a number she knew by heart. How many dinners had sat chilling after she had called that very same number, waiting for her husband to come home? "But he bought me a shot, honey. You can't just ignore it when a man buys you a shot."

She imagined the look on people's faces down at the hospital, the quickly downcast eyes when they saw Paul, smelled the alcohol on his breath. As soon as this thing was over, she would have to have a long talk with him.

And if she didn't call Paul, if she called Sean instead, how would Paul feel about that? "So you thought you were better off with the faggot instead of me?" He would hold up a sarcastic, placating hand. "Hey, it's no skin off my ass if you'd rather be with him. Go ahead." A morose bark of laughter. "Not that there's anything to be jealous of."

The little scenario spurned her on, and she picked up the phone.

*

Sean figured he could do two things while his son was missing. The first was to do nothing, to call into the newspaper, who knew well of his troubles, and tell them he just didn't have the strength to do his job. They would understand. He was already sick of the sad looks of concern he got every time he passed through the newsroom or down a corridor at the paper. The second option, and the one he had chosen, was to throw himself into his work with as much energy as he could muster. Besides, with his position as a writer with the only newspaper in the county, he was in the unique position of being able to keep the public eye focused on his son's disappearance. He made sure that one of the two recent photographs they had of Jason were run in each edition, so if anyone did see him, the photo might get them to call the paper or the police and report it.

So he stayed with his second option, spending twelve-, thirteen-, and fourteen-hour days at the newspaper. It was hard to find enough to keep him busy, what with the paper only publishing three times a week. Once upon a time, this was what he had liked about his job: all the free time it afforded him. The pittance the job paid be damned; he had his freedom. Lots of time to spend with Austin, working on their home, working on their relationship.

And their relationship had suffered. He didn't have time for Austin the past few days. There was too much on his mind at the moment, not enough room for anyone save for Jason.

Now he sat staring at his monitor, trying to make sense of the words in the article he was writing about the city council meeting he had attended earlier that week. He knew he had faithfully reported what had gone on—the zoning permits and the decision to raise funds to restore the limestone on City Hall to its original condition—but the words seemed a jumble, some kind of puzzle he didn't possess the key to figuring out. The cursor winked at him, taunting over and over.

When the phone rang, it caused him to jump, one hand flying out almost of its own accord to knock over his fourth cup of coffee that morning.

"Shit," he whispered, looking down at the rapidly spreading pool on the papers on his desk. He snatched up the phone to quiet its ringing, which seemed to set Sean's nerves even more on edge.

"Dawes. Can I help you?"

"Sean?"

"Shelley." If he was nervous before, the questioning sound of his ex-wife's voice took him to new levels of alarm.

His heart thumped wildly. "Have you found something out?"

"Well, yes. I—"

"Is he okay?" Sean was already imagining two scenarios, one in which she told him their son's body was found and its opposite, in which she informed him that Jason had wandered in early this morning, sheepish but glad to be home. Perhaps he had just wandered too far in the woods surrounding the city and had lost his way.

"I don't know."

"What do you mean, you don't know?"

"That detective, Mr. Allen, called a few minutes ago." Sean conjured up an image of the man and saw an arrogant asshole in his mind's eye, one whom he had the distinct displeasure of having worked with before on many stories—and a man with whom he shared a secret.

"And?"

"If you'd let me finish... He said that a boy had been dropped off at the emergency room."

"Who dropped him off?" Sean already didn't like the sound of where this was going.

"They don't know. He ran off before anyone had a chance to talk to him or find out who he was."

"Jesus."

"Anyway, the little boy pretty much fits Jason's description."

"What do you mean, pretty much? For Christ's sake, Shelley, his picture has been all over the place."

Shelley paused, and Sean realized she was sitting and waiting for him to finish raving before she continued. He shut up.

"The little boy was beaten. I guess his face is pretty bruised, and they're not sure."

"Can't the kid tell them?"

"No. The boy refuses to, or can't, talk."

"So what do they want? You to come down and see if it's really Jason?" Already, Sean knew the little boy couldn't possibly be his son. He was already accepting his fate: Jason would never be found and Sean would be forced to spend the rest of his life cloaked in doubt, wondering if the boy he so loved was even alive.

"Exactly. I'd like you to come with me, if you can get away."

"Of course I can get away. You don't even have to ask." There was a pause. "What about Paul?"

And Shelley, in a voice that held too much nervousness, said, "He, um, is at a job interview."

"Good for him."

"There's more."

Sean swallowed, suddenly at a loss for saliva. The swallow hurt, as if he were trying to force something dry and woolly down his throat. "What is it?" he said, barely able to raise his voice above a whisper.

"Maybe we should go into that when you get here."

"What is it, Shelley?"

"The boy was raped."

The room dropped out from under him, and Sean suddenly felt very sick, his gut churning and a burning sensation rising to take residence at the back of his throat. After he could find enough breath to put behind words, he asked, "Do you want me to come get you?"

"Please, Sean."

"I'll be right there. Gimme five." He didn't wait for her to say anything else. He replaced the phone in its cradle and spun his chair around to look out the window. The sun now peeked out from behind a few clouds, emerging and re-emerging from behind them.

Didn't the world know this type of weather was inappropriate?

Sean grabbed his keys from the desktop and hurried out.

Chapter Five

He was alone. Stretching before him was an endless wood. But this was a wood unlike any in which he liked to play. This wood was the stuff of horror movies and it chilled him, made his hair stand on end. As far as he could see, there was nothing but black trees, their leafless branches stretching up to a sky heavy with slate blue clouds, pregnant with rain. The branches were black and almost looked alive, witches' fingers reaching out to grab the unwary. In one of those trees, he could swear he saw an eye, scarlet irised, the white choked with a yellow film and shots of blood. It blinked and his hand flew to his mouth to stifle the scream. Wisps of fog lay on the ground, and somewhere a wolf howled.

There it was now. A great, hulking black beast, coat matted with spurs. Its eyes, when it swiveled its massive head toward him, were red, hungry.

He turned to run and found a leaden feeling in his limbs impeded any movement he made. It was if his legs suddenly added more weight than the rest of his body, as though they had been filled with cement instead of blood, muscle, and bone. Each step took an extreme effort of will. The boy wanted to cry out, but when he opened his mouth to scream, nothing emerged save for a dry sound: air whistling through his mouth.

He turned and, with all the strength he could muster, began making passage away from the wolf, or whatever it was. He could feel its hot breath on the back of his neck, drawing closer and closer.

Up ahead, his mother held out her arms. If only, if only...

But the beast drew nearer, its heat like a cloud, rolling toward him. The boy could feel it on the back of his legs, could smell its sour breath in the wind.

And yet he made it to within feet of his mother, her blue eyes so familiar, so comforting. He was already imagining the protection her arms would provide, imagining falling into those same arms and laughing as the wolf yelped and turned to run back into the darkness, tail between its legs.

But when he got to his mother, she began laughing and pointing at him, the way the kids did at school when he did something stupid. He stretched his arms out to her, and all she did was turn away.

He took one final step, the step that would lead him into her arms. As he did so, she took flight. With a speed that made a blur of her, she disappeared.

The wolf leaped and then was upon him, furry weight bringing him down hard into the cold earth and the mist, claws digging into his back; and with a triumphant howl, it bit into the back of his neck.

Chapter Six

Shelley stared out the window. Every time she heard the bass of an approaching engine, she would crane her head, hoping for the sight of Sean's red Nissan Sentra.

And each time she would be disappointed.

What was taking him so long? She paced the kitchen, unable to sit. She even picked up one of Paul's cigarettes and put it to her lips, then shook her head and replaced it in its pack, knowing smoking it would only serve to increase her tension, despite what the little addict in her head told her.

Shelley glanced down at her watch. Only ten minutes had passed since she had spoken to Sean on the phone. Amazing how time slows when you're having a tragedy.

The phone's jangle caused her to jump, then frown. *Who's calling now?* she wondered as she hurried to quiet it, making a weird comparison and flashing back to hurrying to Jason's crib when he was a baby to quiet him. Perhaps the person phoning was Detective Allen, to tell her not to bother coming down because they had discovered, somehow, the boy in the hospital was not her son, or he was her son and he had died from his injuries.

"Hello."

The sudden absence of the phone's ringing made the house seem unnaturally quiet. She longed for the sound of the gravel in the driveway crunching as Sean pulled in. She desperately wanted him to arrive before Paul came home. She knew Paul would not like being left out.

"Shelley? Honey?"

"Hi, Mom." Shelley twisted the phone cord around her finger and imagined the woman who had given her life. The cotton candy-like helmet of dull orange hair, the glasses with their big squared-off lenses, and the simple, rectangular house dresses she called "shifts" that no one but her mother seemed to wear anymore. Shelley could also see, behind her mother, on the violet-patterned living room wallpaper, a brass crucifix hanging.

"Have you heard anything yet, honey?"

Shelley paused for a moment, wondering if the best idea might not lie in keeping things to herself, at least until after she had a chance to visit the hospital. Perhaps she didn't want to get her admittedly excitable mother all worked up for nothing. And perhaps, Shelley ruefully thought, she knew that if she told her mother, she would want to accompany her down to City Hospital, and Shelley didn't know if she was up for that. Didn't know if she could stand the clicking rosary beads and the exhortations for Shelley to pray, pray so that Jesus Christ might deliver their little lamb from evil.

Somehow, though, Shelley knew she couldn't *not* tell her mother where she was going. It would be a sin of omission, an indirect lie. And Shelley knew the guilt she would feel keeping this important news from her mother would be a burden she couldn't handle right now, what with all she already had on her plate.

"As a matter of fact, Mom, I'm heading down to City Hospital right now."

"Oh?"

The pause let Shelley know her mother was waiting and she should fill in the blank, even though she didn't want to.

Why hadn't she just let the phone ring? But how could she do that, in the situation in which she found herself? "That detective who was over here, Allen? He called and said a little boy had been left at the emergency room..."

"Left? What do you mean?"

"Someone, they don't know who, dropped off a little boy earlier today."

"Well, is it Jason?"

"They're not sure."

"How could they not be sure? Wouldn't Jason tell them?"

Shelley twisted the phone cord so tightly around her index finger it made her wince. Going through what was happening to her right now would be almost like reliving the phone call from Detective Allen, and all the same anxiety it brought to the surface.

But she had no choice. Mother was waiting.

"It seems that the little boy was pretty badly beaten. His face is all bruised..." And suddenly Shelley felt herself crying, the tears arriving without warning, the sobs escaping her like shudders. For what seemed like several minutes, Shelley struggled to catch her hiccupping breath.

"Oh dear Lord. But still, wouldn't Jason tell them who he was?"

Shelley sniffed, trying to rein in her tears. "Honey?"

"Yes, Mother. It's just that this is so hard."

"Nothing is hard with the help of Jesus."

And next you'll tell me the Lord never gives more than we can bear. Or how about what doesn't kill us makes us stronger?

Shelley rolled her eyes and passed a hand across her face. She blew out a big, quivering sigh. "The boy can't, or won't, talk."

"That doesn't sound like Jason."

"I know." And just then, mercifully, Sean's car pulled into the driveway. The engine died and was followed by the slam of a car door. Shelley leaned over to peer through the kitchen door, just to make sure it wasn't Paul. Sean was mounting the back porch steps. "Listen, Mom, I've gotta get going. They're waiting for me."

"Honey, I can take you. You shouldn't have to go through this by yourself."

"I'm not going alone. Sean just got here."

"Sean?" There was a small note of alarm in her mother's voice. "What about Paul? Where's Paul?"

"Out drowning his sorrows, I suppose."

"Now dear, that's very unkind."

"It's the truth."

Sean tapped at the screen door, and Shelley motioned him into the kitchen. "Anyway, I do have to get going."

"Are you sure this is such a good idea?"

"What do you mean?"

"I mean Sean, honey. Paul should be with you. He is your husband, after all."

"And Sean is Jason's father, *after all*, a fact it seems you'd like to forget."

Her mother snorted. "That's true enough. And I can't understand why you don't feel the same. That man is an abomination."

"Listen, I really have to go."

"I'll meet you down there."

"No, Mom." Shelley thought fast. "The detective said we should come alone."

"Why? I—"

"I've gotta go." Shelley quickly replaced the receiver in its cradle and glanced up at Sean, whose face remained impassive behind sunglasses.

"Let's get this over with."

*

After Sean pressed her for more details and Shelley had been unable to provide them, the two fell silent on the short drive to downtown Summitville and its hospital. The silence in the car was like a third presence, unwelcome, making both of them wish they could let it out at this or that corner. But no such option existed for Shelley and Sean. It was true they had talked very little since the divorce. The fighting, the tears, and the legal maneuvering had just about killed off any feelings the two had for one another. Conversation the past few years had been limited to working out the details of when Jason would be picked up and dropped off for his weekly visitation.

The redbrick building that housed the county's only hospital rose up before them at last. Sean found parking on Third Street, and the two made their way quickly up the front walk. The American flag on a pole outside the main entrance hung limp. The heat and humidity had robbed the air of wind, and the flag looked as tired as the two parents felt.

Through the glass double doors, Sean and Shelley were within the pale green corridors of the hospital, surrounded by air that was chilled to an almost arctic point and perfumed by the smell of disinfectant.

"Where do we go?" Sean asked.

"Fifth floor. It's the children's ward."

As they rode up in the elevator, Sean wondered, "Do you think it's really him?"

"The detective said they thought it probably was."

Sean said nothing for a moment. "I have mixed feelings. Part of me wants it to be him and the other part says no. One way I don't have to face that something horrible has happened to Jason, and the other I at least know he's alive."

"I think we all feel that way."

The elevator doors opened onto a corridor decorated with manila paper-and-crayon drawings done by children. The crude houses, with their attendant mother, father and children, seemed absurdly and inappropriately cheerful for the mission before them. Up ahead was the nurses' station. Shelley left Sean trailing behind her as she strode up to the counter.

An older nurse, a woman with blonde hair shot through with gray, peered up at her through oval lenses when Shelley arrived at the desk, her arms wrapped around herself, massaging.

"May I help you, ma'am?" It was obvious from the anxious way she appraised Shelley that she sensed already something was unusually wrong here.

"Detective Allen called. I'm Shelley Thompson and this is my—the boy's father, Sean Dawes."

The nurse's expression immediately softened. "Of course, you're here to see our little mystery man." She emerged from behind the counter, nylons swishing, to reveal a broad expanse of hips and orthopedic shoes. "He's down the hall this way."

Shelley and Sean followed her. She stopped outside room 515 and turned to address them. "Detective Allen is just downstairs, getting some coffee, I believe. He suggested you wait for him to get back before you go inside."

"That's bullshit." Shelley brushed by the nurse and went into the room.

Sean was right behind her. The nurse stood in the doorway, watching them. Every so often she would lean back, presumably to see if Detective Allen was emerging from the elevator.

But these minor details disappeared for Shelley as she reached out to draw aside the tan curtain that surrounded the bed. A numbness, akin to the one she had been living under since she and Sean had discovered what they thought was Jason's gym shoe at Summitville Power, intensified. It seemed everything that existed in the world around them right now disappeared: the calls over the hospital's PA system, the sounds of carts rolling down the hall to deliver lunches to the patients, the smell of isopropyl alcohol, everything. All that existed for her right now was this bed and the small creature who lay within, covers drawn up to his ears, partially obscuring his face.

Shelley shuddered as she stared at the dark brown hair sticking up from beneath the pale blue blanket. Even though her conscious mind did not want to accept it, playing a game of "wait and see" with her that was entirely reasonable, Shelley knew that hair: the way it stuck up like spikes, the cowlick in the middle of Jason's forehead that ruined any attempt at neatness she'd ever tried to impose.

Shelley froze, listening to the blood pounding in her ears, the beating of her heart, which suddenly seemed too fast, erratic. She suddenly wasn't so sure she wanted to draw back the blanket and witness the injuries to her little boy's face, bad enough that others couldn't identify him with any degree of certainty, even though she had provided them with countless photos.

Her breath caught and a quivering shudder emerged. Sean stepped up behind her and squeezed her shoulder. "Want me to look?"

Shelley shrugged the hand away without looking at her ex-husband. The action was enough for her to take the final two or three steps to the bed.

"Ah, here's Detective Allen now," the nurse said.

Shelley pulled back the blanket and gasped. She turned away, pushing hard against her eyes with the palms of her hands, trying to block out the sobs clamoring inside to escape.

It was him. She had known all along it would be. Coming down here and having a look were both formalities. From the moment Detective Allen told her a boy had been dropped off at the hospital, she had known that boy was her son.

"What have they done to him?" she moaned. Jason's face was a mass of dark purple and sick yellow bruises. His lips were swollen, one eye was swollen shut, his nose had a large lump across the bridge of it, darkening to blue. She had seen pictures once, in a book in high school, of child abuse victims, and this view took her back to those pictures. She never thought a child of hers would look this way. She wanted to touch him, but the pain that touch could bring on held her back.

And his one open eye, looking like something that didn't belong on this ravaged face, stared up at her, unblinking, the green iris taunting, not even seeming to recognize her.

Sean put an arm around her, and this time it was welcome. With her at his side, he approached the bed and drew the covers down farther. He looked at the boy lying there and bit his lip. With a wavering voice, he turned to the detective, who stood impassively with the nurse at his side.

"It's him."

The detective nodded. "Why don't we come out to the corridor? I'll get the doctor..."

"I'll go." And the nurse disappeared down the hallway, leaving in her wake swishing nylons and the smell of some floral-scented perfume, cloying.

"He can tell you what's going on."

"I'm not going anywhere," Shelley whispered, trying to hold back the tears. In spite of herself, two trickled down her cheeks.

"It might be better if we talked outside." Detective Allen, his florid middle-aged face grave, nodded toward the figure on the bed.

And Sean seemed to understand; at least, a look of what Shelley thought of as comprehension passed between the two men's gazes. "Shelley, honey, let's hear what the doctor has to say."

"I'm not leaving him."

"No one's asking you to, ma'am."

Shelley didn't know if she could move: her legs felt rooted to the industrial green tile floor. Sean pulled her close and for a moment, Shelley wondered what the hell he was doing. He whispered, "It might be better if we were outside the room. You know?"

And Shelley closed her eyes with pain. They didn't want Jason hearing the catalog of injuries that was probably forthcoming. After all, even though he wasn't talking, no one had said he was unaware of what was going on around him.

With that thought, Shelley returned to the bed, reached under the covers, and grabbed her son's hand, held it tight. She leaned over and, at last, felt the silk of his brown hair in her hand as she stroked it back from his forehead. She leaned down close to his ear. "Honey? Honey, it's gonna be okay. Mama's here now. And I'm not gonna be far. Daddy and I are just going outside to talk to the doctor, see how we can make you better."

Shelley forced herself to pull her hand away, hiccupped out a short sob, and followed Sean out into the corridor.

*

The doctor was a young Asian woman. She was small, with bird-like bones and a round face topped with black hair, cut short. She wore a blue lab coat, navy skirt, and dark-blue flats. Gold buttons adorned her ears.

Detective Allen said, "This is Ann Wu. She's been looking out for the little boy in there."

"His name is Jason," Shelley said. "It's Jason. It's him." Sean slid his arm around her.

"So then, you're sure?"

"I'm his mother, for Christ's sake."

"Of course." Detective Allen turned to peer down the hall.

"Hello, Mr. and Mrs.?" The doctor had a nice smile; Shelley was glad a woman had been taking care of him. She didn't want to think about why, but the reasons were obvious. For one, the maternal warmth Dr. Wu exhibited made her feel confident that Jason was under good care. For another, whoever had done this to her son was a man, and having another male in charge of his care could be an impediment to his getting better.

"Mrs. Thompson and Mr. Dawes. We're no longer married," Sean said.

"I see. Would the two of you like some coffee? There's a little lounge down the hall where we could talk."

Shelley twisted a lock of hair around her finger, let it go, twisted again. "Do we have to? I think I'd like to stay close."

Sean said, "It might be more comfortable, honey."

"No."

Dr. Wu ran her fingers through her short hair. "It's okay. We can talk here." She took a deep breath. "I'm afraid I don't have much good news. The best I can offer you is that he's going to be all right. There's nothing physically wrong with him that won't be taken care of by time."

"That's good," Sean said.

"But what about the, um, psychological, scars?" Shelley bit her lip. Her eyes were moist.

Dr. Wu nodded. "I understand your concern, Mrs. Thompson. And in that area, I just don't know." Dr. Wu leaned back against the wall. "Let me just go over what we know."

Shelley wasn't sure she wanted to hear this. The little she had eaten that day seemed to awaken, churning in her gut. She tasted bile at the back of her throat.

"As you can see from his injuries, Jason has been badly beaten. There are hematomas on his face, of course, but also a subdural one near his stomach, where it looks like he was kicked."

Shelley gasped and bit her lip.

"He has some lacerations around his wrists and ankles, where he may have been bound, with what appears to have been some sort of wire, or metal cable."

"No, no," Shelley moaned.

Dr. Wu massaged her forehead. It was obvious she didn't want to be delivering this speech. "The worst physical damage was to the boy's, Jason's, rectal cavity. There's been some bad tearing. We've done some stitches to repair the worst of it, but it's going to take a lot of time to heal. We have him on stool softeners and a good antibiotic suppository."

Shelley shook her head.

"Have you run tests for sexually transmitted diseases? AIDS?" Sean's mind clouded over with just how far-reaching the consequences of what had happened to Jason could be.

"We've performed some tests, and so far it looks as if Jason is free from any kind of sexually transmitted disease. As far as HIV, we'll need to wait and see on that. As you might be aware…"

"The window period." Sean's voice was flat, as though he felt numb.

Dr. Wu nodded. "Right. I think he should be tested for HIV in a couple of months, then again in another couple of months. If no antibodies show up after six months, we can pretty much assume there's no problem there. Try not to worry too much about it."

"Try not to worry? Try not to worry?" Shelley's voice was rising with hysteria.

"Shh. Just take it easy, Shelley."

Shelley glared at her ex-husband.

"Mrs. Thompson, Jason is going to need your strength to pull through this. Worrying about what might happen isn't going to do anyone any good. All right?" Dr. Wu's sympathy was evident in her dark brown eyes. "I wish I could offer you more. But I have to give you the truth."

"Doctor, what about his not speaking?" Sean cocked his head. Shelley noticed how pale he had gone over the past few minutes.

The doctor nodded. "We've been unable to find any physical reasons for that. It's not unheard of for trauma victims to experience a loss of speech after the event. But just because it's psychosomatic doesn't mean it's any less real. The good thing is he could snap out of it at any time."

"Or never?" Sean asked.

"That's unlikely. Most of the clinical cases I've looked into, and I have looked into a few, the subjects' speech did eventually return."

"How long?" Sean asked.

Dr. Wu shook her head. "It varies widely, from a few days to a few years."

"Years?" Shelley grabbed on to Sean's arm and squeezed so hard he winced.

"Mrs. Thompson, I want to be honest with you. Your son has been severely traumatized by what's happened to him. In such cases, the best medicine for the psychological damage has been the warmth and caring of people close to the victim."

"Well, he'll certainly get that."

"Certainly," Sean whispered.

Dr. Wu glanced down at the clipboard in her hand. "Now, unless I can answer any other questions—"

"How long will he have to be here?" Shelley asked.

"Two or three more days should be sufficient. We have to watch the stitches and make sure there's no more bleeding." She gently touched Shelley's arm. "I've always believed my patients' best hope lay in recovering at home, in a familiar environment with familiar faces, so we'll do what we can to get him home to you as quickly as possible."

"Thanks, Dr. Wu," Shelley whispered, her voice wavering.

Dr. Wu nodded. "Now, I need to be getting on to my rounds. If you need anything at all..." Dr. Wu dug in her lab coat pocket and produced a card. "Give me a call. My cell number is on there as well."

Leaving the card in Shelley's hand, Dr. Wu disappeared down the hall.

*

Detective Allen turned toward them, and Sean could see he'd just been biding his time while the doctor laid out her horror story. Sean had never liked this big, middle-aged man, with his ruddy complexion and lack of hair. In past encounters with him, Allen had always been overbearing, as if his machismo made him somehow superior to Sean. And Sean couldn't help but wonder if the detective remembered him from a past circumstance that propriety would not allow him to broach. But if he could help his son, Sean was willing to work with him.

"Could I ask the two of you a couple of questions?"

Sean frowned. "Maybe right now isn't the best time."

"Please. Just a couple of minutes. You do want to find the culprit, don't you?"

"What is it, Detective? I don't think either of us has much to tell you." Sean eyed the detective. In spite of the trauma of the situation and his anxiety and grief over what had happened to Jason, he couldn't help but search for some glimmer of recognition in Allen's eyes.

"Well, even so, I'd like you both to think about who might have done this to Jason." He looked pointedly at Sean, who shrunk from his scrutiny. A chill ran through him suddenly as all at once it became clear what the detective was thinking.

Shelley spoke first. "I have no idea, Detective. Jason was a very 'up' little boy. Everyone liked him. Nothing like this... I never imagined anyone could do this."

He looked again at Sean, the pale-blue eyes probing. "How about you, Sean? Any ideas?"

"No. None." Sean stared down at the floor. His face felt hot. The words almost came tumbling out. *Homosexuals like little boys, right, Mr. Allen? Maybe one of my gay boyfriends went after a little something from Jason. Right, Mr. Allen? Or maybe it was me... You should know better, Mr. Allen.*

"Has Jason mentioned anyone to either of you? A new friend? Someone older, perhaps? Have either of you seen anyone hanging around Jason?"

Shelley spoke. "No. There hasn't been anyone. Jason hasn't mentioned a soul. He's got his little playmates, but he's had them since he was so high."

"What about you, Sean? You live in a different neighborhood? Anything unusual when he comes over for the weekend?"

So he's already checked into our situation. "No. Jason usually just hangs out with Austin and me when he comes over."

The detective nodded, looking Sean up and down with slow scrutiny. "Well, if either of you think of anything, give me a call." He handed them each a card. "My home number's on there as well. Call anytime."

"We'll be sure to, Detective." Shelley thought for a moment. "What about the man who dropped him off here at the hospital?"

Detective Allen shook his head. "We're trying to find out who that was. Actually, we're trying very hard. One of the nurses had a glimpse of the man leaving, and she's down at headquarters right now with an artist from Pittsburgh, trying to see if we can get some sort of drawing to put out."

"Good." Shelley looked back into the room. "I'd like to be with him now, if you don't mind."

"I understand. Please keep in touch."

"We're not going anywhere," Sean said.

"I'll talk to you later." Detective Allen flipped the little pocket notebook in his hand shut and started down the corridor.

Sean froze when he saw an older, heavyset woman pass the detective, drawing closer. His mother-in-law. Good Lord, what was next?

Sean followed Shelley into the room.

Jason stared up at his mother. There seemed to be recognition in the green eyes, ringed with long, black lashes. His left eye was now open just a tiny bit. Sean wondered what was going on behind those eyes. Did he recognize his mother? Or was he in some other world, lost to horrors he was suddenly unable to describe?

"Hey, tiger," Shelley whispered, smoothing back the spikes of brown hair. "You've been through a lot, haven't you? But you're safe now, and you're gonna come home soon. Would you like that?"

Jason turned away suddenly, facing the wall.

Shelley gave Sean a puzzled look. She leaned close to her son, and he shrugged up his shoulder, almost as if he wanted to avoid her touch. "Jason? Jason, what is it?"

Before things had a chance to go any further, the voice of Sean's ex-mother-in-law invaded the quiet of the room.

"Well, here's our little boy!" She strode into the room, and the air there seemed to move to accommodate her presence. She set a vase of daisies on the table next to the bed. Almost knocking her daughter out of the way, she leaned over the bed and slid a small teddy bear next to Jason.

Shelley stepped back, regarding her mother with wariness. "Jason, honey, it's Grandma."

Jason turned over on his back, his eyes connecting with the blue eyes of the older woman. She gasped.

She turned to Shelley and Sean. "Oh my Lord," she whispered.

"Please, Mom, not in front of him," Shelley leaned close to her mother's ear to whisper.

"Of course." Mrs. Berry returned to her grandson. "So what do you think of that teddy, honey? He's pretty cute. Don't you think?"

Shelley moved the teddy bear from next to Jason, where it lay, ignored. She set it on the table next to the bed, alongside the flowers. "Mom, I think we need to talk. Can we go out into the hall?"

"Of course. Let's go." She turned to Jason. "We'll be right back, sweetie." She glanced at Sean, who hovered near the corner of the room. When the two women began to leave, he started to follow. Estelle Berry looked pointedly at her daughter. "He doesn't need to come along, does he?"

Shelley began to speak up, and Sean could tell from the three or four words she got out that her speech was to be in his favor, but Estelle cut her off.

"I don't see that he'd have anything useful to contribute."

Shelley began to protest once more, but this time, Sean stopped her. "It's okay, Shelley. I'll stay here with Jason."

"Are you sure? Because it's perfectly all right..."

"No. I haven't really had a chance to talk to him yet."

Shelley nodded. "Okay, we won't be long."

"Take your time."

*

"Jason's doctor said there's a lounge down the hall. Why don't we take a walk down there?" Getting her mother out of earshot from Jason overcame Shelley's initial reluctance to leave close proximity to her son's room.

"I don't see why all this is necessary. I just came to see my grandson."

Shelley led her mother down the hall. "You want to know what's going on with him, don't you?"

"Well, of course I do."

"Well then, I don't think it's wise for us to be discussing it in front of him. He's been through enough."

"You're right, Shelley. I'm sorry."

The two women settled in on vinyl couches. A TV hung on the wall opposite them. A soap opera Shelly didn't recognize was playing and she watched dully as an impossibly good-looking man and woman engaged in a heated argument that ended with them in a sudden lip-lock. Shelley glanced up at it briefly, wondering if she could ever be concerned with the trivial lives of television characters again.

Estelle took her daughter's hands in her own. Shelley didn't like her mother's moist, soft palms, but she let the woman hang on; perhaps it would be easier when she heard all the news.

"So, what do you know?"

Shelley spilled out the scant information she had, beginning with a catalog of Jason's injuries: the bruises and lacerations. When she started to tell her mother about the rest of it, she paused. "I don't know how easy this is going to be for me to tell you."

"There's more?"

"You haven't heard the worst of it yet."

Estelle leaned forward, the red beads she wore clacking against her white blouse. Her blue eyes were alight with concern and, Shelley thought, worry.

Shelley sucked in a great, quivering breath. "There's no nice way to put this, Mom." Shelley pressed her hands to her eyes; she would not cry, not just yet.

"Go on, honey, you can tell me."

"Jason was raped."

Estelle sat back suddenly, almost as if she had been pushed back into the couch. She gasped and raised a trembling, liver-spotted hand to her mouth. When had her mother grown so old? Shelley wondered.

"Raped? What are you talking about? He's a little boy."

"Rape can happen to little boys, Mom." Shelley realized how harsh her tone was and softened it. "There was a lot of tearing, but the doctor says he's going to be all right."

"All right," her mother repeated dumbly, almost as if she was unaware of what was coming out of her mouth. She nodded. "And this is why he can't speak?"

"We think so. The doctor says trauma can do that sometimes."

"Who would do such a thing?"

"We don't know."

Estelle Berry sat very quietly for several moments, staring down at the handbag clutched in her lap. Without looking up at her daughter, she said softly, "You don't know? You don't have any idea?"

Shelley shivered. It was as if her mother suddenly had a clue to this mystery no one else knew. "No, Mom, why should we?" The way her mother couched her question made it apparent she thought Shelley should have some idea who had perpetrated this horror upon her son.

Estelle seemed as if she suddenly was having difficulty breathing. "My God, I'd think you'd have some idea."

Shelley felt sick. Everything going on in her mother's head suddenly became clear. "I don't know what you're talking about."

Estelle Berry leaned close to her daughter, speaking in an intense whisper. "What I'm talking about is your ex-husband. He's a pervert, he and that scumbag he shacks up with... They're both perverts."

"Now, Mom," Shelley chewed on a fingernail. "Sean and Austin love Jason. They would never..."

"And you probably thought the same thing when you got married to him. Good Lord, girl, when will you learn?"

"This is all wrong."

"No, no, I don't think it is. Has anyone even asked where these men were the past couple of days?"

Shelley shook her head.

"Well, I will." Estelle stood suddenly and for a moment, it looked as if she might collapse back into her seat. With a *whoosh* that left a smell of cologne behind her, Estelle was off back down the corridor leading to Jason's room.

"Mom! Mom, wait!" Shelley ran after her mother, ignoring the glances of patients and hospital personnel, who moved away from the older woman's determined stride.

Chapter Seven

She hoped she had done the right thing. In her almost a dozen years at City Hospital, Nancy Clawson had never had to do what she had done earlier that day: describe a suspect to the police, working with a police artist. But she had been on emergency room duty when the little boy, Jason Dawes, had been brought in, or rather, dumped near the emergency room doors.

For once, Nancy was thankful for the pack of cigarettes in her white nurse's smock pocket. If she hadn't been outside on a smoke break then, no one would have seen the man, and that would have been a shame. She had heard what had been done to the little boy, and the thought of it made her stomach turn. What got into people these days? As a little girl growing up just east of here, in Baden, she had never heard of such things.

Nancy pushed the wire-rim glasses up farther on her nose and surveyed the traffic along Third Street as she took one last drag off her cigarette. Her shift was almost over and her feet ached. She wanted to go home and just forget the session with that Detective Allen and the police artist from Pittsburgh, who did all his sketching on a computer screen, something Nancy hadn't even imagined. She had expected the artist to have big sketchpads, lots of pencils, and a big Pink Pearl eraser, the kind she had used in school.

But the guy was good with his electronic tools, and the picture that had eventually emerged on the little screen, Nancy felt, was a very good likeness of the unkempt older man who had so callously dropped his charge off at the hospital.

Had he been the one who had done it? Nancy pushed through the big glass doors and walked into the chaos of the emergency room. Two paramedics raced by her, pushing a cart upon which a bloody young woman had an oxygen mask clamped to her face.

Nancy glanced up at the clock on the tile wall opposite her. Only a half hour to go.

Of course he had been the one. *Why else would he have left the boy without even speaking to anyone, left a very hurt little boy alone out there in the heat to fend for himself?*

Nancy hurried down the corridor to see where she could be of most use in her remaining time. She didn't want to think about this anymore. She hoped no one would ever know it was her finger that pointed and accused.

That, she knew, could have consequences.

*

Shelley and Paul sat in front of the TV, neither of them speaking. Paul guzzled another Genessee, heavy-lidded eyes never moving from the screen, where a young mother was tearfully explaining how it was impossible to keep her promiscuous thirteen-year-old daughter in check. She didn't know how Paul could sit and watch Dr. Phil, drinking beer, while all this was going on.

Shelley, knees drawn up under her on the couch, barely heard the shouting and ranting from the audience. She kept thinking of Jason, alone at the hospital, and wanting so much to be there with him.

But the doctors had said she needed to rest and Paul agreed, insisting she come home with him in the pickup.

How could she rest?

The phone's chirping caused her to stiffen, to drop the nail file she was using without any awareness, and scramble for the phone. Paul looked up sleepily from the recliner, almost as if he didn't know her.

"Hello?"

"Mrs. Thompson? Hugh Allen here. We've had a break in the case."

Shelley swallowed, or rather tried to; all the spit had seemed to have suddenly vanished from her mouth. The idea of what had happened to Jason was bad enough; she wondered if she could bear actually seeing the culprit. It would put everything into too-sharp focus for her. She would be able to picture everything too clearly with the missing piece of the puzzle, and the thought caused the bile to rise, burning the back of her throat.

"What happened?"

"One of the nurses down at City saw the guy who brought Jason in. She did a great job of describing him to this police artist from Pittsburgh. We got the sketch out and what do you know, someone recognized the guy."

"Is he the one?"

"He sure as hell looks guilty."

"Who is it?" Shelley whispered, sitting down at one of the kitchen chairs. Her knees had suddenly gone weak.

"The guy's an old bum, a hermit if you will, who lives up in the hills, just across from your house. Name's Junior Parsons."

Shelley shook her head. She had never seen or heard of this bastard, but she knew well Jason's fondness for playing in those woods. The tiny horror movie began to whir in her brain as she pictured him there, sweeping pine needles together to build low walls for another of his forts. And then a shadow fell across his back, blocking out the sun. Jason looked up, green eyes questioning. Shelley closed her own eyes, willing the image to disappear.

"Mrs. Thompson?"

"What?" Shelley wondered how long the detective had been calling her name. Wondered if she would ever be able to concentrate again.

"Does the name ring any bells?"

"What was it again?"

"Junior Parsons? My men are out in the woods now, tracking him down. We expect to have him in custody any time now."

"No. I've never heard of him before."

"Well, I just wanted to let you know. If this is the guy, we're going to do everything we can to see that he pays for what he's done."

"Thank you." Without thinking, Shelley hung up the phone.

Paul stood behind her, and she jumped when she turned around, seeing him standing so close.

"Oh! I didn't realize you were here."

His eyes, usually hooded brown things, were bright and alive with interest. "Was that the detective?"

"Yes. How did you know?"

"I could hear your half of things, Shel. It doesn't take a genius..."

"Right."

"Well, what did he have to say?"

"They think they've caught the guy."

She watched Paul. His eyes closed, and she could feel the relief coursing through him. He smiled and opened his eyes to regard her. "That's the best news I've heard in a long time."

Shelley felt warm. Paul had been so distant throughout this whole thing. It was good to finally see some emotion from him. And it was good to know he cared enough to be so happy that they'd probably caught the culprit. Never mind that Shelley couldn't muster up any happiness from her own bruised mind; catching the guy who had done this to Jason didn't change anything. Jason still had to endure the pain. Shelley bit her lip to hold back the sobs.

Paul put his arms around her, biceps pressing into her outer arms. He squeezed her. She could smell the beer on his breath and a slight odor of sweat. "Hey," he whispered. "Aren't you happy? It's almost over."

Shelley felt frozen in the chair, her husband's arms nothing more than weights around her shoulders. She shrugged them away. "Nothing's over," she said dully, staring at the steel blue sky outside. "Nothing."

*

Junior Parsons had been sewing when the men came crashing through the woods. His dad had taught him well to take care of himself. After pulling the thread through the buttonhole once more, Junior set the shirt down and crossed to the window. Eunice was putting up a mournful bale at the approach of the men.

They came through the brush, and Junior saw two young, uniformed policemen. "Oh Lord, what now?" Junior said to himself, moving away from the window. The Parsons had never mixed with anyone from town, least of all the police, and he wondered why they were bothering him now.

Had to have something to do with that little boy. Of course. But how had they traced him? He thought no one had seen him and even if they had, how would they know him? Know him well enough to lead the police to his door?

And then a horror dawned in his slow mind. Maybe they thought he was the one who hurt the little boy. After all, it looked pretty guilty, what with him leaving the boy and running off as he did.

They were making their way to his door, ignoring Eunice's furious yapping. Good God, what should he do? They would take him away, and who would take care of Eunice?

Junior scrambled under the bed as the first of their knocks, forceful blows, sounded on his door, rattling the padlock on the inside.

"Mr. Parsons?" one of them cried out over Eunice's barking, the deep boom of his voice causing Junior to scurry back farther under the bed, until he was flattened against the wall.

"Summitville Police. Mr. Parsons, please open up."

Silence for a moment or two. Enough for Junior to take in a few quivering breaths.

"Mr. Parsons. If you do not open the door immediately, we'll have to break it down."

How did they know he was in here? Had they seen him at a window? Junior wanted to cry. He didn't know how to deal with these people. Why couldn't they just leave him alone?

"Mr. Parsons, we'll give you five seconds."

Junior began to tremble under the bed, tremble harder as he heard something slamming into his only door. He shrieked when the lock broke free from the doorframe and the door crashed inward. He tried to flatten himself even more against the wall, watching the two men move into his home.

This wasn't fair! It wasn't fair. Junior was whimpering as he watched the black shoes and bottoms of navy blue uniform pants moving through his little house.

And then the quilt came up suddenly and a dark face with a mustache was peering at him, here in the shadows and the dust.

"Here he is, Pete." The man's brown eyes locked with Junior's. "Come on out of there, *now*, you son of a bitch."

And Junior scooted out, uncertain what fate awaited him outside the protection of his bed.

Chapter Eight

Paul held the phone to his ear, blunt fingers poised above the buttons. He took a deep breath and wished there was a way to make all the beer clouding his brain dwindle away. Most of the time, the slight buzz was a welcome accompaniment to his daily rounds, but today he wished for a way to suddenly summon a clear-headed state.

He put the phone back. Perhaps this wasn't necessary. He leaned back, reached out, and snagged his Marlboros from the kitchen counter. He put one in his mouth and lit it, drawing in deeply, letting the smoke fill his lungs. He glanced at his reflection in the mirror above the kitchen sink and admired himself. Thirty-two years old and he still looked like a twentysomething stud. He smiled, then took a drag off his cigarette and watched himself smoke. His sandy hair was cut short and his mustache was unkempt, but thick and manly. The stubble on his face and the way his broad chest pushed out his T-shirt, the arms tight around his biceps, made him think he could have anyone he wanted.

Enough of this shit! Time to do your duty. With a quick, deep breath, Paul picked up the phone and punched in the numbers for Hugh Allen, whose card Shelley had left by the phone.

As he listened to the ringing, he wondered again if this was necessary. After all, the guy had left Jason at the emergency room doors. Wasn't that evidence enough of guilt? Wasn't that incriminating enough?

Paul scratched his balls and thought that old Junior Parsons could probably use all the help he could get toward getting himself behind bars.

A man answered the phone, and Paul thought there was no turning back.

"Allen here. Help you?"

"Detective Allen? This is Paul Thompson. Jason Dawes's stepfather?"

"Of course, Mr. Thompson. I was just about to call you and your wife."

"Oh?" Shit, what if the arrest had fallen through?

"Yes. I had some good news to share with you."

"Really? Damn, that's great. We could sure use some about now."

"I understand. Well, we picked up Junior Parsons earlier today, and if he isn't guilty, he's sure as hell doing a good job playing the part."

Paul closed his eyes. *Yes.*

"It seems Mr. Parsons hid himself under a bed and wouldn't answer the door when my men came out to bring him in."

"Hell, if he had nothing to hide, why act like that?"

"Exactly. Now, we have no physical evidence tying him to the crime, but I think we'll probably have something very strong if the tests pan out."

"What are you talking about?" Paul twisted the phone cord around his pointing finger, stubbed out his cigarette, and lit another.

"Um, this isn't the most pleasant thing to bring up, but we were able to get a semen sample from Jason's rectum when he was brought in. We can see if it matches Mr. Parsons's blood type. If it does, there's a possibility the crime lab in Pittsburgh could do a more exact test involving DNA," Hugh Allen said. "DNA's like a fingerprint."

"That's great." Paul tried to ignore the twisting nausea that had suddenly risen up in his gut.

"Now, I have a lot to do. Were you just calling for an update, Mr. Thompson?"

Once again, Paul reconsidered what he was about to do. He glanced out the window and decided to go through with it. "Actually, man, I was calling to give you some info."

"Oh?"

"Yeah, I didn't think about it until I heard about this fucker Parsons, but you know what? I saw a real weird dude talking to Jason the day before he disappeared."

"Really?"

"Yeah. Out in front of the house. Jason was on his bike and this strange-looking guy came up to him, and the two had a little talk. Don't know what was said, but I just thought you should know."

"That could be very helpful, Mr. Thompson—"

"Paul."

"Paul. But as I said, I need to get going. I'll probably want to talk more about this later, maybe have you come in and we'll set up a line-up. See if the man you saw was really Parsons."

Paul dragged deep on his cigarette. "Yeah, yeah, sure, whatever I can do to help."

Paul hung up the phone. He noticed the hand holding his cigarette was trembling.

"What was that all about?"

Paul jumped. "Christ, Shelley, you scared me." Paul turned to look at his wife. She suddenly seemed smaller. The puffiness around her eyes seemed not to have disappeared since this whole thing started. Why the fuck couldn't she buck up, be strong for her boy?

"How long you been standin' there?"

"Long enough."

Was there suspicion in her eyes?

"Why didn't you mention this before?"

"Fuck, Shel, I don't know. I guess I didn't think it was important."

"Not important? Not important?" Her voice began to take on a hysterical edge. "How could you think something like that wasn't important? My God, Paul, if you had brought this to the police sooner, maybe they could have found Parsons sooner and maybe this whole thing could have been prevented." She bit her lip, he knew, to hold back the tears. But no woman was going to talk to him this way. No fuckin' way.

Paul leaned menacingly over his wife and liked it when she withered from his stance, almost flinching. Good, good. That's how a woman should behave toward her husband. It was how his mother had behaved toward his father. "Look," he said, making his words slow and measured. "I said I didn't really think nothin' of it at the time. Isn't that good enough for you?"

"I suppose." Shelley hurried from the room.

Christ, Paul thought, *maybe I shouldn't have bothered.*

*

Later, Paul found himself down in the basement. He'd smoked a joint and had a six-pack chilling in the mini refrigerator he had down here in his workroom.

A man needs his space, and for Paul this was it, surrounded by tools hung neatly from pegs above his workbench. Never mind that the hammers, saws, screwdrivers, wrenches, and pliers gathered dust on the wall opposite him. It was his private place.

Paul knew Shelley wouldn't dare bother him down here. She had learned that lesson a long time ago. A good crack to the side of the head ensured she would never disturb him.

The marijuana and the beer weren't working. Paul stared down at the scarred surface of his work table. He traced his fingers in the rough grooves made by saws and his own initials carved there years before with a nail. But no matter what he did, there was no way to forget.

Paul stood and went to stare out the basement window, positioned high on the opposite wall. Outside, the sky was an expanse of white; heat shimmered from the concrete walk leading up the side of the house, running parallel to the driveway. He lit another cigarette and wondered if he should smoke another joint, wondered if the THC would bring on the kind of oblivion he sought.

Or would it just serve to make him more paranoid than he already was? It was a risk, this business with drugs. Hell, you couldn't count on anything, or anyone for that matter, these days. He opted against another joint.

He was still nervous about what he had done, still nervous that, in spite of his admonitions and the beating he had given him, Jason would talk. The fear that he would be exposed caused him to go cold, in spite of the sweat running out of his armpits and down the side of his face.

Jason. The little guy, always there at arm's length. Could Paul help it if the boy taunted him with his little body? He was always hanging around, still occasionally crawling into his lap, in spite of the fact that the boy was going to be nine years old soon, far too old for such behavior.

Paul wanted to feel nothing. All this conflicting shit nagged at him, yammering like little voices, making him so nervous he wanted to just ram his fist through something.

He had always promised himself he would never act on anything. He knew that wouldn't be right. But a part of him had always known he would. And this particular summer, with its oppressive heat and humidity, had unhinged something in him, something ugly and dark, something he never wanted to acknowledge.

Paul giggled, but there was no mirth in it. A single thought ran through his mind: *Must run in the family.*

Cut that shit.

Paul pressed his palms against his eyes. It was going to be okay. No one would ever suspect him—a guy's guy, a vet, a beer-swilling, woman-chasing, deer-hunting man like himself.

He leaned over and ran his fingers across the rough, sawdust-laden surface of his workbench until his fingers fell into a tiny groove. He worked his fingers in the groove and pulled up. Underneath was a small wooden box that he had attached—God, how many years ago?—to the bottom of the workbench.

It was where he had his stash. Most guys had a stash of pornography didn't they? Something to whack the old dick off to when the wife wasn't in the mood? Sure they did.

But another voice, one which Paul wished very much would just go away, told him that most guys didn't have stashes like his. Most guys' stashes consisted of magazines like *Playboy, Penthouse,* or *Hustler.*

Paul's magazines were of a different ilk. You couldn't find them at the local bookstore or even Brook's Newsstand, downtown, that sold the filthiest stuff you could find in Summitville. Paul had worked hard, covertly, to get this collection amassed. And it was at no little risk, what with the postal service cracking down on a man's enjoyment the way they did.

Paul pulled the stack of magazines out lovingly. These magazines had names like *Lollitots, Boy's Lives, The Sexual Maturity of the Prepubescent* and so on. Paul had never seen anything wrong with looking at them.

Who was he hurting?

The mean little voice answered, "Jason." He shut off that portion of his brain.

Fuck 'em. Fuck 'em all. Paul began paging through the magazines, all of which were filled with photographs of naked children or, even better, naked little boys sucking big men's cocks. Little girls, their eyes dead and legs spread too wide. Little boys giving up their asses. Little boys discovering just what Paul had discovered at a similar age, with his Grandpa.

It hadn't been so bad.

And Paul went back. The pot and the beer did nothing to diffuse the memories. They never did. If he could have had the portion of his brain containing these memories excised, Paul would have gladly done it, no matter what the cost, no matter what else he forgot.

But the memories would not be denied. They stayed crisp and sharp in his mind, almost like scenes from an unforgettable movie. The harder Paul tried to forget what had happened when he was a boy, even smaller than Jason, the more the memories forced him to take notice of them.

Why? Why did he have to remember?

And yet, there he was, a little boy of six, a far cry from the tough guy he had become when his teen years unleashed hormones in him, turning him into the kind of man about whom one would never hint at anything feminine.

And yet Grandpa, with his bald pate and hairy belly that hung out over the top of the gray twill work pants he always wore, had seen something within Paul that he felt secure in violating.

What had the old man seen?

The first time it happened was in his grandfather's workroom, a space much like this one, but set up in Grandpa's garage. Little Paul liked to come out there with his grandfather, while his grandmother stood at the stove inside, basting a ham for Sunday dinner.

Had it been Easter the first time? Paul closed his eyes and sucked in a quivering breath. He need not question it: it was Easter, and Paul had been a six-year-old boy, still believing in the Easter bunny, still wearing a chocolate mustache, remnant of the big hollow bunny he had found in his Easter basket earlier that morning.

Grandpa liked to show him the tools, liked to take him on his lap and show him how the different tools worked.

"This here is a Phillips-head screwdriver," he had whispered, drawing his arm tight around the boy's waist. With the other hand, he had shown Paul the grooved tip of the screwdriver, then pulled out a nut with a grooved top, a top that melded perfectly with the tip of the screwdriver. And Paul understood. He took the screwdriver from his grandfather's hand and played with it, twisting its tip into the surface of Grandpa's workbench.

"Not too hard, now," Grandpa had whispered. "You'll mar the wood." And he drew the little boy closer, until his flabby stomach was pressing into Paul's back, until his old man's breath, stinking of cigarettes, heated Paul's ear.

There was something odd in the way the old man held him, something that to Paul, even at six, didn't feel right. He tried to wriggle from his grandfather's tightening grasp, but the old guy held firm. "Now, quit your wigglin'. Ain't nothing wrong with your old Paw Paw."

And Paul, because he was so little and his grandfather was so big, stopped moving. Things suddenly seemed too quiet. The stillness made Paul afraid, made him feel just a little sick to his stomach. He noticed Grandpa's breath coming a little faster, a slight wheeze to it. Grandpa ran his fingers through the boy's hair, and the action caused a chill to run the length of Paul's spine.

"You're a good boy," Grandpa had whispered, pulling Paul close to bury his face in the boy's light hair, the color of honey. As much as Paul liked being held, there was something not quite right about this whole scenario, a fact confirmed by how Grandpa seemed to keep a watchful eye on the door of the garage and its windows, placed up high on the cinder block wall and facing the kitchen where Grandma and his mother were making Easter dinner.

"A very good boy." Grandpa pressed against his back, and when Paul tried once again to wiggle from the old man's grasp, he got, as his reward, a tightening of Grandpa's forearm around his waist.

"Be still now." And Grandpa moved against his back, his breath coming in shorter and shorter pants and the movement of his hips faster and faster.

Paul wanted to tell him to stop, but he had learned little boys didn't bark such orders out at their elders. So he kept still while the old man thrust against him, his lips slick against his ear, waiting for his breathing to return to normal, trying to well down the peculiar nausea that was getting stronger and stronger—so strong, in fact, little Paul thought he might throw up.

And then Grandpa gasped and it seemed everything, even though Paul had no idea then what everything was, stopped.

Grandpa pushed him down from his lap and wouldn't look at him. When Paul tugged on the old man's sleeve, he still wouldn't look at him. Staring at his tools on the opposite wall, Grandpa had said, "Now you go on inside… see if your Grandma needs help settin' the table." And that was how it had begun.

Paul flung a can of beer across the room, where it slammed into the wall opposite, the jagged aluminum opening and sending out a spray of white foam and golden liquid.

"Shit," Paul whispered, rubbing his fist against his eyes.

Chapter Nine

Finally, the heat had abated. Not much, but yet another thunderstorm during the night had changed things. It seemed to Shelley that one of those tremendous peals that left in its wake the smell of ozone and a deafening silence did more than just make noise, but cracked the heat and humidity that had plagued Summitville for most of the summer.

Now the sky was pewter gray, the streets still slick with rain from last night. The air was damp, but during the night the temperature had fallen at least twenty degrees. Not cool enough for a sweater, but cool enough so she could roll down the car windows and let the breeze roll in, rather than trying to force the air-conditioning to work. Each day the air conditioner had to fight harder against the heat and humidity, doing less and less to dispel it. Evidence of the battle was beginning to show. A little pool of water formed under the dash every time she left the air conditioner on for more than ten minutes. Yet another thing in her life that needed fixing, when she didn't have the means for repair.

Jason sat in the seat beside her, and she tried to stay cheerful, calm. But this too was a losing battle. His silence crept into her heart, uncoiling and clenching like a physical pain, causing her eyes to fill with tears. She would brush them away, trying to hide the anger she felt at their presence, disgusted with herself, feeling selfish and ill-equipped for the simple task of driving her little boy home from the hospital.

But she couldn't help but remember how once upon a time the car would be filled with Jason's unending chatter, about everything from how the Pirates were playing this year to the plotline of the latest Batman comic book. Sometimes, the boy's voice got so irritating she would have to tell him to quiet down and even, at times—she felt horrible for remembering this—scream at him to just shut up so she could listen to the radio or drive in peace for five minutes. It now seemed so long ago! But it had, in fact, been only a matter of a few days. Little had she known that she would, very soon, give anything to feel that irritation again.

But now Jason stared ahead, not even a whisper crossing his swollen lips. It was almost as if the boy's soul had departed, leaving behind this shell she couldn't recognize.

To break the monotony, she switched the radio on. Shelley usually listened to a soft rock station out of Pittsburgh, WARM, and thought the music might be soothing, to her and to Jason. Suzanne Vega was singing "Luka," and the song, with its plaintive cry for help from an abused child, was almost more than she could bear.

She punched the AM button and switched to KDKA, where she could rely on news and weather.

When Shelley finally heard the gravel of the driveway crunching underneath the car's tires, she was relieved. All the way home, she had tried conversing with Jason, telling him about the heat and the way it was causing her tomato plants in the backyard to wither and droop, even though she watered them every night after supper. She told him about the Pirates' latest loss and even tried her best to offer an opinion for why the game had been lost, something she would have once felt was well beyond her. She told him how she had heard on the radio that there would be a Star Trek convention in Pittsburgh in October, saving this final and most crucial bit of information for last. The tears welled up again when she got no response, even though she promised to put money back each week so the two of them could attend.

Jason had stared out the window.

Shelley wondered if he had even heard.

At least now she could take him in the house. In his bedroom, surrounded by the trappings of an eight-year-old boy's life, he would be more comfortable, wouldn't he? He could snuggle close to the Smokey Bear teddy he'd had since he was two, could look at the Pirates and Steelers banners on his wall, could turn on the little portable TV in his room and watch the cartoon and science fiction channels as much as he wanted. She wouldn't restrict him as she once had.

But most of all, she could now attend to him, instead of nurses in silly uniforms, adorned with bears and balloons, waking him at odd hours to take his temperature, to note his blood pressure, and change his dressings.

Now Shelley could make all his favorites and serve them to him in bed, read to him while he ate, stories from the old Hans Christian Andersen fairy tale book she had had herself as a child.

Something had to bring him around. A boy as exuberant as Jason just couldn't be kept down long.

Shelley's reverie was interrupted once she put the car in park. She glanced over at Jason, and her eyebrows came together in concern. "What is it, honey?"

The boy appeared to be cowering, bright green eyes staring at the back door with what Shelley could only interpret as horror. He was trembling.

Shelley bit her lip to choke back the sob that felt like a baseball in her throat and reached across the seat to take the little boy in her arms, to nuzzle her cheek against his downy, fine hair. "What's the matter?"

She hugged him tightly, trying with the force of her embrace to stop the shaking in his limbs. "What is it?" Jason's reaction had taken her by surprise; she had thought he would have been so happy to be home. Happy enough, she dared hope, that he might say something, might snap out of this dead state she couldn't have imagined even two weeks ago.

Shelley told herself there was something going on in his mind that had nothing to do with being home. Trauma, she was learning quickly, was powerful and could do strange, unexpected things.

Reluctantly, Shelley released her grasp on the boy and reached into the backseat to pick up the small bag of items the hospital had sent home with him—his medications, the X-Men figure one of the nurses had given him, and the plastic bedside accompaniments the hospital sent home with all its patients. She got out of the car and hurried to the other side. "C'mon, don't you want to go inside?"

Jason leaned back against the seat, staring at her almost as if he didn't recognize her.

Shelley placed the bag on the ground and reached in to gather Jason up in her arms. He clutched tightly at her as she carried him through the door.

"Well, here's our boy!"

The voice startled Shelley as the screen door slammed behind her and she entered the bright yellow light of the kitchen.

"Mom, I didn't know you were going to be here." Shelley had wanted Jason's reentry into the household to be quiet, which was precisely why she had not invited her mother over.

"Hello to you too, dear." Estelle Berry leaned in close to try to get a look at Jason's face, which was buried in Shelley's breast. She reached with a hand Shelley noticed for the first time was too much like a claw and turned the boy's head to face her. "It's Grandma, honey."

Shelley's mother's gaze met her own, giving her daughter a quizzical stare. At least she didn't blurt something stupid out like "What's wrong with him?"

"I'm going to run him up to his room." Shelley started toward the dining room, where the stairs were. Estelle followed. Shelley turned on her. "Mom, could you go outside and fetch Jason's bag for me?"

Estelle's mouth became set in a line. But she said, "Of course."

Before Shelley left for the hospital, she had blown up a couple dozen multicolored balloons and scattered them about the room, sticking some of them to the walls. She had taken care to clean his room and put everything in order. All his favorite toys—the stuffed animals he was getting too old to publicly admit his fondness for, the spaceship models, and the collection of X-Men action figures—were lined up on two shelves above his twin bed. Even though her rational mind told her the efforts might well be received with no emotion, she had still hoped to see Jason's eyes brighten at the familiar and loved items.

Shelley should have learned, through more than just this experience, to listen to her head and not her heart. She thought that if she had one major personality flaw, it was this inability to listen to nothing other than her heart. It had seduced and tricked her into two bad marriages and yet she still never seemed to learn from experience.

The smile vanished from her face as she carried Jason into the room. Dead eyes took in the room with absolutely no brightening. Shelley felt she could have been bringing the boy into any room. His face remained impassive.

Shelley tried to keep her own smile firmly affixed, but it felt all too much like a grimace. "Look, Jason! Isn't this great? When's the last time you've seen this room this clean, huh?"

She might as well have been talking to the balloons. Shelley hurried to the bed, with one hand pulled back the covers, and deposited Jason on the sheets. She knelt to take off his shoes, pants, and shirt, then drew the sheet up over his briefs.

"Listen, everything's gonna be okay. Mom's not going to let anything bad happen to you again. 'Kay?" Shelley brushed her hand through Jason's hair and then let it rest on his cheek. "I know you can hear what I'm saying. I know it. And I know that, as soon as you're ready, you'll talk to us again." Shelley leaned down and quickly planted a kiss on the boy's cheek. "You get some rest now," she said, the words beginning to crack because she was getting too close to a major onrush of tears. "And I'll bring you something great to eat when you wake up." She smiled through her watery gaze. "Nothin' like that crap down at the hospital."

She wanted to stay longer but was afraid if she did, her own emotional state would make the situation with Jason even worse. So she hurried from the room and closed the door behind her. The bathroom was right across the hall from Jason's room and it was there she went, closing and locking the door behind her and then turning on the bath's taps full blast so no one could hear her crying.

When she came downstairs, her mother was drying the few dishes left in the drainer and putting them away.

"You don't have to do that."

Her mother put a mug on the little wooden tree they hung from and then set down the dishtowel. "I know I don't have to; I wanted to. You can use a little help, can't you?" Estelle smiled at her and Shelley was, for a moment, suddenly pleased that her mother was there. The woman could be overbearing at times, what with her always trying to force her Catholic beliefs down her "fallen" daughter's throat, but she was still her mother and it was good to have her taking care of her, even in this small way.

"Yes, I could probably use a lot of help." Shelley sat down at the kitchen table and lit a cigarette.

Estelle frowned. "I wish you wouldn't do that." Shelley rolled her eyes. She should have known.

"It really doesn't make you look attractive, you know."

Shelley breathed in, deeply, and glanced up at the clock. "One of these days, Mother, I'm going to quit."

Estelle sat down at the table and grabbed her daughter's hand. "See that you do. It would make me so happy. I just want you to be around as long as possible."

"Have you seen Paul?" A change of subject was definitely in order.

"He was here when I got here; he let me in. Didn't say much, as usual, just out the door not two minutes after I walked in the kitchen. I don't know where he went."

Shelley didn't either. And, for once, it didn't annoy her. She was glad she had some time to herself, even if she did have to share it with her mother. Paul would have made Jason's homecoming even tenser. But the fact that he wasn't here rankled her anyway. Jason was his stepson, for Christ's sake. "Want some coffee? I just made a pot."

Shelley really didn't, but she didn't want to dismiss her mother's gesture, so she accepted.

While Estelle poured the coffee, the thrum of an engine sounded in the driveway. Shelley stood to look out the screen door and was surprised to see it was not Paul's pickup in the driveway, but Sean's red Sentra.

After the years of wrangling in court, and what Shelley had felt was Sean's betrayal of her, she never thought she could be friends again with this man she once called her husband, but Shelley couldn't deny the happiness she felt when she saw him in the driveway. The last few days had made it obvious he was the one who really cared about Jason and not Paul. This horrible experience, she felt, was forging a new bond between the two parents, welcome or not.

"Is that Paul?" her mother called from the kitchen counter.

"No, it's Sean." Shelley was already opening the screen door when her mother hurried over to stand behind her.

Estelle whispered, "What's he doing here?"

Shelley turned to stare at her mother. "Jason is his son. Or did you forget?"

The older woman's gaze never left the driveway, which Sean was walking up, to meet her daughter's gaze. "I know that. I also know I testified in court that he should be kept away from Jason, and that you were the one who went along with the whole thing. Why this sudden change of heart?"

Sean was almost to the porch. He waved at Shelley and she waved back. "Mother, he's been fine with Jason since we got our divorce. I think he's proved himself."

"How can you say that? In light of—"

But Shelley's mother couldn't say any more. Sean was right in front of them.

"Hey, everybody." He smiled. "Jason home?"

Shelley bit her lip and nodded, suddenly feeling, both literally and figuratively, caught in the middle. "He's upstairs."

She paused for a moment. "Sleeping."

"Oh. I was hoping I could see him."

"That's probably not a good idea right now, Sean," Estelle said.

The smile vanished from his face. Sean looked to Shelley to see if she would dispute her mother.

And, damning herself, Shelley said, "Maybe it would be better if you came back later. I'll call you and let you know when."

Sean nodded. "Sure." And then he was gone, head hung low, walking rapidly back to his car.

Shelley noticed the stuffed purple alligator in his left hand.

"Your coffee's ready. You want some milk?"

"I guess." Shelley slumped down at the kitchen table, cursing her weakness.

Chapter Ten

Twenty years. Hugh had been on the Summitville police force for twenty years. And in all that time, he had never seen a case like this. His daily detective work dealt with trivial stuff for the most part. Domestic violence that resulted in the death of one of the sparring partners, tied up neatly, a confession from some distraught man or woman as a bow on top of the package.

But he had yet to get his hands on a meaty case like the Jason Dawes one. It had everything—kidnapping, rape, and the potential for Hugh to be in the center of it all, garnering as much attention as possible for himself. And who knew where the case might lead? Such a case could get him attention from the big time. Perhaps Hugh could finally leave this dull little town and head for Youngstown or even Pittsburgh, where he could become somebody.

It was what he had always dreamed of, since the days he started on the force, a young, red-faced cop with a lean body and a buzz cut, writing traffic citations. Now Hugh still had the buzz cut and his florid complexion wasn't from the vigor of youth, but from too many happy hours at Hebron's Lounge, out on Route 30, where all the cops liked to gather once their shifts had ended.

He deserved some recognition, by God. He had given his entire life to the force. The wreckage of two failed marriages and two teenagers, a son and a daughter, lay behind him, as unreachable as the North Pole. He had given up everything for his career, and it was time he had a break.

As he gulped down the dregs of a tepid coffee at the bottom of a Styrofoam cup in the cubbyhole he called an office, he thought his break was finally here. He peered into the bottom of the cup, where a little undissolved Coffee mate™ still clung to the bottom.

Junior Parsons was waiting in the interrogation room, which also doubled as a waiting room and storage closet for cleaning supplies. Such were the perks of working for a police force that watched over the rather mild denizens of a town of 12,000.

Hugh stood and slid into his sport coat, a tan seersucker job that did little to make him comfortable in this godforsaken heat and humidity that had risen up from the river and plagued Summitville for the last month. The police station, occupying the fourth and top floor of City Hall, was built at the turn of the century and was beyond the ministrations of modern conveniences like air-conditioning. In the summer the offices buzzed with the sound of rotating fan blades, which did little more than blow the stale, hot air around.

Hugh took a handkerchief from his inside jacket pocket and dabbed at his moist forehead, wishing for a beer.

*

Junior Parsons waited, trembling, in the little room the woman with the bleached-blonde hair had seated him in. The two windows in the room faced a dull, white sky. He was up too high to see any of the buildings below, so Junior's feelings of claustrophobia were not unwarranted. The sky pressed against the glass like dirty cotton, suffocating. The other wall of the room held a large mirror, and Junior knew this mirror was not for freshening up or straightening one's clothes, but for observation. Someone was probably sitting behind the glass right now, watching him.

Not that there was anything interesting to watch. Junior had never been more afraid in his whole life. And the fear inspired in him a kind of shock that made him sit, unmoving, waiting for wheels he didn't understand to begin turning.

He ran a shaking hand through his greasy, dark hair and wished Eunice was here, sitting at his feet. The old beagle couldn't do much to protect him from the mess he now found himself in, but she sure would have been a comfort.

The door whined open and Junior looked up. A man in a wrinkled sport coat filled the door's frame. He looked as hot and uncomfortable as Junior felt. His reddish brown hair was cropped short and his face, with its thin lips and tiny button nose, looked red and angry.

Junior's heart began to race.

"Vernon Parsons?"

Junior tried to swallow but found his mouth suddenly dry. He nodded to the name he had never been called. Vernon was his daddy.

"I'm Detective Allen, and I'd like to ask you a few questions." Detective Allen pulled out a chair from the scarred wooden table at which Junior sat, turned it around, and straddled it, placing himself close to Junior's face. Junior smelled the chewing gum and cigarettes on the man's breath, which made him want to slide his chair back. The man's flushed face frightened him and made a trickle of sweat begin at his hairline. But if he moved away from him, Junior thought it might make the man angry and somehow—even though Junior wondered how it could be possible—might get him in even more trouble. He cast his gaze down at the dark wood floorboards, which wore a coat of dust. Junior nodded slowly, never lifting his gaze from the floor.

"Now, I just have to be sure you've been told what rights you have in this situation, Vernon."

Junior wished he wouldn't call him that! He shifted his weight from one hip to the other, casting a quick glance up at the detective's face.

"When the men brought you in, Vernon, they told you that you could have a lawyer present, didn't they?"

Junior tried to swallow the dry lump of wool in his throat and nodded.

"I need you to speak up, Vernon. Our little talk here is being recorded. You understand?"

Junior began to nod and then mumbled, "Yes, sir."

"Speak up, man!"

The detective's loud voice caused Junior to stiffen, his spine feeling like a spike in his back.

"Yes, sir," Junior said, putting as much breath behind the words as he could.

"You know you can have a lawyer. You know you don't have to say anything if you don't want to. Am I right?"

"Yes, sir." Junior just wanted to go home. How could he refuse to speak to this man? Who knew what would happen to him if he got uppity and refused to talk?

"Good. Now, I'm going to try to start as close to the beginning as I can, and you just let me know if the facts, as I have them, are correct."

Junior nodded, then caught himself and said, "Okay."

"Now, you know about Jason Dawes..."

"Don't know nobody by that name, sir."

"He's the little boy who turned up missing."

Junior flashed on the little boy cowering in the woods behind his shack and wished he had never laid eyes on him. "Yeah, I guess. I just didn't know what he was called."

"Yeah," the detective said, frowning, "I guess getting a name wasn't so important."

Junior didn't know what he was talking about, so he didn't say anything.

"Now, a nurse down at City Hospital says she saw you drop the boy off by the emergency room doors. Is that correct?"

Junior never told lies, but he wanted to now. In fact, he wanted to completely erase everything that had happened the day before and just go back to his old life, the life in which he wasn't involved with any people like this frightening Detective Allen. "That's right."

"What were you doing with that little boy, Vernon? And just tell the truth. I'm here to see that things go much easier on you if you just tell us the truth."

"I found him up in the hills by my place. That's all," Junior said, in a voice barely above a whisper.

"You just found him?"

"Yes, sir. I was out..." And here Junior stopped himself, not wanting to admit he was out hunting. Junior knew enough to know that hunting in August was against the law. "I was out, um, takin' a walk with my dog and she commences to barkin'. I walked over to see what she'd found, and I saw the little guy back there in some bushes."

"What were you doing out there, Vernon?"

Damn...this man was trying to get him to admit he was hunting. And he couldn't do that. "Nothin'. Me and Eunice was just out for a stroll."

"I see. Out for a little stroll."

"Right, sir. And we found the little boy, and he looked hurt somethin' awful, so I just thought I'd just take him down where he could get some help. I don't know nothin' about him or about takin' care of hurt people."

"Well, Vernon, if he was hurt somethin' awful, why would you just leave him like that? I mean, Christ, if you wanted to help the boy, wouldn't you want to make sure he at least got *into* the emergency room?"

Junior didn't know what to say to that. How could this man understand that Junior was afraid of the people in the big brick building that housed the hospital? How could Junior admit that? "I was in a hurry, sir. I thought somebody'd take care of the kid."

"So you just left him there? In this heat?" Detective Allen shook his head. "You're all heart, Vernon."

Junior didn't know what to say to that.

"But you are admitting you are the one the nurse saw?"

It hadn't dawned on Junior to lie, to say that he wasn't the one who dropped the boy off, to just say that he was out in the woods with Eunice when all this happened. But, as Junior saw it, the opportunity for that falsehood was now behind him.

"Yes, sir." Junior moved some of the dust on the floor around with his toe.

Detective Allen was slowly shaking his head. "I just don't get it, Vernon. Why wouldn't you take the little guy inside? I mean, shit, man, I saw him. He was in a bad state. How could you just leave him?"

"I don't know. I was in a hurry." The sky at the windows was pressing in more and more, stealing Junior's breath.

"Well, let's look at something else. When my men came out to your place, just to ask you a few questions, I heard you hid under the bed and wouldn't answer the door. That right, Vernon?"

Junior found he couldn't speak. He stared desperately out the window, the thought of just flinging himself through it crossing his mind. Anything would be preferable to this.

He felt the detective's hand on his face, turning his head, forcing him to look at him. "I asked you a question."

"Yes, sir. I hid because I was...scared." Junior felt a hot flush of shame rise up from his chest to envelop his neck and face.

"Well now, Vernon, it's been my experience that men who have done nothing wrong have nothing to be scared of. Wouldn't you agree with that?"

"I reckon so, sir. But, y'see, I don't have much call to mix with other people. You know, I stick pretty much to myself."

"Yeah, and little boys..." Detective Allen said under his breath, but loudly enough for Junior to hear.

"And you were so scared you hid from the officers?"

"Right."

Detective Allen was shaking his head again. "I don't buy it, Vernon. I just don't buy it. Let me tell you what I think. I think you found that little boy and somehow, by meanness or tricks, you got him up to your little shanty in the woods. I think you were desperate and horny and you did the nasty with this little boy. And when he didn't cooperate, you knocked him around some, just to make sure he wouldn't give you any more trouble. And maybe— you sure as fuck don't look like a killer, Vernon—maybe you accidentally got a little too rough. And even though you'd done wrong with this boy, you didn't have the heart to see him die, so you brought him to the hospital and tried to sneak away." The detective paused to wipe the sweat from his brow. "That's about right, isn't it, Vernon? That's what really happened, isn't it? Now, I told you: you cooperate and it'll go a lot easier. I'll make sure of it."

Junior stared out at the sky for a long time. He didn't have much education, but he was smart enough to know that what the detective said made sense, even if it wasn't the truth. How could he prove he wasn't involved with what happened to that poor little boy? Who would give him an alibi? Eunice? He scratched his head. "That ain't what happened."

Detective Allen was on his feet suddenly and shouting, his deep voice booming and ricocheting off the walls, making Junior shrink down, cowering like Eunice during a scolding.

"Aw, come on, Vernon! Everything you've done points the finger to a guilty man! Innocent men don't do what you did... They don't hide from the police. An innocent man would have taken the little boy right into the emergency room. An innocent man would want to make sure the boy was all right, especially after bringing him close enough to the goddamn doors to the emergency room. Help me out here, Vernon. At least have the balls to come up with a convincing lie."

Junior stared at the floor. What little he had eaten that day roiled and churned in his stomach. He was afraid he was going to be sick. "I didn't hurt that little boy."

"Sure you didn't." The detective blew out a big, disgusted sigh. He put his face right in front of Junior's, forcing him to meet the bloodshot gaze of his pale-blue eyes. "We have other witnesses, Vernon. And we have other ways of proving it was you, even if you don't admit it. Now, I wanted to go easier on you, but I guess that just isn't the way you want it, now is it?"

Junior felt a spray of the man's saliva hit his face but didn't want to make him angrier by wiping it away. He said nothing.

"You know, I don't understand guys like you," the detective screamed. "Not at all!" He stormed from the room, slamming the door behind him so hard it made Junior jump and whimper. He lowered his head and began to cry.

*

Hugh stormed into the observation room next door. The two people inside, a secretary named Monica Griffin and the assistant DA, Veronica Tyconovich, looked up.

"I'd bet my nuts that fucker's guilty, wouldn't you?" Hugh didn't give them a chance to respond. "Monica, call that lab up in Pittsburgh and see if they've got that goddamn DNA test set up and tell them to get on it. I don't know how long we can hold this asshole."

"I'll—"

"And then call that Paul Thompson and get him in here for a lineup."

*

"Can you keep an eye on Jason? I'm going to run out and get some of his favorite stuff to eat."

Paul took his gaze from the Cartoon Network, where Tom and Jerry were about to have another climactic battle, this time involving dynamite, and looked at his wife. Had she always been so mousy, standing before him wringing her hands, her eyes rimmed in red, looking as if she might burst into tears at any moment? Christ, you'd think the woman would be grateful the kid wasn't dead.

"Yeah, sure. Is he sleepin'?"

Shelley sucked in some air and chewed her lower lip. She shrugged. "He might as well be. He's just up there, staring at the ceiling."

"I'll keep an eye on him, honey. Don't worry. Just go on about your business."

"Thanks," Shelley whispered without looking at him. In a moment, she was gone. He listened for the crunch of gravel and the sound of exhaust that indicated Shelley's departure.

Paul sat for a while, simply staring straight ahead, the TV no longer registering. He needed to have a little talk with Jason and would have to choose his words carefully. After a while, he picked up the remote and switched the TV off. Then he stood and rubbed his sweating palms on his jeans. *No time like the present.*

Jason's presence in the house was making Paul nervous. Even though he had never said anything when he was Jason's age, never fingered his old Grandpa, that was no guarantee Jason would keep quiet.

Paul lit a cigarette and drained the last of his beer from the can and set it on the table next to his recliner. He trudged up the stairs slowly. Before he got to the top, the dog, Olive, bounded up after him, her tail wagging and her smashed-in face alight with interest.

He was about to shoo her back downstairs, but then thought better of it. The old mutt might come in useful in this particular conversation.

Just as Shelley had described him, Jason was lying in his bed, the sheet pulled up to his neck, staring at the ceiling. Paul took in the bruises on the boy's face and felt a sudden, sickening wrench in his groin. Had he done that? He groped for some rationalization and went with the fact that the boy deserved it for fighting him the way he had done. If he had just been compliant as Paul himself had been at that age, he might have come out of the experience virtually unscathed.

It was Jason's fault.

Paul took the remaining few steps that would lead him to the boy's bed. Green eyes turned to him, and Paul could see the boy was afraid. There was a shrinking, almost as if the boy were trying to disappear into the wall next to his twin bed.

Paul put a smile on his face, a smile that would tell the boy it was okay, nothing bad was going to happen, and sat down next to him.

Jason whipped his legs away from his stepfather as if, even in this simple touch, danger lurked.

Paul shook his head and reached out, tousling the boy's head of thick, dark hair. He tried to ignore the fact that Jason recoiled from the touch. He told himself the fear was good and gave him less reason to worry the boy would one day talk, telling his mother or faggot dad who the real culprit in this whole scenario was.

"Hey, now," Paul said, making his voice soft, barely above a whisper. He could be gentle when the situation demanded.

Olive's tail thumped on the floor. Paul smiled at the boxer mix and patted the bed. "C'mon, girl, you wanna get comfy with Jason?"

Olive bounded up on the bed. Jason watched her and, for just a moment, a smile flickered across the boy's features. But then he looked back at Paul and seemed to vanish within himself.

Olive settled herself on the bed, snorted, turned in a circle, and finally stretched out next to Jason. Paul scratched the dog behind her ears.

"I just wanted to have a little talk with you, Jason."

Jason stared at the wall. Paul gently took the boy's chin in his hand and, ignoring the trembling this action incited, forced Jason's face to his own. Jason cast his gaze down. Oh well, there wasn't much more he could do. At least Paul knew the boy was listening. And that was the important thing.

"You know what happened between us shouldn't have. Son, I know it too. But someday, when you're all grown up, you'll understand that men sometimes can't control their actions."

Paul searched the boy's features for some sign of understanding. Receiving none, he continued. "You know that if you tell anybody, it'll only make trouble for everyone." Paul sighed, as if he were thinking. "And most of the trouble would be for your mom. Jason, it would hurt her bad, real bad. Likely kill her. Do you understand why you can't ever tell what happened?"

The boy's lack of response was causing a small hum of rage to begin behind Paul's eyes, almost as if a swarm of bees were beginning to touch down there.

"Man, Shelley would be just sick. After all she's been through. She finally finds herself a good man and if you told, it would spoil everything for her. You may not realize it, son, but it would ruin her life. You wouldn't want that, now would you?

"We can just go on, like before. You get yourself on the mend, get better and I promise nothin' like this will ever happen again. And we can just forget it.

"But if you tell, little guy, the horror show never ends. And you know who's fault it'll be?" Paul paused. "Yours."

Paul stared at Jason, desperately wanting some sign of agreement. Surely the boy could understand the trouble he could cause in his own family if he ever revealed the truth about this... mistake. But he got nothing.

He raised his voice a little. "Listen, kid, I didn't want to say this, but if you tell, there'll be more hell to pay than you ever imagined." He glanced down at Olive, who wagged her tail at his look. "That mutt there, for instance, I'd snap her little neck without thinking twice. You wanna be responsible for that?" Jason stared at the wall.

"Damn it, kid!" Paul drew his face close enough that he could smell the boy's breath. "The fuckin' dog won't be the only one to get her fuckin' neck snapped. Do we understand each other?"

And before his rage became overwhelming, Paul hurried from the room.

Downstairs, Shelley was pulling into the driveway.

Chapter Eleven

He doesn't know how he knows it, because he's inside the animal, but he knows it for sure. He's a rabbit. There's the point of view, for one thing. He sees everything from a low, close-to-the-ground perspective. The way the briars brush against his fur is another; they don't scratch but seem to slide off him as he hurries through the thicket. His nose is only inches from the ground. Above him a blue sky beats down, the sun's heat unrelenting, making of his fur a suffocating prison.

And then there's the fear. He can smell it on himself, a hot, sour tang that makes him run, the briars and tall grass a blur as he passes them. His heart pounds and his lungs feel tight in his chest as he springs off his hind legs, bounding blindly forward in his terror.

And then all motion ceases as the trap snaps shut, clamping down on one of his hind legs, razor-sharp teeth digging into the muscled flesh, causing pain that makes him scream—a high-pitched tone that resounds through the forest, causing the birds and insects around him to stop midsong.

His heart pounds harder, so hard it seems the pressure of the blood within will cause it to burst.

Someone is coming. As the shadow, cool, falls across his back, he freezes, waiting for the cruel hand that will claim him.

*

"Honey, honey, wake up." Shelley gently nudged Jason's shoulder, fingers lightly moving over the bony flesh. She had made up a tray of his favorites—Campbell's alphabet soup, a glass of ginger ale, a Granny Smith apple—the kinds of things she had learned were appropriate for a convalescent.

Jason's eyelids fluttered, and then he was looking up at her. Shelley took in a breath of gratitude. The look her son gave her was not one of dull incomprehension, as if she were some stranger, but one of recognition. There was a small kind of communication in his gaze and for that, Shelley could be thankful. She smiled, smoothing his dark hair back from his forehead.

The two days since Jason had come home had been hard on her, hard on her patience. She wanted miracles. Even though Dr. Wu had cautioned her that this withdrawal could last a long time, Shelley wanted to convince herself that once Jason was back in his home, among familiar, loved things like his Smokey Bear, he would awaken and become the chatterbox she had once known.

She pulled Jason up by his arms, wanting to be gentler than she was, but how else did you get someone who didn't cooperate with you into a sitting position? She held him close to her with one arm while raising the pillows behind him.

He seemed to be sitting well enough, and Shelley pulled his desk chair from behind her and seated herself beside the bed, lunch tray balanced on her lap. "Alphabet soup, Jason. Your favorite. Remember how we used to spell your name out with the letters?" She grinned at him and dug into the bowl. She brought the soup near his lips, and he opened his mouth.

Shelley bit her lower lip, never expecting to feel so moved by such a tiny action—Jason opening his mouth to take the soup she offered. She fed him the rest of the soup, chattering, unanswered, about the weather, and how the heat wave would just have to end soon. After all, September was approaching, and he had to get better. Third grade at East Elementary would be starting, and he wouldn't want to miss out on that, would he? Miss Timmons was the nicest teacher in the school; everyone knew that.

Shelley finished with the soup and set the apple and the ginger ale on the nightstand next to his bed. "You can have those whenever you're ready." She leaned over and planted a kiss on his forehead.

As she left the room, she thought she could imagine no finer wish granted than returning to the room and finding his little plastic cup empty and an apple core, turning brown in the harsh light of the sun.

As she was rinsing Jason's bowl in the kitchen sink, the phone rang. Shelley was tempted to let its jangling continue unabated, let the answering machine pick it up.

More and more, she wanted to insulate herself from the outer world, to, in a way, join Jason in his cocoon of silence. What could any of them say? If it was that detective, Hugh Allen, calling to tell her there was a break in the case, what difference would it make? Would it restore the little boy she had lost? Would it return Jason's voice and bring him bounding down the stairs? No, all it would do is keep reopening the wound, exposing its frail pink skin to the sun, bleeding. If it was a concerned neighbor or relative, would good would that do? Their concern only imposed on her a need to put on a brave face, to gently push away their offers of help and expressions of sympathy. If it was Sean, what could she say to him? She would only squash his hopes as she did every day by telling him there was no change.

Except today, she thought, there had been a change. He ate his soup. He looked at her. Would that be enough to send Sean humming to his duties as a reporter for the *Evening View*? And yet it was Sean, and only Sean, who could appreciate the small steps Jason had taken this afternoon. He was the only one with the heart to understand why Jason's small actions upstairs induced in her a small ray of happiness.

Shelley hurried to quiet the ringing of the phone, hoping it was Sean who was calling. It seemed only his voice would be acceptable.

But it wasn't Sean.

"Honey? How are you?"

It was Mom. The woman didn't possess the sensitivity to appreciate Jason's small steps, so there was really nothing to tell her. She tried to keep the annoyance out of her voice. "Hi, Mom. Everything's still status quo. Jason is holding his own." The words were becoming practiced. She could say them without thinking.

"Well, dear, it'll take time. By this time next week, I bet you'll be telling me some good news."

"God, I hope so." Shelley glanced out the window, wondered where Paul was.

"Listen, honey, I was calling for a reason."

Shelley closed her eyes, already not liking the serious tone of her mother's voice. She knew the woman only wanted to help, but—

"What is it, Mom?"

"Well, I was wondering about Sean."

"What about him?"

"Are you leaving him alone with Jason?"

Shelley shrugged. "Sure, when he comes over, I give him some time with Jason. Is there something wrong with that?"

"Don't you think there is?"

Although she knew very well what her mother was getting at, she said, "I don't know what you're talking about."

Her mother snapped, "I think you do," then softened her tone. "Well, you know, Sean's a, um, homosexual. You know."

Shelley could practically hear her mother squirming on the other end. She knew how hard it must have been for the woman to pronounce the word "homosexual." Throughout her divorce, Shelley had listened to her mom's railings against Sean, the quoting of biblical scripture against men lying with men and, most hurtfully, her urgings to deny Sean any kind of visitation based on the fact that he was, um, homosexual. Used in Estelle's arguments were the fears that such men could not be trusted around little boys, and how Sean had deliberately duped her when he married her. After all, Estelle had asked her, hadn't there been men in his life before she came along? Shelley herself had told her mother that. He was just using her when he married her.

"I just think, with his...desires...he might not be so safe around the boy."

"I think I can judge that."

"No, Shelley, I don't think you can. You're in a fragile state of mind. And God only knows why, but you've always given that man the benefit of the doubt."

"Sean loves Jason. He's his father."

"I know that! But doesn't it ever cross your mind that it might have been him? After all, Jason was—oh, I can't bring myself to say it. But that's what men like Sean like."

Shelley sighed, groping on the counter for her cigarettes. She lit one and sucked in hard on the smoke. She felt a perverse desire to shock her mother. "Sean likes to fuck other men, Mother. Not little boys."

The statement got the gasp Shelley was after. "Oh, Shelley. I hardly think we need to use such language."

"And I hardly think we need to be having this discussion. Sean would never do anything to hurt Jason."

"Leaving him wasn't hurting him?"

"No, I mean..." Shelley stopped herself, flustered.

"And even if it wasn't Sean, how do you know you can trust his...friend? What's his name?"

"Austin." Shelley conjured up an image of the blond young man, handsome, broad shouldered, with the kind of blue eyes that once would have made Shelley stop and stare. Her competition. The one who had stolen Sean away. Except that wasn't true. When she and Sean split up, there was no one in the picture. Austin had come along after the final divorce papers had been signed; after, in fact, she had started seeing Paul.

"How do you know it wasn't him?"

"I just do." Shelley wanted to slam the phone down, but she could never do that. Estelle was, after all, her mother.

"I think your certainty is blinding you to the danger of those two men. I think they, or one of them, probably are responsible. And you should at least consider that. Even if they're not responsible, I think you should at least consider it. Think about your child, honey."

Shelley suddenly felt trapped, as if the weight of this whole tragedy had suddenly come down on her shoulders. She knew Sean would never do such a thing to his son, and Austin...well, that just wasn't what homosexuals were about, was it? Wasn't there a word for men who liked children? Pedophiles. Homosexuals were not pedophiles.

"I think it would at least be wise to keep the two of them away from Jason, at least until we find out who is responsible."

"Mom, I can't do that."

Estelle's voice became shrill. "You mean you won't. How can you call yourself a caring mother?"

"That's enough."

"No, I'm afraid it isn't. Maybe you're right. Maybe there's a good chance you're right. But you have to admit there's a chance that my fears aren't groundless. And a good mother wouldn't let even the tiniest chance slip by her. If they did have something to do with it, God knows what their presence might be doing to that boy. Maybe even preventing him from getting well. If they did have something to do with what happened to Jason, then seeing them might just send him back. Every time."

Shelley lowered her head, feeling the tears gathering, the lump forming in her throat. She was sick of crying. She replaced the phone in its cradle, cutting off her mother's voice.

Through blurry eyes, she searched for the keys to the car. *Wait*, she told herself. *You can't leave Jason alone.*

Just for a second, just for a few seconds, so I can calm down. I'll just spin through the park, have a moment to myself. To think. God knows I need to think.

Grasping the keys in one hand, Shelley hurried out the door, rubbing the hot tears away with the hand that was balled around her keys. She threw herself into the car, tripping as she entered and bumping her head on the door frame. Gunning the engine much too hard, Shelley threw the car into reverse and backed into the street, ignoring the blaring horn and screeching brakes behind her.

She roared up the street, watching the light at the next intersection. Once green, she would make a quick left and head up the hill, toward Fawcett Park, with its copses of maple and oak, make a circle of the park, and come home. Five minutes, maybe less, and she would be back.

What if Mother was right? How could Shelley even continue to live in a world populated by such people? She remembered how stunned she had been when Sean had admitted to her he was gay, how she had questioned her own femininity. How the fact that he was attracted to men had never so much as crossed her mind.

Shelley gunned the engine, tearing through the intersection on the tail end of a yellow light.

She didn't even see the station wagon as she made her left. Didn't see it until it was too late, until the pale-blue car, with its wood-grain siding, loomed large in front of her, when, no matter how hard she pressed the brake pedal and threw herself back against the seat for leverage, she couldn't avoid the impact...the metallic boom, the grinding of metal merging with metal and the tinkling of broken glass.

Feeling nothing as she sailed through the glass of her windshield, Shelley had one thought before everything went black. *Who will take care of Jason?*

Chapter Twelve

"And then the ant says to the elephant, 'Take it all, bitch!'"

Paul roared with laughter, slapping the bar. He took a drag off his Marlboro and a swig of his Bud and looked over at his best buddy, Greg Adkins, and grinned. The air in the American Legion was cold, a cloud of cigarette smoke buoyed up on the air-conditioning's current. The darkness was barely broken by the small rectangular windows, situated high on the walls, which let slants of the summer sun filter in, illuminating the smoke and the dust motes in the air. The dark-paneled bar held five or six men, dressed in jeans or work uniforms, all serious drinkers. Dwight Yoakum wailed from the jukebox.

"Where the hell do you get these things?"

"Oh man, I got a million of 'em." Greg chuckled, running his hand through his close-cropped pale blond hair. He downed the shot of Jack Daniels in front of him. "Down at the mill, you just pick 'em up from the other guys." Greg shook his head. "I always had a good memory for jokes." He lit another cigarette and asked the bartender, Dave Simmons, a balding man with a big gut, to bring them another round.

As Dave was drawing the beer from the tap, the phone jangled behind him. One guy shouted, "I ain't here," his voice rising drunkenly above the music's twang. Dave set the beer mugs on the drain below the tap and hurried to quiet it.

"Legion."

Paul was listening as Greg launched into what he described as the "grossest" joke he had ever heard. "So there was this dude, really horny, you know..."

"It's for you, Paul."

Paul rolled his eyes. Ever since this business with Jason, it seemed he never had a moment to himself, what with Shelley always tracking him down with instructions to stop at the grocery store or the pharmacy and pick this, that, or the other thing up. Not to mention the fear that Jason would get his voice back and with it, the ability to accuse. That fear followed him around like a tiny dark cloud, one that would soak him with shit if it ever broke open.

"Hold that thought, buddy," Paul said to Greg as he took the receiver from the bartender.

"Yeah?"

"Mr. Thompson?"

The man's voice was strange and sounded way too official. Damn, if that boy said anything... Ah, maybe it was just that cop, Allen, calling him about the lineup he was supposed to set up.

"Speakin'."

"This is Dr. Caputa, down at City Hospital. You don't know me, Mr. Thompson, but I'm afraid I have some bad news."

Paul's heart began to thud in his chest. What now? "What is it?"

"I'm afraid there's been an accident, Mr. Thompson."

An accident? Why the hell was this guy calling him about an accident? Shelley was home with Jason. How could anything have happened? His mom was down in Florida now, so City Hospital wouldn't be calling about that. "What happened?"

"It's your wife, Mr. Thompson. She was just brought in to the emergency room."

"Are you sure? Shelley's home with our kid. What did she do? Fall down the steps or something?"

"I'm afraid there's been a car accident, Mr. Thompson."

What the hell was Shelley doing out driving? Who was looking after Jason?

"Well, is she all right?"

"I'm afraid there was serious head trauma. We're doing all we can for her right now, but I think you should get down here."

"Oh, Jesus. Sure, sure I'll be right there."

"Just ask for me when you get to the emergency room... That's Dr. Caputa. I'll be waiting." The connection went dead.

"Jesus fuckin' Christ," Paul said to Greg.

"What the hell?"

"When it rains, it fuckin' pours." Paul reached over the bar, grabbed his beer and downed it in two swallows. He belched. "Shelley was in a fuckin' wreck."

"Oh Jesus, man, I'm sorry to hear that. She okay?"

Paul shook his head. "Doctor said something about a head trauma. Jesus Christ, why is it always me?" Paul grabbed his truck keys from the bar and hurried out into the blinding sun before Greg had a chance to say anything else.

The American Legion Post was just around a corner and up a hill from the Thompson house, and Paul thought it would be easy to swing by and make sure someone was taking care of Jason before he headed on to the hospital. He couldn't believe Shelley would have gone out and left the boy alone while she went out joyriding.

The stop would be on his way. Paul headed down Montana Avenue, near the end of which was his green-shingled house.

God, how much time was he going to put in at City Hospital this summer? First Jason and now Shelley. What had he done to deserve this?

And at that thought, a vision of Jason rose up before him with all the clarity of a Technicolor movie. Jason, in the middle of what he called one of his forts—nothing more, really, than pine needles piled a couple of inches high, outlining the edges of rooms. Paul had followed him that afternoon, drunk and horny. He had no thoughts regarding what he was about to do. His mind was a blank as he headed through the trees, the boy's red shirt taunting him, daring him to follow.

The woods had been slightly cooler, because of the shade the trees afforded, but no less humid, with the trees and vegetation holding in the moisture. Insects buzzed in the emerald air, darting for the moisture of Paul's eyes. He batted the gnats away with his forearm, trying not to lose sight of the boy.

Once in a while, on the course of this mission, his rational mind told him to turn back, that what he was after was hitting far too close to home. But a numbness, an advocate of his lust, would shut out the thoughts, returning in their place the same throbbing blankness he had before.

He had felt like an animal, a predator, and as much as he didn't like to acknowledge those feelings, they persisted, conspiring with his lust to think of nothing more than putting one foot in front of the other, to track the little eight-year-old boy ahead of him.

And if his conscience would break through, Paul would tell himself he wasn't going to do anything.

Then why tramp through these hot, moist woods? Why not be in the basement, with a fat joint burning between his fingers and a cold Bud on his workbench? There was plenty to look at down there, plenty of materials to assuage the lust he was feeling. No, it was more than feeling; it was directing him, controlling him, and he was nothing more than a body to deliver the goods to his lust. A lust that on this day could not be satisfied with a mere photograph and his hand.

He had watched for a while as Jason squatted on the pine-cone littered floor of the forest, moving two X-Men figurines through the labyrinth of the fort he had constructed. The boy hummed softly to himself as he made one plastic mutant follow the other, much as Paul had done to him.

Paul leaned forward to get a closer view of Jason's smooth, tanned legs jutting out from the khaki shorts he wore. As he did so, a twig snapped under his foot.

Jason looked up, and Paul could still see the green eyes widening as the boy spotted his stepfather. "Paul. What are you doing here?"

Had there been fear in Jason's eyes? Had the boy already known, on some subconscious level, what was about to happen?

With the image of Jason's eyes burning on the soft pink surface of Paul's brain, he almost rear-ended an old, rusting powder-blue Buick in front of him. He slammed on the brakes and the tires squealed their protest on the hot asphalt.

It was enough time—no impact here, no second accident on a day of accidents. Paul could see the old man driving the Buick stare up in alarm at him in the rearview mirror.

Paul whispered, "Jesus Christ, get a hold of yourself, man."

He navigated the rest of the short course without incident and soon found himself pulling up in the driveway of the frame house he shared with his family. There were no other cars in the driveway, nor were there any parked in front of the house.

That meant Jason was probably alone. "Fuck, Shelley, what were you thinking?" Paul hopped from the cab of his truck and went inside.

*

Jason was sleeping as Paul crossed the threshold into his bedroom. He lay on his back, lips slightly parted, a tiny pool of spittle gathered at the corner of his mouth. Paul stared down at the boy, wondering *Are you going to cause me a lot of trouble?* He crept across the blue-carpeted surface of the boy's bedroom and gently drew back the sheet.

Looking at the boy lying prone in a pair of boxer shorts caused a hot flush to rise up in Paul's face, and he contemplated yanking the elastic waistband of the boy's shorts down.

He would just take a look, just one small look. There was a growing tightness in his jeans as he leaned over the bed, hand outstretched.

The phone jangled, killing the mood immediately, its ring sounding alarming in the quiet house. Paul rushed from the room and into the bedroom he shared with Shelley and picked up the cordless on the nightstand.

"'Lo."

"Paul? Honey, is that you?"

His mother-in-law. Jesus. Paul was trembling, feeling as if he had been caught, as if the woman could see through the telephone and knew what he'd been about to do. "Yeah, Estelle, it's me. Did you hear what happened?"

"Oh, honey, I'm so sorry. I don't know why the Lord places these burdens in front of us. We're good people."

"Right. I was just checking on Jason before I went down to City."

"You mean Shelley left him alone?"

"Looks that way."

"She must have needed something from the store. I can't imagine her leaving him alone like that."

"I can't either, Estelle. Jason is sleeping right now. So I think there's no harm done." Paul paced the room, the receiver pressed hard against his ear. He was sweating; little droplets in his armpits formed and rolled down his side. "Listen, could you come over here and look after him while I go down to the hospital? I know you probably want to do the same, but I don't know who else to call."

"Of course I will, dear. I'll go you one better. Why don't you throw a few of his things in a bag, and I'll come over and bring him back here. With Shelley in the hospital, it might be easier if he just stays with me."

Paul thought about the offer. It would remove from him any opportunity of things getting out of hand with the boy again. Besides, he didn't have time to look after the boy, and who else was going to take care of him while Shelley was gone? The faggot?

"That sounds like a great idea, Estelle. But could you hurry? I need to get down to the hospital."

"I'm on my way. In fact, I'll be there in five minutes. Don't worry about packing a bag. I'll do it."

"You're a sweetie, Estelle. I don't know what we'd do without you."

"Well, I think the boy will be safer with me."

"Right," Paul said and hung up the phone. *Safer?* What could she mean by that?

Chapter Thirteen

Estelle Berry hummed softly as she drove the mile and a half to her daughter's house. As she maneuvered the Chevy Impala down Hill Road, she was surrounded on either side by towering trees: maples, oaks, and black walnuts. The sun filtered through them, making patterns on the road. She tried to concentrate on the play of light and shadow, but all it did was bring her thoughts to how another tragedy was playing itself out in her family. It didn't seem fair. The air-conditioning cooled her, belying the heat outside, making of the day just another beautiful exercise in nature. Jim Brickman played on the radio; she had always loved his music and was grateful for the calming effect it produced. How could everything be so peaceful within the interior of her car, and her world be plunging into turmoil outside its confines?

She tried not to think of Shelley down there at City Hospital, doctors fussing over her. Shelley was her only daughter, only child in fact, and if something happened to her, Estelle didn't know how she could go on. Her husband, John, hadn't been of much use for anything the past several years, devoting his life to the pursuit of televised sporting events and the sampling of snack foods.

"Please, Lord, we've been good people. Always have." She was about to whisper something along the lines of how they didn't deserve all this trouble, not coming so close together, but then humbled herself, thinking better of it. At the red light at the bottom of the hill, she closed her eyes and bowed her head. "It's not for us to understand your ways, Lord," she whispered. "But I accept them with gratitude. I know that these are tests, nothing more, to see how worthy we are. Thank you, Jesus. I know you won't desert me in my hour of need."

Estelle made a right onto Montana and headed down the two blocks that would lead to Shelley's green-shingled frame house. She turned left into the driveway, then saw she would be blocking Paul's pickup truck and threw the car into reverse, backing into the street and parking in front of the house. Grabbing her purse from the seat beside her, Estelle braced herself for the heat and exited the car.

Paul waited for Estelle at the kitchen table, a can of beer in front of him. Estelle worked hard to keep her face from twisting into a grimace, but she wished the man didn't drink so much. And smoke! Lord, the kitchen was enveloped in a fog of the blue stuff. Estelle wondered what effect all this would have on Jason.

"Oh, honey, I'm so sorry." Estelle crossed the kitchen and squeezed Paul's shoulder. "But you have to remember, Jesus never gives us more than we can bear."

Paul nodded. "Right." He drained the last of his beer, stubbed out his cigarette, and stood. "I better be getting down there. See what the hell's going on now. This couldn't have happened at a worse time, not with Jason upstairs needing his mother to help him get better."

"Oh now, he's got his grandma! And you know he's going to be pampered. Now you run along." Paul started toward the door.

"Just come on back to my house after you see her. And please, please, Paul, bring some good news."

"I'd like nothing better."

Estelle stood at the screen door, watching as Paul backed his pickup out of the driveway. She didn't want to wonder but couldn't help it. Why was all of this happening now? Why couldn't it have been she, Estelle, in the accident? She would gladly have taken her daughter's place. But decisions like that, she cautioned herself, were in the hands of a greater power.

But what if something happened to Shelley? The girl had had nothing but trouble, it seemed, all her adult life. Why was she being punished like this? As far back as Estelle could remember, Shelley had always been a good girl, cheerful, quiet, and willing to help. She'd never harmed a soul.

"Stop it," Estelle whispered to herself. "Just stop it. These are not things for you to wonder." Wearily she turned from the screen door and trudged toward the stairs.

Jason was lying awake in his bed when Estelle entered his room. His green eyes stared up at the ceiling.

"Well, how's our little man today?" Estelle said, pushing back all the grief and worry clouding her thoughts. She forced herself to smile as she neared the bed. If there was anything good in this whole mess, it was that Jason didn't have to know what was going on. At least not yet, anyway.

Estelle seated herself next to the bed and snatched up Jason's small hand. It felt cool and slightly moist against her palm. Estelle wanted to gasp when the boy turned to look at her. The look was not one of dull incomprehension, she was sure. Jason recognized her. And, she could swear, the ghost of a smile flickered about his lips.

"I've got some good news, honey." Estelle leaned close to the boy, brushing his hair away from his forehead. "How'd you like to come and stay with your Grandma for a while?"

Even though she knew there'd be no response, Estelle paused, waiting for one.

"Grandma's going to take real good care of her little man." Estelle stood and went to the closet, where she knew she'd find a Pittsburgh Steelers nylon bag. She removed it from the closet and, opening Jason's drawers, began filling the bag with underwear and pajamas and optimistically, a couple of pairs of shorts and T-shirts. She threw in his tennis shoes and some socks and zipped the bag shut. "There," she said, looking toward the bed, "That didn't take too long."

After giving Jason a sponge bath and combing his hair, Estelle lifted him from the bed and started downstairs. About halfway down, she heard a light rapping on the aluminum of the screen door. She quickened her pace, moving down the stairs, through the dining room and into the kitchen as quickly as possible.

Sean and his "friend" stood outside. When he saw her through the screen's mesh, he frowned. "Hello, Estelle."

"Sean."

"I heard about Shelley. I'm awfully sorry."

"Mm-hmm. Could you get that door for me, Sean?"

Sean looked for the briefest of moments at his friend and then opened the door.

"I'd really appreciate a little help from you boys in getting the little guy into my car. Think you could do that?"

Sean said nothing but stood in front of her for a moment, almost as if blocking her way.

"Sean? Can you help me?"

"Where are you taking Jason?"

Estelle laughed. "Well, to my house, of course! I thought you said you'd heard about Shelley's accident."

"I have. That's why we're here."

Estelle didn't understand for a moment. "Well, I'm afraid Paul's already gone down to the hospital." She leaned close, her breath quickening. Even though he was only eight, Jason was a heavy burden for a woman of sixty-five. "I'd wait to go see her, if that's what you're thinking, until Paul comes home."

Sean shook his head. "I do want to see how she is, Estelle. But that's not what I'm here for."

Estelle brushed by him, heading toward her car. She called over her shoulder. "Well, what then? Something I can help you with?"

Sean's pace quickened behind her. Estelle cringed as she felt his hand on her shoulder. "I thought Austin and I could take Jason for a while."

"Oh dear, that's not necessary. I'm sure you boys don't have time for Jason, what with your jobs and all. And me, being a grandma, have nothing but time." Estelle did her best to smile at Sean and...Austin, but the way her heart was quickening made it difficult. She wished Paul was still here.

"Well, grandma or not, Estelle, I'm Jason's father. And I think if anyone's going to take care of him, it should be me."

"But what are you going to do about your job?" Estelle whined.

"I've already talked to the editor. I'm going to take some time. So that's not a problem." Sean came around to Estelle's front, blocking her path. He slipped his hands under Jason and gently tugged. "Give him here."

Estelle held fast. "Please, Sean. Paul knows he's with me. For now I think that's best."

"Well, I don't. You can just tell Paul Jason is over at our place. What's the problem with that?"

Estelle gritted her teeth. She didn't need this. Hadn't she had enough trouble for one day? She sighed. "I just think it's better this way." Lord only knew what would happen to poor Jason left alone with these two.

"Well, I don't. Now give him here." Sean tried to lift him from her arms more forcefully. Estelle stepped back, drawing Jason close to her chest, holding tight.

"No! Now that's enough. I'm not going to stand here and play tug-of-war with Jason in the driveway. The boy's been through enough. If you had any caring for him as a father, you'd realize that. Now are you going to help me get him into the car or not?"

Sean looked over at Austin, and Estelle could read the despair written on his face.

She pressed her advantage. "Now you can make this difficult for all concerned, especially Jason, or you can turn around and go home."

Sean stared at the ground. When he looked up, she saw his eyes were moist with tears. "Whatever," he said, voice barely audible. "Maybe we can make some other arrangements later."

Estelle smiled. And she prayed God would forgive her. "Sure we can, Sean. Now help me get him in the car, would you?" She turned to Austin. "And would you mind running upstairs and getting Jason's bag from his room? It's a Steelers bag." She paused for a moment. "Black and gold."

Chapter Fourteen

They drove most of the way to their house by the river in silence. Sean didn't know himself what words Austin could use to comfort him, but he was slightly annoyed that the man wasn't even trying. Austin just stared out the window, blond hair lifting in the wind, every so often using the Seek button on the car radio to avoid commercials and continue an irritating marathon of electronic dance music.

Outside, the world continued its day as if nothing were going on. Little girls skipped rope, and little boys terrorized them on their bikes. Someone honked at a friend in another car, and the two smiled and waved as they passed each other. The sky was a brilliant blue, the sun, if it were being described in some maudlin, yet overly cheery song, beat its lemon-drop brightness down on the pavement.

In another world, he and Austin might have been out at Beaver Creek, braving the parts of the creek referred to locally as the "tubs," where the water ran deep and the swift-moving currents were not as much of a threat.

Sean pulled in front of the little white Cape Cod with the black shutters he shared with Austin. Behind it, the Ohio River made a turn in its course. A barge was floating on the greenish-brown water, and a powerboat with skier attached buzzed by it. The air was filled with the scent of newly mown grass, thanks to Austin, and the smell of honeysuckle; bushes of the stuff stooped below their front windows, their fragrance attracting bees.

All this belied the turmoil going on within Sean, almost mocking him. It could have been a perfect summer day. What had he done to turn things upside down?

He sat in the car for a moment. He had at least seized control of the car stereo and tuned it to a classical station and now he sat, staring ahead, forcing himself to concentrate on the music the stereo was piping out, something by Brahms, was it? Something that in another time would have been soothing.

"You coming?" Austin was already out of the car, leaning into it, his handsome, chiseled features darkened by the car's interior. That face had once caused Sean's knees to turn to water. And suddenly, Sean realized he'd be just as happy if Austin walked away, leaving him in silence and misery, something only he could own.

"Yeah, sure." Sean snapped the radio off and followed Austin into the house. Inside, there were unfinished projects everywhere. Piled in one corner of the kitchen were rolls of wallpaper and cut lengths of oak for the walls and chair rail they planned on putting up in the dining room, cans of paint for Sean's office upstairs, and in the pantry, Austin's bright red toolbox, open, spilling out its contents on the linoleum.

None of these projects seemed to amount to much anymore.

Sean hurried into the living room, where the stillness bothered him. He squatted down in front of their stereo system and put a CD on, one Austin had bought him for his birthday, a collection of Gershwin music performed by pop stars. Once upon a time, the music would have cheered him. Now all he did was slump on the overstuffed white sofa that faced a bay window looking out on the river. The scenic view did nothing but depress him.

"I wonder when Jason will get a chance to look out this window again."

Austin moved to stand behind him. He dug his fingertips into the muscle above Sean's collarbone. "Jesus, you're tight."

Once upon a time, Sean's dirty mind could not have let a remark like that pass unmolested. Now, he simply said, "What do you expect?"

Austin continued to massage. "It's like you've got steel rods in here. Relax. Take a few deep breaths."

Suddenly the comfort his lover was trying to offer seemed out of place, an affront. It was as if he were ignoring the reality of their situation. "Well, what do you expect, Austin?"

"Being tense isn't going to help anything."

"What do you suggest? Should we fire up a bowl and pop in a movie? Maybe a nice porno?"

Austin stopped massaging for a moment, then pressed his hands back into service. "Loosen up. You'll be able to deal with things better if you're not so tense."

"And just what are those things?" Sean didn't like the way his voice was coming out, strident and snippy.

"I don't know, man. Just relax." Austin knew how to give a good massage, had taken training, in fact, in Pittsburgh, in the Swedish technique. But now the hands Sean had once adored were only serving to make him more tense.

"You don't know? What do you mean you don't know? When I sat down in here I said, 'I wonder when Jason will get to see this view again.' Don't you understand? Don't you realize what that woman's doing?"

"What woman?"

"Shelley's mom, idiot! Christ!" Sean lowered his head, hating himself for the caustic tone and the harsh words. It was almost as if the words had a will of their own, as if the little censor in his brain had shut down, damaged by the stress pulsing like something acidic through his veins.

Austin stopped his massage abruptly. He walked across the room and stared out the window. *Withdrawal,* Sean thought bitterly, was Austin's favorite way of getting attention. *Well, it won't work this time. I don't have the energy for it.* Even as he was thinking these things, he was hating himself for it; yet the invective came pouring out anyway. He just wanted Austin to share in his plight, his fears that once Estelle Berry had her clutches in his son, he might never see him again.

It had been she who had pressed most vehemently to have him denied anything other than rigidly supervised visitation during his protracted divorce proceedings from

Shelley, quoting biblical scripture on the witness stand and urging Shelley to not let Jason visit him until the judge ruled. Estelle had been smug in her belief the law would be on her side. She had even come to court to testify, letting the lawyer lead her through pronouncements of her fears, fears Sean was afraid she would use against him now. That he would molest the boy; that homosexuals were not to be trusted around children, that they set a bad example for a little boy, even the suggestion that Jason would be exposed to the AIDS virus, even though neither he nor Austin was HIV positive.

Shelley had been hurt by Sean's realization that he was gay. Actually, realization wasn't quite the right word. Acceptance would be closer to the truth. But she never wanted to keep him away from Jason. Sean realized now, even though it was unforgivable, that Shelley had gone along with her mother's crazy fears and legal maneuvering to get back at him, to hurt him as he had hurt her. Sean's head slumped as he thought, guiltily, once more that he had been the love of Shelley's life. And, until he couldn't stand hiding behind this self-imposed mask of heterosexuality any longer, their marriage had been good.

Austin turned from the window. "I know you're upset about all that's going on. I'll try not to take it personally when you lash out at me." He crossed the room and knelt in front of his lover, covering one of Sean's hands with his own. He looked up at Sean, his blue eyes searching Sean's face for...what? Sean was too tired to try to figure it out. "We'll get through this. You'll see. In a few months, things will be back to normal."

Sean thought of Shelley, envisioning her at the hospital, hooked up to life support. When he called, they had told him she was in a coma. Without her there to protect his rights, what hope did he have of things ever getting back to normal? And were his fears of not seeing Jason again really so groundless?

"I don't know about that, Austin. Estelle's got Jason now. You know what she thinks of us. She probably thinks one of us molested him. What are the odds she's going to want to make sure Jason can't visit us?"

"The law's on your side, Sean. You have rights. It's all there in the court order, in black and white." He stood. "Want me to go get it?"

"No. I know what it says. But that doesn't mean she won't try to keep him away from me. Who's going to help, now that Shelley's out of the picture?" He laughed bitterly. "Paul?"

"Well, you just can't let this get to you so much. We'll have to cross bridges when we come to them."

"How can you say that?" Sean felt the heat rising to his face, the anger buzzing in his gut, threatening to veer out of control. "How the hell do you expect me to be calm when my son is the most important thing in my life? Now he's been hurt, badly hurt, and Shelley's out of the picture. He's with a hateful old religious woman who hates gays and has a score to settle with the man who broke her daughter's heart." Sean stood up and stared out the window. In a low voice, he said, "I don't know where you get your sensitivity."

Austin said nothing, but Sean could feel his eyes on him, could hear his breathing coming heavier.

At last Austin broke the silence. "Jason is the most important thing in your life, huh? I think it's interesting you didn't add something like, 'along with you.' Well, at least I know where I stand."

And Sean, hating himself but unable to stop, turned and said. "Well, at least you know where you stand."

He stared at Austin, waiting for him to say something back. He was in the mood for a fight, he didn't know why, in the mood to keep pushing and pushing until he made Austin really angry or hurt. Even as he recognized these unreasonable feelings within him, he couldn't help himself. He just wanted to goad Austin, maybe to make him feel a little of the pain and fear coursing through him.

But Austin didn't fight back. His blue eyes clouded over and it seemed as if his whole face went rigid, closing down. He nodded slowly and whispered, "Fine."

Before Sean could do anything but watch in stunned silence, Austin turned and walked out the front door. Sean listened to the gun of the car engine, too hard, too loud, and then the sound of it fading away as Austin made his way out of the drive.

After a moment Sean bit his lip to hold back the tears. He couldn't take all this, couldn't take it.

He hurried to the back door and headed outside, where a breeze was coming off the river, bringing with it the tang of dead fish; the insects and birds around him called out. He walked through the yard where earlier he and Austin had gotten sweaty in the spring sun, laying sod, and moved beyond the tree line, where the earth sloped down to the river's bank.

He found a log to sit on and sat, not thinking for a long time, watching the slow-moving course of the river, its brown water glinting dully in the late afternoon sun.

Chapter Fifteen

Austin took the curve beyond their house much too fast, sending up a cloud of dirt and gravel that pinged against the car's metal finish. He had no idea where he was going and wondered briefly if he should pull over, his heart just about hammering through his chest and his vision blinded by tears.

He didn't pull over, but he did slow the car down, blinking his eyes rapidly to disperse the tears, gulping in deep breaths of air to try to calm himself.

Sean was Austin's first real love. Oh sure, there had been plenty of encounters, some that even lasted a few weeks and months—and some for only a few minutes—over the course of his twenty-seven years, but until he met Sean, he hadn't really known what love was.

They had met one winter afternoon shortly after Sean had left Shelley. Sean was still a married man in the eyes of the law, but his friend Burt from the pottery had seen him as a perfect match for Austin and had invited both men over for dinner. Burt, an older man who worked in the color room, dipping crockery in different colored glazes before it was fired in the kiln, had a weight problem and had just joined the Y, where he had met Sean. Burt had told them both that the dinner was just a casual get-together and not a setup, and even though everyone went along with the story, they all knew Burt was playing matchmaker. By the end of the evening, Burt had made an excuse for getting to bed early and left the two men alone. A simple kiss had sealed their future together. They went out for Chinese the very next night and hadn't really been apart since.

Austin steered the car down a pitted gravel road that ran along the Ohio, making the car bounce and screech on its suspension. The road used to be a major thoroughfare for cars traveling to downtown Summitville, but since the new bridge and highway had been built farther east, the road had fallen into disrepair.

Austin bounced along until he came to the one measly tourist attraction Summitville could honestly boast, the Wharf. An open-air structure built high on the banks of the Ohio, it had a dock and picnic tables and was often crowded with people playing cards, setting out picnics, or just enjoying the views of the river and tree-covered hills of West Virginia.

Austin was in no mood today for picnics or to enjoy the warm air. His mind went to dark places, such as how the Wharf, late at night, was a favorite homosexual trysting spot. He wasn't proud of the fact that he had availed himself more than a few times of the ease of its connections.

But that was before he met Sean and before he settled into a life of domestic bliss, or at least what he thought would be domestic bliss. Austin pulled the car into the parking lot of the Wharf, relieved to see there were few people out on this late afternoon, sunny and warm as it was.

He got out of the car and headed over toward a picnic bench facing the river. His nerves were still jangling from the fight with Sean, and part of him wanted to run home and make sure Sean understood that his storming out of their house did not mean he wasn't coming back.

But he couldn't do that. Not yet. Sean had hurt him.

Austin seated himself on the bench, splaying his long legs out in the grass before him. He watched a barge and tugboat float by and briefly wondered how it would be to work on the boat, to be alone on the river for days at a time. Right now it sounded less complicated than his own life.

He loved Jason, Sean's little boy, he really did, but he wondered if he was too young himself to be a parent and to be involved in all the horrible things that were happening right now. He had friends in Pittsburgh whose lives revolved around going out to the clubs on the weekends, getting laid, and wondering what Lady Gaga would come up with next. Sometimes that vapid life seemed pretty appealing, since Austin had never given himself a chance to really experience it.

Austin ran a trembling hand through his thick blond hair, writing a letter in his mind to Sean.

Dear Sean,

You know I love you and always will. And there are times when I think no man knows the kind of happiness I know when we are at our best together. Being with you has been a dream come true, the family I never had, the culmination of all my hot man fantasies.

And yet, you tell me that I am not first in your life. Your son is. I'm not sure how I'm supposed to take this. Part of me feels like I'm being a real ass for not being more understanding and not willingly taking a back seat to a little boy. A little boy who I know has been through way more than any little guy should have had to endure.

But the selfish part of me wants you to put me at least on the same level with your son. Part of me wants you to say that we are both your family and if you love us in different ways, you at least love us equally. Part of me wants you to look at me as a co-parent, as a team in bringing up your son.

How can I be that if I come second to Jason?

Another part of me, the part that doesn't always think so highly of himself, thinks I am being petty for even considering such things and wishing I had a different place in your life. That part tells me that what I have with you already should be good enough. And that I knew you had a son going into this relationship and that I should understand what it means to be a parent.

And then another voice, a completely selfish one, chimes in and tells me how young I am, still "hot" in the lingo, and that maybe I am settling for something I shouldn't be. That maybe I'm throwing away my youth and the best years of my life to settle into playing house with a man for whom I will always be second banana to his son. Maybe I should go out and play the field, have some fun, enjoy the embraces of many men...party, dance, see what all that online hooking up is about.

Austin stopped composing his letter when someone sat down at the opposite end of the bench from him. He looked up, annoyed at having lost having this bench as his exclusive province.

A young man had seated himself at the opposite end. He was cute, probably no more than twenty-two or -three, with curly, dark brown hair, brown eyes, and a big, straight nose that only served to make his chiseled features more appealing. He wore dark blue cargo shorts and an old faded gray T-shirt with the sleeves cut off. A tribal band snaked around one bicep. His legs, stretched out before him, were long and lean and dusted with dark, curly hair. He wore flip-flops.

Austin swallowed, surprised at his ability, amid all this turmoil, to feel the queasy-giddy sensation of desire rising up within his gut and even farther south. He had come here to be alone and to think, not to cruise. Besides, even if he were here to cruise, the Wharf was not the place for it, not during a bright, sunny summer day. Cruising that went on here usually took place late at night, with furtive assignations taking place in cars or down by the trees that grew near the river's bank.

But Austin couldn't deny he felt something for the young man seated so close he could see the beads of sweat on his upper lip. Beads that Austin could imagine licking away. The man's lips were full, lush, lightly pink in contrast to his deep tan.

The man looked over at Austin and in that one moment, Austin knew the young man was there not just to enjoy the view of the river, but to make a more physical connection. Call it gaydar, or call it the meeting and holding of a gaze a fraction of second too long, but Austin was aware he was being appraised. And he was also aware that he had not come up lacking.

The young man smiled at him, his grin a bit crooked, rising up sexily on one side more than the other and revealing rows of perfect white teeth. There was something complicit in the smile. "Hi." The young man's voice came out deep and at the same time, reedy. "I'm Eric."

Austin nodded. "Austin."

Eric resumed looking out the river. "Beautiful day, huh?"

"Sure is."

Eric turned and met Austin's gaze again, locking him in with irises that were so dark the pupils got lost within them. What was Eric? Italian, maybe? Latino? He had a whole hot-blooded swarthy thing going on, and Austin suddenly found himself questioning if this would be the time he would succumb to temptation and cheat on Sean.

Part of him said that would be a shitty thing to do to a man who was deep into the worst trauma of his life.

Another part told Austin that maybe a little tryst would be just what he needed, something to reassure him he could be number one in someone else's eyes, if only for an hour or two. An escape...

"So, I don't have a lot of time. You here for what I think you're here for?" Eric looked pointedly at Austin, but a grin played about his lips.

Austin knew he could play dumb, press him for details, or act offended, but one thing he had learned in his young life as an adult gay man: volumes often got spoken with simple glances and body language. Austin laughed and knew he needed to make a decision.

"Yeah, I'm probably here for the same thing as you."

"Got someplace we can go?"

Austin shook his head, part of him relieved that the responsibility for betrayal had been taken out of his hands by fate, and the other part disappointed that this would most likely go no further. Otherwise, why would Eric ask if he had a place unless he didn't have one of his own?

But Eric surprised him. "Well, if you don't mind a little mess, we can go back to my house. Only thing is, my ma will be home from work in a couple hours, so if you're up for this, we should probably go now."

And a second opportunity to back out presented itself. But the memory of Sean telling him he came second leaped into his mind, perhaps as rationalization, and all he said was, "So you got a car? Should I follow you?"

Eric looked over to the parking lot. "I'm in the silver Toyota pickup. My place is just a couple miles away."

Eric stood and Austin took in his tall—six three? six four?—frame and his coltish good looks. What was he doing? Shouldn't he just say something now? End this madness?

But the swelling in his groin seemed to have stolen all the blood from his brain, so all he could do was stand wordlessly, indicating he was ready to follow.

On the road, Austin began having second, third, and fourth thoughts, thinking, as they traveled south on the highway that ran along the river, that he could take this exit or that one and leave the guy wondering and hurry home safe—and still faithful—to his man.

But he never did. An absurd sense of decorum kept him on the pickup's trail and in no time at all, they were pulling up in front of a white two-story frame house with a maple tree in the front yard.

On legs that felt weak and shaky, Austin got out of his car. Eric waited near the front porch steps, smiling.

As Austin neared Eric, the young man turned and headed up the stairs. Austin—his mouth dry—watched the calves in Eric's legs bunch and release and the rise and fall of his high, taut ass. Jesus, what was he doing?

Eric said nothing as he struggled to pull a ring of keys out of his pocket and place them in the lock of the weathered wooden door.

Austin followed him into a vestibule. After the brightness of the day outside, it was almost pitch dark and the air was close. He could smell something—beans?—that had cooked the night before wafting in from the kitchen.

And then Eric faced him, his hands massaging Austin's shoulders. Eric leaned in close for a kiss and Austin ducked, moving his head back and away. He laughed to cover the nervousness and—yes—fear rising up within him.

Eric whispered, "Don't like to kiss? It's okay. There are lots of other things we can do." He grabbed Austin's hand and tugged him toward the flight of stairs to their left. "C'mon. Let's go up to my room. We don't have much time."

Austin followed, feeling more and more like this was something he shouldn't be doing and less and less desire for this beautiful young man who had been delivered to him like a gift.

But this was not the answer to his and Sean's problems. This would only make things worse.

Still, there was an absurd little part of him urging to go through with whatever was going to happen upstairs. It would be easier to follow, let Eric kneel before him, suck him off, zip up, and leave than it would be to try to explain that this wasn't going to work—not today.

The absurdity of that line of reasoning made Austin laugh out loud. Eric stopped on the step above him and looked down curiously. "What?"

Austin shook his head, thinking of Sean at home, wondering where Austin was, as if he didn't already have enough to worry him. Austin looked back at Eric. "You're really hot, man, but I can't do this. I'm sorry. I have a boyfriend at home and I've never cheated. I hope you understand. You really tempt me; you really do. But I can't go through with this."

Eric let go of Austin's hand and shook his head, smiling. The smile was so winning and kind it almost—almost—made Austin relent and just push the guy up the stairs and throw him on his bed.

But instead he turned and started tramping back down the steps. "Really, dude, so sorry," he called over his shoulder.

As he was closing the door behind him, Austin heard Eric call, "Are you for real?" He didn't know if he should take that as an insult or a compliment. Either way it didn't matter, because the relief that coursed through him, unmarred by even the slightest trace of disappointment, assured him he was doing the right thing.

Chapter Sixteen

Dusk arrived, throwing its tangerine and purple tinge across the flow of the Ohio. Sean still sat on its banks, feeling weary and defeated. For a while he had listened for the sound of Austin's car coming back, wanting to hear his lover move the brush aside as he headed down the river bank to comfort him. But the only things he heard were the cry of birds and the chirping of crickets and cicadas, which now grew louder as evening approached.

He didn't know where Austin was and wondered how he could have driven his only ally in this whole mess away from him. Before all this, it seemed the pair had always presented a united front to whatever kind of problem that arose. But then, they had yet to weather a problem of this magnitude. And now it seemed Austin just didn't understand. How could he? Austin was younger and had never struggled as Sean had with his sexual orientation. He came out shortly after high school and had never even considered marrying, let alone having children. He had resigned himself to the fact that he would never produce any progeny.

And that made Sean wonder how sympathetic Austin could ever be. What Sean had said earlier, about Jason being the most important thing in his life, was true. Sean knew that he occupied that spot in Austin's life and rationally could not dispute the fact that Austin felt he deserved the same in return.

But it didn't work that way. At least not for Sean. His separation from the boy had only increased his love for him, the guilt at not being there getting all mixed up with his love so that no one could ever take Jason's place. The minute Sean had laid eyes on his son in the delivery room, he had known an ineffable love, one that could never be equaled.

Sean stood and wiped the dust from the seat of his jeans. The gray twilight encroached, warning of the darkness that would arrive in only a few minutes. The darkness would lay its cloak across Sean and Austin's little patch of land so completely, it would be difficult to find his way back to the house. They lived in an area unlit by street lights or commercial establishments.

He headed back to the house, hoping the little red light on the answering machine would be blinking: a message from Austin saying he was sorry things had gotten out of control and he would be home soon, or one from Estelle calling to see what time Sean would pick Jason up this coming weekend.

But the house had never seemed more empty. The answering machine's solid red light taunted him.

He mixed himself a gin and tonic and stood, without turning on any lights, staring out the window that faced on the river, trying to think of nothing as he sipped his drink.

But Jason's face kept rising up before him. His voice rang out in his mind, calling him. "Dad, come over here and look at this," after finding a piece of driftwood that the river's erosion had turned into a Brontosaurus. "Dad, did you know there's going to be a Star Trek convention in Pittsburgh? Can we go, Dad?" *Dad. Dad. Dad.*

The word brought tears to his eyes. He had to see his boy. Estelle was a bitch: there was no getting around that, a woman who twisted Christianity around to suit her own view of morality and how the world should be, Sean thought as he hunted down his keys. But the law was on his side, as Austin had said. And the law had nothing to do with Christianity. "Thank God," Sean whispered and hiccupped out a brief, bitter laugh. In the United States they lived in today, Christianity—or people who twisted its message to give them an excuse to hate or exclude—was alive and well. Separation of church and state, these days, seemed like a quaint concept. And that was what was so terrifying...

There wasn't much the old woman could do to get in the way of a court order.

Was there?

*

"There now, honey, you've got your little bear, and Grandma and Grandpa will be right downstairs. Don't you worry about a thing." Estelle tucked the sheet snugly around Jason's neck and got up from her place on the guest room bed beside him. She gazed down at her grandson, who stared back at her through the dimness of the room, lit only by the pale glow of the night-light plugged into a socket on the opposite wall, and felt despair. There was little recognition in the boy's eyes, only a deadness that tore at her heart. She had read him a story and had run her hands through his dark hair, hoping for something as small as a glimmer of a smile, and had received nothing for her efforts.

Why had this happened? Estelle wondered as she turned from the boy to head downstairs, to join her husband in the living room, where she would take up the afghan she was crocheting while John watched yet another documentary on The Learning Channel. She had been a good Catholic all her life, rarely missing a Sunday mass, and then only when she was sick, and hardly ever missing a holy day of obligation. She had reared Shelley as a vessel of the Lord, not only parochial school but catechism on the weekends, even though it wasn't required. Every night, before she went to sleep, Estelle knelt beside her bed, crossed herself, and prayed, petitioning the Lord for selfless things like the health and happiness of her daughter and husband, the well-being of her grandson, and peace for the world at large.

And yet, she thought, heading down the creaking, sculptured carpeted stairs to the living room where the TV's volume was, as usual, too high, none of it seemed to make a difference. Oh sure, she knew the old rub. The Lord works in mysterious ways...but it seemed to offer little comfort, seeming, more than anything, unfair.

Wordlessly, she sat down on the couch and took up her crochet hook and yarn, not really focusing on the TV set, where a show about dolphins was in progress, and thought of how the Lord seemed to reward perverts like Sean and his "boyfriend" when they had done nothing but hurt her grandson and break her daughter's heart, while decent Christian families like Shelley's experienced nothing but heartache and sorrow.

"The boy asleep?" John mumbled from his recliner.

"I guess so," Estelle whispered. It didn't seem to make much difference. Awake, asleep, lately with Jason the only thing that told the difference was whether his eyes were open or closed. Why wasn't there something the doctors, with all their expensive knowledge and equipment, could do for the boy to snap him out of this?

She had just read in the newspaper a feature article about how AIDS was no longer a death sentence and more of a treatable illness, like diabetes. It didn't seem fair, not when her grandson, who had never done anything but bring joy into the lives of those around him, languished in a world of his own upstairs and when her daughter lay comatose in the hospital downtown.

Estelle guessed the reward for good people didn't come until they were dead.

She dropped her hook to her lap when she heard a rapping on the screen door at the back of the house.

John didn't move and Estelle stood, wondering who had come to call.

*

Sean stood, shifting his weight from one leg to the other, in the yellow glow of the porch light. Queasiness churned in his stomach and icy tendrils of anxiety tickled the nape of his neck. He knew this wouldn't be easy, court order or not, but he wasn't about to leave Jason in this woman's clutches. Who knew what could happen?

In a second or two, Estelle's pinched face appeared behind the screen, a pale oval peering out of the darkness. "Sean! What a surprise! What brings you over here?"

Sean cleared his throat, then forced himself to speak up. "I've come for Jason."

Estelle didn't open the door, and Sean saw her hand reach down stealthily. The action was followed by the click of the lock on the screen door. She shook her head. "I just put him down for the night. Perhaps you could come by in the morning."

"And what? Be told by you that he isn't here? Or maybe you won't even open the door."

Estelle laughed, but there was no mirth in it. "Now, Sean, why would you think that?"

Sean closed his eyes, trying to force out the invective building in his throat. Anger and accusations would get him nowhere. "I remember how things were during the divorce. No offense, Estelle, but how can I trust you?"

"What do you think? That I'm going to keep Jason from you?"

"That's exactly what I'm afraid of."

Estelle, to her credit, didn't try to deny his fears. "Look, Sean, whatever you're afraid of, tonight is not the time for this. We've all had a hard day, what with the accident and all."

"Yes, Estelle, and maybe it would be better if you were there for Shelley while I took care of my son."

"Oh, Sean, don't you have work to do? I'm here all day. I think I can look after the boy better. Who's going to keep an eye on him while you work?"

"The editor has given me some time off. Besides, these days with emails and the net, I can easily handle it at home if anything urgent comes up."

Estelle nodded. "Well, as I said, why don't you drop by in the morning?"

"Because I'd like to take Jason home now."

"That's just not possible."

John, a hulking man with a beer belly and bald pate, appeared behind Estelle. "What's going on, Es?"

"Oh nothing," Estelle snapped, "Go watch your program. Sean wants to take Jason. I told him I just put him to bed."

John leaned closer to the screen. "You heard her. Now go on."

"I will not!" Sean felt the despair rising, hot, to his face. "Jason is my son, and I want to take him home. I won't disturb him. We can just wrap him in a blanket, and I'll put him in the back seat. He'll be fine. He can't have been in bed that long. It's only eight thirty, for Christ's sake."

Estelle's lips straightened into a thin line. "Don't you take the Lord's name in vain with me, mister. Not in my house."

"I'm not in your house. Now let me in so I can get Jason."

"Come on, Estelle. We don't have to stand here and listen to this faggot." John urged his wife away from the door. John pressed his face close to the screen, so it was almost touching. "Now go on, on your way. We don't need any trouble."

"I'm not trying to make trouble! I just want my son with me!" Sean cried, anger and fear twisting in equal parts in his gut. "I have the right. I'm his father."

"Yeah, well you may be his father, but I don't think this is a good idea." John grabbed his wife by the elbow and moved her back from the door. In spite of the heat, John slammed the back door in Sean's face.

Sean began pounding on the door, knowing he was only making things worse but unable to stop himself. After pounding for what seemed like five minutes and incurring the ire of the dog next door, Estelle's angry face appeared, backlit by the kitchen light.

"You heard my husband. Now go on, get out of here! How do you expect Jason to sleep with the racket you're sending up? If you care about Jason, you'll come back tomorrow."

"If you care about Jason, you'll let him come with me."

"I'll do no such thing, young man, and if you don't leave right now, I'm calling the police. You have no business..."

"Go ahead, call the goddamn cops. I'd like to see what they have to say."

Estelle shook her head and closed the door. He watched her cross the kitchen and pick up the wall-mounted phone on the opposite wall. She looked at him, phone in hand for a moment, as if daring him to stay.

He stared back at her.

She turned and began punching in numbers.

*

It wasn't long before a blue-and-white police car, no siren but with blue lights flashing, pulled up in the driveway. "Summitville's finest," Sean mumbled to himself as a burly, middle-aged officer emerged from the driver's side of the car and a younger, hardened woman slid from the passenger seat.

Sean said nothing as Estelle opened the storm door and watched the officers approach.

It was the woman who did the talking. Her frosted hair was clipped short and her boyish features were contorted into a somber expression. Her nameplate read Pickens. "What's the problem here?"

Sean spoke. "They have my son in there, and I just want to take him home."

The woman looked to Estelle, who stood staring out the door. "Ma'am?"

"Officer, it's Jason Dawes, the boy who went missing a few days ago. I'm his grandmother. I tried to tell Sean here that the boy is in bed and for him to come back tomorrow." Estelle snorted and regarded Sean out of the corner of her eye. "He doesn't seem to want to listen."

"Please, Officer," Sean began, "Jason is my son. All I want is to care for him in my home while his mother is in the hospital. There was an accident..."

"Well, what's wrong with tomorrow? Can't you come by and pick the boy up then?"

Sean leaned close to the young woman. He shook his head. "You don't understand. I have good reason to fear that she won't let me take Jason."

"The man's a homosexual. Damn right we have reason to fear." John had once more appeared beside his wife.

Both officers sized Sean up, as if suddenly seeing him in a new light. Sean caught the look. "Look, Officer, I have a court order that I could get, assuring me of visitation rights."

The male officer asked, "You got joint custody?"

"Well, no, but surely the fact that I'm the boy's father carries more weight than being his grandparents."

Pickens nodded. "Ma'am, why don't you let Mister...?"

"Dawes."

"Dawes here take his son home."

Estelle said nothing for a moment, then blurted, "I would, but he isn't here."

Sean stared at the older woman with undisguised disbelief. "That isn't true," he gasped.

Estelle nodded. "One of the boy's aunts came to pick him up earlier. I'm not sure where they are."

Sean felt a sinking in his gut, a snake of anxiety that coiled and twisted inside. "Estelle, how can you say that? You just told me you put him to bed." He thought for a moment. "You just told these people the same thing."

Estelle smiled. "I lied."

"Ma'am, where is the boy?" The female officer took her gaze from Sean to confront Estelle.

"I'm sorry, Officer, but as I said, he's with an aunt, lives up near Pittsburgh, in Aliquippa. I'm not sure where they are right now."

"You bitch," Sean whispered.

"Please, sir, that's not going to help anything."

"I know Jason is in there! I know it. Just let me go inside and check around for him."

The woman in the navy officer's uniform looked to Estelle and John. "Could you let him in, ma'am? Just to have a quick look around? I'll come with him."

John stepped forward, his beer belly bulk a menace. "Not without a court order. I believe we're still in the U S of A and you can't come into someone's home uninvited. Illegal search—you should know that."

"I don't believe this," Sean whispered.

The woman placed a hand on Sean's shoulder. "I'm sorry, Mr. Dawes, but they're right. And I don't think we can get a court order from a judge this late. It'll have to wait for tomorrow."

Sean clenched and unclenched his fists, rage boiling up in him, hot. Despair was rage's companion and the whole combination made Sean sick to his stomach.

"Please, Estelle, don't do this…" he whispered.

"Good night, Sean." Estelle closed the door, a smug grin of satisfaction stamping her features.

Sean stared alternately at the closed door and the departing figures of the officers, watching until they entered the cruiser and backed from the driveway.

He pressed a hand to his eyes, trying to force back the hot flow of tears.

Chapter Seventeen

Sean pulled from the driveway, not sure where he should go now that he had been defeated in round one. He was certain of one thing, though. There were many more rounds to come. He had even discussed with Austin his fears that if anything ever happened to Shelley, he'd have a fight on his hands. Not with Paul, because Paul would probably be relieved to have the freedom to drink himself into oblivion with his buddies. But with Estelle and John. He was certain they would fight tooth and nail to keep him from Jason, their self-righteous so-called Christian morality their justification.

Tonight had proved him right.

Sean cruised down by the Ohio River. The moon reflected off the black water, a distorted oval cast upon its swiftly moving current. He wondered if Austin had returned home yet and was now sitting in their house, wondering himself where Sean had gone to.

He had never felt more hopeless. The rush of tears that had come on the Berrys' back porch had abated, leaving his eyes red and itchy, in their wake an empty feeling in his gut. He pictured Jason in the Berrys' guest room, a sheet pulled up around his neck, staring at the ceiling and puzzled over why the people who *really* loved him were nowhere in sight. The boy lay, he imagined, in the semidarkness, unable to comprehend why all these bad things were happening to him. He was perhaps fearful that the person who had molested him would return, come back to finish the job. First this unknown assailant had destroyed Jason's spirit, and in the wake of fear of retribution, he would return to reclaim Jason's body, shutting him up for good.

As Sean drove west, the lights of Summitville's small downtown appeared on his right, and at the westernmost tip of the town the redbrick facade of City Hospital rose up, yellow windows glowing like a beacon in the night. Sean recalled being with Shelley all night there just a few years ago, and in the morning, they had finally been rewarded with Jason. "We got a boy!" Sean had cried out to the nurses and doctor in the delivery room. Jason was a tiny, red, angry little thing with a crown of thick black hair.

Sean had never loved anything so immediately or with greater passion.

At the next street, Sean signaled and turned left, heading up a hill toward the hospital. He could at least find out how Shelley was doing and discover if this coma she was in was expected to last. Perhaps she just had a mild concussion and the doctors would be releasing her tomorrow, or the next day. If that were the case, Sean had little to worry about.

He knew by now that even if Shelley were around to protect his interests, she would not let Estelle convince her to stop his visitation. Estelle would do that, he knew, because, even though the old woman had never said so, she believed he had something to do with the boy's abduction and rape. And with that belief firm in her mind, she would do whatever she could to keep Sean away from his son. He had to give her some credit: even though her belief was based on prejudice and misinformation, it demonstrated her love for the boy and her need to protect him.

Sean found a parking space on a side street adjacent to the hospital. He got out of the car and headed for the entrance.

*

"What the hell are you doing here?" Paul glowered at him, a cigarette dangling from his lips, hazing around his grizzled face and bloodshot eyes.

Sean closed his eyes for a moment, sucking in a deep breath. This was the last thing he needed, and he decided right then not to let the man rile him. Another confrontation tonight, Sean feared, would put him over the edge.

He tried to keep his voice even as the man's stare bored into him, his hatred and jealousy almost palpable in the air. Sean knew, from inferences he had made from Jason's description of their home life, that Shelley had been much happier when she was with Sean. And he sensed that Paul picked up on that. When one factored in

Paul's obvious homophobia, he could understand why the man was so resentful and even fearful of him.

"I just came to see how Shelley was doing."

"She's in a coma. Visiting hours are over. The exit's back there." Paul sucked in on his cigarette, dropped it to the floor, and ground it out under the heel of his work boot. *Didn't this asshole know smoking wasn't permitted in the hospital?* Stupid question.

"Paul, there's no reason to take that tone," Sean said, hating himself for the way his words came out, wheedling. He knew Paul could take that tone and twist it into a portrait of the effeminate homosexual. He forged onward. "We both care about Shelley. And I just wanted to see how she was doing."

Paul lit another cigarette, exhaling the smoke angrily through his nostrils. "Sure. But there's nothin' to know. She cracked her head on the windshield, and the doctors don't know nothin'."

"Any idea how long this could last?"

Paul shook his head. "Her doctor told me she could come out of it tomorrow."

Sean brightened.

"Or next year."

Sean frowned, staring down at the green-tiled floor.

"They say it's hard to predict with shit like this."

For a moment Sean was tempted to plead his case with Paul, tell him about the Berrys. But he knew almost immediately that such pleading would be useless. Paul would be on their side, 100 percent. "Any chance I could look in on her?"

"Like I say, visiting hours are over." He grinned. "You can bring her some posies tomorrow."

Tomorrow. Tomorrow. Everyone wanted him to do something tomorrow. Why was he convinced tomorrow held no different scenario for him than today?

Sean was suddenly very tired. There was no fight left. "Okay, well, if she does come to, would you tell her I'm rooting for her?"

"Yeah, I'll be sure to do that," Paul said in a voice that dripped with sarcasm.

Sean turned and walked down the corridor to the main entrance. It had been a long night. He wanted to just go home, pull the covers over his head, and sleep.

He angrily pushed through the glass double doors, stepping out into the humid night, where insects chirped and the rush of traffic on Seventh Street greeted him. *Perhaps, it would be best if I just never woke up.*

Like Shelley, like Shelley. In spite of the heat pressing in, Sean felt chilled.

*

When Sean got home from the hospital, he was relieved to see Austin's car outside. Warm yellow light spilled from the windows of their house, and the feeling of homecoming did a lot to offset all the trauma he had been through in the last few hours.

He slammed the car door and gratefully headed for his and Austin's house. He didn't know what he'd find inside, whether it would be a contrite Austin, an Austin who wanted to talk, or an Austin who was packing a bag. He was simply glad Austin had come home.

As he neared the screen door, he could see into the kitchen. Austin was inside, his back to him, barefoot, wearing only a pair of cargo shorts as he put away the dishes from the dishwasher. The cargo shorts were loose and hung low on his hips, revealing a strip of white where his skin hadn't tanned. The light caught on his blond hair, making it look like wheat. His shoulders were broad and his arms beefy from hours of working in the yard.

Sean stood silently, watching. He felt weak in the knees with gratitude and warmth...just from this simple, homespun vision. Austin turned and saw him standing there. He grinned. "Are you coming in or are you going to stand out there all night?"

And Sean went inside and directly into Austin's waiting arms. There were no words. Just a quick glance into one another's eyes, which spoke volumes about need, forgiveness, comfort, shelter, and lust. In seconds, Sean covered Austin's face with kisses, gentle ones on his eyes, hard-sucking ones on the stubbly line of jaw, nipping ones at his ear lobes, until finally his lips found Austin's mouth. His tongue plunged inside, hungry and exploring. With one hand Sean fumbled with the button and zipper of Austin's cargo shorts, pushing them down. Austin's cock, hard, flopped against Sean's belly when it was released, and Sean dropped to his knees, his eyes closed, engulfing Austin in his mouth like a starving man.

He looked up at Austin to see his eyes shut tight with pleasure, pleasure Sean was giving him. Sean resumed his ministrations, alternating his pace, stopping to kiss and lick Austin's thighs, his balls. He was excited too, and yet couldn't help but think that all of this, although lustful and certainly passionate, was also an expression of love, of caring and of a kind of contrition. Sean understood now that the two of them were a pair and, together, they could see the worst life had to offer through. Success or failure, each would have the other to comfort, console, and, hopefully, celebrate.

Yes, Sean loved Jason with all his heart. But he could do the same with Austin, simply in a different—and no less meaningful—way.

After a while Sean stood, pushed Austin back on top of the kitchen table, and threw Austin's legs on top of his shoulders. He quickly unzipped and without preamble, Sean entered Austin with a grunt. Austin cried out and grabbed Sean's thighs, drawing him in deeper. Mixed in with the groans, the grunts, and the sighs, both of them whispered, "I love you." Both men's faces were wet with tears.

Chapter Eighteen

Estelle awakened, lying in the gray darkness of early morning. John snored beside her. She turned on her side to consult the little brass alarm clock that adorned the maple nightstand, along with a small blue ceramic lamp, a doily, and John's glass of water, half full, bubbles clinging to the sides. It was 5:37 a.m.

What had caused her to wake so early? She had never been one to sleep in, always up and ready to meet the day by six thirty or so. But she lay still, listening. There had been a sound, she was sure of it.

She heard something: movement downstairs. Estelle's gut tightened, the fear causing her heart to race. Whoever had done this to her grandson—and in spite of what Sean thought, she was at least open to the possibility of another assailant—that person was still out there, fearful that Jason might regain his voice and use it to accuse.

Perhaps that someone had broken into the house and was coming to make sure her grandson never spoke again. She glanced over at John, unsure if she should wake him. She thought of how useful he would be, what with the bursitis in his hip and his large frame, bloated from too many beers and pizzas.

Estelle shook her head and, swinging her legs out of bed, sat up. There was a creak of floorboards from the kitchen below. It was too hot to put on her robe, so she padded through the bedroom and into the hall, barefoot, standing finally at the top of the stairs.

Now that she could hear more clearly, she was certain someone was down there, in the kitchen. She could hear what sounded like the slap of the refrigerator door closing, which seemed odd in light of what had prompted her fears. Someone doesn't break into a house and then check to see what the refrigerator held.

Cautiously, with one hand on the wall, Estelle headed down the stairs, fingering the small brass crucifix around her neck.

When she reached the kitchen, she gasped.

Jason was at the breakfast set, a bowl of cereal in front of him, eating. She had bought the Froot Loops, Jason's favorite, only yesterday, and the brightly colored rings filled his bowl. A shaft of sunlight streamed in through the kitchen window, laying its brightness across Jason, making a swatch of his dark hair lighter.

Estelle smiled, the relief coursing through her like a drug. "Jason!" she cried. "It's so good to see you up." The boy had dressed himself in a pair of red cotton shorts and a blue-and-white striped T-shirt. He looked up at her, cheeks full of milk and cereal, and grinned.

"Are we finally talking?" Estelle moved toward the table, pulled out a chair, and sat adjacent to her grandson.

Jason swallowed and smiled more broadly at his grandmother. He then cast his gaze down at the Formica surface of the table and shook his head.

"What, Jason? Can you talk?"

He met her gaze and then shook his head more firmly. He continued eating his cereal.

Even though he wasn't talking, this was real progress. Prior to this morning, the boy had been in a state not so dissimilar from his mother's. But now, it seemed he was at least back among them.

"You finish up your cereal, Jason. Grandma's going to run upstairs and throw some clothes on, honey. Okay?" she asked finally, to test him.

Jason nodded.

And Estelle hurried to run upstairs, wake John, and get herself dressed. She would do whatever she could to make sure Jason didn't have a relapse. Perhaps it would be just a small step to get him to talk once more and when he did, she thought, perhaps he could tell just who had done this to him.

As she slid into a green-plaid housedress, she thought of the calls she needed to make. First Paul, of course; he would be delighted with the news. Wouldn't he? Estelle felt a rush of pleasure, being able to tell her son-in-law that his boy was coming out of it, that he was on the road to recovery, she was sure.

And then she would call Milton Hughes, the attorney she had used to draft her and John's wills a couple of years back. Mr. Hughes attended the same church as she did, St. Aloysius, and she knew he was a good Christian man and that he would understand her need to keep the boy away from the danger of his father.

At no time did it occur to Estelle to call Sean.

*

The cherrywood-paneled offices of Wright, Hughes, and Donovan made Estelle a little uncomfortable. She sat in the waiting room, wringing her hands, consulting the framed Degas hunting prints on the wall while trying to think best how to present her case.

But it didn't really matter, did it? She thought of Milton Hughes. The man was old, that she couldn't deny. He had founded the law firm, the best known in Summitville, more than fifty years ago, as a young pup just out of law school. But his age didn't give her any concern. Milton Hughes might have been in his seventies, but that made him no less vigorous. Tall, probably six four or more, his head was topped with a thick shock of snowy white hair. His suits, always impeccably tailored, adorned a frame as vigorous as that of a man of thirty-five. And when she saw him in church, bringing up the offerings or doing a reading, there was a purposeful stride to his walk, unmarred by the shuffling that had overtaken so many of his geriatric brethren.

The phone on the receptionist's desk buzzed. The woman behind the mahogany desk, wearing a simple linen sheath, her dark hair pulled severely away from a tanned face, lifted it with a manicured hand. She consulted for a moment in a low voice, then hung up and smiled at Estelle.

"He'll see you now, Mrs. Berry. Just go on in."

As Estelle stood and was about to ask behind which of the mahogany doors she would find Mr. Hughes, the door to the extreme left of the outer office opened, and Milton Hughes filled its frame.

"Come on in, Estelle, come on in!" His smile was as big as the booming voice that exhorted her inside.

Estelle followed, head hung low, staring at the tough matte of the gray Berber carpet. She passed Milton Hughes and went into his office, a room easily as big, if not bigger, than her living room at home. Two large picture windows looked down on the Ohio River and the tree-choked hills rising up from its banks. Milton's office was crowded with glass-fronted bookcases, containing leather-bound legal tomes. His desk was mirror reflective, the wood's grain unbroken except for a telephone, a blotter upon which sat a sheaf of papers, and a leather-wrapped penholder.

"Have a seat, Estelle. Make yourself comfortable. Did Maggie offer you some coffee? A soda?"

Estelle smiled and sat down, growing increasingly uncomfortable in the plush surroundings, the quiet and the frigid chill of the air conditioner making her feel miserably out of place. "Yes," she whispered, then cleared her throat and spoke up. "She was very kind. But I'm fine."

Milton hurried around to the other side of his desk, leaving in his wake the aroma of some woody cologne. He shoved the stack of papers on the blotter to one side and pulled a yellow legal pad from one of his desk drawers. He uncapped a black-and-gold-trimmed fountain pen and held it ready.

"Now, I assume you're here for more than just a social call." Milton's voice was deep and had a commanding tone. He was so different from the men who surrounded her in her everyday life. He might as well have been from another planet.

Estelle traced an outline around the pattern of a peony on her skirt, then finally looked up, meeting the lawyer's blue-eyed gaze. She wished he would ask her about church or something, make some small talk before launching into things. But she knew Milton Hughes hadn't gotten to where he was by making small talk. The man she knew—not well, not well at all—had always been direct, bordering on overbearing.

"Well, it's about my grandson," Estelle began. She looked up at Milton, whose attention was focused almost too much on her. "Could I change my mind? I'd like a glass of water, please."

Milton got on the phone, and within moments Maggie was standing over her with a cut crystal glass. Estelle took it and drank gratefully, hoping Milton would say something, hoping to divert, just for a moment, the attention away from herself.

But he didn't.

"As I said, it's about Jason, my grandson. Maybe you heard about him?"

Milton's expression changed into something stern yet sympathetic. His bushy eyebrows creased together. "It was in all the papers, Estelle. I'm very sorry."

Estelle nodded. "It's been very hard."

"I'm sure. But what's brought you here today?"

Estelle smiled weakly. "It seems like this summer hasn't been a good one for my family. A couple days ago, my daughter and Jason's mother, Shelley, was in a car accident."

Milton shook his head. "That's tough, Estelle."

"Yeah. And I'm sorry to say it wasn't a little fender bender. She's down at City now, in a coma."

"The Lord sometimes gives us a lot to bear, but never more than we can handle."

"Oh, I know that. That's a fact I try to hold on to every day."

"And what he gives us makes us stronger."

"You're absolutely right."

"But I'm still not sure what I can do for you, other than offer my support."

"Well, Shelley was married to Sean Dawes. He's a reporter for the newspaper. Maybe you know him?"

"Can't say that I do."

Estelle swallowed. "The man's a homosexual, Milton."

He nodded. "I see."

Estelle was grateful for the look of distaste that passed briefly over the attorney's features. "He wants Jason. He wants Jason while Shelley is getting better."

"And you don't want that. Is the boy with you?"

"For now," Estelle said. "But Sean is threatening to take legal action if I don't let him have the boy." Estelle stared down at the carpeting once more. How could she voice her fears? They were something she preferred to keep hidden. "I'm afraid, Milton." Tears, for just a moment, clouded her vision. Angrily, she wiped them away with the back of her hand. She swallowed hard and took a deep breath. "You know, maybe, that my grandson was...raped." The last word came out in a whisper. "No one knows who did it, but I have my fears." She sat up straighter in the leather wing chair. "I mean, you can understand. The man's queer."

Milton nodded. "Any other reason, besides that disturbing fact, for you to suspect Mr. Dawes?"

"Well, I think that's reason enough. Don't they all like little boys?"

Milton frowned. "I don't know much about what they like. But I do know the boy's father is an abomination before God. And that alone, to my way of thinking, is enough to keep him away from the boy." Milton shook his head. "Such a horrible example to set."

Estelle was relieved. She hoped Milton wasn't just agreeing with her for the sake of being sympathetic. "I agree. I agree so completely, Mr. Hughes."

"Milton, call me Milton for goodness sake."

Estelle smiled and whispered, "Milton...fine."

Milton jotted something down on his legal pad. "Now, you and I both know the fact that this Sean Dawes is queer is enough to keep him away from a little boy, especially one who's been through so much, but I'm not sure the courts will agree. Depends a lot on the judge we get. Old Dan Simpson, now if we get him, we wouldn't have to say much more than that. But a lot of these judges nowadays, well, they've got more liberal views."

"So you think there's nothing I can do to stop him?"

"Oh-ho! I didn't say that. Didn't say that at all. But we could use some more ammunition. You know and I know we've got enough but, as I said, it may not be enough to convince the courts. Did this Dawes fella ever abuse the boy?"

Estelle shook her head. Sean had never been anything but loving toward Jason, often to the point of spoiling him. If he had ever laid a finger on the boy, she had never heard of it. Now, if they were talking about Paul... Estelle began to wonder if she was doing the right thing. "Not that I know of."

"Is this Sean a...how do you say it...obvious? Is he, you know, effeminate?"

Estelle pictured Sean. There had been nothing during his courtship and subsequent marriage to her daughter that would indicate to her that he was a homosexual, no limp wrists, no prancing walk, no breathy way of speaking. "No. He's a pretty regular guy. Not big on sports or hunting or anything like that, but not sissified either."

"Hmm." Milton tapped his pen against his chin. "How does the man live? By himself?"

"Oh no, he and his so-called lover—" A grimace passed over Estelle's features. "—share a house down by the river."

"So this other man; what's his name?"

"Austin Phillips."

"This Austin... Does he live there with Sean full-time?"

"Yes, they're just like a married couple."

"And does Jason visit them together?"

Estelle nodded. "Yes, for the past couple years. I didn't want it, let me tell you. But Shelley insisted. I think it's a horrible thing for a little boy to see."

"We may be able to do something with that. Especially in light of the boy's rape. Even if the father and his 'friend' had nothing to do with what happened, it still might be traumatic, considering what happened to the boy is something that probably goes on in that house every night."

Estelle shivered, and it wasn't because of the air-conditioning.

"Does the boy ever see them kiss and hug?"

"Oh yes. I know he sees that."

"Well, Estelle, I think we may have something to go on here."

"Really?"

"No promises, but I think we can make a case at least for the time being that this unwholesome environment could be traumatic for the boy. Especially in light of recent events."

Estelle paused for a moment, asking herself if she was certain she wanted to proceed with this. She thought then of Jason, earlier this morning at the kitchen table, the sunlight slanting across his dark hair, highlighting his button nose. He had smiled at her. He was beginning to come around. But could she take this boy from his father? *The father's a queer!* a little voice shouted back. *What's the Bible have to say about that? It's an abomination, that's what.* Estelle knew her Bible, and the Bible was very clear. Why, in Leviticus it said, "If a man lies with a man as one lies with a woman, both of them have done what is detestable. They must be put to death; their blood will be on their own heads." These were the same thoughts and verses she had used on Shelley when they were going through the divorce and Estelle knew, in her heart, that the best thing for her grandson would be to never see his father again. After all, evil begets evil, and if Jason was exposed to such perversion, he could be swayed, growing up to be just like his father.

How could she not proceed?

"What do we have to do next?"

"Beat 'em to the punch. I can file a motion, a sort of restraining order, this afternoon. We'll try and make you the boy's legal guardian while his mother's in the hospital. Shelley's remarried, right?"

"Yes, to a wonderful man, Paul Thompson."

"Would he go along with letting you be the guardian?"

Estelle laughed. "I don't think that'll be a problem."

"Good. Good. Then why don't you let me get to work here, and I'll call you as soon as I know something."

Estelle stood, smoothing her floral skirt against her lap. She extended her hand. "Thank you so much, Mr., er, Milton."

Milton took her hand, grasping it. "Not at all. You and I, we go to St. Al's. It's good to know there are still a few right-thinking people in this world. I'm only glad I can help."

Estelle left the office. Round one fired. She knew Sean would be hurt, but she had to do the right thing. And this was it.

Chapter Nineteen

Paul grimaced and whispered, "Fuckin' commercials," punching the buttons hard on his pickup's radio, searching for a station. After several attempts, the Texas twang of ZZ Top came through, loud strains of "Gimme All Your Lovin'" rocking the truck's interior. Paul eased back in his seat, lighting another Marlboro.

John had called about fifteen minutes ago, asking if Paul wouldn't mind coming over to keep an eye on Jason while he went out to get a few supplies for his garden. Even though Paul was just about to leave the house to shoot a few games of pool with his buddies at the Legion, he couldn't very well say no. He could head up to the Legion a little late, with plenty of time for a few beers and to whip those fuckers' asses. His cue stick, in its leather case, was in the compartment behind the seat.

John was waiting on the porch when Paul pulled up in the driveway. The old man waved at Paul and Paul waved back. He flicked his cigarette out the window.

"How's it goin', John?" Paul mounted the steps to the back porch where his father-in-law stood, wearing gray work pants and a white T-shirt, bald pate glinting in the sun.

"Pretty good, Paul. Hope I didn't interrupt any plans."

"Not at all. How's my boy doin' today?"

John stepped down a couple of stairs and smiled. "Well, actually better."

Paul shivered.

"He's not talking yet, but he was up this morning already when Estelle woke up." John smiled. "Estelle heard him down in the kitchen." He barked out a short laugh. "She thought we had a burglar or somethin'. But it was just Jason, fixing himself a bowl of Froot Loops."

"Great," Paul mumbled.

"Yeah, the boy, uh, seems to be snapping out of it a little bit. You know how he was so withdrawn? Well he's at least smiling now, little bit. And when you talk to him, he'll nod or shake his head." John shook his head. "Damn fine thing to see."

Paul clenched his fists, feeling the thrumming of his heart beating rapidly. "That's great news. Why don't you head on out, and I'll go on in, keep an eye on him."

"Sure. Maybe you could bring him outside for a while."

"Right! Maybe I can see if I can get him to toss a baseball around with me."

"That'd be great. Don't know if he's ready for that much yet or not, but it sure can't hurt to try."

Paul watched John drive off and headed into the house, the screen door slamming behind him.

After the bright sunlight outside, it was difficult to see, but the manic sounds of cartoons, at high volume, led him to the living room.

Bugs Bunny was all dressed up as a female rabbit to try to fool the Tasmanian Devil. The colors on the screen seemed too bright, lurid even, in the dimly lit room. Paul stood just outside the entrance to the room and watched his stepson. He didn't think Jason had heard him come in, so intense was his interest in the cartoon. A smile flickered about the boy's lips as he tugged unconsciously at his dark hair. Jason was wearing shorts and a striped T-shirt, bony legs sticking out of the red cotton fabric, bare feet hanging over the edge of the recliner, not touching the floor.

Paul took a deep breath and entered the room. "How's it goin', pardner?" He forced a big grin to his face but wasn't sure it worked. A queasiness had risen up in his gut, causing the beer he had drunk earlier to gurgle.

Jason looked up at his entrance, and the delight that had been on the boy's face moments ago vanished. Jason seemed to shrink into the avocado green fabric of the recliner's upholstery. His eyes dulled as he spotted his stepfather, and his lips turned down into a frown.

Jason cringed when Paul strode across the room and ruffled his hair. Paul wished to hell he had never let things get so out of control. *Never spit where you eat*, his old man used to say. And Paul wished now he had taken the crude advice to heart.

He squatted down on his haunches beside him, wishing Jason wouldn't have drawn his legs so tightly to his chest, hoping Jason would meet his gaze. But the boy looked off, concentration intense on the television screen, even though Paul wondered if Jason even knew what he was seeing.

"Listen, Jason, sometimes adults do stupid things. I sure as hell ain't no exception. I'm sorry for what happened between me and you, but someday you'll understand why it happened. It shouldn't have, but as I said, sometimes grown-ups are just plain dumb. You bein' afraid of me isn't gonna help nobody." Paul reached over and took hold of the boy's face. The boy sucked in his breath. His skin was so soft, still like a baby's. He stroked the boy's chin with his finger and then forced the boy's head to face his. "You know what I'm sayin', Jason? You keep this up and it's just gonna cause problems for the family, for your mother and me."

Paul thought for a moment, idly stroking Jason's face. He knew the boy didn't know what had happened to Shelley, but maybe it was time. A voice in his head told him no, the boy's been through enough and this kind of bad news might send him right over the edge. But another voice, this one husky and more seductive, countered by telling Paul that the news could be used, if done correctly, to help ensure his mistake would never be discovered.

"Listen, I ain't s'posed to be tellin' you this, but your ma's in the hospital." Jason looked at him then, and his small eyebrows came together in confusion.

"Yeah, she had a car accident. See, Jason, she was so upset by what's goin' on with you that she wasn't thinking and plowed head on into another car. Your grandma's prayin' she'll be okay and I am, too, but if she hadn't been so worried about you, this might never have happened."

Jason closed his eyes, which caused a couple of tears to run down his cheeks. He opened his mouth as if to sob, but no sound emerged. The boy's chest heaved, and finally he covered his face with his hands. Paul pulled them away, forcing Jason to look at him once more.

"Hey, I know a lotta guys say it's not good for guys to cry, but you go right ahead." Paul gently lifted Jason from the recliner and carried him over to the couch. He sat down and positioned Jason on his lap, stroking his dark hair as he spoke. "I think she's gonna be okay, Jason. But she's in the hospital right now. She hurt her head pretty bad, and she's in what they call a coma. That just means she's in kind of, well, kind of a deep sleep."

Jason bit his lower lip, and Paul could feel the small body trembling in his arms.

"Now, I think she's gonna wake up real soon. But she can't have any kind of stress, y'know? And if you were to tell anybody about the mistake that happened between us, I'm pretty sure that'd just about kill her. I'm not just talkin' here, son; I'm serious when I say it could kill her. We both wouldn't want that to happen, now would we, Jason?"

The boy stared up at him, his green eyes bright with tears. He shook his head slowly.

Paul blew out a big sigh, glad he had made the right decision in telling Jason about Shelley.

Paul held the boy close to him in his lap while he wept, the boy shaking in his arms, his chest heaving. It was weird, having a little kid cry like this without making any noise. Paul reached down and touched Jason's exposed legs. The skin there was so incredibly soft and smooth, even more than a woman's. He couldn't help it, running his big callused hands up and down Jason's legs. The skin felt so good.

This is just the kind of thing that got you into this mess in the first place, the sensible little voice inside his head cautioned.

He closed his eyes and set Jason down on the floor. *Oh God, don't do this.* Paul allowed himself only a minute to think of what he was about to do—and to take a grim kind of pleasure in it—then he picked Jason up again, roughly from the floor and set him down, hard, on the couch.

"Watch your damn cartoons," he said, breathless.

Suddenly the world re-emerged: the silly voices blaring on the TV set, accompanied by manic music, the dimness of the living room with its curtains drawn and its maple and plaid early American living room suite, the traffic rushing by on the street outside.

Paul looked down at Jason, who stared resolutely at the screen. Had he understood how close they had come? And the shame came then, borne on a wave of revulsion so great it made Paul fear he would vomit. He looked back once at Jason as he left the room; the kid seemed to be watching nothing as he slumped on the couch. Who knew what he was watching? The kid was in a world of his own.

You used to go to that world, Paul. Remember that secret place you went to? The only place you could get away from Grandpa.

Chapter Twenty

Art's Tavern had been in downtown Summitville for as long as anyone could remember. Situated on the corner of Fifth and Main Streets, its darkened window facing the street held a neon Rolling Rock sign since before the beer had become trendy, from back in the day when the Latrobe brew was nothing more than a local beer, popular at summer picnics and parties. Art's was the kind of place that was a second home to serious drinkers, alcoholics, and women who had nothing more to hold on to than the chance of meeting a man who would show them some attention, even if it was only for an hour in a filthy motel bedroom. It was also home to a number of bikers: fat, unkempt men long past their prime, dreams of being a Hell's Angel never realized. Art's never lacked for a fight, which sometimes stumbled out onto the street, where the police could no longer ignore the tavern known for its low-life patrons. Inside Art's the air had a perpetual haze of blue-gray cigarette smoke near the ceiling, twangs of the Rolling Stones or the Grateful Dead blaring from its juke in testimony to bygone days. The air was heavy with the smell of stale beer and tobacco smoke. A television was a silent sentinel above the bar, largely ignored except when its snowy screen broadcast a Pirates or a Steelers game.

It was here that Paul found himself a couple of hours later, after leaving Jason with Estelle, whose cheerful demeanor wilted when Paul informed her that the boy had "had some kind of relapse." He didn't know why. Estelle went immediately to the living room, where Jason stared, sullen, dumb, at the TV screen. No glimmer of recognition crossed his features when he saw her.

"But he seemed so happy when I left today. It really seemed like he was beginning to snap out of it." She had rustled the boy's hair and frowned at him, then turned back to Paul.

"These things take time, Estelle. He'll probably be up, then down, a few times before he gets better."

"I suppose so." Estelle paused for a moment, staring out the picture window at the traffic on the street in front of the house. "There's something I need to talk to you about, Paul. Let's go in the kitchen. Want some coffee?"

"John got any beer?"

The tiny grimace on Estelle's face didn't prevent her from hunting around in the refrigerator until she found a can of Iron City. She handed it to him.

Paul gulped the beer gratefully, half a can in one swallow. He hoped Estelle did not detect the slight trembling in his hands as he lifted the beer to his lips. "What's up?"

"Well, I was just downtown, talking to Milton Hughes."

Paul knew the name. Summitville had a short list of attorneys, and Hughes's name was at the top of the list.

"I wanted to talk to him to see if he could keep Sean away from Jason, at least until Shelley got out of the hospital." She shook her head. "I just don't trust those two around Jason. Not in light of what happened."

Paul felt hopeful. Anything that would divert the glare of suspicion from him was welcome. "Does he think he can do anything?"

"Milton's a Christian man, Paul, a good Catholic. He agrees with me, and he's going to file a motion... probably this afternoon."

"That's cool by me."

"Anyway, we may need your support. You might need to testify or sign some papers, whatever's necessary for something like this." Estelle crossed the kitchen to place her hand on Paul's forearm. "Can I count on your support?"

Paul didn't have to think long. "Anything it takes, Estelle. Anything I can do. Never have felt comfortable having that fag around Jason."

And now, as Paul pulled up a stool to the dark wood bar, sticky with the residue of a thousand spilled beers, he was glad Estelle was taking legal action against Sean. If she succeeded, people might suspect Sean, thinking the law was on the side of protecting the boy from this "dangerous" homosexual. What with Junior Parsons still under major suspicion—was he still in jail? Paul would have to check with Hugh Allen—Paul knew no suspicious eyes would ever be cast his way.

Unless the boy talked. Unless Jason told...

Paul downed his first beer and signaled to the bartender. "Hit me again," he said, lighting up a Marlboro, "and bring me a shot of Jack with that, would you?"

"You got it."

Paul knew he was drinking too fast. Knew and didn't care. There was an ache in his gut he couldn't quite put his finger on. A more astute man might have called it remorse, but for Paul it was just another discomfort, one he knew could be washed away with enough alcohol, with the relentless pursuit of liquors amber and gold.

Paul downed the shot and began sipping the beer, staring at his reflection across the bar as he smoked. Why had he touched Jason that afternoon? Why couldn't he leave the boy alone? What was wrong with him? Nothing had ever led Paul Thompson around by the nose; it was a goal he had made certain to achieve all his adult life. And now here he was, doing dangerous things, things that could ruin his life as he knew it, and yet in spite of the admitted stupidity of such actions, he was letting himself get out of control. He pictured Jason's dead face in his mind's eye, and the portrait made his stomach turn.

He drank down his beer and ordered another.

By the fourth beer, Paul was no longer thinking about Jason. In fact, his mind was absorbing a comforting kind of murk, woolly-headed, his mental state making oblivion of the day and his desires. The bass of a Grateful Dead song, "Truckin'," pounded in the background, making his temples throb, but it was good to have something other than his own tortured thoughts to irritate him.

And yet other demons called to him, increasing his feelings of helplessness, his low opinion of himself.

"Son, get out here and help your Grandpa. There ain't no reason for a boy to sit around in the house with the ladies when there's work to be done out in the workshop."

The big man loomed above him, impossibly powerful, able to bend little Paul to his whims. To make him do anything...

"Go on, Paulie. You heard your granddaddy," his grandma, stripping green beans at the kitchen table, had exhorted him. Her careworn face looked tired, mouth sagging at the corners, eyes listless, dull. It was almost as if she knew what went on out there but was a conspirator, wanting it to happen, even as she insisted innocence.

And little Paulie had followed, Keds making no noise on the pavement of the driveway, then the grass, as he trailed his big grandfather out to the garage.

He would be waiting, Paul knew, half sitting on the high stool of the workbench, pants undone, waiting...

Stop it, Paul told himself, the words even mentally beginning to slur. Perhaps it was time to go home and sleep this off. Sleep offered another kind of oblivion, and Paul thought for a moment how half his days were spent seeking oblivion.

"Hey, stranger. I never seen you in here before."

Paul turned slowly at the sound of the woman's voice. Turned to regard a woman who must have been well into her forties, with dyed black hair, blue eye shadow, heavy eyeliner that had smudged. Her lips were painted a lurid red and her sagging jowls sported two upsweeps of pink blush. She wore a pair of shorts, thongs, and a midriff top that showed off large sagging breasts and a layer of fat around her middle. She reeked of red wine and a perfume his mother used to wear, called Tabu.

Paul didn't return her hopeful, desperate smile. "That's 'cause I don't come here much. Usually down at the Vets or up at the Legion."

"Oooh, a military man. I like that." She winked at him and climbed onto the stool next to him. She placed her drink—what looked like a Whiskey Sour—unsteadily on the bar.

When she put her hand on Paul's thigh, he recoiled, drawing his leg back.

"What's the matter, sweet? Playin' hard to get?"

"I ain't playin' at all," Paul said glumly, staring at the rows of bottles behind the bar.

The woman said nothing, sipping her drink until the last dregs of it were washed down her throat, the straw making a draining noise in the ice. "Buy me a drink? I've been known to be very nice to gentleman who are generous."

Paul signaled to the bartender, sliding some of his money across the bar. "Get the lady here another one."

"Nice man. Nice-looking too," the woman mumbled. But her gaze defied her, watching the bartender hungrily as he poured her another. She gulped down half its contents once the drink was placed before her, then turned back to Paul. She grabbed his upper arm and squeezed. "Where'd you get muscles like these?"

"From slappin' around women like you," Paul whispered, seething, under his breath.

He slid from his stool, and then grabbed on to the bar for support as the room tilted. He hurried out of the place without looking back, or he would have seen the woman's expression: a stunned O indicating humiliation and shock.

*

She had been going to Lake Juniper since she was fifteen. That was a year ago, and it seemed Marcy Gregson had grown a lot between her fifteenth and sixteenth years. There were other clubs she could have gone to, she knew, since she looked at least five years older than she was.

Marcy stood five foot eleven and weighed 125 pounds. Everyone told her she should go into modeling, and Marcy had even sent for the brochures from the John Casablancas school in Pittsburgh, but she had to finish high school before she could begin to run after such dreams. Besides, the wait would give her a little more time to work on her look. She knew this was important because she had learned there was a lot of competition out there.

Her parents didn't approve of the lake. "Too many boys there with one thing on their minds," her mother had often said, when Marcy had tried to legitimize her Friday night forays.

What Mrs. Gregson didn't know was that her fears about boys with one thing on their minds were unfounded. Or at least a couple of years too late. Marcy's willowy stature and her dark good looks had been enjoyed by an innumerable number of boys over the past two years.

Now, as Marcy walked along the winding dirt road that led up to the old dance hall overlooking the lake, she thought she was beginning to grow tired of teenage boys, who took and took and took and seldom gave anything in return. The frantic, always too quick couplings in the woods near the dance hall and cramped back seats had completely lost their charm for her.

Marcy longed for an older man. One preferably with his own place. An older man who knew what to do and who could perhaps bring Marcy what she dreamed of now with increasing frequency: her first orgasm.

She wondered why she was even bothering going to the lake now anyway. It would be the same crowd that was there every Friday night. But for Marcy, there was always a possibility somebody new would turn up.

As she rounded a bend in the road and the barnlike structure of the dance hall came into view, Marcy saw something unfamiliar on the side of the road. A pickup truck, not new but in great shape, was pulled over to the side of the road, jacked up on the driver's side.

And crouching near the jack was the most beautiful man she had ever seen. Not a boy, but a man. Even in the dusky light, she could see that no boy at the Friday night dances could ever hope to hold a candle to him. Marcy swung her long black hair over one shoulder and dug in her purse for a cigarette. Once she had it lit, she approached the car.

The man was busy pumping the jack and making its rear end rise up. His shoulders were broad, and even beneath the cotton material of his shirt, Marcy could see the strong muscles in his back working.

"Do you need any help?"

The man turned and regarded Marcy with wary interest. She took in his pale eyes and the chiseled features of his stubbled face, a face unlike any other she had seen. The face of a god.

Marcy took a drag off her cigarette and pulled out her cell. "I could call someone. A tow truck, maybe."

The man stood, and Marcy was delighted to find he stood at least three or four inches taller than she. "Well, aren't you the most considerate thing? A good Samaritan, are you?"

Marcy smiled and stared deep into his eyes. "I like to help out when I can."

"I bet you do."

The man let his phrase hang in the thick summer air for a moment. "But I really don't need anything. I can change this flat myself."

"Are you sure? I'd hate to see you get all dirty." Pause. "Especially when you look so nice."

"You don't look too bad yourself. Headed up to the dance?"

"Yeah." Marcy dug in the road dust with the toe of her sandal.

The man barked out a short laugh. "You don't seem thrilled."

Marcy loved the way he talked, the timbre of his voice deep, scarred by cigarettes, manly, so different from the boys she knew. "It's just that it's gotten kind of old, you know?"

The man nodded. "You look a little too good, sweetheart, for the likes of that fuckin' place."

"Thank you." Marcy was glad he had noticed. "It's just that there's not much else to do around here. You know."

"Yeah, I know." He paused for a moment, as if thinking. "Listen, if you're not that interested in the dance, maybe I could persuade you to take a little drive with me. I mean, once I get this fuckin' flat fixed."

Marcy looked down at the ground, and for the first time noticed the tire lying near the car looked perfectly all right and there was no spare in sight. She shrugged. Maybe he had a pump or something. Ignoring the doubts that came with the sight of the perfectly good tire, she said, "You know, that'd be a great idea. I just have to be home by twelve." She rolled her eyes. "Parents."

The man held up a hand to stop her from further explanations. "Got it. And you gotta understand..." He grinned then, pausing. "With me, your parents will be the least of your worries."

Marcy laughed and watched as the man squatted once more and began fitting the tire back on the car. She noticed how the faded denim gripped his ass and wondered what it would be like to hold those hardened half globes in her hands, pushing him deeper inside her. She felt a flush rise to her face and suddenly, it seemed harder to draw air in the moist twilight.

After Marcy finished watching Paul, as he had told her his name was, tightening the lug bolts once the tire was in place, she smiled at him as he stood. "All set?"

"Ready. Still wanna take that ride?"

"I wouldn't have stayed here if I didn't."

"Then let's go."

After they pulled out onto the road, Paul asked, "You like to party, Marcy?"

And now she found herself here, in his house, only a little over a half hour later. The place wasn't much; she'd expected better. But this could be fun, she thought, as she took another sip of the vodka and tonic Paul had made for her.

Paul sat next to her on the couch, arm casually draped across the back of it. Marcy's drink was almost gone, and she was already feeling the warmth of the alcohol as it pulsed through her, making her feel both languorous and light-headed at the same time.

Paul slid his arm down so it lay across Marcy's shoulders. This was going well, better than she expected. Marcy leaned back, pressing herself against the arm at her back.

Paul leaned over and turned Marcy's face to his. "You're hot. How old are you?"

"Nineteen," Marcy lied.

"Really? Come on, now."

So he knew. "All right, I'm sixteen, but..."

"Very mature for your age?"

Before Marcy could reply, Paul brushed his lips across hers, so gently it felt like the flutter of tiny wings. Marcy felt warm. She put down her first drink and took a big gulp of the second. Then she turned to him and with what she thought of as a nineteen-year-old's boldness, kissed Paul deeply, exploring the inside of his mouth with her tongue. Inside, despite the acrid taste of cigarettes, whiskey, beer. She wanted him to know she was no kid.

She reached down and caressed the crotch of his jeans, delighted to find him getting hard.

She pulled back suddenly and looked in his eyes. "Is this all right?"

"Better than all right." Paul leaned into her, and this time the kiss was deep and passionate. He leaned over so his body was pressed against hers, and the room suddenly got hotter. Marcy ran her hand up and down his back, feeling the powerful muscles there. With the boys from the lake, all she felt were skinny, immature boys' bodies. This was a man, and the prospect of what was surely to come made her feel so excited, she was almost giddy. She pulled him on top of her, wrapping one of her legs around his thigh.

After a while, he pulled away from her. "You're a wild one, aren't you?"

"Count on it." The liquor and the drop-dead handsomeness of this man were making Marcy forget all her inhibitions. She groped for his belt buckle, and then his zipper. Once she had his jeans open, she pulled down the elastic waistband of his briefs. Nestled in a mound of black pubic hair was the largest dick she had ever seen. Marcy squeezed it, pulling it out and away from Paul's stomach.

And then, lowering her head effortlessly, she took him in her mouth. He sprawled back against the couch as she sucked, gently squeezing his balls and swirling her hand around his shaft on the upstroke. He thrust into her mouth.

Finally Paul pulled her head gently away, whispering, "Let's go into the bedroom."

They undressed quickly in dim light spilling out from behind a half-opened closet door. Marcy ran her hands down his hairy chest, gripping his sex in her hand and squeezing. A pearl of clear liquid oozed from its tip.

Marcy licked it off.

"I want you to fuck me."

Paul didn't say anything. Marcy noticed his eyes had gone dull, the lids at half-mast. It was creepy and sexy all at once. Almost as if she weren't there anymore. He pushed her down on the bed and slid his lips over her body, stopping to work her nipples, tongue her navel, and at last to lap up the juices flowing from her. Marcy clutched the sheets beneath her, grinding her hips against his face.

When she thought she could take no more, she tugged at his thick hair. "Now," she whispered, words tinged with urgency.

He rose above her, his face shadowed in the dimness. Marcy spread her legs apart, drawing her knees up close to her chest. "Now," she said, reaching down to grab his ass and draw him closer. "Oh, please, now."

He entered her slowly, sliding and pushing so gently, so slowly, Marcy wriggled herself down to get more of him inside her.

And then she rolled her head to one side on the pillow, lost in the pleasure of him deep inside her.

"Oh, that's good," she moaned. "Fuck me hard." And he did.

And then Paul was rising above her, knees braced against her thighs, fucking so hard it hurt.

And then Marcy froze as he lifted the pillow next to her head, lifted it and brought it down, covering her face and shutting out the world, stealing her air and changing the scene from one of passion to one of terror, where the desire to come was replaced by the desire to breathe. She squirmed under him, her hands futile tools drumming against his chest, her legs loose from him now, kicking helplessly into the air. Her scream was a muffled sound, ridiculous. Who would hear?

By slow degrees, the struggling subsided and Marcy drew one last quivering breath as everything around her went black.

*

The room was dark when Paul was finally awakened by the low grumble of thunder outside, by the chill air blowing the curtains of the bedroom in, bearing a smell of rain. The muscles in his arms felt tight, slightly cramped, as if he had been working hard. The hair on his chest was matted with sweat and his temples throbbed.

"Jesus Christ," he whispered, sitting up, the action causing a thousand pinpricks of pain to shoot through his head. "Fuck! I really tied one on this time." He slid his feet to the floor and lowered his head so it was supported, almost between his legs, by his hands. His stomach gurgled.

He groped on the nightstand for his cigarettes and when he didn't find them, he turned around slowly—even the smallest movement caused the ache in his head to enlarge—to lean over and see if they were on the floor on the other side of the bed.

And that was when he let out a startled cry and sucked in his breath. For a moment his rational mind deserted him. It had to be Shelley lying next to him, chilled by the breeze blowing in, but it took only a second, even in his addled post-drunk state, for him to recall that Shelley was lying in a hospital downtown and not here in their bed, next to him.

"Fuckin' Christ." Paul stared down at the lithe young body and the swell of breasts, the triangle of pubic hair, looking black in the wan light of midnight. A pillow hid the woman's face, and Paul remembered the sleazebag in the bar. He thought he had left her there, but hell, he was drunk, and who's to say what he did?

He sure as fuck didn't remember her having such a fine body. He yanked away the pillow lying like a stuffed animal over her face and gasped.

With a mouth almost too dry to form words and a heart racing so hard the blood thrummed in his ears, he whispered, "Who the fuck are you?"

And when the woman didn't reply, he shook her, harder, harder, until his hands dug into the cold, cold flesh, until he gasped and finally cried out, raw, anguished.

Chapter Twenty-One

Milton Hughes rubbed his forehead, setting aside the three-page document he had been reading. His secretary, Ellen, had done her usual job, an homage to perfection...no spelling errors, no extraneous punctuation, the margins wide. He swiveled in his chair to stare out at the bright summer day, stratocumulus clouds low on the horizon, and thought about what he was doing. The request for a restraining order was not an easy motion to file. Of course, the man in question's perversion was despicable, something Milton couldn't bear to think of in any real sense, something he could consider only in the remotest of abstractions. Besides, Milton had always thought of himself as a God-fearing man, one who had been inclined all his life to rigidly follow the rules. And the rules of the Bible were the supreme directives of how to live a good life. Injunctions against homosexuality were clear. One had only to read the stories of Sodom and Gomorrah to know what the Lord thought of such sick behavior.

Milton picked up his Montblanc fountain pen and signed the bottom of the document with a flourish but with little glee. He knew the Bible, and he could point with confidence to several Old Testament references that made it clear God had not meant for "man to lay with another man." *But*, Milton thought as he shoved the document away from him, *I know the New Testament too, backwards and forwards, and Christ preached only love, acceptance, and forgiveness.* Nowhere, that Milton could think of, had Christ said anything against homosexuality.

Family law. For the most part, Milton had stopped practicing it years ago, sick of being involved in the heartache that divorce and custody battles caused. He had seen too much tragedy, had purported much of it himself being the advocate of this or that husband or wife, to want to continue working in such a field.

But Estelle was an acquaintance, a woman he saw in church every Sunday morning, grasped her hand and smiled when offering the sign of peace, stood behind her in line for communion. He couldn't send her to someone else, couldn't turn his back on her.

And yet the words of the motion rankled him, the request, basically, that Sean not be allowed any visitation until the mother was present to supervise or until the person who had raped the boy was found, clearing his father. The document cited how Sean Dawes was setting a bad example for his son, how his living openly with another man in his son's presence was thwarting the boy's psychological development, how even the boy's own stepfather was in concurrence with his grandmother. He had backed up his work with documentation from the divorce trial of Jason's parents, using language culled from the court-ordered psychological evaluation of Sean

Dawes, excising only the most unflattering verbiage to bolster his case. Milton glanced down at some of the report, which he had included in his motion.

"...a very self-absorbed individual who is interested in his own needs, impulsive gratification, and perhaps using the child as a narcissistic extension of the self...to brag, show off or demonstrate and prove he is a 'man.' Mr. Dawes also exposed Jason, in a rather blunt manner, to a lifestyle which may be overwhelming to a young, developing ego, showing no sensitivity to Jason's need of a relationship with his father unencumbered by all of the confusion, anxiety, and tension or overstimulation evident in an atmosphere where young adults are trying to sort out their relationships and issues."

There was more, so much more, all the allegations made by Shelley at the time, the citing of various references that discussed children being exposed to the "primal scene." A large issue during the divorce proceedings was that Jason had crawled into bed with Sean and Austin once; enough that Milton thought, in light of the current circumstances, it would be enough to convince the judge to at least issue a temporary restraining order, allowing the boy to recuperate in his grandmother's home.

And yet, Milton thought as he stood and shrugged into his suit coat, there was something not quite right about all of this. Something he, as a Christian, didn't feel was the correct road to travel. He didn't know Sean Dawes, and the picture of him that emerged from the words of court-appointed therapists was not a flattering one. But Milton knew how that game was played and wasn't convinced by the impressions to be had from court-appointed mental health professionals. They were often as guilty of bias as anyone else.

But if he was erring, he would rather it be in favor of little Jason Dawes and not in favor of his father, who, at the bottom of all this, remained suspect. At the very least, a little caution was probably wise.

Milton closed the door to his office and let Ellen know he would be over at the courthouse.

*

Sean sat alone. Austin was at work, an uneasy truce between the two men settled the night before, a truce that was fragile and could explode with even the slightest provocation. Sure, the sex was good, passionate, almost frantic, a balm on all the wounds the pair had endured over the past few days. Yet once the two had climaxed and reality seeped back in, it was obvious to both of them, Sean was certain, that they needed to talk more. For one thing, Sean had to be sure Austin understood the difference between a father's love for his child and that same man's love for his partner. The two were not the same thing, not at all, and there was no point in trying to compare or compete.

He had filled the CD player with classical music: six CDs ranging from Bartok to Mozart, from Beethoven to Philip Glass. The music, which he had hoped would allow him a kind of oblivion, did little more than depress him, in defiance of the bright sun outside and the cries of birds as they swooped over the muddy waters of the Ohio River.

He hadn't seen Jason in several days. Each time he had gone to the house, Estelle or John barred him entrance and once, and Sean recalled this with a twisting nausea, Estelle had told him he could not see him until the court resolved the issue.

What had she done? Sean wondered, pulling one of the pillows off the couch to his chest. What had she done? He had thought all the legal maneuverings regarding Jason were over once the divorce decree was final and all its attendant miseries were meted out, in measured legalese, regarding child support, division of assets, and most importantly—to him, anyway—visitation.

Estelle had refused to elaborate on what she meant, and now Sean was left alone with anxiety, the fear that some judge downtown would see things differently, in light of the abuse Jason had suffered and his mother's in-effect absence.

All he could do was wait.

Sean threw the pillow from his chest and sat up, more alert, as he heard the low roar of an engine approaching the end of the driveway. The sound of the mail truck had once been familiar, with happy portents, but now it inspired only dread.

Sean hurried outside into the heat, the chirping of insects, and made his way to the mailbox at the end of the drive. He opened the mailbox and found a letter from the law offices of Milton Hughes, along with an electric bill and a preapproved acceptance for a Visa gold card.

Walking back down the drive, kicking up dust as he went, Sean tore open the buff-colored envelope, knowing, with a sinking feeling, what the letter would contain.

A brief note from Hughes, directing him to the court order, issued by a Judge Daniel Simpson, of temporary suspension of parental rights to visitation.

It seemed the sky clouded over and the birds stopping singing. Sean was afraid his breakfast would come up as he read the cold, hard words over and over, until he had to sit in the dust of the driveway, holding the letter away from him like something disgusting, the slimy corpse of an insect or a snake. "No," he whispered. "No, I can't go along with this."

Chapter Twenty-Two

Hugh Allen sat in his office, biting the end of a Bic pen. The pen's tip was already gritty to the touch, subject to many previous anxiety-ridden chewings. On his desk, amid the stacks of reports and the Styrofoam cups of cold coffee, some filming over, was the DNA report from the lab in Pittsburgh. He had sent the semen sample taken from Jason Dawes at the City Hospital emergency room and the saliva sample culled from Vernon Parsons. He had hoped there would be a match, something further to go on. He had imagined the results coming back matching and he could make his arrest final, an airtight case, a case closed.

But there was no match. The semen taken from the boy's rectum was definitely not that of Parsons. In spite of the circumstantial evidence pointing at Parsons, the new high-tech test cleared him. Not that he was completely free from suspicion; he could have played a part in the boy's abduction, could have aided and abetted, as the legal lingo went, but Hugh doubted it. Crimes like the one perpetrated against Jason Dawes were usually done by someone alone, someone filled with shame and perhaps even remorse, driven by urges uncontrollable. Besides, Parsons was a hermit, fearful of almost anyone. Hugh very much doubted the man was in cahoots with someone else.

He had seen to it himself that Parsons was released, had given him a warning, a seemingly useless warning, that Parsons should stay in the area in case any further questions arose. The one bright spot was the grateful look on the hermit's face when he was freed from the little cell in the basement of City Hall, gratitude that shone out even under the film of suspicion and fear that clouded his features. The story Parsons had given them, Allen thought, was most likely true.

Who, then, was the culprit? Hugh shook his head. He knew most people suspected Sean Dawes, the boy's father, or even Austin Philips, his partner, but Hugh was not so small-minded.

He spun around in the creaking vinyl-covered chair and looked at the bright blue sky outside. Turning his back on the cramped and cluttered cell—reeking of cigarettes and old, sour coffee—he called his office and knew it was only ignorant, bigoted people who would suspect a man of pedophilia simply because he was a homosexual.

Gay men liked other gay men. Period. They had no more interest in little boys than straight men had in little girls, or little boys, for that matter.

Hugh knew that well enough. And how well he knew it was his most closely guarded secret. He tapped the pen thoughtfully against his chin. Not many people knew how Detective Allen spent his weekends in Pittsburgh, not many at all. And he planned to keep it that way. What would his girlfriend, Mary Alice, think? What would the department think?

And it was just this kind of wondering that made Hugh consider the fear of discovery if he championed the cause of Sean Dawes too strongly.

It was a sad little world...here in Summitville, PA. Hugh wondered, for about the thousandth time, why he didn't just get out.

Hating himself but knowing he was doing what would be expected of him, Hugh picked up the phone. After all, the buzz around the station was why Allen hadn't brought in Sean Dawes for questioning. "You sweet on him?" One of the uniforms had smirked, gaining him an ice glare from Hugh.

He had his reasons for not wanting to call in Sean Dawes, but they were reasons he didn't even want to recall, much less fear they would be brought to light by an angry, hurt, and outraged man who saw Hugh as one of the spokes of the bureaucratic wheel rolling over him.

He listened to the distant ringing and finally a metallic recorded voice.

"Neither Sean nor Austin can take your call right now. Leave a message and we'll get back to you."

Hugh closed his eyes for a moment, breathing in courage. Sometimes he hated his job.

"Sean, er, Mr. Dawes, this is Detective Allen down at Summitville headquarters. I need to speak with you. Please give me a call as soon as possible." Hugh hung the phone up, feeling his heart race a little faster. Had Sean even remembered him? There had been no glimmer of recognition when they had met at the hospital, but still, Sean was under a lot of stress at that time.

Hugh sipped some tepid coffee and wondered what Sean would say about him, the detective in charge of the case, if he were angry and backed into a corner.

It was a risk he'd have to take. Leaving him out of it was just as much a risk.

"You sweet on him?"

Chapter Twenty-Three

Paul lit another joint and considered just how lucky he was that he and Shelley had bought the chest freezer the fall before, just after deer hunting season when Paul had bagged a buck. "Honey, where are we going to put all this meat?" Paul had wondered when Shelley complained that the freezer would strain their meager budget too much.

"All this meat" was now rapidly thawing in the garbage cans in the backyard. Since Jason and Shelley both hated venison, Paul was certain it would be a long time before the roasts, steaks, and ground meat would be discovered missing.

Now, Paul thought, the freezer held a different sort of meat. He pinched the roach between thumb and forefinger and took one last drag. He flicked the tiny bit of paper and ash away from him, where it sputtered and died on the basement's concrete floor. Paul stood, wiped his hands on his jeans, and walked from his workbench into the adjoining room of the basement, where the washer, dryer, and freezer were housed.

Outside, the sky shone darkly in through the high basement windows. A light rain spattered the glass. Paul pulled the cord that would flood the basement room with illumination. There was a nausea growing in his gut, like a snake uncoiling, twisting to wrap around his innards and squeeze.

He paused at the large chest freezer positioned along one wall. He laid a hand across its cold enamel surface. Why did he want to look? There was a part of him that wanted to be sure the other morning, when he had awakened with a dead girl beside him, was even real. He took a great quivering breath and threw open the lid.

A cloud of vapor obscured the freezer's contents for just a moment, and then Paul found himself staring down, with horror, at the frozen features of a young girl. Her skin, almost pure white, was now tinged with blue. Frost clung to her face, a face that held cold dead eyes that were filmy but stared back at him no less accusingly.

His gut twisted, and the Hostess apple pie he had consumed for breakfast seemed to liquefy, shooting bile up to the back of this throat. He felt unsteady, as though the room were listing beneath his feet.

Paul slammed the freezer's top shut with a bang, sending out a cloud of steam that evaporated quickly.

He rushed to the drain, nothing more than a round hole in the floor of the basement, certain his breakfast was about to come up. He gripped the wall as the retching made his throat convulse but was somehow able to hold things under control.

Eyes watering and gasping, Paul leaned back against the brick surface of basement wall.

"Jesus Christ," he whispered, wiping a shaking hand across a forehead slick with sweat.

"I've got to do something about her," he whispered. "Can't share this place with her no more."

Chapter Twenty-Four

Jason could hear them downstairs. He drew his knees to his chest and wished there were a way he could shut his ears so he wouldn't have to listen. Jason stuck his thumb in his mouth and sucked. It was a habit he thought he had given up long ago, when Mom had commended him for being such a "big boy." But the thumb, resting gently against the roof of his mouth, seemed to comfort him better than anything else ever could. Better than the Smokey Bear that lay beside him, better than the stuffed chimp Grandpa had bought him, better even than the X-Men figures lined up on the nightstand beside him.

There had been a lot of screaming lately. First there would be the low roar of a car engine—his father's Sentra—the gravel crunching beneath its weight in the driveway. This sound would trigger the TV going off downstairs. Then loud whispering that ended with pounding on the aluminum screen door.

Jason rolled over on his side, staring wide-eyed at the cream-colored wall his bed was shoved against. The words were always the same...his father pleading, begging them to let him see his son. His grandmother's sharp tone, lashing out at his father, making Jason cringe, telling him something about a judge, something about a court order she could not go against. His father would always reply that it was his grandmother who instigated this whole damn thing and even if it wasn't, who was to know if he came in and sat with Jason for ten or fifteen minutes? Then Grandpa would pipe in, repeating, in a calm yet menacing way, that they would not go against the law. If his dad said anything more, Grandpa would threaten to call the cops and have him thrown in jail.

"The law, after all, is on our side," Grandma would say.

"Now go on, get out of here," Grandpa would say.

And then Jason would lie, sad, fingers nervously rubbing the sheet, listening as his father backed from the driveway.

After a few minutes and a few low words exchanged between his grandparents, the TV would come back on and things would return to normal.

Jason wondered if anything would ever be normal again.

*

Sean drove through the town, knowing he was going too fast and not giving a damn. Rain spattered his windshield, and for a moment he wished it would spatter his vision enough to blind him, so he too could run head-on into some other vehicle, granting him the same oblivion his ex-wife now had. *Just an end. I just want an end to this whole mess, the pain and the misery.*

As he drove through the streets of Summitville, with their curves and rises as the concrete mapped out a destination on the hills, he couldn't help but think what a contrast the little city presented: the beauty of the hills, rising up above the town, tree-covered, the Ohio River twisting through its valley, all scarred by the evidence of human habitation. The houses perched, clinging to the hillsides, most of them in need of paint or repair, the rusting carcasses of cars littering many of the driveways. People, too poor to afford air-conditioning, sat on front porch stoops fanning themselves, staring dumbly at the traffic passing their homes. Sean wondered why he even bothered to live there. He was a good, if not great, writer, passable enough to maybe not write the great American novel as he had once dreamed of doing, but adequate enough to at least work at a larger newspaper in someplace like Pittsburgh or maybe even Chicago. But he knew the reason he stayed. And it wasn't because his roots were here. Nor was it because of Austin, whom he had once figured would be happy to pull up stakes and follow him anywhere. Nor was it because of his job, which valued his writing ability at the majestic sum of $32,000 per year.

No, he stayed because of Jason. To be near his little boy. The only child he would ever have. He wanted to watch his son grow up, to shepherd him to adulthood, to make sure he grew up compassionate, without the bigotry and ignorance so rampant in this little town by the river.

His vision blurred for just a second as he pictured the little boy tossing a Frisbee in the backyard of his home, sunlight brightening his dark features, his hoarse laugh that never failed to charm him.

Jason was all he had. All he'd ever had. It seemed he loved the boy perhaps even more intensely than he should. But all his life, Sean had dreamed of children, of being a father. And now that fate had decreed it, he realized Jason was the only offspring he would ever have.

Shelley's parents couldn't have possibly realized how thoughtless their decision to keep him from Jason was. They probably imagined, with characteristic self-righteousness, ignorance, and chauvinism, that because he was a man, having Jason around or not could not matter that much to him. *After all*, Sean imagined them reasoning, *if he loved Jason and being a father so much, he would have never left their daughter in the first place.* For people like them, Sean knew, homosexuality was an abominable choice. Nothing more. Case closed.

Sean shepherded the Nissan south, toward the river, bouncing as he crossed railroad tracks. Ahead of him was the River Road Wharf, a sad little structure that had once seen better days, the wood now fading, the steps on one side leading down to the river, rickety and a danger. Sean sped by, taking a glance over: a barge floated by and a few mallards swam lazily in the water, bouncing on the wake from the barge, waiting for someone to come down the steps and feed them.

He stopped by his mailbox and sat with the motor running, the little aluminum box with its rounded top taunting him. He hated to open the mailbox, fearful that yet another serpent lay coiled inside, waiting to pounce, to destroy his happiness.

But when he opened it, the only things inside were a grocery store flyer and a reminder to renew his subscription to *Entertainment Weekly*. Sean snorted and thought how there was no such bird as entertainment, not anymore. He shook his head as he bumped down the driveway, thinking he had to pull himself out of this funk if he was to be there for Jason, one day, when all of this blew over.

He planned on making himself a very strong vodka and tonic, putting some good Bruckner on the stereo, and just closing his eyes until the darkness in the room matched the darkness beneath his eyelids.

But that was not to be the case. He entered the house just as a crack of thunder sent a downpour to the earth, the rain thrumming on the roof. On the desk near the entryway, the answering machine's little red light blinked. Once a happy omen, the little red dot now filled Sean with dread.

His finger hovered a moment over the button, unsure if he even wanted to hear whatever news awaited him. *What could it be?* he thought sarcastically. Maybe some other guy calling for Austin...the paper calling to tell him he'd been fired...or a new legal maneuvering that would prevent him from seeing his son for the rest of his life.

He punched the button. His brow furrowed as he recognized the scarred voice of Detective Hugh Allen, issuing forth from the little gray machine. "Mr. Dawes, this is Detective Allen down at Summitville headquarters. I need to speak with you. Please give me a call as soon as possible." Sean sat slowly down in the desk chair and listened as the detective gave his number.

Sean placed his head in his hands. He had known this was coming. There was little doubt what the detective wanted to talk to him about. And he didn't think it was a repeat of the blowjob he had given him at a rest step on Route 7 two years ago. "Christ," Sean whispered. "Where's that vodka?"

Chapter Twenty-Five

The room was stuffy, little more than a broom closet. A mirror covered a good part of one wall, the glass darker than a regular mirror. Sean knew he was being watched. What did the person on the other side of the glass see? A young man, perhaps grown a little too thin over the past few days, wiry limbs pressed into a rumpled T-shirt and jeans that had stretched, hanging loose on his hips. The face, one he had once considered attractive, was now pale, wearing a light sheen of sweat, which gathered on his upper lip and around his hairline, where a drop or two would trickle down his forehead, pause at his eyebrow, then make its way down to his eyes, where it would sting, causing him to wipe angrily at it. His thick eyebrows were gathered together to match the frown he wore. Dull, listless stare. In front of him, a scarred wooden table, its only contents a blank yellow legal pad and two Styrofoam cups filled with tepid, sour-tasting black coffee, untouched.

Sean stared over at Hugh Allen and wondered what the man was thinking. Allen was a few years older than he, with dark brown hair, thinning at the crown, and a gut that spoke of too much beer and pizza and not enough exercise. Sean had trouble deciding what color the detective's eyes were, because he had hardly looked at him since he had led him to this miserable little room about a half hour ago. Sean wondered about that, wondered why an interrogator would have trouble making eye contact with his subject. Sean would have thought one of the first tools a detective would have would be the ability to stare down a subject, make him uncomfortable enough to not only talk, but not to lie. And yet Allen's gaze seemed to be everywhere but on him: out the window on the wall behind him, staring down at the table, absorbed in adding a packet of sweetener to his coffee.

Sean knew why Allen didn't want to look at him. They both did. And the knowledge hung unspoken in the room like a third presence. Sean had made some mistakes on his journey toward coming out, and one of them was relieving his sexual frustration at a certain rest stop on the outskirts of town. The day was cloudy in his memory, details forgotten, but he was sure he and Allen had once had a furtive and anonymous tryst in a green-painted bathroom stall, scarred with graffiti. How could either of them have known they would meet again, and under such circumstances? And which of the two, Sean wondered, was more uncomfortable?

Sean, in spite of his position, wanted to reassure the detective, to tell him he wasn't about to let anyone in on their dirty little secret. But there was that mirror and the mystery of who sat behind it. If he said anything to put the detective at ease, it would be as good as blabbing it to the whole department. So instead he grew more and more uncomfortable, hands fisted, nails digging into sweaty palms.

Finally he spoke. "Look, you never said. Am I under arrest here?"

"No, of course not, Mr. Dawes. As I said before, we just wanted to ask you a few questions." Allen rubbed his hand over his head, leaving a shock of brown hair standing up near the back. "And as I said, you're welcome to call a lawyer if you want."

"Why the video camera?" Sean nodded with his head to the small wall-mounted camera above them, barely noticeable.

"Always helps to have conversations taped." Allen attempted a thin smile and lost. "It helps later if there's any disagreement over what was said."

"Uh-huh." Sean chewed at a hangnail. "What else can I tell you?"

"Go over your whereabouts on the day Jason disappeared."

"I was working all day. You can check that easily enough. Just call the paper."

"I already did that. They said you were out of the office for part of the day, researching a story."

Sean nodded. "That's right. I was at the library."

"Talk to anyone there?"

"Not that I can recall. But you know Pete Hinkle, don't you? I'm sure he saw me in the reference section."

Allen wrote something down. "I'll ask him. What times were you there?"

"God, I don't know. A good part of the morning."

"What were you researching?"

"A feature article about the origins of the pottery industry in this area. The article ran the following weekend. You can check."

"Okay." Allen tapped his pen against the surface of the table. "Look, Mr. Dawes, I'm going to be honest with you. You don't have exactly what the movies would call an airtight alibi. And your open homosexuality has some people concerned."

Sean's mouth dropped open. Even though he'd been expecting the allegation, it still came as a shock. "Being gay isn't being a pedophile. You should know that." Sean forced Allen to look back at him this time, his gaze relentless. If he remembered their encounter, it didn't register in his eyes.

"I do know that. But a lot of other people don't. And, even with that fact thrown out, things still look a little suspicious. In a town this size, Mr. Dawes, when something like this happens, the first place we look is usually the family. Child abuse is a sad, but all too real, part of life. I've seen more of it than I'd ever care to."

"What about Paul Thompson, the boy's stepfather? Have you talked to him?"

"We've had several conversations."

"Uh-huh."

"And he isn't under any suspicion at the moment."

"And I am?"

"I understand that Judge Simmons issued a restraining order, so that you're not currently able to see Jason." Sean's back went rigid. He didn't say anything. "Why do you think that's happened?"

"Because of a narrow-minded holy roller mother-in-law."

"Does she have control over the judge?"

"Don't even try..." Sean put his hands to his face, where they slid around in the sweat. He wanted to be anywhere but here.

"That court order, Mr. Dawes, is not a factor in your favor, regardless of how unmotivated you think it is."

Sean shook his head slowly. The walls seemed to move in closer. It was getting more difficult to breathe. "Is there anything else?" Sean thought back to the rapid-fire questions he had dealt with when Allen had led him to this room and wondered what else the detective could possibly want to know.

"Did you have anything to do with what happened to Jason?"

Sean shook his head slowly once more. "No." His voice was barely above a whisper. "God, no. He's my son. I would never—"

Allen stood up. Sean felt dizzy, sick. "Mr. Dawes, I have nothing more to ask you right now. You're free to go."

Sean was on his feet in an instant and heading toward the door, wondering where the closest men's room was. The bile burned at the back of his throat.

"One more thing."

"What is it?" Sean snapped, hand on the doorknob.

"Don't leave town without telling me."

"Well, I'm sure you'll be keeping an eye on all the roads leading out of town." Sean paused and stared at the detective. "From the rest stops, maybe?" He didn't wait for an answer, but hurried from the room.

*

Austin was waiting when he got back. For the most part, ever since Jason's disappearance, an atmosphere of strain hung between them like static electricity, rising up to shock at the most unexpected moments. After their brief moment of passion the other night, Austin had once again grown quiet, disappearing into a paperback novel or the TV. When Sean tried to talk to him, to get things to the surface, he was rewarded with a shrug or, at best, a noncommittal "There's nothing wrong" followed by that age-old excuse, "I'm just tired."

He knew Austin felt the strain of all that was going on and wished he knew some way to bridge the gap of outside tension that lay between them like a chasm, but it just seemed like there was no way. It was like there was an out-of-control river rushing between them. Sean knew this wretched moment in time would be the ultimate test of their love for one another.

As Sean came in the door, he thought how he'd like nothing more than to have a smile from his lover, to feel the protective warmth of his arms. God, he needed that contact! Needed to feel there was someone else in this world who was on his side, who was there for him. And he didn't feel he should have to ask for it. Asking for it would ruin the whole gesture.

So he lingered near the door, watching Austin, whose back was turned to him, an old black-and-white movie on the TV. The back of Austin's neck was red, a sharp contrast to the dark blond of his hair. Once upon a time, Sean would have kissed that reddened neck and asked him if he had been working in their vegetable garden.

But today he stood nervously near the door, almost as if he were an unwelcome guest in his own home. For the first time, he felt like an outsider, like someone moving into a space where he wasn't sure of his welcome. It left him feeling hollow in his gut.

"Hello," he called out.

Austin turned to regard him, blue eyes moving across his features almost as if he didn't know him, as if a life together was something he had tried to build with someone else. "Hey, how's it goin'?" Austin gestured toward the TV. "*Casablanca*. God, I haven't seen it in years."

"Good movie."

Silence cloaked the house once more, its presence almost palpable, an invader and violator of the peace that had somehow vanished the same day Jason vanished.

Sean moved across the room and sat down on the opposite end of the couch. He stared at the movie for a while, but couldn't force his mind to focus on what was happening with the characters. He linked his fingers together, unlinked them, did it again.

"Austin?"

"Yeah." Austin did not turn his gaze away from the movie. He reached down to the floor, picked up a can of Diet Coke, and took a swig.

"You've seen *Casablanca* before, haven't you?"

Austin laughed. "More times than I can count on both hands. But you know, it never seems to—"

"Then maybe you wouldn't mind shutting it off...so we can talk?"

It hurt Sean to see Austin roll his eyes. But Austin snatched up the remote from the coffee table and turned the TV off. "What did you want to talk about?"

"Don't you want to know where I was today?"

"I assumed you were at work."

"Austin, I haven't been into work all week."

Austin turned to him and finally met his gaze. "Then where were you?"

"I was down at the police station."

"Oh?"

"That detective, Hugh Allen, called me in for questioning."

Sean wanted his simple statement to be enough. Austin would immediately know why—any idiot would—and he would comfort him.

"What did he want?"

Sean bit the inside of his mouth and told himself to be patient. But he hated this, hated feeling he was in this all alone.

What was a partner for, anyway, if he wasn't there for you during the bad times? *And times*, Sean thought, *didn't get any worse than this*. "He was asking about my whereabouts on the day Jason disappeared."

Austin regarded him with little change in his eyes. Maybe he just didn't know what to say, but Sean wanted—no, needed—so much more.

"Austin! They're starting to think maybe I had something to do with this."

Austin snorted. "That's a good one."

"Will you take this seriously? Do you know how many people out there have the impression that gays like little boys?"

"That's ridiculous."

"Yeah, right, you know that, I know that. Hell, Shelley even knows that, but she's not saying much."

Silence again. Austin stared straight ahead.

"Is this making you uncomfortable?"

"No, no of course not." Austin's Adam's apple bobbed as he swallowed. Sean could see that his lover's last statement was a lie.

"Hugh Allen said it doesn't look good that my whereabouts can't be very well verified on that day. He says it doesn't look good that a judge ruled that I can't see my son for a while. He says that it doesn't look good that I live in an openly homosexual relationship."

Austin said nothing. He rubbed at his thighs, hands moving over faded denim.

"Don't you have anything to say?"

"What can I say? I'm sorry all this is happening."

"Are you?"

"Well, of course I am."

"You have a funny way of showing it."

Neither of them said anything for a moment, but the tension thrummed in the air like an electric current.

"Well, I'm sorry if I can't be more supportive. This hasn't been easy on me, you know. Down at the pottery, everyone's turned kind of a cold shoulder to me. Some of the women in the color room were even whispering when I walked by them the other day. So yes, I do know what you mean when you talk about people suspecting you of this just because you're gay."

Sean bit his lip. How dare Austin compare his torments at the hands of stupid gossips to his? Austin wasn't losing the right to see his son. Austin wasn't suddenly under the glare of suspicion for a crime that tore at his heart, knowing how awfully his son was hurt. "Well, I'm sorry if what's happening in your life is making things a little uncomfortable for you at work."

Austin turned to him, and the glare was unmistakable.

"What?" Sean cried, full of disbelief.

"You say that so sarcastically."

"Well, what the hell do you expect? Have you even gotten a clue in all of our time together how much I care about Jason?" Sean lowered his voice. "I had assumed you did too. You told me once you thought of him as your own son."

"That's right."

"Then why haven't I seen any of the concern? Where's the grief over what's happened to that little boy? All I see is someone who just wishes the problem would go away so life could return to normal."

"And what's wrong with that?"

"What's wrong with it is that it's not just going to go away. And your lack of sensitivity is heartless."

Austin nodded slowly. "I see. I'm heartless now."

Sean blew out an exasperated sigh. "You're missing the point."

Austin stood suddenly and went to stare out the living room window, where the river sparkled in the wan light of the dying day. His fists clenched and unclenched. Was he angry because he knew what Sean was saying was true? "I don't think I'm missing anything. I think you're missing something. Ever since this happened, it seems as if I don't exist anymore. I mean, shit, it's awful what's happened to Jason, but it's almost like I'm not here. And it's been that way since this whole fucking mess started. You haven't even been here, not in any real way."

"So now you're blaming me for being upset that my son, a little boy, was raped?"

"That's not it!" Austin yelled. Sean was surprised to see the tears on Austin's face and to hear the tremor in his voice. "I just think in times like these couples should hang together, to comfort each other, y'know?"

"That's exactly what *I* think! Goddamn it, Austin. Why don't you ever come up and put your arms around me, like you did so much before any of this shit happened? Why don't you just seem to...seem to...care?"

"Because you're unapproachable. You're always brooding. Every time I come near you, I get a fuckin' chill."

"Oh, that's just great. So you keep away from me, you don't even try."

"I don't know how to deal with this!"

"No, a gay boy like you never expected to have problems raising a kid, let alone something of this magnitude. Your life's been nothing but going up to Pittsburgh and going to the bars: drugs, dick, and disco. That's all your life was until I met you. It must be hard having to settle down with a man who has the baggage of a kid."

"That's the shittiest thing you've ever said to me. And you know it's not even true. That picture you paint... You know that was never me."

"And the way you've been treating me lately is the shittiest way I've ever been treated. I'm going through the worst crisis of my fucking life and I...feel...so...alone!" Sean turned his head and wiped angrily at his own tears.

"This isn't easy for me either."

"No, I imagine it's just breaking your heart."

"It is."

"I don't see it, Austin. I just don't see it. If anything, all I see is the concern of someone who's seen this stuff on the news. That's it."

"I loved Jason."

"Loved?"

"You know what I mean. If you think I feel this way, why are you even here?" Austin chewed on his lip.

"Oh, so it's come down to that question. I'm here because I love you, Austin. And I don't think it's too much to ask for a little comfort from you."

"It's hard to comfort someone who isn't here."

"And I imagine it would be too much trouble to try and break through?"

"Why should I have to?"

Sean shook his head. An instinct to flee was rising in him, almost a primal urge. The acid in his stomach churned. He was sorry he had ever started this whole thing. "You should have to because I thought that's what people did when they loved each other. It's what Shelley would have done." Sean regretted the words the moment he said them, knowing their power to hurt. A statement like that was never fair. But damn it, he couldn't help it. In spite of the fact that they were both attracted to men, he and Shelley really did love each other, still did, for all he knew. Oh God, he thought sickly, where was this going?

"Shelley?" Austin whispered. "That's fucking great."

"I didn't mean that." But he did. Oh yes, he did.

"You did mean it, Sean. And that's the sad thing."

"If you had just been here for me..."

"Like she would have been?"

"That's not fair."

"No, what isn't fair is the fact that you've decided to play martyr and shut me out."

"I can't believe you see things that way."

"I see what I see."

There wasn't much more to say. The silence that hung between them was filled with dread for Sean. Conversations like these always ended the same way. But that couldn't be, could it? Not after all their dreams, all the togetherness and happiness they shared. One conversation, bad as it was, couldn't destroy all that.

Could it?

"I need to be alone for a while, Sean. This is too much for me to deal with. And I think you need the time too. Plus it might look better for you right now if we weren't together anyway."

"Thanks a lot."

"Really, just a little time apart."

"Just go."

Sean watched as Austin turned to climb the stairs. Then he ran outside, to sit by the river and wait for the dying sound of Austin's car heading out of the driveway.

Chapter Twenty-Six

Jason was in the woods again. The woods, he thought as he tore through them, scratching his ankles on briars and maneuvering, avoiding trees and low-hanging branches as if this were a maze, the woods where he used to have so much fun. Now, the way the trees blocked out the sunlight caused the path beneath him to disappear and fill this once happy place with menace.

The woods had once been the home of squirrels, red-winged blackbirds, blue jays, cardinals, robins, and maybe the occasional possum, raccoon, or fox. Now the woods, with darkening thunderheads above, were populated by snakes, lying in wait in the briars, just watching for a chance to slither out and grab an unwary and frightened boy's ankles. Or perhaps a bear hid behind the boulder up ahead, nothing cute like a cartoon or stuffed bear, but a grizzly with huge fangs and claws, who would swipe at the boy, knocking him flat and leaving a row of bloody cuts, deep and fragrant, alerting the bear to the meal that lay struggling beneath his towering bulk. And perhaps the darkness had alerted the bats, giving them a false signal of twilight, making them take wing and head out into the electrically charged air, looking to swoop down on a small dark-haired boy, hair fine and silken, perfect for tangling their claws in.

Jason ran. The wind was getting colder now, and he was afraid to look behind him. His pursuer, a dark shadowy figure, was behind him, edging closer; Jason could feel the heat of his body near, a sinister contrast to the chill.

This was all so familiar. He felt he'd been through this before. These thoughts came in flashes of rationality: mostly his mind was concentrating on getting away from the terror that flew like a demon behind him, strides long and loping, no match for the frantic pace of a little boy.

He knew it was inevitable. And when he tripped over the fallen branch of oak, he knew there was nothing more to be done than to curl into a little ball, head between clasped arms, shut up like a bug, to try to hold off what was coming.

And he knew what was coming. Not like that first time, when the pain and the rage were played out on an unsuspecting body. No, this time he knew what would happen. Knew the white-hot pain that would tear through him, making him want to die. And somehow, being armed with the knowledge made the fear of the pain that much more intense. Knowing what was coming, anticipating it, Jason knew, would make everything hurt worse.

He lay still, an animal hoping not to be noticed, as the darkness of the panting figure caught up with him, stood over him. Jason began to whimper, to wish there was some way he could stop what was about to happen.

The pain was worse than anything he ever knew, and he would trade places with anyone in any kind of pain, no matter how bad, to be released from this.

The panting slowed, and then there was a low rumble of laughter, deep and dirty. Jason felt the sweat trickle down from his armpits, felt his stomach twist and turn, almost as if something alive had invaded his innards. His breathing seemed to increase just as the monster's above him decreased. He was panting, gasping for air, unable to utter even a word as simple as no.

He hugged his shoulders up tight to his head, recoiling from just the idea of the touch he knew was coming. He could hear, maybe even feel the monster bending low, his hot, alcohol-tinged breath coming closer. Jason squinched his eyes, every muscle in his body tightening, becoming metal, trying to will away the touch of the dirty, callused hand as it turned him, forcing him to open his limbs.

And then something that shouldn't have happened, did.

"Stop!" A voice commanded from behind. "Stop it right there!"

It was his daddy! All he had ever wanted the last time was for Daddy to be there to rescue him and this time, he was.

"What the fuck?" the slurred voice of the monster came out, unable to speak without using bad words.

There was a scuffle in the brush behind him, and Jason turned to see what was going on. The monster, with his grizzled face and red-shot eyes, was being slammed into the bark of a tree by his daddy. When his back came in contact with the rough bark, he let out a little grunt, then whispered the word "faggot." Jason didn't know what the word meant, but he knew it was really bad and hurt his daddy more than any dirty word could.

Daddy doubled up his fist and slammed it into the monster's ugly face. The monster cried out, an almost wolfen howl of rage and pain, but turned and ran off into the brush.

The rain came then, cleansing, and his daddy was picking him up, to carry him through the woods.

To carry him home.

Jason awakened. The room was dark, and for the first time since that awful day, he didn't feel afraid. He actually felt kind of happy. Perhaps it was only in a dream that his real father could protect him. Perhaps not. But for the first time, he felt a little bit like himself again.

Jason put his thumb in his mouth and pulled Smokey closer under the sheets and drifted back to sleep.

*

Sean sat up late. The house had never seemed more empty, all the clichés present and accounted for: the lonesome click of the deco clock on the mantle, the sound of the wind moving through the trees outside, and the creaking of the house as it settled for the night, no longer a slave to the movements of its human inhabitants.

Inhabitant?

There was no sleep for Sean. A bizarre plan, one that could ruin his life, or at least change it away from any course he had ever considered, was forming in his mind.

The kind of plan taking shape in his mind was the stuff, he thought, of TV movies and tabloid-style talk shows.

But suddenly, it seemed the only way out.

Everything was closing in on him. Once upon a time, Shelley was around, an ineffectual buffer against those who sought to keep him from his son. But a buffer nonetheless. And now she was gone. He prayed she would rouse herself from the head injuries that had caused this lengthy slumber, but he couldn't count on that.

People like Judge Simmons, Detective Allen, and Estelle Berry were conspiring to make sure he never laid a hand on his son again, no matter how innocent and love-filled that hand was.

And what if they succeeded? Sean couldn't bear a life apart from Jason, the only person who had ever really made a difference in his life. The only one who really let him feel what love meant.

But there was the plan. And, in his love for his son, Sean had to consider if he would be hurting the boy as well. Had to make sure his own needs weren't usurping those of the boy's. Sean couldn't be selfish.

Sean had to consider whomever had harmed his son was still out there somewhere, capable of doing the same thing to Jason again...or worse, in the interest of silencing him.

Besides, what kind of life did Jason have to look forward to? With Shelley out of the picture, he might be raised by his maternal grandparents, with their bigotry and their coldness. He knew what Shelley's life had been like, growing up in that house with a silent, brooding father and a mother who was nothing short of a zealot, never seeing anything without the frame of reference of the most rigid, literal interpretation of the Bible. And if Shelley did come back, there was the iron fist of Paul Thompson to be considered. Was Jason really better off with him?

Sean didn't think so. He knew, firsthand, what it was like to grow up under the caprices of an alcoholic father. His own was much too fond of drink, as so many men were in this little town on the Ohio River, just west of Pittsburgh. He remembered never knowing, growing up, what kind of mood the alcohol would induce in his father. There were the happy times, but even those always guarded, when his father would squeeze his shoulder, call him his prince, and stare into his eyes as if he were something new, something he had never seen. The times when his father would grasp him in a drunken embrace, pull him close, and murmur his love for him.

The hugs and the love were something Sean had been starved for, but these touches and proclamations always rang false, no matter how much he wanted to believe them. And then there were the other times, the bad times, when his father would come home from the "beer joint" brooding and sullen, and the other members of his family tiptoed around the house, afraid and not knowing what move they would make might ignite the silent brooding into rage, rage that could be taken out on one of them, or on the dishes his mother had left in the drainer on the sink to dry, or the eggs in the refrigerator, whatever was handy.

Jason could grow up with that kind of life. It wasn't hard to imagine, especially when Jason, in his own way, told him such things were already happening.

So, no, Sean didn't think he would be hurting his boy all that much if he took him away from all that.

Of course, there was Shelley to consider. The boy loved his mother, and the feeling was mutual. Shelley loved Jason with a fierceness and intensity that matched Sean's. Could he take him away from that love? This was the part that hurt Sean the most; the thought of the boy being without his mother was a pain, a wrenching in the heart.

But who knew when Shelley would return from her vehicular-induced slumber? And when and if she did, would she be the same woman? Or would she be a quiet invalid, putty in the hands of those around her? If that were the case, Jason would be no better off than if Shelley had stayed in a coma.

Sean knew thinking this latter way was, in large part, rationalization. There was no way to excuse taking Jason from his ex-wife. Jason's *mother*. There lay the core of his selfishness.

He couldn't bear the thought of being without him, and he would do whatever it took to make sure that didn't occur.

But how to get Jason from the protective fortress his grandparents had built around him? That was the challenge. Jason was never alone, as well he shouldn't be, given his age and what had happened to him. And the Berrys were not even comfortable with letting Sean come in and sit on the edge of the bed and talk to his son, let alone leave him alone with him, long enough to spirit him out of the house and to go God knew where.

Sean had never been a kidnapper before. And he knew he would never even have the nerve to do such a thing, were the consequences of not doing so dire.

He suddenly felt very tired. The fatigue engulfed him and his brain could barely function. Tomorrow, he would think up some sort of plan, and then he would put it into motion. Things had to be done very quickly. The image of Hugh Allen's suspicious face burned in his brain, spurring him onward.

If he didn't do something really fast, the chance might be taken from him.

And then where would Jason be?

Chapter Twenty-Seven

Estelle Berry awakened early on the morning when everything changed. She would look back on that morning, wondering if she had done something out of the scope of her normal routine, if the outcome would be different. But when things went awry in life, Estelle had found there were always other paths one could have taken, other ways of doing things to affect how things turned out. All of that was beside the point. The Lord moved in mysterious ways; she had heard the saying a hundred times growing up and used it herself often, but never had she been so challenged to accept his will.

Estelle rose that morning at five, slid into her pale-blue cotton housecoat and slippers and padded down the hallway to Jason's room, peeking in on his slumber, making sure the room did not reek of sweat or urine, as it unfortunately had a few times since her grandson came to stay with her, then headed downstairs to put the coffee on and make herself something for breakfast. John still snored in his bed, a lifetime of rising early to labor in the steel mill not seeming to affect his postretirement ability to sleep late.

No, Estelle had to tell herself—and to comfort herself somehow, in the dark, self-accusatory hours—there was nothing she could have done to prevent what was coming. Nothing at all.

Estelle scrambled a couple of eggs and put two slices of bread in the toaster while the coffee brewed. She switched on the little portable TV on the kitchen cabinet and watched the morning news as she ate.

It was always good to keep up with what was going on in the world.

*

Sean had been up since the false light of dawn invaded his house by the river, making gray shapes of the furniture, with a promise to add color later.

He toured the house, making a last inventory. He might never see the home he had once so loved again. A home forged with dreams and a hope for the future with someone no longer there. The dreams and the work he and Austin put into the house were meaningless now, he told himself. *Meaningless, right?* he wondered, running his hand across the back of the sofa they had bought the previous winter at IKEA in Pittsburgh. Meaningless: the almost completed deck facing the river. Meaningless: the new tiles in the bathroom and on the kitchen floor. Meaningless: the sleigh bed, with its cream down comforter. Sean snorted; this last was now especially meaningless. A beautiful bed with no one to share it with became just a mattress and box springs, a place to toss and turn the night away.

In the pale light, brightening more with every second, he dressed and thought about what he was about to do.

If he were caught, and there was a good chance he would be, this could look even more awful for him, in the microscope of suspicion he was beginning to come under. How perfect for the culprit of the little boy's abduction and rape to try it again.

What could possibly look worse?

That was why Sean knew he had to make sure things went off without a hitch.

He slid into a pair of shorts and an Iron City beer T-shirt, a pair of Nikes. His bag, filled taut with essentials, was on the bed, waiting to be loaded into the car.

He sat in front of the window facing the river and watched its lazy course. He had to wait until at least eight thirty, when he could leave and go down to First National and empty his account of funds.

He had a feeling of being in a dream. This whole thing seemed so unreal, so far removed than anything he had ever known. Was he actually going to do it? He couldn't know until he attempted it.

*

Estelle washed her breakfast dishes and set them in the drainer to dry. Standing at the kitchen window, she watched the flight of a robin redbreast as it swooped down from the summer sky to land on the branch of an apple tree in the yard next door. The bird had a nest built there, and Estelle could see a few small, downy heads cheeping up at the mother and at the wriggling earthworm she held in her mouth.

The toilet flushed upstairs, alerting her to the fact that her husband had risen. She was glad she hadn't wiped out the cast iron skillet she had used for her eggs. She pulled a mug from the cupboard, set it near the coffee maker, and padded across the kitchen to take a couple more eggs from the refrigerator.

Looking back, the day seemed infused with tedium, not a momentous day at all. Just another day of small talk, television, and the preparation of meals.

Perhaps if she hadn't gone to see that lawyer, perhaps none of what followed would have happened.

But regrets were for the rest of the world.

She just hoped that when Shelley awakened, she wouldn't long for the coma once more...and wouldn't blame her own mother for being unable to properly watch over her son for just a few days.

John came into the kitchen, wearing a pair of Bermuda shorts and a white T-shirt. His bald pate glinted from the kitchen's overhead light.

Estelle crossed the room to kiss him good morning, then turned to the stove to begin making his breakfast.

"Gotta go downtown today," John said. "Pay that damn electric bill. I swear it gets higher every month."

Estelle set a plate of eggs and bacon before her husband, along with his coffee, and said, "I wish you wouldn't use that kind of language in the house. How many times do I have to tell you?"

John said nothing. He broke the yolk of one of his eggs with a toast point and began eating.

So humdrum. It didn't seem right.

*

Sean drove toward the river, following the course of a bumpy brick road toward a poor neighborhood that had been called for years "Little England."

Little England was quiet this early in the morning. Down here, by the river, the houses were old, ramshackle affairs, most in need of a good coat of paint. Those that didn't need paint hid behind cheap tar paper masquerading as brick. Shells of old rusting automobiles stood forlorn in many yards, and the pothole-filled streets were not lined by sidewalks. Here, the smell of the river rose up, overpowering the little neighborhood with the smell of dead fish.

Quiet was just what Sean had been hoping for. He turned down a street he knew ended at the banks of the Ohio. And there, parked near the street's dead end, was a rusting Chevy Impala, its green coat worn almost gray by the sun. But the items Sean sought were there, intact, on both the front and back bumpers.

Sean pulled to the side of the road and shut the car off. For a while he listened to the cries of birds circling out over the brown water and the dying fan of his car engine.

Quiet.

Sean looked around him and saw no one about. He then reached down to the floorboard, where a screwdriver lay. He grasped it, liking the feel of its heft in his hand. He looked around once more, then quickly exited his car.

Keeping a watchful eye out for early morning strollers or faces behind windows, Sean stooped behind the Impala and began to remove the first license plate. He knew he was shielded as he crouched low by his own car and tried to work fast. The work made him anxious, the grip of the tool slippery in his sweaty palm.

Finally he had all four license plates exchanged and stood, wiping his hands on his shorts, and let out a trembling sigh. He had vowed to this course of action and promised himself he would not question again if he was doing the right thing. The way he saw it, there was no other choice. And yet the feeling of being trapped in an outlandish dream persisted; he had never done anything criminal in his whole life, and to start with something this momentous seemed beyond belief. Unreal.

Sean looked around once more and saw no one. He got in his car and started to drive off, headed for the bank downtown. After depleting his savings and checking accounts, he would be faced with the exciting part: the challenge of getting his Jason out of the home of the evil grandparents.

This was all just a story, wasn't it? Soon he would awaken to find that none of what had occurred over the past few weeks had happened, and Jason, on a weekend visit, slumbered in the room next to his and Austin's.

If only...

*

Estelle waved as John backed out of the driveway, then headed back into the kitchen from her post on the back porch. Jason probably wouldn't awaken for another hour or two; he had been sleeping later and later in the mornings, and the time alone would give her a chance to do a little picking up around the house.

She debated whether she should have another coffee and allow herself to sit and watch the *Oprah Winfrey Show* before beginning her cleaning. After all, the house wasn't that messy, and she deserved a break. But her sense of duty nagged at her. It seemed almost sinful to sit in the living room recliner with her feet up when there was work to be done. In the end she decided she would at least make a good start on things and see how far she got in a half hour. As her reward, she could sit and watch the last half hour of Oprah.

Just as she was gathering a week's worth of newspapers from the living room, the phone rang. Estelle hurried to answer it, not wanting its chirping to awaken Jason. The boy needed his rest. Estelle shook her head and thought the real reason she didn't want Jason to wake up was so she could have a little more time for herself. "Hello?"

"Mrs. Berry?"

"Yes?"

"This is Howard Keeler, down at the Amoco on Fourth Street."

Estelle was sure she didn't know a Howard Keeler, but the Amoco on Fourth was familiar. She and John had taken their cars there for maintenance for years. Why on earth would he be calling her this morning?

"Look, Mr. Keeler, if this is a sales call, I really don't have time. We're not due for an oil change for at least another month."

The man on the other end laughed. "Nothin' like that, Mrs. B. Nothing at all." There was a pause, and just as Estelle was about to ask why he was calling her, the man continued. "Seems your hubby's had a little car trouble."

"Oh?"

"Yeah, and he left the car here with us. I don't think it's anything too major, nothin' like needing a new one, but we do have to replace some bands and it'll take a while."

"Is John there?"

"That's the thing, Mrs. B. He went on over to the diner, you know, the one where Shelley works, and said he's gonna get himself a cup of coffee."

"Why are you telling me this?"

"It's just that John asked me to give you a jingle, see if you wouldn't mind coming down with the other car to give him a lift home. We're probably going to have to keep his car here at least overnight, with parts and all."

"Well, I have my grandson here. John knows that. He's been sick, and I don't know if I can leave him."

"Oh, don't worry about that, Mrs. B. John told me to tell you he'd be waiting outside. Won't take you all of ten minutes to run down and pick him up."

"Why didn't John just call me himself?"

"Now that's a question you're going to have ask John. I guess it was just easier for him to have me give you a call."

Well, at least that sounded like John, always looking for someone else to do for him. She'd learned that lesson over and over in their forty-two years of marriage.

"All right, Mr. Keeler. I'll see what I can do."

"Much appreciate it."

Estelle hung up the phone and sighed. No cleaning. No Oprah. And what of Jason? What if he awakened to find her gone? Estelle shook her head. She had half a mind to give that diner a call and to tell John he could walk home. But then she thought of how angry he'd be and how she'd never had the nerve to make a move like that before, so why start now?

Estelle hunted around for the keys. Ten minutes was about right. It could even be less than that, if the lights were with her. She supposed Jason would be all right; most likely he wouldn't even know she was gone.

As she pulled the door closed behind her, she reassured herself that nothing could possibly go wrong.

*

Sean cruised by the Berry house slowly, making sure there were no cars in the driveway. It wouldn't take long for Estelle to find she had been duped, and his window of opportunity was very small. He was thankful there was an alley that backed up to the yard. That way he could park his car unnoticed and do what he needed to do without the prying eyes of neighbors.

He situated the car as close as he could to the garage and let himself in through the back gate. The day was typical for August: sunny, with a few stratus clouds up high, the air warm, smelling of newly mown grass from the yard next door. The ordinariness of it contributed to Sean's feeling of unreality.

He mounted the back porch steps and found, to his dismay, the door locked. Moving around to the front door yielded the same result. "Damn," he whispered, after yanking on the door a final time.

What if Estelle had simply loaded Jason in the car with her? That would have made sense; that way she didn't have to shirk her responsibility to the boy to come to her husband's aid.

If that was the case, Sean would have to wait for another opportunity, come up with another plan. And with Detective Allen closing in, time was a commodity Sean didn't think he could afford to squander.

Sean returned to the back door and knocked, tentatively at first, then harder. If there was no one home, it would make no difference, but if Jason was sleeping upstairs, as Sean suspected he was, he would be happy to open the door to his father.

It seemed like he pounded on the aluminum of the screen door for a long time. Long enough, he feared, to bring the neighbors to their windows to see what the racket was about.

And then Jason was there and Sean forgot about the neighbors.

He wore a pair of flannel boxer shorts and an oversized T-shirt, dark hair tousled, rubbing sleep from his eyes. He was frowning, but when he saw Sean, the corners of his mouth turned up in a grin, and he rushed to unlock and open the door.

"Daddy!" he squealed, the delight and joy radiating through his voice.

Sean paused with his arms outstretched. He had heard Jason's bubbling voice so much in the past—his loquaciousness almost having been a sore spot before all this occurred—that for a moment, it didn't register that the boy was actually speaking.

And when he realized the first word to break the silence was his delighted squeal of the word "Daddy," Sean couldn't help but get a lump in his throat and watched as his vision blurred from the tears.

Jason's arms hung at his side, and his eyes were wide with wonder. It seemed he was as surprised as Sean to have finally found his voice.

"Jason! Oh, Jason! It's so good to hear you speak."

The boy rushed into his father's arms, and Sean felt no lover's embrace could ever match the sheer joy of holding the little boy in his arms, especially after being separated from him, especially after being told by a court of law that he was not allowed to do what he was doing right now. He buried his face in Jason's sweet-smelling hair, drinking in the feel of him, the solidity of his little body, something he feared he might never be able to experience again. And losing that would be the worst torture he could imagine.

A car horn sounded outside, and it alerted Sean to the fact that he didn't have much time. Squatting down by Jason, he said, "Son, how would you like to take a little trip with your old man? Get away from these old folks and have some fun?"

Jason nodded, his grin broadening. Sean thought that maybe, just maybe, Jason was as starved for affection as he was.

"Well, let's go upstairs and throw some of your things into a bag. What do you say?"

"Is Austin coming?"

Sean grabbed his son's hands and led him into the dining room and up the stairs. "No, Jason, Austin...is going to be busy here. He has a lot to do."

Sean hated lying to his son this way, but he saw no other avenue. Eventually Sean would have to tell the boy everything, in terms he could understand, but there was no time for that now.

Once in the bedroom, Sean began emptying Jason's drawers into the nylon bag he had brought with him when the Berrys brought him home. His muscles felt taut with anxiety and tension. He could imagine the sound of Estelle Berry's car pulling into the driveway, the feeling of being trapped as the woman entered her house and called out for Jason, puzzled at being tricked into a quick trip downtown and the back door being unlocked and open.

So he moved quickly, while Jason watched from his seat on the bed.

"Don't we need to wait until Grandma gets back?"

Sean stiffened. He realized suddenly this wasn't going to be easy. He had worried about the legal ramifications of what he was doing, along with his fears of how he might be changing the course of his own life and career for what could definitely be the worst, but he hadn't given much thought to what this would do to Jason.

He had a sudden jolt of guilt. The boy loved his grandparents; Sean couldn't fault him for that. And the worst part was that he might never see Shelley again. In spite of the horrendous divorce and her subsequent marriage to a brute, Shelley and Jason loved each other very much. And to take this boy—any boy, really—from his mother, was a pain Sean would have to bear the rest of his life.

He just hoped Jason would not hold it against him, his resentment growing to hatred as the years passed.

It was too late. He had come this far and couldn't stop. Not now, not when he thought of what could very well happen if he should stay here in Summitville. It might not just be the Berrys who prevented him from seeing Jason, but prison bars.

Sean zipped the bag closed and rustled Jason's hair. "C'mon, sport, we gotta go."

"But Grandma?"

Sean swallowed hard. "Grandma's already given her okay. I called her last night."

Jason looked at him doubtfully. Sean realized the boy could have easily overheard Sean's heated pleas to his grandparents to let him see Jason. Even an eight-year-old would be puzzled by his grandparents' sudden change of heart. "Really, Jason, it's okay. Now we gotta get on the road." Sean stooped to undress Jason and put a T-shirt, shoes, and a pair of shorts on him.

"Let's go. Okay?" Sean grabbed Jason's hand and tugged him.

The boy stood still, his green eyes probing. "I want to wait for Grandma. Gotta say goodbye, at least."

Shit. He hadn't anticipated this. He glanced down at his watch and saw that fifteen minutes had already passed. Estelle Berry would be pulling into the driveway any minute now.

"Jason, we have to go. Please. Grandma's going to meet us downtown." Sean hated himself for lying.

Finally, Jason followed him.

In the yard, Sean could see Estelle coming down the road. Thank God the old woman drove slow.

"Let's run!" Sean shouted with what he hoped sounded lighthearted rather than desperate. He swooped Jason up in his arms and rushed through the gate. He deposited Jason in the passenger's seat and was just hurrying around to the other side of the car when Estelle's car slowed in front of the house, her left turn signal blinking. Thank God there was a line of traffic preventing her from turning.

She pulled into the driveway just as Sean gunned the car out of its space and down the alley.

Chapter Twenty-Eight

Thick. The air seemed so thick, she could almost touch it. It weighed her down like a solid thing, making even the slightest movement real effort. Around her were trees, hanging low with dead fruit, strange leather-winged birds perched on their limbs. Shelley moved through this dark wood with one thought on her mind: finding Jason. She knew he was in the woods somewhere; she had heard his faint cry in the distance. But it seemed everywhere she turned was another dead end, another completion to a circle she had made a hundred times before.

"Mommy!" The cry, almost strangled, cut straight to her heart. She had to find him, had to protect him before whatever it was that was causing him to scream did, closing in and stifling his voice.

Something foul-smelling swooped above her head, blocking out the feeble light and chilling her with the flap of its wings.

"Jason!" Shelley cried out. "Jason, where are you?"

"Mommy!" was her only reply. It seemed the voice could have come from a thousand directions; it echoed and reverberated through the trees.

Oh God, let me find him, she thought, the anxiety causing her to quicken her pace more. More. She rushed headlong, not knowing where she was going, but the urgency moved her forward. Somehow she would have to come upon the boy, but only if she kept moving.

But the air! The air was so heavy it gripped at her legs, weighing her down. If only she could rest for a moment or two. If only she could lie on the mossy earthen floor of the forest and just sleep. Perhaps her mind would clear, her energy revitalize itself.

But there was no time for that! No time at all. Jason could be in grave danger. In fact, she was certain he was.

Up ahead, a clearing. The sun shone more brightly there. And it was toward this light that Shelley moved. Perhaps in the clearing she would be able to get a more useful perspective of where she was.

Into the light and everything changed. Shelley's eyelids fluttered and her head was seized with pain unlike any she had ever known. A monster-size headache throbbed behind her eyelids.

She opened them and the dream dispersed, falling in fragments to wither away and die, leaving in their wake only a vague feeling of dread and paranoia.

The first thing she saw was the IV bag hanging above and to her left. She traced its course down, its clear line going into her arm. She was in a hospital, she realized.

Oh God, what had happened to her? Where was Jason? She tried to hoist herself up on her elbows, but the movement sent white-hot shoots of pain through her, and she collapsed.

It was then she heard a voice. Her mother.

"Nurse! Nurse! Oh, where is that darned call button?" Whisper of movement, and then her mother saying, "My God, she's woke up. Thank you, Jesus."

And then, in a blur, her mother's pinched features were above her, staring down. "Shelley, honey, can you hear me?"

Shelley nodded. She wanted to say so much more, to burst the dam of questions buzzing and chattering inside her, demanding answers, but her throat was dry and her tongue was thick; she couldn't muster the energy to say anything.

Not yet.

And then a nurse was above her, concerned features below a thick mop of dark curls. She checked Shelley's pulse, forced her eyes open more to peer into them.

"Mrs. Thompson, can you hear me?"

"Of course she can! I just asked her."

The two women exchanged annoyed glances.

Shelley touched the nurse's hand; it was cool. When the nurse looked back at her, Shelley nodded her head, slowly, deliberately, even this small movement causing her head to ache more.

"I'll go see if I can find a doctor."

"Thank you," Estelle said. She began stroking her daughter's forehead, and Shelley wanted to slap the hand away and would have, had she the energy.

She licked her lips, trying to muster up some saliva. She didn't care about the pain, could stomach it. What she could not stomach was not knowing what had happened. Why was she here? Was Jason all right? She knew something bad had happened to him but could not remember what.

"Jason?" She managed to mumble.

The communication was enough to bring a frown to her mother's face. The frown told Shelley more than she wanted to know; an answer to her simple question that she had hoped would not be.

Estelle glanced desperately at the door. "Shh," she whispered, back of her hand to her daughter's cheek, a gentle stroke. "Shhh, the doctor's coming. You don't want to strain yourself. You're weak, honey. We'll talk in a little bit."

Something had happened to Jason, she was sure of it. Her mother's face never could hide anything. Maybe that was why she was such a devout Catholic: she was physically unable to tell a lie.

"Jason?" she repeated. "Okay?"

Estelle patted Shelley's hand. "In a minute, honey, we'll talk."

"Jason!" Shelley screamed, the anxiety twisted in her gut like some foreign creature. "Jason!" she cried, causing the pain to radiate, to throb, to torture.

Finally her mother looked down at her, eyes full of pity and concern. "Jason is all right, dear. I'm sure he's all right. There's nothing to worry about." The lies spilled from her lips; even Shelley, in her fragile state, could detect the falsehoods on her mother's breath.

"I...don't...believe...you," Shelley said, each word punctuated by a gasp.

Estelle laughed, trying to convey how silly her daughter was being. "Don't get yourself so worked up, dear. I don't want to see you have a relapse."

Shelley's eyebrows came together in confusion.

"You've been in a coma, honey." Estelle searched her daughter's features, looking perhaps for understanding. "There was a car accident—"

"Jason?"

"No, you were alone. But you had a bad bump to the noggin, and you've been sleeping for a few days, almost a week. We weren't sure you'd ever come back to us." Estelle brushed some stray hair away from Shelley's forehead. "But now you're back, and I'm sure you'll be feeling right as rain real soon. But you mustn't tax yourself."

Shelley swallowed, her throat dry, painful. "Jason is okay?"

"Yes. Yes, now relax. I think I hear the doctor coming."

Shelley let herself lie back on the pillows, staring up at the ceiling. Mom was right about one thing: she didn't need a relapse. Something was very wrong; she didn't know what yet, but she wouldn't find out unless she regained some of her strength. She tried to breathe deeply but found she was growing very tired, the grogginess overcoming her like a drug.

The nurse was coming back into the room, and there was a young man with her. *Please*, Shelley begged mentally, *please help me get better. I need to be somewhere else.*

I need to be with Jason.

*

Paul couldn't believe it. The phone call had come only moments ago, a call for some reason he hadn't expected.

Estelle was talking so fast and with so much excitement, he had to make her slow down and repeat herself.

"Shelley's come to, Paul. Isn't that wonderful?"

"Yeah, it's great." Paul glanced around the mess the house had become: the living room floor littered with beer cans and pizza boxes, some still containing dried slices that looked like cardboard. The ashtrays were overflowing and there was clear evidence—roaches—that he had been smoking pot, something Shelley put up with, but never in the house proper. Magazines and newspapers were everywhere and some of the magazines, hauled up from his basement workshop, could get him in a lot of trouble. His clothes were all over the house, wherever he happened to drop them when he came home from yet another late night, there to be sorted through the next day and put back on, providing the smell wasn't too overpowering.

It looked like his bachelor days were over, and Paul stared out at an overcast sky, mourning them.

Things had been going so well! Ever since Estelle called and said that Sean had taken Jason and she had no idea where they'd gone; Sean's account drained of funds, his little boyfriend clueless, everything seeming to turn around for Paul. With Jason out of the picture, it didn't seem as if Paul would have much to worry about. Even better, Sean taking the boy as he did—with stealth and trickery—cast an even bigger shadow of suspicion on the faggot.

It was perfect. Paul didn't care where Sean had taken the boy. Paul wished them well, wished them an unfindable hiding place. Because with the two of them gone, no one would come sniffing around him anymore, searching for answers.

And with Shelley in the hospital, Paul enjoyed a taste of freedom he hadn't had since he and Shelley had stood up in St. Aloysius church and taken their vows. In sickness and in health, sure thing.

And now it was all coming to a close. Shelley would be desperate, frantic to find Jason, and Paul would have to bear the brunt of it, get her trained all over again to not make too much of a nuisance of herself. He felt for the poor girl, he really did, but he couldn't stand her moping around the house, crying and wondering. He hated to do it, but a few good cracks should change her mood. Change it considerably.

But he'd have to be sure to avoid her head. That could be a problem, in light of what had happened.

He'd have to get the house cleaned up. Paul was sure he'd have a few days to do it, but he despised the prospect: cleaning was women's work, but Shelley would have a relapse if she came home and saw what had been wrought on her home in her absence. He had half a mind to just have her do it, but he couldn't be that heartless. Besides, she probably wouldn't be able to do a proper job, having just come out of a coma and all. He chuckled as he thought of her creeping around the house, hand to woozy forehead, trying to pick up.

And then there was the matter of what was in the freezer. Yes, that would have to be taken care of. Wouldn't want Shelley heading for the freezer and finding filet of slut for dinner.

*

In a matter of a few hours, Shelley felt much better. She wondered if the headache would ever go away, but at least it had lessened in intensity, the ache behind her eyes now nothing more than a dull throb that would, at times, rise up to remind her it was still there and would not be taken for granted. But at least now Shelley could raise the bed to a semisitting position, so she could cast her gaze around the hospital room, with its green-tiled floors and cream-colored walls, the beige curtain hanging half open around her bed. At least now she felt well enough to drink the protein shake the nurse had brought her, to even take a few spoonfuls of Jell-O.

And well enough to know what the hell was going on. Mother had gone home to tell her father the news, backing out with a sheepish grin and a promise to return soon, to let Shelley in on all she had missed.

But Shelley didn't want to wait for her mother's fumbled proclamations and her couched, vague description of what had happened to her. So when she spotted the young Asian woman who had treated Jason passing her room, Ann Wu—funny the things one remembered when memory was nothing but a cloud, changing shape, indefinable—Shelley tried to well down the stabs of pain in her head as she sat up straighter and called to her.

At first, it seemed the doctor hadn't heard; she kept right on making her way down the hospital corridor. Shelley slumped back down on the warm sheets, her disappointment rising up to torment her in much the same way the ever present pain in her head did.

But Dr. Wu came back, her small features creased with concern.

"Yes?" she said, dark eyes moving over Shelley's supine figure in bed, a glimmer of recognition beginning to form there.

"You're Dr. Wu, right?"

"Yes, and you're..."

"Shelley Thompson. You treated my son, Jason." How long ago had it been? Shelley didn't even know if she had lain in this bed for a few hours, a few days, or a few weeks.

Dr. Wu nodded, the mystery completely solved. "That's right. I heard about your accident, Mrs. Thompson."

"Could you do me a favor?"

"Anything I can help with, I'd be glad to."

"I just need to know what's been going on. I guess I've just come out of some kind of...coma."

Dr. Wu bent to take the chart from its slot at the foot of Shelley's bed. She briefly consulted it, then came over to sit on the edge of the bed, near Shelley's feet.

"Mrs. Thompson, you've been in a coma for about a week. Hasn't anyone told you that?"

"No one's told me anything," Shelley said thickly, reaching for a glass of water.

"Well, from what I can gather, you were in an automobile accident and had trauma to the head."

"No shit?" Shelley asked, shocked at the sarcasm in her voice. "I'm sorry. What I really want to know is what happened to Jason."

"He was released a few days ago."

"Was he better then?" Shelley pictured a full recovery, with Jason chattering happily to the orderly who wheeled him to hospital's front door.

"His physical injuries were quite a bit better, in fact. I wanted to see him every few days, to continue to check on his progress. But he still hadn't gotten his speech back when he left. I don't know if he has yet."

"What?" All this past-tense bullshit seemed out of kilter, causing bright points of anxiety to blossom within her.

Dr. Wu moved closer up the bed and took Shelley's hand. She scratched behind her ear, stared out the window for several moments.

"What is it?"

"It seems, um, Jason has disappeared, Mrs. Thompson."

The room seemed to dip, to swerve, like the floor of a boat on the high seas. Shelley gasped. "What do you mean?"

"Just yesterday. It was on the news. Jason disappeared from his grandmother's home." Dr. Wu's deep brown eyes bore into Shelley's. "I'm so sorry."

"Do they have any idea who took him?" Nausea roiled in her. It had to be the man who had raped him, wanting to silence him forever. *Oh God, please no...* Shelley longed for two things: to jump from the bed, physical limitations gone, and to sink back into her coma, to leave behind the melodrama her life had suddenly become.

"From what I've heard, they suspect your ex-husband, Sean Dawes. He's also turned up missing. Many of his personal belongings are gone from his house." Dr. Wu couldn't look at her. She relayed the information in a dull monotone, staring out the window. "His bank account had been drained, and his car is gone."

Shelley sank back into the pillows, willing the tears to come, but her eyes were dry. Sean had taken him? Why? Why? It was so out of character for him to do something like that. One thing of which she had been certain was that he would never do anything to harm Jason. And now he had gone and done this? "Why?" she asked, aloud.

There was an odd component of relief in this news, bolstered by the bedrock of faith Shelley had that Sean would never harm his son. He loved the boy more than he loved his own life. Anyone could see that. Anyone, that is, except her mother.

"I don't know why, Mrs. Thompson. Maybe those questions could better be answered by your family."

And, as if on cue, clicking footsteps preceded Estelle's entrance into the room. She smiled when she saw her daughter and nodded to the doctor. "Well, it looks as if you're feeling better."

"If you'll excuse me," Dr. Wu said.

"Oh, sure," Shelley said, never taking her eyes from her mother.

Dr. Wu hurried from the room, with a promise to stop in soon to see how she was doing.

The two women stared at one another for a moment. "Jason is missing. Why didn't you tell me?"

Estelle laughed, mirthless. "You had just come out of a coma, dear." Estelle crossed to sit on the bed and brush back a strand of hair from Shelley's forehead. "I had to think of you."

Shelley paused to consider that. She felt annoyed but knew her mother was right. "When did this happen? How could it have happened? Where was Paul?"

Estelle brushed at the sheet, smoothing and straightening. "I don't know where Paul was. Jason was staying with your father and me. I thought he might be better off there after you had your little accident."

"Uh-huh."

Estelle swallowed hard. Shelley could see her throat bobbing.

"Where were you, Mother?"

Tears welled up in the older woman's eyes. "I'm so sorry," she whispered. "He tricked me. That Sean... He tricked me."

"What are you talking about?"

Estelle told her how she had been duped. "I knew it would only take a few minutes. And Jason was sleeping. Oh God, Shelley, I had no idea. I'm so sorry. When I got back, they were gone."

Shelley stared down at the sheets, feeling helpless. She had to get better as fast as possible. It suddenly seemed to her that it was only she who could put things right, who could find Sean and Jason. The longer she lay here, the further they could slip from her grasp. But one thing still nagged at her...

"Mother, why would Sean do such a thing? What about Austin? What about his job? Sean could have taken Jason whenever he wanted in the past. Why would he want to now?"

Shelley watched as her mother's face went pale and the guilt, like a shadow, moved across her features. "Who knows why he would want to do such a thing."

And Shelley knew... "You do, Mother. You know, don't you?"

Estelle didn't say anything for a long while. Long enough for Shelley to consider grabbing her and shaking her, causing the answer to fall from her mother's mouth like coins from a shaken piggy bank. "I suppose it might have had something to do with the court order."

"Court order?"

"I thought it was for the best. There was no one but me to decide, y'see. I had to do what I thought was right."

"Court order?"

Estelle grabbed her daughter's hand, squeezing it so tight, Shelley gasped and pulled her hand free.

"You have to understand, dear. Sean could have been the one. Even you must see that."

"I never—"

"No, no, he could have been the one. With his perverted ways, it was only the next logical step."

"Mother, Sean would never do anything to harm Jason." Even though the pain in her head bloomed into agony, she screamed, "It wasn't Sean who raped my boy! It wasn't!"

Silence. Then Estelle blurted, "Well, I believe it could have been! I thought it was at least possible. And so did my lawyer. And so did the judge. All I got was a simple ruling that Sean couldn't see Jason until you were better."

Shelley couldn't believe it. "You went to court and had them bar Sean from seeing his own son?" A welling nausea joined the pain in her head. Shelley was afraid she was going to be sick.

"I thought it was for the best. There was no one but me to decide. I had to do what I thought was best." Estelle began to sob, just a little. "I only did it out of love and concern for Jason."

"Keeping him from his father was a loving thing to do?"

Estelle had no reply. "Well, what's done is done. We'll find Jason. The whole police department is on it. They're not going to let this rest. And by the way, that Detective Allen thinks that Sean could have been responsible too. He told me that Sean had no good alibi for the day Jason disappeared. None at all. And he thinks that his pulling a stunt like this makes him look even guiltier."

"Well, of course Sean would do this, Mother! Haven't any one of you stopped to consider..." Shelley pressed a hand to her pounding forehead. The room was spinning and her vision slipped out of focus for a moment. *Calm down; please calm down.* "Has anyone stopped to consider that Sean might have done this, not out of guilt, but because he loved Jason so much he couldn't bear to be apart from him?" Shelley hiccupped out a sob. "Maybe even to protect him?"

"Oh now, why wouldn't he just wait and see how things went? There are other channels he could have taken other than kidnapping. Surely."

Shelley slumped back down on her pillows. Rest now, she told herself. *Rest. Don't say another word. In a world full of imbeciles, someone has to take charge, and I need to be the one.*

Chapter Twenty-Nine

Sean drove west. The view was getting boring: endless rows of cornfields and flatlands. Silos, barns, and housing developments were the only things to look at. Near the turnpike exits, fast-food restaurants and oversized gas stations jockeyed for space just beyond the point where one would leave the road. Vast expanses of emptiness. Who had said "America was a vast wasteland"? He couldn't remember; only that Will Rogers had quipped that it was now only "half vast."

He wished there was something to look at. Wished he had taken the time to gather up a few CDs from the cupboard near the stereo, just to have something to listen to other than waxing and waning radio stations...country-western hits, talk radio, teenybopper tunes, a whole panoply of nothingness. A void.

He wanted to think of something else. Anything. Anything other than what he was doing. He had been driving for almost six hours, and there was nothing to occupy his thoughts other than the guilt and anxiety that wrenched at him, that made him want to turn back and do the right thing, as he had always done. Always the good little boy…from as far back as he could remember.

Jason sat silently in the passenger seat, gazing out at endless stretches on either side of the road, not ceasing their boring existence until they reached the steel blue sky. Perhaps it was more interesting for the boy, who had never seen anything other than the dips and swells of hilly western Pennsylvania. Perhaps there was some novelty in it.

Frustrated with the radio's chorus of competing commercials, idiotic DJ banter, and songs too mediocre for him to even consider listening to, Sean snapped the thing off. "So what do you think, Jason? Never been in Indiana, huh?" Jason said nothing.

"Jason, I'm talking to you." Sean reached over and gently tickled his son just below his ribs. In the past the action had never failed to provoke a reaction from him. This time it did: Jason squirmed out of his reach and continued to fix his gaze outside the window, where now there was a field of black-and-white cows grazing, looking sullenly at the traffic swarming by on the turnpike.

"Jason?"

The boy turned to stare at him. "I have to pee."

Good. At least he was talking; at least he hadn't slipped back into the state he had been in…the muteness that had tugged at Sean's heart and made him want to die, made him want to exchange places with his boy so he could bear the pain that caused it.

"There's an oasis coming up in a couple miles." Sean had seen the big blue sign just a minute ago. He was leery of going into such places. He didn't know how fast police departments could work, didn't know how much interstate talk there would be about Jason's disappearance. Perhaps an officer, plain clothed, would be waiting at each oasis for the pair to appear.

As he swung the car onto the exit ramp, he tried to reassure himself how unlikely it would be that there would already be a nationwide manhunt—boyhunt?—in progress. He did know one thing from his days as a reporter—how slowly legal wheels turned, especially when they crossed state lines. He knew he could have pulled over to the side of the road and found some bushes and let Jason relieve himself there. But he couldn't do that to him. Somehow he would have to give the boy as normal a life as possible. As normal a life as one could have in hiding, anyway.

A sickness clenched at his gut. This wasn't fair to Jason, he told himself; this was the height of selfishness. But he pressed down on the gas pedal anyway, propelling them farther and farther away from the only place Jason had ever called home.

He and Austin had once upon a time wanted to take Jason along on vacations with them. He had told Shelley it would broaden Jason, that it was unfair of her to deny Jason the experience of, say, climbing through Native American cave dwellings in New Mexico or beachcombing on the Gulf Coast of Florida. She had never agreed, and he assumed her mother and that lout she had married had soundly bolstered her disagreement.

The white brick facade of the turnpike oasis rose up before them as Sean shut the ignition off. He sat for a moment, listening to the whir of the cooling fan. What would he say if someone should recognize them? It was a chance he'd have to take. There was always the option of just picking up the boy and running, running as fast as he could to the car, where he would slam and lock the doors, and take off, all squealing tires and kicked-up asphalt.

Sean took Jason's hand as they went inside. An assortment of travelers milled about the overly bright building: an overweight couple staring up at the menu at Hardee's, a trucker on one of the pay phones, a group of teenage boys staring at the big map of Indiana on one wall. All of them unconcerned with this father and son entrance.

Or at least Sean hoped.

Sean led Jason into the bathroom and got him settled in a stall, then headed to one of the urinals. A man to his left sized him up, and Sean wondered if he was trying to cruise him or maybe, just maybe, he recognized him from a photograph displayed on the news or a description beamed out over the radio.

Sean kept his eyes down, paranoia eating at him and wishing Jason would hurry, hurry.

Finished, Sean led the boy out. "Want something to eat, sport? They've got ice cream." Jason shook his head.

"Well, I think I'll get us a couple burgers. Two guys like us can't go for long without nourishment. Right?" Jason said nothing.

Sean had an idea. Maybe, if there had been any bulletins about what he had done, it would look better if he weren't walking around with Jason, in full view, just asking for apprehension.

"Listen, why don't you wait in the car while I get us some food?"

Jason followed complacently, saying nothing. Sean got him situated in the car. "I'll be back in a jiffy." He winked at the boy, smiled, tousled his hair.

No reaction.

"I know the Dawes appetite, and you'll be feeling much better once you get some food in your belly."

Sean closed his eyes in relief when Jason finally smiled at him and nodded. He took comfort from the weak smile, as forced as it was obvious. He made sure the car was locked, the windows cracked open, and hurried to get them some Hardee's hamburgers.

The line inside was too long. *Damn it, why now?* Sean looked down at his watch and saw it was a little after three in the afternoon. An off-time, right? But the place was a beehive: travelers milling about with trays balanced, searching for that ideal seat. He shifted his weight from one foot to the other, wishing things would go more quickly.

Finally, his turn arrived and he said, "Two burgers, two small fries, a large Coke, and a milk." The portly woman behind the counter, all nervous fingers, uncertainly punched in his order on the computer, peering through thick lenses to find the selections he had ordered. Sean held himself in check from pointing them out to her.

Finally the woman had their food bagged, took Sean's cash, and uncertainly made change. Sean tried to keep his annoyance in check but couldn't resist saying, "New, are you?"

"No, why?" the woman responded, peering at him from behind thick lenses. She turned away and went to wait on another customer before Sean had a chance to say anything further.

He hurried back to the car.

At first, he thought the sun was playing tricks on his vision, obscuring his view of Jason's dark hair by creating a blinding glare across the windshield. But his pulse quickened along with his pace anyway.

The car appeared empty.

His heart sank when he saw that the front seat was indeed empty. He looked inside anyway, opening the door and throwing the bag of food on his seat, peering into the backseat, checking the floorboards.

But the car was empty.

Jason was gone.

Sean stood away from the car, nerves jangling, and scanned the parking lot. No sign of Jason. Oh good God, what now? Had a police officer seen him, already settling the boy into the backseat of an unmarked car? The officer had seen Sean and was right now saying to his partner, "There he is. Let's go get the bastard."

But no one came running up to him. Sean closed the door and strode quickly back to the oasis. Inside, there was no trace of Jason, not near the pinball machines, not in the restroom, not in the little gift shop that sold Indiana souvenirs and saltwater taffy.

Heart thudding and a line of perspiration beginning at his hairline, Sean ran to the parking lot. All busy commerce there...cars coming and going, people walking their dogs in the grassy area to the east of the white brick building. Sean headed for that area, praying Jason would be there. He stopped in the grass, shielding his eyes from the sun with one hand, and looked around.

"Jason!" he called, "Jason!" trying to keep the terror out of his voice. He circled the building, going around to the back, and came up with nothing.

"I shouldn't have done it. I shouldn't have done it," he whispered. Wouldn't it be just his luck if some sickie had seen Jason alone in the car and had decided to seize the moment...and his son? Wouldn't that just be ironic?

Sean's shoulders sagged, his hope withering in the humidity of the day. He closed his eyes, wishing the blood rushing in his ears weren't so loud, wishing the nausea rising up within him would go away and leave him to think.

He looked around. Behind the oasis was a clump of trees, maples mostly, and Sean wondered, could he possibly be there? Taking long, quick strides, Sean rushed to the covering of trees and slipped into their shadows.

"Jason!"

And of course, after a moment or two of his eyes adjusting to the change in light, Sean saw his son. Jason squatted by the bark of a tree, back against it. His thumb was in his mouth and he was crying.

Breathless, Sean rushed up to him. "Jason, oh Jason. You shouldn't have left like that. I didn't know where you were." Sean got down on his haunches in front of the boy and brushed his tears away with his thumb. "Come on, why the waterworks?"

Jason looked up at him, all green eyes, terror and remorse stricken. "I want to go home," he sobbed.

Of course, Sean thought, this had all been too much for him. "Oh now, c'mon, sport. We're going to have an adventure. This'll be fun. Do you know where we're going, Jason?"

The boy bit his lower lip and shook his head.

"I thought we'd head on to Chicago. It's a big, beautiful city, Jason...on a lake as big as the ocean. There are skyscrapers there, some of them the biggest in the world. We'll go up to the top, you and me, and can look down on the whole world. Now, doesn't that sound like fun?"

"It would be more fun if Mommy was there."

"Well...who knows, Jason? Maybe in a little while, she'll come out and see us." Sean pictured the reunion, with a tearful Shelley clutching her son and Sean being led away in handcuffs. But if he could just get Jason there, get a sort of life set up for them, he knew Jason would eventually be all right. Sure, he'd miss his mother, but wouldn't that eventually fade?

Who are you trying to kid?

Sean took Jason's hand. In a monotone, he said, "Come on, the food's getting cold, and we have to get moving if we're going to make it to Chicago before it gets dark. I want you to see that Lake Michigan. Boy, it's something."

Jason went with his father. His steps were slow, and he was sniffling, trying to rein in his tears.

He will hate me, Sean thought, *and I will be more completely shut out of his life than any court order could ever hope to do.*

Back in the car, Sean briefly considered gassing up and heading back to Pennsylvania. He could drop Jason off in Estelle's block and hurry away to continue his life as a fugitive, on the lam for loving his son too much.

He closed his eyes and put his head on the steering wheel. After a moment, he started the engine.

Chicago, here we come.

God help me.

Chapter Thirty

He had to get rid of the body. Paul had just hung up the phone, damning Shelley, her voice watery and hopeful, saying the doctors had told her it would be all right for her to come home the following day. She had interrupted the Pirates game he was watching and now had ruined any hopes of returning to it with any concentration.

"I'm coming home tomorrow, honey. Isn't that great news?"

And Paul had lied, saying he couldn't wait to see her. "And once you're here, sweets, we can find Jason. Be a family again."

The whisper of her breath came through the phone, quivering, and he knew she was sobbing. Christ, he had thought, won't this be great? And the image of the young girl in the freezer, her eyes clouded over by blue-white frost, rose up to torment him.

Paul lit a cigarette and went out to the front porch, where he could smoke and pace, pace and smoke, and try to figure out what he should do with the body. Sure, the solution was simple enough, four words really: Get rid of it. But how? But how?

It would have to be done in the morning, early, early morning, when there was just enough light to see but too little for the rest of the world to be roused.

"Shit," he whispered to himself. There was so much to do. Clean the place up, get rid of a body, try to make himself ready to fuck Shelley again...somehow none of the above had any appeal for him.

But the weariness, along with the six beers he had consumed, washed over him, and he wanted nothing more than to collapse into bed and wait until tomorrow to face his problems. They sure as hell would be there another day.

Paul trudged up the stairs, accompanied by the low grumble of thunder outside. "Go on and fuckin' rain," he whispered. "Make it easier to dig."

Paul stripped out of his clothes and flung himself across the sheets, warm and dirty, stained with come and sweat, crunchy with crumbs, and fell asleep.

*

Harriet Schmidbauer was old. Beyond senior citizens' groups, beyond AARP, at ninety-two Harriet found it hard to remember what she'd even looked like with dark hair, a frame that wasn't bent and withered, and skin that wasn't contracted into too many wrinkles to count.

But she bore her ninety-two years with pride. While almost everyone her age was dead, the very few remaining drooling in nursing homes and trying to remember who their children and grandchildren were, Harriet was still fit—other than the occasional bouts of arthritis in her hands that made opening the goddamn aspirin bottle so difficult—and able to get around just fine. There were no problems with her memory either. She could remember what she had for breakfast as well as her wedding day, now almost seventy years past.

But Harriet's greatest pride was her eyesight. Not many women could claim to have perfect vision at her age. Not many men either. Most of the people her age wore bifocal lenses so thick they weighed down their faces.

And Harriet was most thankful for this strange and almost unheard of gift from her Lord, Jesus Christ. She thanked him each and every Sunday at Mass, which she attended faithfully at St. Aloysius in downtown Summitville. She was grateful because it allowed her to continue with her passion: bird watching. Harriet had a notebook filled with sightings over the years, cardinals, finches, sparrows, hummingbirds, mockingbirds, doves, and various unusual species Harriet particularly prided herself on.

Now, as she tramped through the woods overlooking the Ohio River and the banks of West Virginia on the other side, Harriet was wondering if she shouldn't just give up for the day.

It was hot. The humidity pressed in close, like another presence in the woods with her. Insects buzzed, loud enough to be annoying. Harriet tried to ignore them. But she was tired and had only seen two blue jays that morning, hardly worth her effort. At home a pitcher of freshly squeezed lemonade waited for her, along with the big corduroy recliner her husband had once so loved.

Harriet started to make her way toward the dirt road that would bring her down the side of the hill and to her car, an ancient Buick.

As she began to see the dusty ribbon of brown that cut through the greenery, Harriet paused. The sound of a motor coming up the hill caused her to clutch her binoculars and wonder what was going on. The old road was deep and rutted, filled with holes and precipitous drop-offs on one side. It was seldom used for anything other than foot traffic.

Whoever was trying to maneuver their vehicle up the hill at the moment had to be out of their mind. *It has to be kids*, Harriet thought; no one else would be stupid enough to attempt that hill in anything other than a Jeep. Harriet moved down the embankment a little more, moving a low-hanging walnut tree branch out of her way. She leaned back against the big, rutted bark of the tree as the bass of the engine grew louder.

Harriet didn't know why—perhaps it was simply the oddness of a pickup truck coming up the road, a thing Harriet had seldom laid eyes on—but the approaching truck gave her pause, made her want to wait and see what was going on. She leaned against the tree and tucked her field binoculars into the case hanging from her shoulder.

Across from Harriet was a crime. The whole side of the hill on the other side of the road dropped off suddenly and, if you stood at the right level, all you saw were trees at the other side of the valley. But once on the road, all one had to do was look down to see the charade some residents of Summitville had made of this beautiful woodland setting.

The other side of the hill, plunging rapidly downward toward a tiny, mud-brown creek, was covered with garbage.

White and black plastic bags, torn open by forest foragers, littered the side of the hill, along with their contents: cans, bottles, boxes, disposable diapers, and almost anything you could imagine. Harriet had even seen an old rusting refrigerator and a couple of old bicycles, abandoned to this undignified graveyard by their owners.

Harriet leaned back, making sure the walnut tree covered her as the vehicle making all that ruckus rounded a bend and came into view. A red pickup climbed the hill with effort, sending up clouds of dust as it went, ruining the peaceful solitude of the woods with its complaining engine. Harriet shook her head and thought it might be a good idea to just linger here for a moment longer, until the truck passed.

But the truck didn't pass. Harriet watched as it swung over to the side of the road, sitting dangerously on the edge of the ravine. The driver cut the engine and there was a moment of silence, filled almost immediately by the buzzing and chirping of insects, the cries and coos of birds, the knock of a woodpecker, and the rustling of the leaves in the tree tops. Harriet wished the breeze would filter down to her. She brushed a line of sweat from her hairline and wondered what these fool people were up to.

Probably dumping garbage, she thought, *further ruining the sanctuary I've come to for years.*

The thought infuriated the old woman. What was wrong with these people, anyway? Weren't the city garbage collectors enough for them? Or, if they lived outside city limits, were they too cheap to pay the few dollars it would take to have someone haul away their trash on a weekly basis? Good Lord, couldn't they see what they were doing to the woods? Didn't they care that they were spoiling it?

Apparently not, Harriet sniffed. In spite of the signs posted above this makeshift landfill, warning violators of a $500 fine for dumping, it was still used on a regular basis.

Harriet's blood was boiling. And this time she would not sit silently by. She had caught these folks red-handed, and she would do her best to see that they paid for violating nature this way. Harriet reached into the deep pocket of her smock and pulled out the little notebook and pen she kept for jotting down her bird sightings. She located a blank page and leaned around the tree to see if she could make out the license plate number.

It was a Pennsylvania plate. *Leave it to them to soil their own backyard!* Harriet thought, growing more and more angry at these thoughtless people. She jotted down the number, MHK 369, and looked again to make sure she had gotten it right.

She was so mad she was tempted to just go over there and give the guilty person or persons a good piece of her mind. And then she would report them. But that, she thought, would probably do no good, since whoever it was in the pickup would probably drive away without committing the crime, only to return later when no one was around.

So Harriet waited. She didn't have to wait long; the door swung open and a young man, muscular, potbellied, and grizzled, emerged. Harriet didn't recognize him but thought a strong man like this surely didn't need to stoop so low. The man had sandy hair and roughhewn features, putting her in mind of a young Charles Bronson.

The man went to the back of the truck and lowered the gate, then paused to scan the tree-choked hillside, hand to his forehead to shield his eyes from the sun. Harriet stood back, hiding herself behind the big walnut, praying she would be able to make her accusation stick. To be witnessed would ruin everything. And Harriet was on a mission.

The man sat down on the gate of the truck and lit a cigarette with trembling fingers. *How nice*, Harriet thought. *He's nervous. I wish his conscience extended to thinking first about what he was doing.*

But Harriet could well imagine the stuffed-full white plastic bags and their hateful contents: chicken bones and TV dinner boxes, empty shampoo bottles, and spent toothpaste tubes.

When the man moved into her sight again, Harriet gasped and had to grab the tree for support. The man was carrying the body of a young woman.

"Oh God," Harriet whispered to herself, shrinking against the bark of the tree. The young woman had long dark hair, stiff; an unbearable burden. But the bulge in the man's arms gave testimony to the fact that he was strong enough to bear the load.

Harriet began to tremble. What if he spotted her? What if her yellow smock stood out against the foliage? *Leave no witnesses.* The phrase ran chillingly through Harriet's mind as her stomach churned.

But it didn't seem as if he had seen her. She was sure his gaze had never lit on her.

But that didn't mean it couldn't. Harriet squatted down in the brush, positioning as much of herself behind the tree as she could.

She couldn't see much, but could see enough to know what the man was doing, wading down the side of the hill, having trouble because of his terrible burden.

Once the man was over the hill, Harriet could no longer see him, and it seemed as if she was alone in the woods once more. Should she make a break for it while they were occupied?

Even though Harriet prided herself on her good health and her stamina, she knew if she were spotted, there would be no way an old woman like herself could get away from this man. And if he had killed the girl he carried into the woods, what would he do to her?

Harriet's heart raced. It was hard to resist the urge to slide down the rest of the hill, hop onto the road, and run for the safety of her car. She knew that would be the stupidest thing she could do, yet she wanted to so badly.

Harriet held herself in check, listening.

It didn't take long. After about ten minutes, but what seemed more like hours, Harriet spied the man coming back. His face was smeared with dirt, and his hands were filthy.

Harriet scrunched down more, trying to disappear into herself.

She watched, and began to breathe again, once he got back in the truck.

Harriet waited for a long time after the thrum of the engine was nothing more than a memory before coming out of her hiding place. What if he had turned around at the top of the hill, up by the park, and was coming back down the hill just as she was making her way down it? Would he run her down? Or would he force her inside and take her somewhere else and kill her, so that the sight of a run-over old woman in the road would not arouse suspicion about what might lie in the garbage dump?

Harriet allowed herself a quick glance over the side of the hill and saw nothing more than the usual mess she saw every time she made her way up here to do her birding.

And then her eye caught on something down near the creek. No one else would have noticed the pile of trash, looking almost neat in the sunlight. No one else without her knowledge, that is. Harriet leaned over, peering, and gasped when she saw some hair sticking out from under the garbage.

And Harriet, in spite of her stiff, brittle bones, began to gallop down the hill, a scream suppressed in her throat.

He would not get away with this.

*

Paul sat exhausted in the mess of the living room. Christ, if someone had told him what he'd be up to this morning, he would never have believed it. Although—and this was the part of the whole thing that chilled him—in spite of the fan blowing right on him, he had a weird sense while he was burying the body in the trash dump at the side of the hill. There was a word for the feeling, and he knew if he just didn't try so hard to grasp at the odd word, it would come to him. What was it? *Déjà vu*...that was it. He didn't know what the French words meant literally but knew it meant a feeling that you'd done something before. And that was just how he felt. The whole bizarre scene had the ring of familiarity to it. He didn't know how that could be. He had never done anything like that before. He sure as fuck would have remembered if he had tried to hide a body, one he had presumably killed. But the feeling nagged at him, even now, right down to a memory of dirt beneath his fingernails, unexplained dirt.

He closed his eyes, wishing he could have a few beers, smoke a joint. They would bring him oblivion, deliverance from this awful gift of false memory. But he couldn't do those things. There was much to be done before Shelley's return home. Normally he would have never considered lifting even one finger to do housework, but at least this one time, he had to break down and do it. Shelley would be in no condition to clean, at least not for a few days, and he couldn't leave the place looking as it did... a bachelor pad from hell. He grinned, but there was little mirth in it.

What would happen when someone finally stumbled upon the body, as they were sure to do? Paul was pretty damn sure he wouldn't be connected to it. And since he hadn't really buried the body, he knew it wouldn't be long before it was discovered, making even more news for the little town for which a Fourth of July parade was the biggest local news story of the summer.

He thought it odd, again, that he had seen nothing in the news about the disappearance of the girl. All the time she chilled in the freezer, there hadn't been one word about her.

He assumed whoever would have an interest in her disappearance would have just written her off as a runaway. The flashes of memory he had from that night told Paul that the girl who had come home with him was pretty wild, no stranger to sex and alcohol. Girls like that, he supposed, turned up missing all the time.

And got what was coming to them. Paul felt no guilt, save for the fear of what could happen to him should he be tied to her disappearance in some way. What if someone had seen her get in his clearly recognizable pickup truck? What if, and this gave him a shiver, there was a way to trace the tire treads he might have left up by the makeshift dump? But Paul was pretty sure the dry, dusty August weather would be his ally, blowing away evidence of his presence at her impromptu burial. And, well, if anyone had seen her get into the pickup, they had to have been pretty well concealed. He knew there were seldom people on the road from which he had plucked her.

Plucked her, fucked her...now I gotta kill you, a little singsong rhyme went through his mind, and Paul stood on uncertain, weary legs to begin the task of cleaning up.

At least Jason wouldn't be around to mess things up again. There were a few things to be thankful for. And "mess things up" had layers of meaning Paul didn't even want to think about.

He stooped to pick up a kiddie porn magazine. *Step one.*

Chapter Thirty-One

Harriet Schmidbauer didn't know what to do. The pleasant chill of her apartment in the retirement building she had wound up in and the show on Discovery about native birdlife in Florida made her so much just want to forget what she had seen on the hillside earlier that morning. Just forget it all, be like people were nowadays and just look the other way, let someone else deal with it. What if she called in her sighting and found, one night, this man she had seen, standing above her bed, out on parole and out for vengeance. The girl was dead already; going to the police with this information wouldn't help her a wit.

If she didn't do something, other young girls out there, with their whole lives before them, could turn up missing, could turn up dead.

And how would Harriet feel then? Grudgingly, as she took a sip of her iced tea, she knew she could never just let this rest. If another girl died, she would feel at least partly responsible. And that was a responsibility she didn't think she would be able to deal with.

So Harriet set her glass down on the doily on the end table and wandered out to the kitchen. She sat down on the little step stool near her wall phone and picked it up.

Should she call 911? This wasn't exactly an emergency. She grabbed the slim volume that contained the phone numbers for Summitville and a couple of other little burgs gathered along the Ohio River and looked inside the front cover. There, along with an ambulance company and the fire department, was the number for the Summitville Police Department.

Without giving herself time to reconsider or lose her nerve, she punched in the number. As she listened to the ringing, she wished, more than anything, that it had been someone dumping garbage instead of a body. Funny how one could be so zealous over a minor crime and so reluctant to report a major one. "Summitville Police. May I help you?"

Harriet took a breath and prayed she was doing the right thing.

*

Hugh Allen had never felt more frustrated in his entire career. Everything was spinning out of control. A rape, a disappearance, and a kidnapping...all in the space of a few weeks, and he had nothing, nothing to go on. Combine his whole ten-year career here in Summitville, and the crimes did not add up to what had gone on this summer. What had he done to deserve this? He had thought the job would be a piece of cake.

There had been pressure, subtle at first and then not so subtle, for him to do something, to make an arrest. The citizenry was getting restless. A joke was starting, here and in neighboring towns, one where the punch line was giving Summitville the moniker "Crime Capital of the United States." It looked bad for the little town, so many "unsolved mysteries." Hugh knew there was talk of bringing someone else in, since he obviously wasn't very effective at getting his job done. The chief, a tough, steel-haired woman named Marion Hartley, had told him that things were getting too big for him to handle, and perhaps it was time to call in extra reinforcements. "We could put together one of those task forces, a countywide thing, and see how that would go."

Hugh, a man for whom pride was in no short supply, had pleaded for another week. But another week had almost gone by, and he was still as clueless as the rest of the people in town. Junior Parsons had looked so good; why couldn't that have worked out? And Sean Dawes, by his disappearing act with his son, had raised suspicions all over the place about his part in Jason's rape, not that they weren't there to begin with.

Intuition was something a detective had to have, and intuition told him Sean Dawes was not responsible. And Hugh thought he knew why. His own fantasies, when he dared to let them seep out, cautiously, because they might overwhelm, were never about little boys. They were about hairy-chested men, the kind of men his mother had once called burly.

What happened to Jason Dawes had been the work of someone who had a thing for kids, and not even necessarily male kids. It had crossed his mind that the same person was responsible for all the crimes in Summitville that summer. And, if that were the case, there were going to be more.

Almost on cue with that thought, Hugh's phone rang. He prayed the call would not be from his girlfriend, Mary Alice, but from someone who wanted to provide a good, solid lead.

"Allen here." Jean Kelly, the woman who worked the switchboard, briefed him about the call.

"Older woman says she saw a body dump. Decomp by the park."

Hugh rolled his eyes. "Shit," he whispered just before Jean put the woman through.

"Can I help you, ma'am?"

"Um, I saw something this morning I think you should know about."

"Can I ask to whom I'm speaking, ma'am?"

"Do I have to tell you?"

"No, but it would help if you would cooperate fully. Besides," Hugh said, "we have a very sophisticated Caller ID system here. After I hang up, it'll only take a second to find out who you are."

The woman sighed. "Oh dear." There was a pause. "Harriet Schmidbauer, over on Ravine Street, Officer."

"Thank you, Ms. Schmidbauer. Now you were saying?" Hugh pulled a pad and pen in front of him.

"It was up by the park, early this morning. You know the dirt access road that leads up there?"

"I sure do." Hugh had spent countless summers taking that very same road to the park's swimming pool as a boy.

"Well, you know how people dump garbage on the side of the road?"

Hugh bit his lip, resisting the urge to hurry the old woman along. "Uh-huh."

"This morning I was out in the woods above the hill. I like to go up there and bird watch—"

"And what did you see, ma'am?"

"I saw a man pull up in a pickup truck and take the body of a girl from the back." Harriet hesitated. "I'm positive she was dead."

"I'm sorry you had to see that, ma'am. Were you able to get a license plate number?"

"I sure was, Officer."

Hugh closed his eyes. Could this be it? Could this be it?

Chapter Thirty-Two

It was hard getting up the stairs. But before she even gave her husband much of a greeting, before she even looked to see what kind of condition her house was in, she had to go up there. She didn't know why; there was just an irresistible pull toward the stairs and then...here.

Shelley paused at the entrance to Jason's room. The door was closed and her hand rested on the doorknob. Two emotions warred within her. One telling, insisting, that she go on in. And the other, perhaps more sensible, saying to leave the door closed, that the emptiness that lay inside would only cause her more anguish.

She opened the door...and stood frozen at the threshold to the room. She did not dare let her eyes focus for a moment, did not dare take in the details. She knew already how much this would hurt.

She looked anyway. There was Jason's twin bed, made up neatly with the navy blue bedspread with its constellation of stars and planets. "Mom! Mom! They've got this really cool bedspread with our solar system on it. Can I have it? Please?" Shelley moved quickly across the room and ran her hand over the bedspread's quilted surface, hoping more than anything to feel a trace of warmth there, knowing it was impossible but wanting it just the same. She dropped to her knees and buried her face near the pillow, praying some essence of Jason would be left there, some simple smell. But there was nothing. Not even a trace of sweat. The bedspread smelled of nothing more than cotton and polyester. Shelley stayed like that for a moment, on her knees, head down on the bed, resting, fingers moving lightly over the surface. How many nights had she sat here, the bedspread beneath her, as she read Jason a bedtime story; images of clean-smelling hair, pajamas, and just-brushed teeth ran through her mind.

Shelley stood. She felt almost dizzy, as if her legs would, at any moment, refuse to support her. Her gaze roamed about the room, taking in the bookcase, made of knotty pine, that she had, once upon a time, put together and finished with a simple coat of satin polyurethane. All Jason's favorite books lined its shelves, books by Richard Scarry, Dr. Seuss, E.B. White, and Maurice Sendak. There was the Golden Book of the planets. There were several books having something to do with *Star Trek*, a couple of spin-offs of *Star Wars*. Her collection of Hans Christian Andersen fairy tales. *The Poky Little Puppy*. Shelley ran her fingers over the spines, wondering if Jason would ever take them from the shelves again. "Mommy, I want to hear this one tonight," the book held in little outstretched hands, urging her.

Oh God, why had she sometimes refused him? Why had she sometimes just been too tired, wanting only to have a few minutes to herself, putting him off with a stern, "Get to bed, Jason. You don't need to hear a story every night." Now she would read to him, and read, and read, and read...

If only she had the chance.

The walls were covered with pennants: Pittsburgh Steelers, the Pirates, the Chicago Bulls. Framed posters of Spock, Darth Vader, laser-dealing starships. There was his toy box, shut. She opened it and looked down on X-Men action figures, Hot Wheels cars, G.I. Joes, and Tonka trucks. A pile of stuffed animals, loved more than the rest but not now admitted to, stood unloved, like orphans, between the toy box and the walls.

Shelley wandered back to the bed, lifting up a little wool sock monkey as she went. She cradled the monkey in her lap, lowered her head, and wept. *Oh, Jason, will I ever see you again?*

*

Paul had waited long enough. He stood in the kitchen, shocked by how Shelley ignored him when she came through the door. Estelle had brought her, discreetly letting her out near the back porch and then driving away, probably so as not to intrude on the happy couple's reunion.

Bullshit. Paul cracked open another beer, sat down at the table, and lit a Marlboro. He would have thought she would have been happy to see him, overjoyed to see the fruit of all his hard work: house neat as a pin, ready to pass a white glove test.

Women. They're the first to complain when you do something wrong and the last to notice when you do something right. It wasn't fair. His mother had always been there for his father. The old man had had to do little to keep her in line. And when he did have to do something, Mom would always understand, do what was required of her, realize that her missing something or taking too long to accomplish a task would get her punishment. She knew she deserved it and didn't complain.

Paul had thought Shelley would be the same when he married her. She had been beautiful when they met... just a little thing, with reddish brown hair pulled into a ponytail, freckles across the bridge of her nose, standing all of five foot two. Paul had thought *That's for me* and had gone right after her, pursuing her with a zeal he had never invested in anything before.

Of course, he had thought she was much younger. When he learned, during the course of their first evening together at the Oasis, a little bar down on Vine Street, that Shelley was divorced and had a kid, he was stunned.

But her age, which was about fifteen years older than he would have guessed, did little to dampen his enthusiasm for her. It wasn't the age that counted, it was how old she looked.

From the moment he had laid eyes on her, learning of her love of country music, Patsy Cline especially, and of her secret dream to one day sing as her idol did, Paul was hooked. He did whatever it took to make Shelley love him. He sent flowers, made lots of calls just to see how she was doing, took her to the best restaurants, and made passionate love to her. How could a girl say no?

But after they were married, everything changed. Was it his fault that courtship and marriage were two different things? Once he had her, he didn't need to constantly demonstrate his affection. She should have known, from the fact that he married her and took in her little boy to raise as his own, that he loved her.

It was her turn to show her love for him. And she could do that by taking care of him.

Was that asking too much?

And now, was it asking too much for her to show a little happiness at being home with him? To show a little gratitude for all the work he had done getting the house ready for her arrival? Paul didn't think so.

He cracked open another beer and downed it in two or three guzzles. Cracked open another.

Sure, he understood she was sad about Jason. But there was someone else in this house she was supposed to love as well. Didn't having a husband mean something too? Paul wished he could just go back and undo what had happened with Jason, but that wasn't possible. Life moves on. Jason would be found again, and then the faggot would go to jail. That ought to cheer her up. And if Jason wasn't found, well, hell, he was perfectly capable of making another baby with her.

In fact, he thought, standing on unsteady legs, maybe that's what I should propose to her right now.

*

She heard the creak of the stairs. Paul. Shelley swallowed hard, realizing a simple fact. She didn't love this man anymore. She wondered if she ever had.

And now he was coming up the stairs. Shelley sat up straight, brushing the tears away. He stood in the threshold, glaring at her. And all at once, a cold fear gripped her. It was as if Paul was someone she didn't know. The cold look in his eyes returned no love; there was only menace in his gaze.

Shelley stood but did not walk near him. "The doctor says I need to get a lot of rest, and this trip home took everything out of me," she announced. "If you don't mind, I think I will lay down for a bit." Shelley brushed by him, not liking the feel of him against her back, the hot breath soured by beer and cigarettes.

Who was this man?

She heard him silently padding down the hallway behind her, toward their bedroom. Suddenly Shelley longed for her old hospital room, longed for the security she felt there.

Shelley entered the bedroom and looked around. The bed was neatly made up, but a layer of dust clung to the wood surfaces. She pulled the comforter and sheets back, folding both over the footboard. Paul's eyes were on her the whole time, not saying anything. She turned and gave him a feeble grin. "Let me get a little rest, and then maybe I can fix us something to eat. Okay?"

Paul said nothing. His arms were folded across his chest as he leaned against the doorframe.

Shelley took off the white shorts and red-and-green floral print blouse she had worn home from the hospital.

It felt as if she was undressing in front of a stranger.

She dropped her panties and bra, got her nightgown from its hook on the back of the door, pulled it over her head, and lay down. She reached forward to pull the sheet up over herself.

Paul caught her hand. She looked up at him, gaze questioning, and was surprised to find she was trembling. There was something horrible in his eyes: something predatory, something black.

Paul stopped her when the sheet was up to her thighs.

"What are you doing?" Shelley whispered, fear stealing her breath.

Paul continued to grin, but there was nothing happy in that smile...no kindness or warmth. The smile looked cruel.

"It's been a long time, Shel. Don't you have something you want to give me?"

At first she didn't understand. The very thought was too outrageous to even consider that he might be serious. And then, with a sickening certainty, she knew he was. She tried to laugh, but all that escaped from her was a hysterical little hiccup. Why were words failing her now? Why was her heart thudding in her chest? Why did she feel little pinpricks of electricity coursing through her, increasing the trembling in her limbs? "Honey," she whispered, "I'm not quite ready for that yet."

"It was your head you bumped," Paul said dully. "Not your cunt."

Shelley stared at him, wide-eyed, and all at once a dream rushed back to her, the one she'd had the morning after Jason's disappearance. She shook her head, not believing this was happening, trying to convince herself she was mistaken. Paul wasn't that heartless.

He pulled her toward him. She would not take her eyes from him, searching for something human in the pools of green flecked with yellow, something she had once called love. Love, she knew, or at least thought she had, would not play out this scenario. There was a simple pleading in her gaze.

"Paul," she whimpered, finding suddenly there wasn't much breath to put behind her words. "Paul, please."

He pushed her back on the bed, and she felt vulnerable, exposed as she sat down hard on the mattress, which squeaked. She continued to stare up at him, her eyes a silent plea.

He used his body to cover hers, to push her back, prone, on the crisp white sheets. He bunched up her nightgown and pushed it up. She wanted to scream, wanted to tell him, with rage and certainty, that she was not ready for this. But her tongue held fast, an unmoving conspirator in this dance of horror.

He kissed her, lips moving like slugs across hers. Shelley tasted bile at the back of her throat. She was too weak to fight. She clamped her legs together and feebly placed her hands against his chest. "No" came out, an almost silent exhalation.

His hand moved down between her thighs, pushing them apart. She wished for a moment there was at least some sort of physical pleasure in this, if nothing more. At least that way, it wouldn't hurt so much.

But she knew he wouldn't wait. Knew he would take and take and take.

He pushed her legs apart and slid between them. She could feel his need pressing against her dry opening, and she attempted to move her hips backward, up the sheets, but there was no movement under the thick weight of him. He pressed into her, forcefully at first, then when no entry was made, savagely.

Shelley gasped as he entered her, the hot pinpricks of pain shooting, like dark tendrils, throughout her being.

He was in her, and it seemed as if all the air in the room left with his savage thrust. She couldn't breathe, and the pain was causing swarms of silver light to swim before her eyes. She clutched his back as he pressed deeper, feeling as if she would be rent in two. Her nails dug into the iron muscles of his back, and she closed her eyes, turning her head into the pillow beneath her, praying that this pain would not last long. If it did, she wasn't sure she could manage to stay alive through it.

He thrust, the movements causing a small amount of lubrication to begin, and the pain seemed to lessen, but not much. She brought her thighs up, cooperating and damning herself for it, her legs gripping his bulk as he rode into her. She looked up at him, attempting eye contact, but Paul had gone somewhere else. There was a deadness to his eyes, as if his soul had departed and he had become something animal. Fucking.

Tears pooled in her eyes, born of pain and outrage, trickling down to tickle her ears and dampen the pillowcase below. She grunted along with him as he rode her, bucking and slamming into her. She wondered if the damp she felt down there was lubrication or blood.

And then he stiffened and she swore, through her dryness, she could feel the spastic throbbing of his cock as he came.

She closed her eyes as he rolled off her. He slapped her thigh.

"Take a little nap," he said. "And then we can see you make good on that promise of something to eat."

She watched his figure depart from the bedroom, disbelieving.

Shelley lay there for a while, the ache between her legs dull and throbbing, pulsing into screaming white heat when she moved. She felt cold in spite of the sheen of sweat that covered her body. Nausea roiled in her gut. She remembered one of the nurses telling her how patients usually began a quicker recovery once they got home, and she almost laughed at the bitterness and irony of the comment. With treatment like this, she would be back in the hospital in no time, if she wasn't dead.

Staring, lying on her side, out the pale blue, priscilla curtain-framed window at the dull sun reflecting off the Adams's roof next door and the top of a black walnut tree in the backyard, Shelley was seized with a pain more intense than any of the cramps she was experiencing. A sudden realization hit her all at once and it made her gag and try to hold back the bile. The thought that distressed her began *If Paul could rape me...* Shelley closed her eyes, trying to breathe. It seemed the cream-colored walls were closing in, sucking in air, becoming smaller as she resisted the completion of the thought... *If Paul could rape me, then maybe he could have raped Jason.*

She thought of how Paul had behaved after Jason was found in the woods, how there was almost a sense of disappointment in him. At the time she attributed this feeling to her own belief that Paul had always really wanted it to be just the two of them, and that if a child should intrude on their marriage, it should be from his own seed and not that of the "faggot." It was too farfetched to believe this man of men could do something like that to a little boy. But the primal hunger, the craziness even, in his eyes as he thrust above her just moments ago, told another tale.

Could he have done it? Were there signs she should have seen?

Shelley's nauseated revelations were interrupted by a loud pounding at the door downstairs, which came almost too quickly, almost simultaneously with the sound of cars pulling up in the gravel driveway below her. She took a deep breath, swung her legs over the side of the bed, and hobbled to the window. She looked down on the driveway and saw two police cars, blue lights whirling, in the driveway below.

What was going on now? The pounding sounded again, more insistent. Then a deep voice cried, "Open up! Police!" Shelley shivered and went to the back of the bedroom door, where her pink quilted bathrobe hung. She slid into it and started carefully down the stairs, each footstep making her wince. The pounding sounded again. "Open up or we break down the door."

Where was Paul? Why hadn't he answered the door?

Somehow, she managed to get downstairs and to the back door. "I'm coming! I'm coming!" she shouted to quiet the pounding, which had become continuous.

She showed herself in the locked screen door, peering out with confusion at the three uniformed officers and Hugh Allen, standing stoic on her back porch.

She put a hand on the latch that unlocked the door and asked, "What is it?"

Detective Allen looked for a moment as if he weren't sure what to do. He looked first at Shelley, and she knew what he saw—a pale woman, almost a ghost, too thin with watery red eyes, radiating pain and fatigue. Then his gaze moved to the yard, as if disbelieving, as if he had seen a ghost. His gaze moved back to her, and he seemed to compose himself. Whatever was going on, Shelley thought, it was monumental. She had never seen a man look as nervous as Detective Allen.

"We need to speak to your husband, Mrs. Thompson. Could you call him? We know he's in there; we've been watching the house."

"You've been watching... What's going on?" Mingled with Shelley's confusion, there was a growing sense of elation, almost joy.

And she couldn't quite put her finger on why. Perhaps the idea of Paul being punished brought a sense of happiness to her. The absurd thought rose up that these men were here to arrest her husband for raping her. As if, like God, they were watching over and protecting her. But neither God nor the police had offered much evidence of watching over her lately.

Then she thought of Jason and the thought that had occurred to her only minutes ago. Had someone else made the connection? Had they found some sort of proof linking Paul to what had happened to her son?

"Have you found Jason?" Shelley blurted out.

Her disappointment was swift as the detective's face clouded over with confusion. "No. Could you get your husband out here?"

It was then Shelley noticed the uniformed officers had their guns drawn. A chill went through her.

She leaned back and called, "Paul? Paul, could you come out here? Someone wants to speak to you."

The only response to her watery cry was silence. She leaned back farther, looking through the kitchen and into the dining room, expecting to see her husband.

But it appeared the house was empty.

"He was just here…" she said and then turned. She felt Detective Allen's hand on her shoulder.

"Step aside, please."

She watched, mute, stunned, as Detective Allen let the two officers, with their guns drawn, precede him.

"Mr. Thompson, please don't make this difficult. We have a warrant for your arrest. There are officers stationed at the front door. Please come out."

Shelley moved to the kitchen table, on legs she was sure would give out at any moment. She sat down hard on one of the maple chairs and stared at the surface of the table, too weak to even ask why they wanted to arrest her husband. When had her life turned upside down? Why had things gone from low-drone mediocre to high melodrama?

She could hear them moving through the house, doors squeaking open, floorboards creaking, calling for Paul. She hoped they would find him, lead him away in handcuffs, and that she would never have to see him again. She was surprised at her hunger for retribution.

She hoped he would get the death sentence, for whatever it was they were here for.

She closed her eyes, the hatred and rage inside her boiling, but her body and voice too weak to use as tools of their expression.

Detective Allen was first to return to the kitchen. He looked at her, eyes flaring with accusation and something else... anger perhaps. "All right," he said sharply. "Where is he?"

Shelley lifted her head slowly to stare back at him. "I don't know. He was just here."

"Is there any other way out of the house, other than the front and the back door?"

Shelley shook her head. "No, no, I'm sure... Wait a minute." She thought of the basement, and the glass-paned door down there. The door led to a flight of stairs that went up and into the backyard. She swallowed hard, already feeling as if she was playing a part in whatever was going on. "There's the basement," she said. "The basement has a door that goes up and into the backyard."

Allen looked to his men, two guys not much older than boys, both with dark complexions and expectant brown eyes. "Well, let's go!" he barked.

And then they were gone once more from the kitchen. Shelley stood. The room seemed to move slightly, tilting like a boat riding the crest of a wave, then returned to normal. It hurt to walk, but she began to follow the sound of the men, the feet thundering down the rickety staircase to the basement.

She made her way down, sidestepping to lessen the pain, and saw them gathered at the rear of the basement, where the chest freezer and her washer and dryer were. Allen had his head on the doorframe, and she caught a glimpse of the two officers heading up the stairs.

The door stood open.

"Damn," Allen whispered over and over again.

"Damn, damn, damn."

Chapter Thirty-Three

Paul ran down the back alley, feeling as if vicious dogs, Rottweilers or Dobies, maybe, were snapping at his heels. He could almost feel their fetid, imaginary breath on his calves. He was stunned at the speed and agility with which he moved, stunned that he was able to run like this, after so many years of two to three packs of cigarettes a day and all the pot smoke he had inhaled. But he continued to move, not slowing to consider from where this curious gift of speed had come.

Because he knew that speed and movement, his heels hitting the brick pavement of the alley hard, springing off on his toes, were the only ways he could save himself. He supposed adrenaline had a lot to do with it; he could practically feel the stuff pumping through his veins, electric, like a drug.

He pumped his elbows, felt the sweat slicking his face, the air going raggedly in and out of his mouth to fill his lungs—not enough, never enough, but adequate to keep him in flight. A painful stitch had begun in his side and he had to ignore it, along with the air that seemed to disappear more with each step he took, each leap he made.

But this was about survival. This was life and death, and it didn't get any more serious than this.

He had been sitting at the kitchen table when the cars rushed up the driveway, causing the gravel to crunch and ping against the side of the house, sending up a cloud of gray dust. Immediately the terror ran through him, almost simultaneously with the realization that these sounds were accompanied by flashing blue lights.

It was almost as if he didn't need to think. He knew why the police were here. It wasn't because they had found Jason. He knew, just knew, they had found the body of the girl...perhaps someone had seen him. He could have sworn he had felt observed when he dumped her body among the garbage on the hillside. But Paul was never one who was big on feelings...until now.

Call it what you want. Paul knew they were here to take him away. Something inside, something smarter and more calculating than he was in everyday life, took over. Before the car doors slammed, he was on his feet, bolting for the basement. He knew the basement exit was his only hope for escape.

And he was right. He had wanted to scream when he threw open the door and pounded up the cement stairs. Wanted to scream in giddy terror and triumph as he emerged into the yard, barely passing that detective guy and a couple of uniforms.

He had wanted to leap into the air to avoid the cries of "Halt!" he was sure were coming, followed by the reports of revolvers and the smell of cordite hanging in the thick air.

But there were no cries, and now, as he ran along the alleys that turned and twisted toward the Ohio River, he wanted to laugh, if his lungs would have permitted it, at the sheer stupidity of the Summitville Police Force.

A quick turn and he was no longer running on the bucking surface of old bricks, but on dirt, his black Cons kicking up dust as he went. The river was ahead of him, its greenish-brown current twisting, and Paul wondered if he should just keep heading downhill, until he was at the river's edge. He could dive in the water, its cold embrace invigorating him and erasing the weariness that gripped him, threatened to undo him. He thought of the river's powerful—and unforgiving—currents and how many lives they had claimed throughout the years.

He twisted through the brambles and low-hanging tree limbs that lined the river's edge, a branch scratching his face and starting a warm freshet of blood at his cheek. He wiped angrily at it, swatted at the mosquitoes and gnats dive-bombing for the moisture in his eyes.

Without thinking, he sprung up in the air, almost losing his balance among the pebble-choked damp shore, and dove in. He knew he was stronger than any current.

In a second he was underwater and in a green-filtered world. He swam underwater for what seemed like a long time, wondering how his lungs were managing to achieve this feat. He swam along the bottom of the river, pausing to examine the discarded tires and rusting cans that lined the bottom. He felt as though he could stay in the muddy green water's embrace forever.

Yet he broke to the surface and turned immediately to look along the shoreline, where the River Road passed, expecting to see the blue-and-white police cars heading downhill, toward the river, nose-diving as they sped over the railroad tracks, but there was nothing save for an orange Mustang, circa 1964, that he would have once coveted.

He turned in the water and began swimming, long hard strokes that were leaving him breathless, churning and fighting the current. The hills of West Virginia, on the other side, looked miles and miles away. The sky had an odd, reddish tinge to it that Paul thought he had never seen before. The world was bizarrely still. The hills were silhouettes, looking like beasts waiting for him on the shore.

And yet he swam toward them, thinking of nothing but his goal.

And then what? And then what? He sunk below the surface once more, yearning to feel that cool green embrace again...

Chapter Thirty-Four

Shelley stood in the basement after they had gone, feeling as if some sort of whirlwind, a tornado perhaps, had blown through the house. She felt drained, as if she were the one the police were looking for, as if she were the one who suddenly found herself on the lam.

She wandered back through the basement. There was the big gas heater, with its ducts lining the ceiling above. There was Paul's workbench...the curious place where he spent a lot of time but never seemed to get anything accomplished, nothing created or repaired.

She moved toward the bench, its carved wooden surface rising up before her, its neat rows of nuts, bolts, nails, and screws lined up orderly on the shelves above the work surface. Various tools, hammers, screwdrivers, pliers, and wrenches, hung from a pegboard on the wall. She ran her fingers lightly over the tools, thinking how Paul possessed all this stuff to show the world he was a man. He never used them.

Shelley sat on the stool at the workbench, wondering, not for the first time, what it was Paul spent time doing down here. Of course, she knew he smoked pot. It was a place to get away from Jason's prying, questioning eyes. Too many times she had seen Paul disappear when they were having some sort of family day, only to return red-eyed and grinning after a few minutes. Shelley hated those red-tinged eyes, hated the man who hid behind them. And she wondered then how long she had hated him. As if the hatred in her heart had been there for a long time, unacknowledged and unchecked, grown too familiar to even be recognizable.

But suddenly, even though it made a hypocrite of her, she thought of how the pot she knew had to be hidden down here somewhere might offer her an escape, soothing the pain, obliterating the trouble that had just occurred. Getting high, eating some cereal from the box, and falling asleep suddenly sounded very appealing.

Shelley was aware that Paul knew of her disapproval of his pot smoking with Jason in the house. Had she had the courage, she would have insisted he never smoke pot in the house, instead of forging with him a weak compromise to make certain Jason never knew of the drug's existence. Paul had been good about it. She had to give him credit for that. In the years since they had been married, she was sure, Jason never knew anything of his father's substance abuse. Shelley knew too that Paul would have found a good hiding place for the little plastic sandwich bags filled with resinous buds.

She stooped over, wrapping her ankles around the stool's bench for leverage, searching underneath the surface of the workbench for a hiding place. In the cool, musty-smelling shadows, she found nothing, no small pigeonholes where the pot might be stuffed, no hidden drawers or cubbyholes. Nothing underneath but the dark, unfinished surface of the wood, backed by the cinder block dividing wall. She let her fingers scramble over the surface like blind crabs, the tips sensitive for any imperfections in the smoothness of the wood's surface.

It didn't take her long to find the rectangular groove cut into the wood. She let her fingers rub around the small cut lines, roughly nine by twelve inches. And there, on the left side, was a small hole, just big enough to hook a finger inside. Shelley paused before lifting the wood, knowing what she would find: the pot and its accouterments: a pipe, a one hitter, a packet of EZ Wider rolling papers. All of this seemed so much the domain of her husband that she considered for a moment just leaving it alone. She was so conditioned by fear that it almost seemed like an act of monumental rebellion to actually invade his privacy this way.

But she knew her relationship with Paul had been turned upside down within the last half hour. Detective Allen had told her he was wanted for questioning in the murder of a teenage girl. The detective had, in fact, warned her that if she knew anything about her husband's whereabouts, she too could be arrested as an accomplice. But Shelley saw the warning as a relief, a small gift of salvation from the man who had made her life rotten, who had all but stolen her youth and certainly her interest in life.

So, she decided. There was nothing to stop her from going into his secret little-boy cubbyhole and stealing his marijuana. Hell, perhaps she would smoke it all, just to spite him.

If he ever returned.

The thought gave her a chill, even though the fact of it was something she realized she had wanted for a long, long time.

She hooked her forefinger into the opening and pulled up. The wood creaked and protested, almost seeming to pull back. Shelley yanked harder and the wood came up. She let her hand slide all the way under to grasp the panel more firmly and lifted it, laying it face down on the surface of the table.

What she saw inside made her forget all about getting high, although she wished more desperately for oblivion than ever. When she first saw the magazines, she thought for a moment, they were just skin mags, the kind of things most men looked at: *Playboy, Penthouse, Hustler*...but she knew she was deceiving herself, trying to turn away from the truth of the pornography buried beneath the little wooden panel.

The covers were enough for her. Some of them were very graphic in their depictions of adult/child sexuality. Enough to make her gag, to make her cast her eyes anywhere but there.

How could he have looked at these? The room was starting to spin, and Shelley grabbed on to the edge of the workbench to keep herself from toppling from the stool.

She had lived with this man for years, and she had no idea who he was. She was tempted to open the magazines, to see just how sick the man she had shared her life with was, but what was the point? The idea of just looking at such things made her sick, really sick, her stomach roiling and churning, the bile splashing up to burn the back of her throat.

With one hand, she swept the magazines to the floor and found herself screaming. She kicked them across the room, their pages fluttering in midair to land among the shadows of the basement.

"How could you?" she screamed. She went to one magazine, picked it up, and in a frenzy of loathing, ripped the magazine apart, with a strength she didn't know she had, especially now. She stomped on other magazines, twisting on top of them until the pages tore, until the perverted, grim pictures within twisted beyond recognition.

Finally, when every magazine had been destroyed so thoroughly that no one would ever again gaze lovingly on exploited children, Shelley collapsed, cross-legged, to the floor and wept.

The worst thing was not the secret Paul had kept from her, but what it confirmed.

A sick pounding had begun at her temples, and already tiny voices, shrill, were yammering at her with accusation and blame. *It was you! You were the one who brought him into this house! If it hadn't been for you, Jason would never have been raped! Everything would be different! It was you! You! You!*

Shelley placed her hands over her ears, as if the action would block out the voices, but it served only to isolate them. She rocked, humming, trying to drown out the accusations, which seemed almost distinct from her own mind, rocked and hummed, until at last the hum broke into a moan and finally ascended to a shriek.

Chapter Thirty-Five

Darkness and the steady thrum of tires on asphalt were Sean's only company. Jason had again lapsed into silence, but a different, less threatening void this time: that of slumber. Sean had turned the radio off miles ago and left the car windows open to the night air. For a while he let his mind drift, thinking of nothing. The engine had a soothing hum, the road stretched out straight and orderly before him, disappearing into blackness at the horizon. There were other cars to look at, license plates to check out.

But Jason's slumber was a troubled one. The little boy on the seat next to him, head dangling over the seat belt, was not a quiet sleeper. Not the way he used to be, Sean thought, the memory rising up to wring his heart, making him feel pain he didn't know was possible. Jason's sleep was punctuated with sighs, whimpers, and terrified moans.

Sean would reach over and gently lay a hand on the boy's shoulder at times when the nightmares must have been getting particularly bad. But it seemed that only made things worse. The boy would flinch, recoiling from his touch.

And so Sean kept his hands on the steering wheel, eyes focused on the road, and tried to blot out the occasional strangled cry coming from his son. Tried to ignore the pain. Tried to ebb the frustration he felt, the fear that there was nothing he could ever do to rescue his son.

Chicago loomed ahead. They had passed Gary, Indiana, with its smokestacks rising up, twinkling, in front of the dark void that was Lake Michigan. And then Sean followed signs that led him to a section of highway called the Skyway. Sean imagined a great road, thrust up on pillars, miles and miles above the ground that would lead him into the city, where cars would cruise on a parallel with the tops of skyscrapers.

He was getting tired. He didn't know where he'd go once he got into the city proper. Chicago was little more than an arbitrary choice: a place of some, but not great, distance away, big enough to lose oneself in, to begin a new life, one where there wouldn't be too much suspicion or interest in a single man living alone with a strangely quiet boy.

He drove on, wondering what was happening back in Summitville. If there was a search on for him, if the radio and television stations in Pittsburgh had picked up on things yet, if bulletins were being flashed.

He knew he needed to get hold of a newspaper. He was kidding himself if he didn't think word was out, and in a big way.

He wondered what his colleagues at the newspaper were thinking. Sean had always been quiet, responsible, and able to be counted upon for overtime, for doing more than just what was required of him.

At last he got a glimpse of the skyline, its towers rising up majestically against the black sky. The city seemed beautiful but cold. The traffic was heavier now, L train stations popping up between the lanes of the freeway, everything busy with people who belonged here, people who knew what they were doing.

How would he survive?

How would Jason survive?

Chapter Thirty-Six

Paul sat, gasping, on the West Virginia bank of the Ohio River, looking across at the tree-choked hills of Pennsylvania and the little town of Summitville, the town he had grown up in, clustered around the base of those hills.

Home had never seemed so far away. In fact, Summitville could never be his home again. He felt as if he'd already been cast out and banished. What was the word? Exiled?

It was dusk and milky purplish light was turning the trees to silhouettes. The light in the sky had an odd quality, almost unreal; it was a sunset Paul had never before laid eyes on. Near the horizon the light was pale lilac, but as it went up, the light vanished, becoming a black void. It was like the sky was gone and the world had ended. *Shit, stop thinkin' like that. It's stupid.*

Lights were coming on in windows, warm yellow pools that did nothing but make him feel excluded.

He longed for a cigarette. His life had just been turned upside down. He was wanted for murder. Already wheels were turning to trap him: manhunts, roadblocks, interstate bulletins, wanted posters, his handsome chiseled features at last enjoying a kind of fame. Paul grinned at that and grinned that even with all the shit coming down, he still had a lot of time to think about how much he needed a smoke and a beer.

His clothes were still damp, clinging and sticking to him, attracting the interest, with their rank fishy smell, of numerous flies, gnats, mosquitoes. Paul slapped angrily at the insects, but no amount of rage or punishment or even killing slowed the onslaught.

Paul wished the bugs were people. Then he could take care of them.

Something would have to be done soon, he thought, standing. He needed dry clothes, some food in his belly, and of course, tobacco and alcohol—how had he ever lived without them? He wandered through the brush and low trees lining the river bank, stopping to look out at the water, which was becoming deeper and blacker by the minute as the sun disappeared behind the hills, wondering if he would see a police boat cruising among the barges, a spotlight trained on the river bank. He shivered as he thought of the light picking him out and exposing him. An unpleasant association: a bug squirming as it was exposed when someone lifted a rock.

Well, he wasn't a damn bug, and the only thing on the fuckin' river was a couple of motorboats. He climbed up the embankment, pulling himself along by grabbing hold of trees and bushes, falling only once.

He looked back as a rock tumbled down the hill behind him to the shoreline below. And what he saw on the shore made him stifle a scream, made him shut his eyes and reopen them.

He thought he had seen his own body lying there, wet, bruised, and tangled up in river weeds.

He turned back to his ascent, chastising himself again for being so stupid. In the dark, probably all he had seen was a bag of garbage caught on some reeds.

That was all. Surely.

At the top he stood, knowing what he must look like: one of those damn bums that camped out by the river. Those guys had been around since he was a kid, when he and the other guys in the neighborhood would torment them, beat them up, wreck their pathetic little campsites.

It was funny. A scream.

And now, here he was, Paul Thompson, looking no different. Good thing it was dark.

He stood on a strip of grass about ten feet wide. Across from him was the town of Chesterton, West Virginia, a little town whose chief claim to fame was a couple of potteries that made dishes for hotels and restaurants. Paul had worked in one once, for a couple of years actually, where he was being trained to work as a caster, one of the guys who actually made the pottery, pouring liquid slip into molds that would one day become an urn, a pitcher, a decanter. But that wasn't for him.

No, the town's chief claim to fame, for Paul, was the fact that when he was a teenager, he could come over to Chesterton and drink, because the legal age there was only eighteen.

Seemed like such a long time ago. Carefree days. Getting high, listening to heavy metal, headbanger shit.

There were always lots of guys around, always someone to do something with.

Oh fuck it! he thought, kicking a can into the quiet street before him. *Fuck it, I don't have time to reminisce.* The houses lining the street he was on were grand ones. The ones with views of the river usually were, unless you were down low, where the neighborhoods were prone to flooding. Those houses were covered in tar paper, or dilapidated frame jobs in need of paint, the kind Paul had grown up in.

If I could get in one of those places, I could clean myself up. Make myself look presentable again. Surely there's a guy lives in one of them places who must be pretty close to the same size. Hell, I could even get myself disguised. Need to do that anyway.

Paul walked the length of the grassy strip opposite the houses, looking for some clue, some way to know that what lingered inside was what he needed. But curtains were drawn and the most he got a glimpse of was the blue flickering of a TV screen and once, a woman in T-shirt and shorts headed through the living room with a plate in her hands.

Paul felt invisible. The thought should be comforting, but it gave him a chill.

And then Paul froze. He hadn't heard anyone walking near him. In fact, the street was dead quiet. But suddenly, there was a flare of match in the darkness and then the orange glow of a cigarette. It made him gasp and almost cry out... He was that startled.

He couldn't see who was smoking a few feet away from him. But he could smell the cigarette, and it made his mouth water.

I'd kill for a smoke, he thought and laughed softly to himself, wondering how true the statement was. He stood still, thinking maybe the figure in the dark wouldn't see him if he didn't move.

How intense was the search for him? Had his picture already been broadcast on TV? Had it graced that evening's edition of that Summitville rag? Most important, would the person sharing this little strip of grass recognize him?

Paul thought it unlikely. After all, what had it been since the cops made their little call? An hour, maybe less. Hell, those Keystone Kops were so stupid, they were probably still searching his neighborhood.

In the still darkness, Paul's panic began to slow, the beating of his heart to ebb. He began to make out features of the man—yes, he could see that much—standing before him. Even though he was little more than a silhouette, it was obvious to Paul that the guy was roughly the same size. "Thank you, Jesus," Paul whispered.

And then the man was walking toward him. Paul sensed that he really was moving toward him and not just in his direction. He could feel the man's gaze focused on him, kind of like a cat stalking a mouse.

Paul sucked in some air, wondering why he was suddenly feeling this acute paranoia. There was something almost predatory about the way the man was moving toward him, slowly, the way one would approach a wild animal, no sudden movements.

Paul stood still. Maybe the guy did know. Maybe there was a reward and this dude's head was filled with thoughts of being a hero.

"What's goin' on, man?" Paul finally called out into the darkness, just to break the odd feeling of being stalked, of being sized up, appraised.

"Just enjoying the night," the man returned. "I do believe it's gotten a bit cooler."

Paul grinned. In one quick flash, it all came clear. The guy was a fag. It was obvious from his womanish voice and the prissy way he talked. And, well, Paul suddenly understood why he was staring at him so intently, why he didn't want to startle him off. Even stinking of the river, he knew he still would be a hot number for this middle-aged pansy, who just happened to be about the same size.

"You got an extra smoke on you?"

The man walked up to him, and Paul was able to make him out more clearly. He had thinning blond hair, a pair of gold-framed oval glasses, and thin lips that made Paul think of worms. He wore a black T-shirt and a pair of baggy gray cargo shorts, sandals. He reached into one of the pockets of his shorts and pulled out a pack of Benson & Hedges and shook one out, handed it to Paul, and lit it for him.

"My name's James," the man said. "What happened to you, fall in the river?" He hiccupped out a short laugh.

"Don't you know it. I was just down on the bank, man, not watchin' where I was goin' and kaboom, down I went. You can't trust that bank to stay level."

"I suppose not. Good thing you made it. Those currents can suck you clean under."

James stared at him, his eyes moving up and down restlessly over Paul's body, a body hard and roped with muscle. Paul knew he still looked good, in spite of all that had happened. He then had a thought. "You live around here, James?"

James's face seemed to light up, even in the dark. "Why yes, yes I do. Just down the block, the house with the pillars on the corner."

"Live alone?" And Paul made sure to temper this question, so he didn't spook James. He made sure to make long eye contact with the man, holding it and then releasing with a suggestive raise of the eyebrows.

The man smiled and then sighed. "Up until a couple of weeks ago, the answer to that question would have been no. But yes, I live alone." The man sighed again, his gaze meeting Paul's after a moment. "What did you say your name was?"

"Jake," Paul said. He paused for a moment, considering. Then he thought he might as well take the plunge. Life was full of plunges these days, anyways, rash movements that so far had gotten him somewhere. "You lookin' for company?"

The man laughed, a finicky little hiccup of a laugh. Paul hated him already. "Why, Jake, what an impertinent question!"

Paul laughed too, even though he didn't know what the hell the guy was talking about. He dragged hard on his cigarette, unsure, even if it was a desperate measure, if he could go through with the plan forming vaguely in his mind. "Yeah, well..."

"As a matter of fact, I could use some company." James looked Paul up and down once more, appraising him. "And you could probably stand to get cleaned up. I probably have something dry for you to put on."

"Sounds like a plan." Paul took one last drag on his cigarette, then flicked it into the brush. "Let's go."

*

Paul had never seen a house like James's. It was filled with old-fashioned furniture, curving settees with carved wooden arms that looked too uncomfortable to sit on, claw-foot tables, lamps with stained glass. James moved toward a big, dark wood cabinet and opened it, revealing a full bar: bottles lined along the back of the cabinet on two tiers, a silver ice bucket and tongs, a neat row of glasses of various sizes below the liquor.

"I don't suppose you'd like a drink, er, Jake?"

"Fuck, man, it's just what the doctor ordered. Got any Jack?"

James lifted a bottle. "Right here."

"Just put a couple splashes of that on ice." Paul watched as James unscrewed the bottle's cap and followed his instructions. Paul took the glass from him almost before he had a chance to hand it to him and swigged it down in two long swallows. He belched and handed the glass to James for a refill. "Good man."

James refilled the glass and handed it to Paul, turned to mix himself a gin and tonic. Tanqueray. The guy was all class.

James came toward him. Paul could see the predatory look in his eyes again, and it made rage buzz in his head, pounding and throbbing behind his temples like a headache. He bit down on his tongue, trying hard to ebb the wave of darkness cresting within him. He smiled and hoped it didn't come out like a grimace.

"You're a very handsome man," James said and laughed. "Even if you have been dipped in the river." He took a tiny sip of his drink, then took out two cigarettes and lit them, handing one to Paul. As he did, he locked eyes with Paul. "Very handsome."

Paul grinned, not with delight at the compliment, but in ridicule of this pathetic little sissy. He wondered if James had ever done Sean. He knew how these fags were, going around blowing anyone with a willing dick.

James said, "I suppose you wouldn't mind cleaning up. A shower, perhaps?"

Paul set his second drink, empty, down on an end table. James made a face and swept the glass up. He rubbed at the little circle of water droplets on the dark wood surface. "That sounds cool. I probably don't smell too great."

James nodded toward the staircase just outside the living room, in the foyer, with its curving banister. "Just go on upstairs. First door on your left. You'll find everything you need—clean towels, soap, shampoo...even a bathrobe."

Paul started up the stairs.

"Why don't you toss those clothes down to me? I'll throw them in the washing machine."

"You're a saint, James."

Paul dropped his clothes as he went up the stairs, then stooped, naked, to lift them and throw them down, in a ball, to James, who stood at the bottom of the stairs, blushing and staring. Paul threw his clothes hard enough to make the old fag gasp when he caught them. Paul hated the way he eyed his naked body...intense.

Once in the bathroom, Paul took stock: for one thing, the place was nicer than his own living room. Done in shades of peach and emerald green, the bathroom was huge, with bright white ceramic tile, pedestal sink, a separate glass-doored shower enclosure, and claw-foot tub.

He crossed the room and opened a cupboard. There were towels stacked neatly inside. The bottom shelf held a pharmacy full of cosmetics and over-the-counter remedies. There were several Fleet enemas, which made Paul snicker. A bottle of Rogaine. Paul picked it up and snorted. "Figures," he said to himself, setting it back in its place.

But there, near the back, was something he thought would suit his purpose perfectly. In a small leather bag was a Wahl clipper with different attachments. He took the clippers out and moved to the mirror.

To his reflection he said, "You've had this hair for a long time, buddy. Kiss it goodbye." He flicked on the clippers and watched his coarse hair disappear as he ran the clippers over his head. The curls fell to the sink, a contrast to the white porcelain.

When he was finished, he regarded himself in the mirror. He still looked good. The shaved head made his eyes stand out more prominently. He reached into the bag and brought out a beard trimmer and got rid of his moustache too.

A different man gazed back at him.

And a different man was what he needed to be right now. Difficult circumstances had made of him a different man.

He stepped into the shower.

The water felt hard against his skin, its needles hot jets, biting. Paul searched for something to reduce the water pressure and found nothing. He turned quickly in the spray, wincing when the sharp jets hit his dick. A cockroach crawled up one tiled wall and Paul snickered... *Even in a fancy-schmancy place like this...*

So this is what it's like. Cockroaches and too much water pressure. Life ain't so different on the other side of the river.

Another cockroach crawled drunkenly from the drain. Paul stomped on it, feeling a sickening crunch as he crushed it. He slapped the other one on the wall, getting it after three or four tries. A smear of brown indicated where its life had ended.

He heard movement behind him and turned to see James stepping into the shower. He grinned, but there was no mirth in it, only malice. Then he saw that James had shaved his entire body, even the pubic hair. James was thinner than Paul had first thought, his ribs sticking out. It reminded Paul of a boy's body.

Oh God, he thought, what is this? His dick began to rise at the sight of the smooth, hairless body.

He said nothing as James reached for him. He did nothing as James's hands, soft as a woman's, slid around his waist and drew him closer. Under the hot spray and engulfed in mist, Paul did nothing as James's lips sought his, did nothing but pull James closer, roughly, smearing his mouth and tongue across his face.

*

He awakened to a chorus of birds arguing outside the bedroom window. For a moment he thought he was back home, in bed beside Shelley. There was a warm body beside his, but when he turned to throw his arm around that body, he discovered it was not Shelley with her small waist and bee-stung rise of breasts, but the body of a man, with a gut that stuck out, hard, covered in coarse hair. He opened his eyes, groggy and saw the back of a bald pate, ringed in coarse gray hair.

He coughed, then spit some water on the pillow. A water bug, its black hard-shelled back repugnant, scurried out of the inside of his mouth.

He gagged.

And then the body next to him turned and Paul could not stop screaming.

When the eyes opened, only inches away, to face him, Paul saw who it was.

Grandpa.

*

The kids, Randy, Jack, and Billy, hurried along the West Virginia side of the Ohio River. Randy was the tallest of the three, with pale brown hair, streaked with red, already growing a dust of fine hair on his upper lip. The natural leader. Then there was Jack, a stout boy of ten, with his father's dark Italian coloring and the straight nose and pale eyes of his German mother. He had a wide smile, a chipped tooth, a dusting of brown freckles across the bridge of his nose. And Billy trailed behind the other two, only seven, towheaded, bucktoothed, pudgy, and already made fun of because of his eyes: one brown, one blue.

They had all been told repeatedly by their mothers to stay away from the river. It was not a place for playing, each mother said, singing the tired chorus of the same song other mothers who lived along the river had always sung. *There are currents in the river. Currents that will suck you under. Currents you will not be able to fight.*

In evidence, mothers could always bring readily to mind a death list: other boys who had not listened to their mothers and had met the same fate, their lungs filling with water instead of air as they fought, panicked, against the downward pull of the river.

But the river held such treasures. Its rich fishy smell, the sight of a riverboat, maybe even the Delta Queen, floating by, the pieces of driftwood that could be fashioned into something smooth and beautiful by a boy. And then there were the smooth stones found in the rich soil along the bank. The best ones could be fodder for skipping contests and boasting rights.

Always, there was the temptation to swim, to brave the warm brownish-green course of the river, to even make it out to the little island in its middle. The nameless island where people with boats had set up lean-tos and campsites with roofs, picnic tables, and little more.

So they scampered along the bank, Randy and Jack in the lead, Billy struggling to keep up but never abandoning the idea of not staying with his friends, these older boys who granted him a kind of stature. What did he care if they made fun of him, tried to ditch him? In the end they always let him tag along, and his association made him something more than the other boys of his age in the neighborhood.

His mother would kill him if she knew he was down here. Drown him in the murky waters herself.

Billy stopped for a moment to catch his breath, wishing the other two would slow down. What was their hurry anyway? Who knew what they might be missing? He rubbed at his eyes and watched as the boys grew smaller in the distance, but his lungs would not allow him to follow them. He fingered the inhaler in his pocket, embarrassed about bringing it out in front of them: a sign of weakness.

Good. He could see they were stopping up ahead. They must have found something interesting that had washed up on shore. It would give him a chance to catch up without running, and maybe he wouldn't have to bring out his inhaler. Already, his breathing and beating heart were slowing.

Billy had not taken more than two steps when he heard Jack's high, watery scream. It sounded like a girl's, and it made Billy want to laugh, but only for a moment. It didn't sound like he was playing.

The two boys ahead of him stood still in the brilliant sunlight, their bodies blocking whatever it was that had caused the scream.

It looked like a photograph: the boys standing so still, the sunlight illuminating them, casting black shadows, mirror surface of the stagnant river not moving. Only the wind rustling the tops of the trees made it real.

Billy stood frozen for only a moment, watching. Stood wondering, for only a moment...if they were setting up yet another joke to play on him.

Then Randy's cry cut through the sluggish air as he sunk to his knees, turning to retch onto the pebbled bank.

Billy sucked some air into his lungs and began to run, covering the short distance by trundling his stubby legs, pumping his meaty arms, wondering what this burst of running, this sprint really, would do for his asthma. But he was scared...and fear spurred him on.

Whatever was up there was no joke, and Billy didn't want to be by himself. Even if it meant seeing what was up there.

He stood behind his friends, gasping, almost wanting to claw at his throat, to force it open to accept some of the humid air all around him, pressing in but giving him no breath.

"Don't look, kid. Just don't look," Jack said, his voice no longer the deep timbre of adolescence, but a high watery cry that chilled Billy in spite of the August heat.

Telling Billy not to look was no different than roughly grasping him by the shoulders, taping his eyes open, and shoving him in front of whatever it was that was causing so much alarm.

At first he didn't want to believe the body was real. It looked as if it had been fashioned from rubber. It was bluish, marred by bruises and cuts it must have gotten as the river's fast moving current pulled it into sunken trees, roots—God only knew what else. The eyes were open, milky, undisturbed by the pounding sun.

Billy wanted to scream too. But there was no air to put behind it. He reached desperately for his inhaler, clutched it, and brought it to his mouth, unable to take his eyes from the drowned man before him.

He knew even then that this bloated corpse would haunt his nightmares for years to come.

Chapter Thirty-Seven

Shelly woke from restless dreams, their images scattering, dispersing with each measured ring of the phone. The heat surrounded her, dampening the sheets, making them heavy as she threw them off to hurry to the phone to quiet its insistent ringing.

Maybe they had found Jason. Oh God, please let it be that.

She stood above the ringing phone for just a moment, waiting, heart pounding, somehow knowing that this was the one. The call was not from her mother, something instinctive and as real as motherhood told her that.

She lifted the receiver from its cradle, snatching it up with annoyance, as if it should have known she was there and piped down.

"Hello," she said into the phone, putting some breath behind her words, trying not to sound as if the call had just roused her from a restless slumber, more prison than rejuvenation.

"Mrs. Thompson? Shelley?" Hugh Allen. She had grown to recognize the voice over the past few weeks. And thought, this is it, this has got to be it.

Knowing that Sean had Jason meant that the news could not possibly be bad.

Sean would never harm their boy. Maybe the nightmare was about to end.

It was about time.

"Hugh? What is it?" Shelley said breathlessly, in a rush.

"Shelley, I have some news. Can I come over?"

"What is it? Have you found Jason?"

There was a pause. "No, nothing like that. I can be there in five minutes."

Shelley's heart sank...a stone, disappearing without waves or bubbles, beneath the surface of the Ohio. What news could he possibly have that would interest her other than the news they had found her baby? "What news?"

"Five minutes."

"No!" Shelley screamed to stop the detective from hanging up. "No, you tell me now. I don't have five minutes to spare."

She could actually hear the detective considering, deciding whether he should tell whatever his news was. Finally, he said, "It's about Paul, Shelley."

"Paul?" she wondered. Blessedly, she had forgotten for several minutes on this heavy, hot day that her husband even existed. The events of the previous afternoon, the attempted arrest of her husband, the subsequent chase, and the buzz of gossip already floating around town had gotten lost somewhere in her addled brain. And why shouldn't it be addled? Look at what she had been through. For a moment she even looked around the house for him, listening for him. The house was not revealing anything.

"Yes. Give me five minutes, Shelley."

"Tell me now," she said simply, forcefully, in a way that gave no room for other alternatives.

"Um. Someone found a body this morning."

Shelley gasped, grasping for something to hold onto. She settled for the bottom of the T-shirt she had worn to bed, balling some of it up, worrying it. "A body?" she said thickly.

"Yes, there were some boys..."

Shelley couldn't hear him as it all rushed back...the police storming the house, ready to arrest him for the murder of a young girl, someone she had never heard of. "What?" she whispered. "Could you repeat that?"

"A drowned body washed up on the West Virginia side. Some boys discovered it less than an hour ago. It might be Paul. Do you think you could make an identification?"

Shelley sat down hard on the floor, gripping the phone as if it would keep her from falling farther, as if it would keep her from descending into an abyss that opened blackly right before her. Would she awaken in a minute?

"I... I think so."

"I'll be there as quick as I can." The line went dead.

*

Shelley found her Newports and lit one with a trembling hand. The smoke tasted sour in her mouth, leaving nothing behind but an acrid aftertaste. Still, it was something to do, something to fill the minutes until Detective Allen arrived.

She went upstairs and opened drawers, searching for something to wear. Suddenly she began laughing. "What does someone wear to identify a body? Do you wear black or what?" she choked out, the laughter spiraling up, ascending to giddy heights that finally left her breathless, her cheeks moist with tears.

She sat on the bed for a moment, certain she would hear the detective pulling up in the driveway, and here she was: stringy hair, no makeup, wearing only an old, graying T-shirt with a moth hole in the side. Again, she began to giggle but reined it in.

She took a sundress and a pair of flats from her closet, clipped her hair back, and looked at herself in the mirror. "Good God, woman, you've aged twenty years in the past few weeks." Her skin was sallow, eyes sunken. She turned away, disgusted, from her reflection, remembering when Paul used to tell her how she looked like a little girl.

What a compliment that was...then. Now his words came back to her, cloaked in a chill that was creepy. Was her little-girl appearance what had attracted Paul to her?

The gravel in the driveway crunched and Shelley realized, grabbing some lipstick and putting it on, that her question might now never be answered.

The morgue wasn't what she expected. She thought it would be like the rest of the hospital, with nurses going by, talking, carts of food and medication being wheeled around by orderlies.

She didn't know why she thought the morgue, housed in the basement of Summitville City Hospital, should be as she supposed. After all, this was not a place for the sick.

This was the home of the dead.

It was quiet there, hushed. Other than the occasional squawk of the PA system, all Shelley heard were a few murmurs coming from offices. Ahead of her were two swinging stainless steel doors. She knew Paul would be behind them. Or maybe not. Wasn't this what she was there for? To make sure? A part of her hoped the body on the slab would be that of a stranger. But there was another part, larger, that flashed forward to the relief she would feel if it was Paul. She already knew what she would whisper in his ear.

She gripped Detective Allen's arm. Beyond briefing her on the facts of what had happened earlier that morning, the detective had little to say to her.

The two proceeded forward. When they got to the doors, Shelley was glad Allen didn't make a gentlemanly gesture and let her go first. He went through the swinging door, rubber edged on the bottom to maintain the quiet. Shelley stood for a moment, paralyzed, staring at the closed doors in front of her.

Then she went in.

The body was there, lying on a stainless steel table, sheathed in a white sheet. Already Shelley was trying to make out if the form was that of her husband, as if the hills and valleys under the sheet would have some sort of identifying characteristic.

Detective Allen's arm slid around her shoulder, and he urged her forward. She noticed for the first time there was someone else in the room, a dark-haired woman with thick-lensed black glasses. The woman stared at her and said nothing.

The woman moved forward. Her hand gripped the edge of the sheet. "Are we ready?"

Allen looked at her, his eyebrows coming together. "Shelley?"

Shelley bit her lower lip and nodded.

The woman pulled back the sheet.

Shelley closed her eyes as the sheet fluttered back, kept them closed for a moment.

Then opened them.

She gulped. Paul lay before her. There was no doubt of it. Even with the bloating and the cuts and bruises where he must have hit submerged rocks and branches, there was no mistaking his face. Even in this condition, he still retained the chiseled good looks. The same thick hair, the bushy mustache. For a moment Shelley went back, seeing him in a hundred different guises: an abashed smile on his face, clean-shaven and holding out a bouquet of irises for her to take, the face sleepy above her after they had just made love, his features chiseled in anger, the eyebrows close, his mouth open to yell, to frighten her.

"That's him," she whispered. Then she turned to the detective and said, with formality, louder now, "That's Paul Thompson."

Her eyes were welling with tears; she didn't know why. With the back of her hand, she brushed angrily at the moisture. A ball formed in her throat, making it hard to swallow.

How could she feel any sorrow? Her mother's voice, absurdly, came to her: "You loved him once."

"How could I?" Shelley blurted out.

"What?" Allen asked.

"Nothing, nothing at all." Shelley turned her back on the body and crossed her arms across her chest. "Could we go now?"

"Of course." Allen grabbed her arm and began leading her from the room.

Just as they neared the doors, Shelley stopped. "Wait." She hurried back to the table, not caring about the gaze of the detective and the woman.

She leaned in close to Paul, hand hovering just above his head. She got her mouth down close to his ear, hoping some vestige of him remained to hear her whisper, "You can never hurt me again."

Chapter Thirty-Eight

A fugitive. That's what he had become. Sean grinned at the absurdity of it. Him. A fugitive. He thought briefly of the old TV series and later, the movie with Harrison Ford, the one-armed man pursuing him. It all seemed romantic. Adventurous.

Not a life for someone like Sean, who had seldom taken risks, who had always lived on the right side of propriety. Hell, he had never even smoked pot until he was thirty.

He lay back on the rough bedspread of the Motel 6, here on the South Side of Chicago. Through the heavy drapery, he could just see the dawn sky tinged with gray, the light filtering in and making the furniture in the room into vague shapes. Blessedly, Jason was asleep in the other bed. Sean looked over to watch the small face on the pillow, at last uncreased with premature worry and anxiety. Jason's breath fell slowly, evenly, deeply.

Full morning waited for Sean like a threat. If abducting his son was hard, what would the rest of his life bring? What would he do with the next day and the next and the next? And would he ever be able to stop looking over his shoulder? He drifted back into an uneasy slumber.

*

Morning's light brought with it a little more optimism. Sean reawakened to a bright line of sunshine peeking in where the heavy curtains did not close all the way and Jason sitting on the bed opposite him, staring at his father, his expression unreadable. He had already dressed himself in a pair of blue jean shorts that ended just below his knees, red high tops, and a green T-shirt with a Summitville County parks logo embroidered across the front, a stand of pines and a lone bird circling above them. Jason was still, hands folded in his lap. He had made his bed, combed his hair, and looked completely clean. Sean missed the days when Jason would spend the weekend with him and Austin and Sean would have to come upstairs and tickle him awake. This silent, too-well-behaved boy seemed like someone else's son, a changeling.

Sean grinned at him. "Well, sport, today's the big day. The day we get started. We're gonna go into the city and see if we can find ourselves a home. Won't that be fun?"

Jason regarded him with an unreadable expression. Sean couldn't read any of his own son's emotions from the boy's poker face.

As the day wore on, well into afternoon, a sobering discovery confronted Sean. At each apartment he tried to apply for, he was turned down. All the management companies he went to told him the same thing. "We need to run a credit check." And Sean did not, could not, give them the information that would make that possible. He had once done a story for the paper, about how easy it was for people to get information about you, because of all the computerized data banks. He couldn't risk being found so easily. He shuddered as he thought about what that could mean.

The credit check was a hurdle he had not expected he would have to jump. In Summitville, most apartments were owned by people who had refurbished the space above their garage. Leases were sealed with a signature and a handshake.

He had money enough to pay the first few months of rent up front, but even that would not convince any of the landlords to forgo the credit application. All of them had procedure to follow, wanting solid tenants in their buildings, rather than this nervous-looking young man with his son, who could not give them any personal information.

The day was getting on. It was not quite dusk when Sean passed the large redbrick home on the far north side of the city, a neighborhood whose banners proclaimed that this was Rogers Park.

Jason was getting tired. Sean could tell by the way the boy did not keep up with him as he had during the day. Now he lagged along behind him, stopping every so often as if he were lost, deep in thought.

Sean had brought him up here mainly because he had wanted to think, and he had simply driven, following

Lake Shore Drive north until it became Sheridan Road, until they had passed a curve where the campus of Loyola University was situated.

He had thought Jason might enjoy stopping up here, where the two of them might park near a beach and gaze out at the churning blue waters of Lake Michigan, so unlike the Ohio River at home.

Home. Would this cold city ever become that? With its millions of people and skyscrapers, would it ever welcome the two of them? Would the streets ever become familiar, so that he and Sean could walk them with knowledge and confidence?

"Is that the ocean, Daddy?" Jason had asked when they stopped at a beach at the end of Touhy, a place grandly named Leone Park, although the only signs of a park were a narrow strip of grass with a few trees, the beach, and some playground equipment. At home, parks were acres of green, forests with trails where one could lose oneself for an afternoon. Sean had explained, "No, Jason, that's Lake Michigan. Even though we can't see to the other side, it's still not an ocean. But it sure is pretty, isn't it?"

Jason had stared at the waves crashing against the shore, saying nothing in reply.

They were on their way back to the car when Sean spotted the building. The Kmart-issue black sign with fluorescent letters saying nothing more than FOR RENT, with a phone number below, told him that this building probably was not under the aegis of a management company, that it might be owned by someone who occupied one of the floors, someone who might not be so adamant about a credit check, especially when Sean could pay the first few months up front.

The building was a simple redbrick house, with a big wraparound front porch and wide steps leading up to oak double doors with leaded glass windows. The yard looked well-kept, with neat rows of irises skirting the front walkway. Sean looked up; empty windows told him that what was probably for rent was on the second floor. In spite of the care the lawn had been given, Sean could see it was a losing battle. Here and there bits of paper, a Pepsi can, bird feathers, and other detritus had caught in the long stems of the grass.

Sean did not let his weariness slow his thought processes down. The building, looking solid enough despite the obvious lack of care, could be an opportunity. And an opportunity was exactly what he needed.

He grabbed Jason's hand, walked up, and consulted a row of three buzzers. The middle one had no name. He picked the first floor. The name beneath the buzzer was Duchene.

He heard a metallic buzz from within and then a squawk. A voice, so metallic it was impossible to discern even gender, issued forth. "May I help you?"

"I'm interested in the apartment."

In reply, unintelligible metallic gibberish.

"What?"

"I said you should call the number on the sign and set up an appointment."

Sean looked down at his shoes, noticing the Nikes' soles were wearing thin. He shook his head. He was about to turn and walk away when the door opened.

"Goodness gracious! I didn't know you had a child with you!"

Sean turned to see the biggest queen he had ever encountered. There was just no other way to put it. The man was older, midsixties maybe, rail thin with a shock of thick white hair. Even though he wore a plaid shirt and khakis, both pressed with lots of starch and razor-sharp creases, there was something so feminine about him that one wondered for a moment if this was a man or a poor excuse for a dyke. Sean caught the telltale signs of the drag queen: a little blusher on the cheeks, a little eyeliner and mascara. The man smiled at them with impossibly even, white teeth. His blue eyes darted quickly from father to son.

Sean smiled, uncertain of whether he should stay. But the man wore a slightly bemused expression that exuded warmth... There didn't seem to be any predatory component to his gaze. There was something about him, and his obvious delight in seeing them, that caused any discomfort to evaporate. It was as if this man was in on some big joke, and Sean couldn't wait to be let in on it as well. "Well, yes, I have a child with me. And we've come all the way from the South Side just to have a look at this place you've got for rent. Now, you're not going to turn us away, are you?"

"What do I look like, the guard at the entrance to the Emerald City?" The man barked out a short little laugh that ended in a yelp.

"Actually, I was thinking more along the lines of Orville Redenbacher." Sean suddenly decided the association might not be so flattering, however true. "A young Orville, I mean."

The man pursed his lips. "I have half a notion to slam this door in your face. The only thing stopping me is this sweet child. I couldn't do that to him."

Sean grinned. "Thank you. That's Jason. And I'm Sean."

"How cozy! We're already on a first name basis. Do we have last names?"

Sean debated. Perhaps even linking their first names together was danger enough. He couldn't dare risk using his own last name. There must have already been some publicity, even if it hadn't reached as far as Chicago.

"It's Gale." Sean's only inspiration was the *Wizard of Oz* crack, and he hoped this man wouldn't pick up on the illusion.

The man nodded. "George Duchene, at your service." He paused for a moment. "Well, gentlemen, why don't you come on inside and we'll talk about the place."

Sean followed George, pulling Jason along by his hand. The living room they entered was like nothing he had ever seen. The whole room was populated by teddy bears, some dressed for high tea, in lace and satin and gathered around a child-size table, others dressed in Western garb, one even dressed as a monk. There were too many to take in all at once.

"Daddy, look at all the bears!" Jason shouted. It was the happiest he had sounded since this whole fiasco had begun. And it was probably the most he had spoken all at once since before this nightmare had invaded their lives.

"Aren't they...great?" Sean asked. He didn't know whether he should give in to delight or suspicion.

George knelt down in front of Jason. "It's my special collection. Do you know I have some bears from when I was your age?"

"I have a Smokey Bear," Jason confided.

This was about as much as Sean had heard Jason speak in weeks. Suddenly he didn't care what condition the apartment above them was in... He could already see this character would be good for Jason.

"Oh, that's charming, lad!" George clapped his hands together. "I have a Smokey too. He's in with the rest of my collection." George's eyes got big. "I only let people who really appreciate teddy bears see the rest of it. Would you like to see?"

Jason nodded eagerly.

Jason's eagerness was what really sealed the deal between Duchene and father and son. Sean could tell Duchene was a lonely man, and having a little boy who appreciated his taste in teddy bears in the house was some kind of gift for the older man. In spite of the warmth Duchene exuded, Sean made a mental note to never leave Jason alone with him. As childish and wondrous as the teddy bear collection was, it was also downright creepy.

But Duchene had two things all the other landlords Sean had encountered that day lacked. First, he was willing to let them move in that day. It turned out it was not the entire second floor that was available, but a spacious bedroom, already furnished with twin beds, a desk, loveseat, TV, dressers, and an en-suite bathroom. This suited Sean's purpose just fine, at least for now. And the price, which seemed steep by Summitville standards, was cheap enough that Sean's savings would not be depleted as quickly as some of the other places Sean had looked at that day.

But the second advantage this place offered was the real winning factor. Duchene agreed not to run a credit check. It wasn't easy to convince the older man to forego this formality, but he would do so if Sean would agree to put down a deposit on a major credit card.

"I won't even put the charge through, but I have to protect myself here, you understand."

Sean was reluctant but knew the alternative would be either sleeping in the car—dangerous, uncomfortable, and hot—or spending another night in a high-priced motel. Besides, the man had said he would not put the charge through, so he figured he was safe from being traced.

He had handed George Duchene his Visa. Duchene glanced down at it and then back up at Sean. He opened his mouth, and Sean's heart sank. He knew what was wrong. It did not say Sean Gale on the credit card; it said Sean Dawes. How could he explain?

But the older man said nothing other than "I'll get this back to you after I run an impression."

"And you won't put a charge through?"

The gleam that had been in Duchene's eyes seemed to have vanished. "Oh no, it will be just like I said."

Sean wasn't so sure what would happen, and the fear that Duchene might run the card or report him caused anxiety and tension to ratchet up enough that he felt a small trickle of sweat run, crawly, down his spine.

But at least now, as the day gasped out its dying last rays of light, Sean and Jason had a place to call home. It hadn't been that hard.

Jason had already settled on one of the twin beds—they both had white Chenille bedspreads with pink roses—aimed the remote at the portable TV, and located Cartoon Network with surprising speed.

Sean took out a few of their belongings and placed them in drawers. He could empty out the car later.

"We'll go out and get some supper in a minute, sport, okay? I think we passed a pizza place on the way up here, and it's probably close enough that we could walk. I just want to check my email first." Jason didn't say anything as Sean withdrew his laptop from his backpack and set it on the desk. Duchene had told him that the building had Wi-Fi, which was a big selling point, although hardly the greatest of its enchantments.

Sean plugged in the power cord, powered up, and was online in no time. He googled the home page for the *Review* and clicked on the resulting link in the findings.

And wished he hadn't.

Sean swallowed, suddenly feeling like he had no spit left. His heart thudded uncomfortably in his chest, blood roared in his ears, his temples pounded, a single line of sweat trickled down to pool in the small of his back. He stared at the computer screen as though staring hard enough could erase the truth revealed on its bright surface. "Oh shit," he whispered.

The headline—with accompanying photos—was the first thing to give him pause. The headline, broad and spanning the whole screen, was simple: SEARCH FOR

MISSING BOY INTENSIFIES. The second thing was the recent pictures: his very own press photo for work, and Jason's last year's school picture. Was this stuff already on the AP and UPI wires? How long would it be before Duchene saw these pictures and picked up the phone?

In spite of the warm, verging on hot, air blowing in through the window screens, Sean felt a chill. His stomach dropped.

He read the story and saw that he did not come off looking good. The article talked about Jason's recent abduction, and thankfully, maybe out of consideration for the boy, did not mention his molestation, making a clear case for both abductions being related.

But the thing that really caused his heart to stop was the line, "The boy's mother, Shelley Thompson, sends out an impassioned plea to anyone who may have seen her son to contact the authorities immediately. 'Jason is everything to me. I just want him home. Please, please, if you see him, get in touch with the Summitville Police Department.'"

Sean shut the lid of the laptop and stared out at the night. He whispered to himself, "Shelley's out of the coma. She's okay."

He hadn't spoken loud, but what Jason said next seemed almost in response to Sean's whisper. "Is Mama coming out here? When can I see her again, Dad, huh?" Sean shut his eyes tight.

Jesus Christ, what am I doing?

Chapter Thirty-Nine

The house was empty, a shell. The simple frame house, with its green shingles and run-down interior, had never felt more like a house and less like a home. Shelley didn't know how she could bear it. One of the men in her life was gone forever and she was glad; he hadn't deserved to breathe even the same air as she had. She had loved him once, she supposed, but that love had been for a shadow, a made-up man, someone she wanted him to be, but who was not really Paul. Shelley couldn't wait to clear out his things, maybe even go against city regulations and build a big bonfire in the backyard until all that remained of Paul Thompson was ashes.

If only she had this one loss, singular, with which to cope. But the other male in her life, Jason, was also gone. And losing him meant losing everything.

Shelley sat down heavily on one of the maple kitchen chairs, looking at the dull, tired morning sky outside, thinking she should at least try to keep busy. *For God's sake, girl, make yourself a cup of coffee. Can you do that much?* But she didn't have even the strength to carry out such simple tasks as filling a carafe with water, a filter with ground coffee, putting them together, and pressing a button. It was as though all she really had the fortitude for was sitting and staring at the polyurethane top of the kitchen table.

Jason was gone. The fact of the matter was she longed for him with a desperation that bordered on grief, yet the longing and the stress of her loss was tempered by the fact that she knew, with almost total certainty, that Jason was with his father. She closed her eyes, picturing Sean in her mind's eye. Their relationship and marriage had been happy, she thought, until that fateful night when they had argued and he had blurted out his attraction for men. It was one of those watershed moments, a bridge that, once crossed, self-destructed behind it. The revelation opened one door and closed many others.

After she had gotten over her anger, her loss, her despair, she had finally come to understand one thing: Sean was a good father who truly loved his son. His homosexuality had nothing to do with his being a good dad; the two were mutually exclusive, much as her own heterosexuality had nothing to do with her being a good mom...or not.

She knew wherever they were right now, her son was being well looked after. She snorted and thought he was probably now more out of harm's way than he had been in his own home.

The thought sent an icy chill up her spine. The hairs on her neck rose as if electrified. *Did I allow a molester into our home? Am I partly responsible for the horrible thing that happened to Jason?* A sob caught in her throat, and she stood on unsteady legs to begin preparing coffee, because if she didn't do something, she would collapse into hysterical tears, hitting her own head on the table over and over again. It wouldn't be the first time she had hurt herself, and even Shelley had sense enough to know that such an action might land her right back in the hospital.

As she pulled the Folgers down from a cupboard and searched for a paper coffee filter in one drawer's unkempt mess, she had a nauseating thought of the magazines she had found hidden in Paul's workspace. The thought of some of the photographs—and especially the children's dead gazes in them—made bile, acidic and sour, rise up in the back of her throat, burning, before she forced the images out of her mind.

She sat at the table, waiting for the coffee to brew and pulled out the newspaper to find the crossword puzzle—anything to keep her mind off her situation.

But Fate saw to it that Shelley did not need a paper, black-and-white distraction, when a living one had just made her way up to her front door. That distraction was now peering in the screen door at her daughter as she tentatively knocked, saying, "Yoo-hoo."

Oh Christ. Maybe being alone isn't such a bad thing, when you consider the alternatives. Shelley forced herself to smile at her mother, but she felt like she was straining and knew the smile probably looked more like a grimace. No matter. Shelley knew her mother would be oblivious to such subtleties.

"Oh good, I can smell you have the coffee brewing."

"Come on in, Mom."

Estelle bustled in, wearing, for her, the rare pair of slacks—polyester with a sewn-in crease and elastic waistband—topped with a flowing floral print top. Her dull orange hair looked as though it had just been permed. Her lips were a smear of pink not found in nature.

How was I ever borne of this creature?

Shelley wearily headed to the cupboard to get a couple of mugs.

"Now, now, dear, I don't want you tiring yourself on my account. That's why I came over, to help you out while you got better. Now just sit yourself back down and let your mom take care of you."

Shelley debated whether she should say anything about the fact that Jason had been abducted while under her mother's care and then thought better of it. What was the point? She would have been too tired to fight against the wave of Estelle's self-righteousness and defensiveness. Besides, until the accident that put her in a coma, Shelley herself would have said Jason was much better off with his father than with his grandparents.

Shelley turned a kitchen chair sideways and plopped down in it, her legs splayed out before her. Let the old woman wait on her. It was the least her mother could do.

Just as Estelle set the mug of steaming coffee before her daughter, the kitchen wall phone rang.

"Want me to get that?"

No, I most certainly do not. Shelley smiled once again at her mother. "Don't trouble yourself, Mom. I've got it. How about getting that Coffee mate in the fridge?

It's hazelnut." Shelley hurried to quiet the ringing of the telephone, unable to stop herself from fervently hoping it was someone calling with good news of her son.

Detective Allen was calling. "Shelley, I've just gotten some news."

The room seemed to shift slightly. Shelley let out a little gasp. "What is it? Have you found Jason?" She looked over at her mother, who paused in front of the refrigerator, straightening just a bit so she could listen better.

"We're working on that. And this does concern your boy, but it's not the kind of news you probably consider good."

Shelley had long ago placed a little collapsible folding step stool by the wall phone in the kitchen. She dropped onto it, not certain what she was about to hear, but sure the news was not going to be good. "What? Tell me."

"It's about Paul, your late husband."

"Okay..."

"I have in front of me a report from the DNA lab in Pittsburgh. During his autopsy, we were able to obtain DNA from Paul, and we had it checked against the sample taken from your son after he was, uh, tampered with."

Shelley knew what was coming. It was simply confirmation. "I'm pretty sure I know what that report said, but go ahead."

"It appears that the samples from your son and your late husband matched. It's, uh, pretty conclusive evidence that he molested Jason."

The words caused Shelley to put a hand to her forehead; true and expected as they were, his words were still painful and nauseating to hear. She felt a hot rush of tears at the corners of her eyes and blinked them back. For her mother's benefit, because she knew Estelle was hanging on her every word, and Shelley felt like saying something that would vindicate her faith in her ex-husband, she said, "So, let me get this clear in my head. You're saying you have pretty conclusive proof of who molested my son."

"Yes."

Estelle closed the refrigerator door and set the Coffee mate on the table. Her gaze locked with Shelley's.

"And that person is—" Shelley paused for only a second, but a second freighted with tension. She realized she was taking perverse pleasure in this moment, even though so much heartache and pain surrounded it. "Paul Thompson?"

"Yes," Allan sounded like he was getting impatient, as though he were dealing with someone with flawed comprehension.

"Sorry, I just wanted to be sure you said Paul. And not Sean."

"That's right. If he were still alive, we would be arresting him right now. And the DA would have a very strong case."

Estelle had seated herself at the table. She was pouring creamer into her coffee and staring into the dark liquid intently. Suddenly, she seemed resolute not to meet her daughter's gaze.

Shelley sighed, twisting the phone cord around her finger. "Thanks for letting me know. You should probably know that I found something very incriminating in Paul's work space in the basement."

"Oh?"

"Yeah. Not that it matters now, but I found a hiding place, and inside it were several kiddie porn magazines. I know that, in and of itself, these would not constitute any proof, but with the DNA match, I think there's no doubt that my husband was a monster." Shelley's voice caught on the last word. She had to steel herself not to burst into sobs. How had she gotten to this hideous, dark place?

"Do you still have the magazines?"

"No. I destroyed every one of them. And I felt good doing it."

"I understand." Allen paused. "I also wanted to let you know we have gotten hold of Sean Dawes's credit card numbers and are tracking them to see if anything like gas or motel charges show up, so we can locate him."

"That helps a lot. I'm glad you're working to find my boy." Shelley paused, considering her next words. "Mr. Allan, I want you to understand one thing. If Jason is with Sean—and I think he is—I do want him found. But I won't want to press charges. Jason is his son...and this is not a kidnapping. Do you understand?"

"I do. I do understand. And I will do what I can to not only find your boy, but to work with you to see your family reunited."

"Thank you so much." After a few brief exchanges and promises on both sides to keep the other posted, Shelley hung up.

Now, Estelle looked up from her coffee. Her mouth was slightly open, and she stared at her daughter with undisguised disbelief.

"What?" Shelley sat down at the table and pulled the mug of coffee her mother had poured toward her, adding creamer and sugar.

"I don't know if I can believe my ears." Estelle shook her head.

"You mean about Paul?"

"Well, that, yes, but also what you said at the end. What was it? Something about not pressing charges? What's wrong with you? That man stole your son right out from under my nose." Estelle's voice was veering into shrillness.

Shelley rolled her eyes. *Stay calm. You do not have to defend yourself. But she is your mother and you can make an attempt, however misguided, to explain.* And although the easy thing to do right now would be to accuse her mother and say how easily someone "stole" Jason while on her watch, Shelley resisted the impulse. She took a breath and began, "You know about a parent's love for a child, right?"

"What a question for a daughter to ask her mother. Of course I do!"

"Then I would think you'd understand that Jason is not just *my* son, he's Sean's and my son. And if Sean *stole* him, as you call it, I believe it was only because he had our little boy's best interests at heart. He didn't know I had come out of my coma. And he didn't know when, or if, I would. And he did *not* molest Jason, so maybe removing him from the environment where our little boy was hurt was the right thing to do. Don't you think, *Mother*?"

Estelle glared at her daughter. "Whatever you say, dear. But I would think the man would at least have the decency to call you if he does have Jason. And if he doesn't, Lord knows where that child is."

Shelley put a hand to her forehead, which was throbbing. She suddenly felt nauseated. Her mother was offering her nothing like comfort, and she wondered why she let the old woman continue to sit here and challenge and torment her. Where was a mother's loving embrace? Shouldn't Estelle be taking her daughter's side? *Why do I sit here like a lump and just take this abuse from her?*

I don't have to.

Shelley looked over at her mother, slurping her coffee, and felt a wave of repulsion. The faded, cotton-candy hair, the sagging jowls, the out-of-date polyester clothes...and the complete lack of sympathy replaced by self-righteousness painted a portrait of a woman Shelley wasn't ever sure she knew or wanted to know. She didn't think she could ever look at her mother in the same way again.

"Mom. I need to be alone."

"I don't think so, honey. Let me stay here and take care of you."

"Mom." Shelley waited until Estelle's gaze met her own. "You are not taking care of me. You are aggravating me and causing me pain. Now, would you just go?"

Shelley watched as bright tears sprang to her mother's eyes. The older woman opened her mouth to speak, then looked as though she thought better of it.

Shelley stared down at the floor as she listened to the slam of the screen door and her mother's receding footsteps. "Jason, my Jason, where are you?"

Chapter Forty

The last of the sun's dying rays reflected on the murky brown water of the Ohio River as Austin pulled up to the house. The sky was fading to twilight, pale lavender near the horizon, deepening into navy blue higher up. Austin put the car in park, pulled the keys from the ignition, and sat listening to the ticking of the engine as it cooled down.

Their house sat before him, its windows looking black in the dusk. He remembered returning home to this very same place at other times when twilight was approaching and seeing the lamps illuminated with yellow light, welcoming. He wondered if he would ever feel the same sense of homecoming and warmth ever again. Now the house almost had a foreboding aspect, as if its emptiness was a vacuum that would suck him in and drag him down.

He got out of the car and pulled out the duffel he had hurriedly filled when he rushed out of the house a few days ago, his anger and hurt throbbing in him like physical pain. He had gone up to his mom's house in Baden, and she had been glad to have him for a few days.

He had purposefully avoided talking about Sean, or Jason, or all the horror that had transpired. And his mother, who was almost blissful about denying her son's sexuality, was only too happy not to ask any questions about Austin's life with Sean.

It had been easy to sink back into his role as son, going off to work at the pottery in the morning and returning home to be taken care of. Mom would have supper on the table and waiting; she would hand him the remote when they settled in the front room for TV. But easy lasted only so long. He saw in the papers that Sean and Jason had disappeared...and the news came as a revelation. Their absence seemed almost like a death, and Austin had spent the night in his boyhood bedroom, surrounded by old athletic trophies, Pirates banners, and other remnants of his youth, sobbing into his pillow. In the morning he had repacked his bag, kissed his mother goodbye, telling her he would not be coming back that night, and headed off for work.

And now he was home from work, the feeling of déjà vu nearly eradicated by the empty house and the knowledge he didn't know where his partner and his son were. His steps were heavy as he approached the house, and he wondered if he'd ever see these two people he loved so much ever again.

The thought was not unreasonable. What if Sean had taken the boy and left the country? What if he feared horrible recriminations and consequences if he came back? What if they—and this was the worst—never intended to leave for a long period, but had just taken a quick car trip and something too terrible for words had befallen them? What if Sean's car was lying at the bottom of the river right now? And, finally, what if the man just felt there was no longer anything here for his son and himself in Summitville?

Austin couldn't blame him.

Why hadn't he been more supportive? Had that been too much to ask? But no, Austin had to try to assert his place in their little family's hierarchy. And look where it had gotten him...

Wearily, and with a fatigue that had nothing to do with the day's work, Austin unlocked the back door and entered the kitchen. Often Sean would beat him home from work, and when he came into this very room, there would be the smell of garlic, onions, and tomatoes from their garden simmering on the stove. Sean would have the radio tuned to the classical station out of Pittsburgh, and he would smile as Austin came in. There were times when Austin would go in to shower off the day's clay dust, and Sean would lower the heat on whatever he was making and would slip into the shower with him, naked. Austin closed his eyes, allowing himself to savor the feel of Sean's hairy chest, slick with wet, pressed against his smooth back.

How had he let everything slip away? *Why is it that we see how valuable things are to us when they are gone?* Who made up that ridiculous rule that had seemed to plague mankind since the beginning?

Austin plopped down in one of the kitchen chairs without bothering to turn on a light, even though the kitchen was only dimly lit now from the rising silver moon outside. He felt numb, without even the directive of hunger prompting him to do anything other than sit here and wonder if he ever would have a chance to reclaim the life and love he once had.

Austin didn't know how he should behave now that his world, once as comfortable as an old pair of slippers, was in disarray. There were no roadmaps or guides for how to behave under the kind of trauma they had all been through in these few sweltering hot weeks of summer.

But even though the house was empty and silent, mockingly so, Austin would keep vigil here, just in case the phone rang, just in case there was word, just in case Sean and Jason drove up the crunching gravel driveway in homecoming. What a welcome sound that would be!

Just as he thought of the gravel crunching, he heard that very sound, signaling the arrival of someone at their house—Austin would never think of it as *his* house. He got up from the table and flipped on the overhead light, looking around quickly. There were still dishes in the drainer and a newspaper folded neatly on the counter. Seeing these prosaic signs of life made Austin long all over again for a life he hoped had only been misplaced.

He glanced out the window and saw Shelley getting out of her car. Austin watched her approach, thinking of how he had always thought of this slight woman who looked even younger than her years as his rival, as someone who had once laid claim to territory he now claimed as his own, exclusively. Sometimes he had hated her, in selfish moments, envious of the irrevocable bond of parenthood she shared with Sean, something he wasn't sure the two of them could ever have. Not in the same way, anyway.

But now, as she approached the deck and mounted the first step, Austin smiled, relieved to see Shelley. Before they even spoke, he knew the two of them were now united in adversity, and that both of them wanted the same thing: for Sean and Jason to be home.

Austin pushed open the door, grinning. "Hi! Come on in."

Shelley glanced up at him, shyly, as she edged by him to enter the kitchen. "Hey, Austin, did you hear the news?" Shelley sat down at the kitchen table, her hands folded in front of her.

For a moment Austin's heart stopped. Had Sean and Jason been found? Were they back? Why hadn't they come here?

Before he could ask anything, Shelley cocked her head. "About Paul? You heard about Paul, right?"

Austin blew out a big sigh. Since he'd been up in Baden, he'd paid little attention to the news. "What about Paul?"

Shelley smiled, and Austin would think the smile peculiar when he heard what she said next. "He's dead. It looks like he drowned in the river." Shelley continued to smile, as if she were imparting the information that Paul had bowled a perfect game.

Austin wasn't sure how he was to react to this: the smile and the news were at such odds with one another. "I... I guess I'm real sorry to hear that, Shelley."

Shelley shook her head. "Don't be. He was a monster." She bowed her head so her hair fell down over her face, obscuring it. "He's in hell now." Austin heard her sniffle. When she looked back up, her eyes were bright.

"He was the one who raped Jason. He also killed a young girl. I don't know how you couldn't know about this stuff."

Austin didn't know what to say. He leaned back against the counter, folding his arms across his chest, then unfolding them.

"Never mind. It doesn't matter. What does matter is that you and I both know Sean has Jason—he's got to. And he's on the run. He doesn't need to be. I'm not gonna press charges. You have to believe that. We need to find them and get them home."

Austin closed his eyes, grateful. This was the kind of unity he had hoped for when he saw Shelley walking toward his kitchen door. "Want a beer?"

"Sure. Then let's talk."

Austin got two Iron City beers from the fridge, opened them, placed one before Shelley, and sat down across from her.

"Austin. We both want them back. So I need you to be honest with me. Do you know where Sean is? I wasn't lying when I said I don't want to press charges. Under the circumstances, I kind of don't blame Sean for running. But Jason is my son too, and it isn't right that he's without his mother...without me."

Austin took a swig of his beer, and before he felt self-conscious about it, he reached across the table and took Shelley's hands in his own. "Listen. We fought and I left. Maybe if that hadn't happened, Sean wouldn't have made such a drastic move, but with you in a coma and your parents angling to take Jason away from Sean for good, he probably felt he had no other way out. I'm not defending him, but I can understand what he did."

"So do you know where he is or not?"

"I wish I did. Honest to God, Shel, if I knew, we'd hop in the car—together—right now and drive there. But I haven't heard anything. I have no idea." He paused and looked meaningfully at Shelley. "I wouldn't lie. If I knew, I'd tell you."

"I hope you would." Shelley gazed off into the distance, gnawing at a hangnail on her thumb, perhaps peering into the darkness pressing against the window over Austin's shoulder.

The pair sat silently for a few moments; then Shelley's cell phone rang. She reached into her cargo shorts to quiet it. "Hello?" Shelley's gaze met Austin's as the person on the other end began to speak. Austin was sure her look meant something significant was being imparted.

"Really? Oh, that's good news." Shelley listened for another minute or two and then said, "So, if you do find them, remember, no arrests, please. I just want them to know we're here and just want them home." She listened again. "I understand that. And I know you'll do your best, Hugh." Shelley nodded. "Right. I know there are things beyond your control, but the important thing is that both Sean and Jason get home safely. Okay, okay, talk to you soon."

Shelley clicked shut the clamshell phone and smiled at Austin. "We have maybe some good news."

"Yeah?"

"Yes. That was Hugh Allen, from the police, and he says they were able to track Sean's Visa card to the address of some kind of rooming house in Chicago."

"Chicago?"

"I know... Who knew? And maybe that was Sean's point."

"So, what happens now? Should we gas up and head out to Chicago? We could be there in seven, eight hours." Austin felt adrenaline course through him, wanting and needing to do something now that he felt seeing Sean and Jason was within reach...maybe.

Shelley smiled. "I don't know if that's a good idea. Detective Allen said that they would get in touch with the Chicago police and ask them to pay a visit to the place and see what they could find out. Because it's a residential place, they're hoping maybe Sean and Jason will be there, and all this mess can be cleared up and drawn to a close."

"God, I hope so."

"I told them that there were to be no arrests and that they could just come home without worry."

"I heard you say that. And they'll do that?"

"Allen's gonna try his best. The important thing is finding them and getting them back."

Austin closed his eyes. "Maybe by this time tomorrow, they'll be back with us."

Shelley squeezed Austin's hands. "From your mouth to God's ear."

Chapter Forty-One

Sean lay in bed, eyes open wide in the darkness. Jason, in the bed across from him, burrowed under the sheet, thumb tucked into his mouth, asleep. His breathing was regular and even, and Sean knew if he pressed his face close to his son's, the air that would come out of his mouth would be sweet. No matter how hard Sean tried, though, sleep eluded him. His brain wouldn't shut down, not for an instant. It was crowded with worries. What if he had done the wrong thing? It was one thing when Shelley had been in a coma, but now that he knew she was back to normal, how could he call it fair to take Jason away from her? And how could he deprive Jason of his mother? In spite of the home environment with that lout, Paul, Sean knew how much Shelley loved the boy.

Perhaps he should just pack up the car in the morning and head back, try to explain why he had left. Would the authorities be sympathetic to a father who feared losing his only son? A father whose ex-wife lay in a coma, at least at the time? A father who was gay? Sean's stomach churned.

Or perhaps he should just pack up the car and head even farther west...or south. How long would it take to drive to Mexico? Maybe he should shave his head and dye Jason's hair blond. Maybe he should look into how one acquired things like fake birth certificates, so maybe he and his son could truly vanish and reinvent themselves? He pictured himself as the quiet man next door with the adorable little boy, someone who kept to himself.

And then, again, he thought of Shelley, her wounded gaze as she watched out the window for the return of a boy she loved...and would never see again. How could he do that to her? How could he do that to Jason? Separating a mother and child was a violation, maybe even as bad as what had happened earlier in the summer to Jason.

And what of Austin? He loved the man, really loved him, and if Austin had some growing up to do, why, so did Sean. Had things been broken so badly they could never be repaired? Would he be allowed another chance?

Sean rolled over on his side, knowing this was the wrong path. He stared at his sleeping son, and his heart swelled with love for the boy. He knew being a good father meant doing what was right for the child and not for himself.

He rolled back over on his back. He needed to sleep. Tomorrow morning they would have a long drive ahead of them. And then who knew what awaited him at the other end? Whatever it was, he would have to accept the consequences for his actions. Taking Jason away had not been the right thing to do, and the only way back to any semblance of right was to return the boy home.

Just as he was about to lapse into a restless slumber, Sean sat bolt upright, his heart thudding in his chest.

"Oh God, no," he whispered, flinging the sheet off himself and staring frantically at the blue-and-red lights flashing on the bedroom walls. He could hear the squawk of metallic voices outside, engines idling.

He crept to the window and saw the two Chicago Police squad cars parked in front of the building. The sight made his face burn and caused bile to splash at the back of his throat. What had Duchene done? It couldn't end this way.

Quickly he crossed back to the beds and shook Jason awake. The boy looked up at him, blinking, confusion stamping his otherwise smooth features.

"Son, we have to leave...fast. I need you to get up and get dressed as quickly and quietly as you can."

Sleepily, Jason got up and reached for the lamp on the shared nightstand between the two beds. Sean grabbed his hand away, whispering furiously, "No! No lights. Just hurry up and get dressed."

Luckily they hadn't really unpacked, so Sean had the duffel bags ready and by the door within a minute. He struggled into his clothes, recalling the back stairs Duchene had shown him earlier that led into the kitchen. He hoped and prayed they could slip out the back door. He didn't know where they would go or what they would do, but he couldn't allow this to happen. The boy had been through so many traumas already. He didn't want to put him through some scene where his father was dragged away in handcuffs, and Jason himself taken to a foster home.

In spite of these thoughts, Sean knew he wasn't being rational as he shepherded Jason out of the room, ignoring the boy's request to use the bathroom. "Can you hold on for just a few minutes, Jason? We need to get outside."

Jason pulled away from his father and stared up at him, his green eyes—so like his father's—looking back, defiant. He folded his little arms across his chest. "What's going on, Daddy?" Jason's gaze moved to the reflections of the flashing blue-and-red lights on the bedroom wall. "Are we in trouble?"

There would be time enough to discuss everything later, but for right now, Sean simply needed to get the boy and himself out of the house, before the police stormed up the stairs. He reached out for one of Jason's hands, and the boy turned his body so both hands were out of reach. His small voice was on the verge of tears, but had a stubborn edge. "I want to go home!"

Sean knelt down. "That's what we're gonna do. But I need you to come with me."

Jason looked away and took two steps back, away from his father. "The police will take me home."

"No. No, that's not what's gonna happen, son. Look, I don't have time to argue."

Sweating, Sean scooped the boy up and hurried out the door, leaving their duffel bags behind. He could hear the police talking to Duchene downstairs. The conversation was unintelligible from up here, but Sean had a pretty good idea what they were saying.

Quickly he turned to the left and walked as briskly and as silently as he could down the short corridor that led to the utility stairs descending into the kitchen. Sean had a sinking feeling in his heart that if they actually were here to arrest him, there would be officers stationed at the back of the house, and his apprehension was really only moments away.

But he had to try.

The kitchen was dark. From Sean's viewpoint, the small backyard and alley behind it appeared similarly dark... and empty. He saw no movement among the bushes in the yard or farther back, where dumpsters were stationed along the fence. Sean took a deep breath and plunged out into the night air, heavy and thick with humidity.

He couldn't believe there was no one stationed in the back. He put Jason down and said simply, "We have to run. We're going to the big lake we saw earlier. Lake Michigan? Maybe we can even go for a midnight swim!" Sean prayed the boy didn't pick up on the desperation in his father's voice.

And father and son took off into the night, without the sound of footfalls in pursuit behind them.

It didn't take them long to reach the beach at the end of Jarvis Avenue. There was a small retaining wall where the street ended and the beach began, and it was here Sean sat down, breathless, with Jason at his side.

Sean's heart was racing. He expected sirens, flashing lights, and the footsteps of many men and women—armed with guns—to be heading toward them at any moment.

But there was nothing. The only sound was the flow of traffic farther west, along Sheridan Road, and the relentless crash of the waves against the shore. Still, Sean couldn't help glancing over his shoulder every few seconds.

This was the way he was going to live? This was the life he thought was better for his child?

Sean looked over at the little boy staring out at the water. Jason's face was sad; his eyes were dull, his mouth turned down in a frown.

This was a little boy who simply wanted to be home and with his mother.

This was a little boy who should be tucked into bed now, dreaming.

Sean blinked back tears and told himself that didn't mean this was a little boy who did *not* want to be with his father, but a mother was an essential ingredient in the package, and Sean could not take it away. He didn't have the right.

So he took an ATM receipt out of his wallet and a pen from his pocket. He scrawled something on the back of the receipt, stood, and brushed the sand off the back of his jeans. He held out his hand to Jason. "Come on, let's go find the car."

"Where are we going now?" The weariness and upset came through Jason's voice, and Sean wanted to kick himself.

"You'll see."

*

Jason hopped into the Sentra when his father opened the door for him. He just wanted to go to sleep. It seemed like all the grown-ups in the world had lost their minds. Where were they going *now*?

Daddy wasn't saying as he started the car and pulled away from their parking space. He went a few blocks and came to a busy street that Jason could read from the street sign was called Clark. There was a little park with a tennis court to one side of them and a fruit market on the other.

His father rolled down the window when he saw a young African American man walking down Clark. "Hey! Excuse me."

Jason watched as the Black man stopped to regard his father with a wary stare. He looked almost afraid of his dad. He took a few steps toward their car.

"Yeah. What do you need?" The man's voice was deep.

"Would you happen to know, um, where the closest police station is?"

"Sure. Just a few blocks south on Clark." The man came closer to the car and peered inside at Jason. He smiled.

"Everything okay, kid?"

"Yeah," Jason managed to breathe, his voice barely above a whisper. "I'm just here with my dad."

"Okay," the man turned his gaze to Jason's father. "Everything okay?"

His dad blew out a sigh. "Everything's fine. Thanks for your help."

Clark, before them, was pretty quiet, and his father gunned the car to make a left so he could head south. It took them only a few minutes to reach a squat, white brick building on the west side of Clark. Jason could read the word Police lit up on the outside of the building.

His dad pulled over to the curb, switched off the car, and turned to regard his son. Jason could see that his dad was blinking back tears, and it made him feel weird, sort of panicky and sick to his stomach.

"What's wrong, Daddy?"

His father didn't really answer but said, "Can you be a big, brave boy?"

"What do you mean?"

He looked out the window. Jason could see his father's shoulders shake. He just wished they would drive home, even if it took all night.

His dad took a deep, shuddering breath and turned back to Jason. He tried to smile, but the attempt was pathetic. He groped in his pocket and brought out the little slip of paper he had written on down by the beach and handed it to his son.

"I need you to go inside and give this note to the first policeman or policewoman you see, okay?"

"Why? Aren't you gonna come in with me?"

He shook his head. "There are some things I've got to do. I would if I could, you know." Jason felt his father's hands on his shoulders as he leaned in close to his face. "I need you to be brave for me just this one time. You wanna see your mom? They'll make sure that happens. I promise."

"But I want you to come!" Jason felt the ball in his throat that signaled tears were on their way.

His dad gripped him more firmly. "I can't. I can't go into why right now. I just need you to do this for me. Please...son?"

His father sounded scared, and Jason had never heard him sound quite this way before. He thought all he had to do was get out of the car, walk into the building, and hand the note to somebody. He could do that, couldn't he?

He clutched the slip of paper more firmly in his hand and reached down to open the car door. "Okay, Daddy. I'll go."

Jason swung his legs outside the car, then looked back at his father, whose face was twisted up all funny, like he would burst into sobs at any minute. "You sure you want me to go?"

It seemed like his daddy could barely catch his breath as he whispered, "Yes."

"And you'll come back, right? I'll see you in just a little bit, huh?"

"Yes," his dad said, staring out through the windshield, not looking at him.

Jason hopped out of the car, then stopped. He scrambled back in and hugged his dad, kissing him on the cheek. "You're coming back, aren't you? You promise."

His father just nodded, pulling him close. They sat for a moment like that, wrapped in each other's arms, then his dad pushed him away. "Go on, now."

And Jason hopped from the car and started toward the brightly lit glass doors of the police station. He turned once to look back, and his father was pulling away from the curb to merge into traffic behind a bus. Jason raised his hand to wave, but Daddy wasn't looking.

He unfolded the note. Now that there was enough light, he could read it: "My name is Jason Dawes. My mother is Shelley Thompson in Summitville, PA. Her phone number is 412-555-9408." Jason folded the paper back up and went inside.

Chapter Forty-Two

Shelley awakened all at once, unsure where she was. She could hear her cell phone ringing, but she couldn't recall where she had left it. In the darkness, she knew enough to know she was in an unfamiliar place. She felt the fabric below her. A couch?

And then she remembered that Austin had convinced her to stay here at his house the night before, in case Sean should try to get in touch or if there was further word from Detective Allen. It made sense. The only thing that surprised her was that she had managed to sleep.

Groggily she put her legs on the floor, remembering her cell was on their kitchen table. The device stopped ringing just as Shelley got to it, after barking her shin on an end table.

Impatiently she flipped on the light switch and glanced down at her phone.

"Who was it?" Austin's voice behind her made Shelley jump. She turned to look at him, in a T-shirt and boxers, rubbing his eyes.

"That's what I'm about to find out. What time is it?"

"A little after five."

Shelley saw what she knew: that she had one missed call. She pressed the button that would bring up who had called. It was Detective Allen. Shelley's heart began to pound. Holding the phone up so Austin could see, she said, "It's him. He called."

"Allen?"

"Yes!"

"Well, maybe it's good news."

Shelley turned away from Austin to listen as the phone rang, thinking: pick up, pick up. Please don't make me wait.

Allen answered and Shelley jumped right in. "It's Shelley Thompson. Do you have news?"

"Yes...and it's good. Your son is on his way home."

Shelley flopped down on one of the kitchen chairs, dropped her phone, and covered her face with her hands. From almost out of nowhere, the sobs came, hard and uncontrollable.

Austin bent to pick up the phone. "She'll be just a minute." Austin waited for Shelley to compose herself, then handed the phone back to her.

"Let me make sure I heard you right," Shelley said, struggling to regain control of her breath. "You said Jason is on his way home?"

Shelley swore she could hear Allen beaming through the telephone. "Yes, Jason is being brought back from Chicago as we speak by Officer Rebecca Tippie of the Chicago Police Department. She's doing this on her own personal time, in her own personal vehicle. Apparently your boy made quite an impression on her."

"That's wonderful! How soon do you think they'll be here?"

"I would imagine they should be getting here within a couple of hours."

Shelley couldn't believe it. She grinned up at Austin and whispered, "Jason's on his way home!"

Austin smiled back, but there was caution in his expression. "With Sean?"

Shelley shook her head and held up her finger for Austin to hold on as she listened. "Should I come down there to the station?"

"Yeah...that's where we told Officer Tippie to bring the boy."

"I'll be right there." Shelley snapped the phone shut and looked up at Austin, letting the joy leave her face like a sunray going into shadow. "I'm sorry, Austin, but what happened was that Jason was dropped off at the police station. He was alone." Shelley shook her head. "I'm sorry. He had a note with him, and I suspect Sean wrote it."

Shelley saw the distress on Austin's face and, without questioning herself, she stood and put her arms around him. "Sean probably thinks he's in a lot of trouble and did the best thing he could for Jason to get him home." She pushed away so she could look into Austin's pale-blue eyes. The young man looked shell-shocked. Shelley could sympathize. "Listen, I'm sure they'll get the word out. There's been a lot of coverage of this story. And Sean is bound to see that he's not in trouble, right?"

"I don't know," Austin said doubtfully. "I've been trying his cell over and over." He shrugged. "It always goes right to voice mail." Austin pulled Shelley close to him again and whispered into her hair, "I hope you're right."

*

Shelley could not take her eyes off the street before her. She sat on the front steps of City Hall as the morning grew brighter and hotter. She had been told Officer Tippie drove a maroon Altima, and her gaze hungrily scanned each vehicle that passed by, even if it bore only the most passing resemblance to a Nissan.

To her left there was a gathering of media: reporters from print, television, and radio jockeyed for position, each wanting to capture the emotional mother and child reunion. She was surprised to see outlets from as far away as Pittsburgh and Youngstown had shown up. But their excited chatter and positioning of cameras, microphones, and other recording devices were no match for her attention, which continued to be steadfast on the road.

Detective Allen waited quietly beside her, along with two uniformed officers—a man and a woman—flanking him. It seemed Allen intuitively understood the magnitude of the moment and respectfully didn't talk to Shelley or ask her questions. He and the uniformed officers kept the rest of the crowd at bay, onlookers who had gathered on the sidewalk below the steps leading up to City Hall.

It seemed the entire town had turned out...and there was an excited clamor that was almost a buzz.

Austin was among them. Shelley knew he was happy for her, yet anguished and distressed that Sean was not part of this homecoming. Her parents were down there, too, somewhere. She had met her mother's gaze for an instant earlier and could see how hungry the old woman was to join her daughter at the top of the stairs, to be part of this moment.

Shelley had simply looked away.

And then she saw a maroon Altima coming down the street. For a moment her vision turned into a smear as her eyes welled up with tears. She stood on uncertain legs, as if at the end of a long journey...and in a way, she supposed that's exactly what this was. She told herself that the car was a common model and this could be anyone.

But she knew it was her son. Knew even before she could make out the license plate and see that it was not a Pennsylvania plate. Knew before she could see Jason's small, dark-haired head in the passenger seat.

She gave out a little cry when she saw, for sure, that Jason was in the car. The crowd went silent, and everyone turned to peer into the street.

It all became dreamlike, almost like sound and motion had been stilled, slowed.

The car pulled to the curb, and the uniformed officers hurried from Shelley's side to hold back the crowd of media and onlookers that swarmed toward it, as if it contained celebrities.

Rebecca Tippie, a strong, solid woman with masses of curly auburn hair and a kind face, got out of the car, looking surprised and uncertain at the crowd, the flashing lights, and the questions already being tossed at her like machine-gun fire. She ignored them all, crossed in front of her vehicle, and opened the passenger door.

"Oh!" Shelley cried as she watched Jason step down from the car, wearing shorts, a striped T-shirt, and new red Chuck Taylors. His dark hair stuck up, and he blinked as if he had just awakened and now was being plunged into a weird dream.

"Oh!" Shelley cried again, a lump large in her throat and tears rolling down her cheeks. She hurried down the steps, the crowd parting before her, her focus intent on one thing: her little boy.

"Jason! My Jason!" She rushed to him, her arms outstretched, and dropped to her knees before the boy, gathering him up in her arms. She pulled him so close she feared crushing him, but nothing in the world compared to the radiance of this moment, of having her little boy back in her arms. His solid weight, his breath on her cheek, the brush of his fine, soft hair against her skin, and his whisper of one word—*Mama*—made her just about collapse with joy. She closed her eyes, breathing in Jason's scent, reveling in the nearness of him...and the crowd around her, for just a moment, seemed to disappear.

All that existed, for one shining interlude in time, was mother and son.

Chapter Forty-Three

Sean watched the little family from a picnic table not five feet away. Before him was an empty soda can and a wrapper from a Kit Kat bar: the remnants of a horrible lunch that did nothing to nourish him, but provided lots of sugar for a short burst of energy. His eyelids were heavy, and his stomach felt filled with nothing but bile. Yet he couldn't take his eyes off the small family tableau before him.

The little family at the next picnic table, here at this rest area off the Indiana turnpike, were oblivious to him, and they were obviously eating better. The mother, a blonde with wide hips and a caring face, had set out apples, sandwiches, and containers of yogurt for everyone. There was milk for the little girl, a towhead with a serious demeanor far beyond her six or so years, and bottles of Propel for Mom and Dad.

They were laughing, probably relieved to be out of their vehicle for a short time, on this bright, sunny summer day. Sean imagined they were on their way to a family reunion or maybe a camping trip. He pictured an

SUV packed with camping supplies, overnight bags, food, toys.

The father, a redhead with lots of freckles, was slicing up the apple for his little girl, smiling as he held out each bite-sized piece in his hand and watching as she took it from him and ate.

Sean bit his lip and felt something stir inside at this simple scene, the father feeding his daughter. *Do you know how complete and how beautiful you all look? Do you realize what a portrait of love you paint sitting here in the sunlight, sharing a simple meal together? There is nothing about you that's cloying or sweet, and if you realized you were being observed, you probably would become self-conscious. But all this is about, right now, is family being together, sharing time and sustenance, an impromptu picnic that will probably quickly be forgotten once you hit the road again on your way to Grandma's house or wherever you're going. Mom and Dad, cling to these moments! You never know when you might not have them to treasure. If nothing else, time will pull your little angel from your grasp...*

Stop it, now, you're just getting sentimental. Still, Sean wished he had a camera, so he could memorialize the scene before him. But even if he did, if the family had seen him taking a picture, they more than likely would have been weirded out by it. *What a world we live in, when something as simple as wanting to remember a family scene could be viewed with suspicion or even fear.*

Sean looked away as the family packed up the leavings from their lunch.

"I'm tired, Daddy! Carry me."

The little girl had her arms upraised, and the father stood to sling the little girl over his shoulder, not unlike a sack of potatoes. She giggled. The threesome started through the rest area park to go back to their car, which was, as Sean thought, an SUV.

He looked down at the scarred redwood of the picnic table and knew what he had to do: cross the remainder of Indiana, to Ohio, and then into Pennsylvania. His son was there, and he needed to be there for him. So was his partner, he hoped.

Consequences might be waiting too. But whatever their cost, they could not exceed the price of all he would give up if he continued to run.

He pulled his car keys from his pocket and started toward his car.

Epilogue

Austin wondered if the house would ever seem like a home again. His car complained on its suspension as he headed down the dusty road toward the river and the house he had shared with Sean. He was tired; the day at work had been a long one, hot, sweaty, and grueling, lifting molds for urns all day that strained all his muscles and left him aching.

He ached inside too. Ached for a love he once had. Ached for the simple bliss of coming home to the man he loved. The loss of that simple kiss, a peck on the lips when he came in the door, seemed huge, something that could never be replaced, its value far outstripping its reality in time and gesture.

He could hear the buzz of a mosquito near his ear, and he swatted at it. The Ohio River rose up in front of him, looking like a great, flowing brown snake, its surface slick and unmoving. Humidity hung heavy in the late afternoon summer air, and Austin hoped for a thundershower to break the humidity...at least for a while. His heart might have been broken, but did he also have to be mired in sweat and air so heavy he felt he could scoop up handfuls of it?

He parked the car next to the house, pocketed his keys, and stood for a moment looking out at the water, its silent flow, the smell of fish faintly assailing his nostrils. He thought of just stripping down, running across the grass and pebbled dirt beach, and submerging himself in the water, letting its green-brown surface swallow him up, floating down in its strong current.

Maybe then he could forget the scene he had seen yesterday in front of Summitville City Hall—Shelley and Jason's joyful reunion, how it seemed everyone in the world was united, for just a moment, in happiness as parent and child came back together and began the process of putting their pain behind them.

Austin moved toward the water, stopping to kick off his work boots and roll up his jeans. He waded in, the almost too warm water grasping at his ankles, and wondered if he was a horribly selfish person for feeling left out as he'd watched Shelley scoop Jason into her arms and cover his face with kisses. He closed his eyes, recalling the moment, remembering how there was a paradox: of course he was happy for them, but at the same time, he felt hollow and more alone than he ever had in his young life.

He didn't like to admit the tears on his face were ones of loss and not of joy.

He had turned away from the scene and hurried home, not wanting to see any more.

He waded a little farther into the river, the water dampening his jeans.

"What are you doing?"

He smiled. He could swear he heard Sean's voice behind him. Austin shook his head to clear it.

"Didn't your mother tell you that river is dangerous?"

Austin bit his lip and closed his eyes. Was this real? He got an answer to his question as he felt strong arms wrap around his midsection and looked down to see those familiar arms, dusted with dark brown hair, pull him close.

Austin turned and Sean was there, with him, standing in the shallow part of the river. Sean searched Austin's eyes with his gaze and smiled. He reached up and touched Austin's face, tenderly running his fingers across the stubble on his chin and cheeks.

"Are you really here?" Austin whispered, reaching up to run his fingers through Sean's dark hair, to revel in the simple reality of it.

Sean nodded and pulled him close, his mouth at last finding Austin's. Their lips and tongues found each other, and the kiss was more than a kiss. It was an affirmation, forgiveness, and a new start all rolled into one. And Austin understood, finally, what Shelley must have felt yesterday morning.

About the Author

Real Men. True Love.

Rick R. Reed is an award-winning and bestselling author of more than fifty works of published fiction. He is a Lambda Literary Award finalist. Entertainment Weekly has described his work as "heartrending and sensitive." Lambda Literary has called him: "A writer that doesn't disappoint..." Find him at www.rickrreedreality.blogspot.com. Rick lives in Palm Springs, CA, with his husband, Bruce, and their fierce Chihuahua/Shiba Inu mix, Kodi.

Email: rickrreedbooks@gmail.com

Facebook: www.facebook.com/rickrreedbooks

Twitter: @rickrreed

Website: www.rickrreedreality.blogspot.com

Other NineStar books by this author

Unraveling	*A Face without a Heart*
Sky Full of Mysteries	*Bigger Love*
The Perils of Intimacy	*Torn*
IM	*The Secrets We Keep*

Chaser

Raining Men

Blue Umbrella Sky

Third Eye

Legally Wed

Hungry for Love

Big Love

The Man From Milwaukee

Bashed

M4M

The Couple Next Door

Homecoming

Dinner at the Blue Moon Cafe

Also Available from NineStar Press

Connect with NineStar Press

www.ninestarpress.com

www.facebook.com/ninestarpress

www.facebook.com/groups/NineStarNiche

www.twitter.com/ninestarpress